FINDERS KEEPERS

"Torvik is a good tracker. He'll find your daughter." Raven spoke with a hint of panic.

"I don't want another tracker. I want *you.*" As Raven tensed, Beckett quickly finished his statement. "To find Ciorstan. I know you can do it." Raven had to agree with him. He couldn't trust anyone else.

"I...I'll think about it."

Beckett controlled his elation. She would find Ciorstan. He knew it. "Thank you," he murmured.

Her defiant gaze met his. "I haven't said I'd do it."

"I know." *But you will.* Already he understood a little of how this woman thought. But not enough...not nearly enough. He suspected Raven held many secrets.

Watching her swallow, Beckett found the movement of her slim throat strangely erotic. Despite his concern for Ciorstan, Raven affected him more than any woman he'd met. His body responded to her nearness, to her wide eyes, to her full lips. He lifted his hand to trace the line of her face. She stared at him, her gaze confused. "I trust you, Raven. I need you."

Her eyes widened, but she didn't pull away.

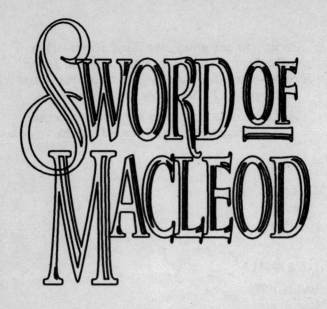

SWORD OF MACLEOD

KAREN FOX

LOVE SPELL ✦ NEW YORK CITY

To my critique group, the Wyrd Sisters—Pam McCutcheon, Deb Stover, Paula Gill and Laura Hayden—who gave unselfishly of their time, talent and support. I wouldn't be here without you.

And to Jessica Wulf, who provided wonderful encouragement when I needed it most.

LOVE SPELL®

January 1997

Published by

Dorchester Publishing Co., Inc.
276 Fifth Avenue
New York, NY 10001

Printed in the United States of America.

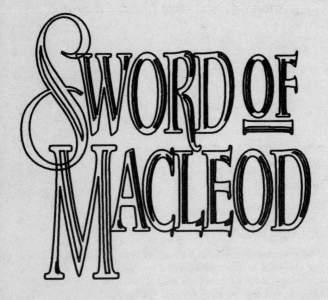

Prologue

Da isna going to like this. Ciorstan MacLeod grimaced. If her father caught her near the merchant's spaceship, he'd drag her away without hesitation. He'd told her more than once that he didn't want her around this area, but she found the aliens fascinating. Wouldn't any nine-year-old?

Hearing voices, Ciorstan ducked behind a large crate as two men walked past, engrossed in conversation. She didn't dare let anyone see her—not now.

The crate towered over her and she cautiously peeked around the edge. No other humans were around; only the aliens known as Dweezles, small fur-covered creatures with tiny pointed ears, stood by the merchant starship.

Clutching a small pouch to her chest, Ciorstan darted up the ramp into the ship and froze. She considered herself quite grown up, but she'd never seen anything like this. The vessel looked enormous enough from the outside, but the interior was even worse. Her whole village could fit in here with room to spare.

She swallowed the lump in her throat, debating the wisdom of her plan. Why had she thought this so important? Squaring her shoulders, she lifted her head high. No one else believed she'd solved the riddle, but no one else knew what she knew.

If her mother had lived, perhaps Ciorstan could've made her understand, but for now Ciorstan was on her own. She knew she was right.

A new planet had been discovered at the edge of the known universe—a planet with a huge canyon, a vast desert and a towering rock formation that resembled a dog. Just like the riddle. Everything fit.

However, even her own father wouldn't believe her. He'd been adamant in his refusal to venture a foot off his planet and wasn't about to help her. He no longer believed in old riddles and legends. She *had* to sneak away. If she didn't go, people on Alba would continue to starve.

Ciorstan drew a deep breath. Legend said that the Sword of MacLeod would bring prosperity when held by a MacLeod. And Alba definitely needed prosperity. Others might consider her a child, but Ciorstan was a MacLeod as much as her father. She would do this.

Gripping the wide handrail, she slowly climbed the spiraling steps until she discovered an open area bustling with unusual creatures and strange-looking equipment. For a moment she hugged the wall as her glance darted from one object to another, gleaning bits and pieces of desired knowledge. As much as she wanted to know more—much more—about the universe beyond her planet, she couldn't help being afraid . . . just a little.

An angry voice disturbed her fascination and she lifted her gaze to meet that of a round creature with an oversized head, his height equal to hers. Was this one of the merchants? He appeared to be in charge.

Swallowing hard, she struggled to recall the name of his race. Saluit . . . Saluram . . . something like that. He babbled in a language she couldn't understand, but anger was universal—he wasn't pleased to see her.

8

She waited for him to finish, then forced a smile. "I need passage to a planet," she said, relieved that her voice didn't quiver.

He barked at her again and waved a stubby four-fingered hand in her face.

"I *must* have passage." Ciorstan reached inside her pouch and removed a heavy gold chain, a present from her father on her last birthday. As much as she treasured it, this trip was more important. "Is this enough?"

The alien lifted the chain from her hand and tested its weight. He held it up to the light, an expression similar to a smile crossing his face. He nodded and spoke again, waving his hand in the air.

A furry Dweezle ran up to Ciorstan and indicated that she should follow him. She matched his rapid pace through narrow hallways until he stopped in an open doorway.

Motioning her inside, the Dweezle showed Ciorstan how to sit in a reclining seat and fasten the padded belts securely around her. By the time he finished she could feel a rumble reverberate through the ship.

The engines.

They'd be gone soon. The merchant ship never stayed long at Alba, just long enough to trade food for woven tartans.

The Dweezle left. Ciorstan trembled, her fear rising. What if she was wrong about the riddle? What if she never made it back home? What if she never saw Da again?

She removed a paper from the pocket of her skirt and unfolded it carefully to read the words she'd long since memorized.

> *Hie away, Clan MacLeod,*
> *Hie away, mystical sword*
> *'til the edges of time draw near.*
> *Linger not at the bottomless depths*
> *nor tarry amidst the burning sand.*
> *Journey far and seek the guardian who points*
>   *the way.*

9

Hie away, Clan MacLeod.
Bow before the rainbows pouring from heaven.
Claim the mystical sword, Clan MacLeod.
Through wisdom, find prosperity,
In faith, claim your destiny,
With love, discover the magic.

No one else believed in the old legends anymore, not really. They laughed when she told them about this new world . . . about finding the sword. The sword would solve all of Alba's problems. She had to find it.

A tremor shook the ship as a heavy weight pushed against Ciorstan's chest. She closed her eyes, offering a silent prayer, convinced death was only moments away. At the point the weight became unbearable it ceased abruptly, and Ciorstan released a sigh.

A flicker of movement at the corner of her eye caught her attention and she turned her head to stare out a small window. The typical night sky had grown to several times its size. Blackness dotted with bright lights stretched on without end.

She was in space.

At least she had left her father a note explaining her mission. She had a month to locate the Sword of MacLeod and return to Alba—a month before the next merchant ship stopped at her planet.

She had to be back by then or else her father, as much as he detested modern technology, would come after her.

And he wouldn't be very happy.

Chapter One

Beckett MacLeod couldn't stop staring.

Gripping the doorframe, he blinked, trying to focus on the aliens inside the noisy bar. He'd lifted a pint of ale or two in a pub back home, but even drunk he'd never seen anything like this. Creatures of varied shapes and sizes sprawled in the oddly curved seats in the establishment. Some of them had populated his nightmares.

Strange words sounded behind him and Beckett looked around to find a being, easily a head taller than himself, whose face resembled a wild boar . . . with three eyes. The light from the glowing sign above the doorway glinted off its tusks as it growled. Finally comprehending, Beckett stepped aside and let the beast enter.

Beckett frowned. He didn't belong here. He didn't want to be here. He could no more read the sign over the entrance than he could understand the conversation spoken inside.

"Newcomer."

Beckett looked around until he found the alien he'd hired. It stood inside the bar, its head cocked to one side. He struggled to remember its hard-to-pronounce name—Rajix or something like that.

Rajix waved at him. "You want tracker? Yes? No?" The creature's high-pitched voice matched its unusual appearance—that of an oversized squirrel, complete with bushy tail.

Nodding, Beckett entered the bar. Though dimly lit, one corner vibrated with light and he glanced over to see some creatures—no, just one creature with three heads and six arms—playing some kind of loud music. He winced. At least, he thought it was music.

As he passed through the jumble of unusual beasts, Beckett's head throbbed. The myriad of odors and types of speech overwhelmed him. This was nothing like home.

And Ciorstan was alone in this world—somewhere.

Clenching his jaws, he reached his guide. "Where's this tracker you promised me?" Beckett demanded.

Rajix chattered some indecipherable speech and tugged at Beckett's arm with a pawlike hand. Beckett brushed off its grip but followed the scampering creature to the back of the large bar and through another doorway to emerge outside again.

He found himself in a large alley illuminated only by the light from the open doorway. He tried to see into the black depths but failed. Gripping his guide's thin limb, Beckett whirled it around. "Where's this Raven person?"

"Raven be here." More chatter followed this until Beckett heard something he could understand. "Raven best tracker in galaxy."

"Actually, I'm the best tracker in the universe."

Beckett released Rajix and glared into the darkness. Slowly, a figure stepped forward, pausing in the shadows. "You're Raven?" Beckett asked.

"It depends." Raven made a short hand movement and Rajix scampered away.

Though Beckett couldn't make out Raven's features,

the tracker was definitely humanoid, half a head shorter than himself and slight of build. "I need a tracker."

"Why?"

The low-pitched voice intrigued Beckett. Even better, he could understand Raven's speech without difficulty despite the unusual accent. "My daughter's run away. I must find her."

"And you think I can do it?"

The baiting tone irritated Beckett. "Dinna you say you're the best in the universe? That's what I want."

"Are you sure?" Raven stepped into the dim light and Beckett inhaled sharply, surprised to see the smooth features and distinct curves of a female.

"You're a woman." He spoke before he could stop himself. Of course she was.

"So?" The gently rounded chin lifted slightly.

Eyeing Raven, Beckett found it difficult to believe she was a tracker. Though not much shorter than himself, she gave the impression of frailty with her lengthy slimness and finely shaped cheekbones. Her short black hair capped her head in a riotous mass of curls while her long dark lashes surrounded flashing eyes of an indeterminate color. Her full lips, pressed tightly together, begged to be kissed, and the one-piece blue suit she wore molded to her figure, accenting her small breasts and narrow waist. The only disturbing piece of the portrait was the belt slung low around her hips, drawn down by the weight of some type of weapon.

He met her stare and smiled. Though nothing like the women of his planet, she was definitely interesting. He briefly wondered what Nessa would've thought of Raven. Though if his young wife had lived past Ciorstan's fifth birthday, he probably wouldn't be here now. "I dinna mean to offend. I still need your help."

Her expression didn't change. "Tell me about your daughter. How old is she?"

"Nine."

"I don't do children." Raven turned as if to leave, and Beckett jumped forward, his hand outstretched.

"Wait." He'd never find Ciorstan without help. Not in this culture. "I'll pay well."

Slowly Raven pivoted back to face him. "How much?"

Beckett reached inside his shirt and removed his gold medallion. Though marked with the seal of the Clan MacLeod, he hoped it would be worth something off his planet. He held it out.

She snatched the medallion from his palm and held it up in the dim light. "Is this gold?"

"Aye."

As she ran a small metal box over the medallion, tiny lights flashed in the darkness, then disappeared. "It's real."

Beckett caught her note of awe. "'Tis enough for your fee?"

"Perhaps." Raven hesitated, staring at the medallion. "Who are you? Where are you from?"

"I'm Beckett MacLeod from Alba."

"Alba?" She spoke derisively. "I thought no one ever left Alba, not since it was settled almost two hundred years ago."

"We prefer to keep to ourselves. I'd nae have left except for Ciorstan."

"Your daughter?"

"Aye."

"And why did she leave?"

He sighed. How could he explain without sounding a fool? "There's a legend. Actually, more of a riddle." Hearing Raven's exasperated sigh, he plunged ahead. "Ciorstan's trying to find the magical sword of Mac-Leod."

"A magical sword?" Disbelief tinged her voice. "Why?"

"We've had two years of drought. Our crops have failed. The people are starving." Beckett ground his teeth together as he recalled the meager amounts of food they had left. Even with supplies from the merchant ships, it wasn't enough.

"She believes this sword will fix everything?"

"Aye," he said, his heart heavy. He'd failed not only

his people, but his daughter. Else she'd never have defied him, never risked her life in this forsaken world to
find a legendary sword. "She left a note saying she'd
solved the riddle and would bring back the sword."

"Then let her do that. She might surprise you."

"No." He clenched his fists. "I'll nae leave my daughter alone in this . . . this chaos."

Raven paused and extended the medallion so that the
dim light gleamed off it. "If I agree to find your daughter, the medallion is mine?"

Beckett quickly snatched the medallion back. "*After*
you find my daughter."

Even though Raven gave no outward display of emotion, he sensed her anger . . . and something else, too.
Something more . . . unnerving. A sudden knot of longing swirled in his chest—a longing tied to this Raven
person.

Frowning, Beckett dismissed the idea. He needed to
find Ciorstan, not dally with some woman, even if she
was physically appealing. He extended his hand. "Will
you find my daughter or nae?"

Raven drew an audible breath and released it slowly.
"I'll do it."

Wrapping his fingers around hers, Beckett measured
her strength. Her callused palm told him she wasn't
afraid of hard work. "We'll work together fine."

She jerked her hand from his. "I work alone. Let me
know where you're staying and I'll deliver Ciorstan to
you. Do you have a holo of her?"

"You dinna understand." Beckett didn't try to keep
the coldness from his voice. "Ciorstan is *my* daughter.
She's alone here. I'm going with you."

"I—"

"I go or I find another tracker."

"You won't find another as good as me."

"I'll take that chance." Beckett noted the spark of intelligence in her eyes as she apparently weighed both
sides of the problem. Her glance darted once more to
the medallion, and he closed his fingers around it. So,
she was mercenary. He'd use any advantage he could.

15

"If you find her in less than three days, I'll throw in a bonus."

"You'll only slow me down. You're from a backward planet," she snapped. "In the two hundred years since it's been settled, Alba hasn't progressed at all. If anything, it's regressed."

Beckett straightened and adjusted his Clan MacLeod tartan sash. "We live the way we do because we choose to."

"You know nothing about the real universe."

"I already know more than I cared to learn. Find my daughter and I'll be gone. I've nae desire to remain here."

She glared at him, the angry fire in her gaze fueling the low heat already brewing in his gut. To his surprise, she nodded curtly, then brushed past him to enter the bar. "I need a drink."

So do I. Beckett grimaced and followed her inside. Seating himself in one of the cuplike floating chairs, he stiffened as it adjusted its height to match his long legs. A smirk played at the corner of Raven's lips, and he forced himself to relax.

As much as he hated to admit it, she had a valid point. He didn't know much about any world other than Alba, and what knowledge he did have came from books over two hundred years old. But he learned quickly.

Raven motioned to the bartender, a purplish creature with a long thin nose and huge globular eyes, and held up one finger. Following her example, Beckett did the same. Raven quirked an eyebrow at him but said nothing.

Leaning back in her chair, Raven studied him through narrowed eyes. Beckett returned her steady gaze. She was not about to intimidate him. He'd faced tougher challenges than her.

Their stares broke only when a tray containing two odd-shaped flasks floated over to their table. Raven removed the cups and placed her thumb against a small glowing disk on the tray. It flashed once, then beeped, and the tray slowly drifted away.

Beckett accepted a flask. "What did you do?"

"I paid for our drinks."

"With what? Your thumbprint?"

"Exactly. Nemeth will add the cost to my account."

"And when do you give him real money?"

"Money? Oh, credits? When *I* get paid."

He frowned. "You'll get paid when you find my daughter."

"So you've said." She lifted the mug to her lips and took a quick swallow. "How did you get here?"

"A merchant ship stops at our planet once a month. Ciorstan left a month ago. I persuaded the captain of the next ship to bring me after her." He grimaced, remembering his methods of persuasion. He'd been ready to rip the hideous alien's oversized head from its body in order to secure passage. Ciorstan had already been gone for a month. Anything could have happened to her. Fortunately, a supply of tartan fabric provided suitable payment for his trip.

"I'm surprised your planet allows merchant ships."

"Only for the past two years." Beckett remembered the wave of fear his people had experienced when the first merchant ship had landed in the fields near his castle. If not for the already failing crops, the ship would've been sent on its way. Ciorstan had persuaded him to trade with the merchants for food—food that had sustained them that first long, cruel winter.

The clansmen of Alba continued to trade in order to survive, but now they had little left to barter. Though their distinctive plaids, the only ones in the galaxy still made from real sheep's wool, were in demand, the weavers could barely produce enough to purchase the food they needed. Especially with sheep dying from the drought as well.

Guilt stabbed at Beckett. Though he couldn't control the weather, he still felt responsible for his people's hunger. Something had to be done. If only the sword were real . . .

Gripping his mug, he gulped the contents, then gasped for air, his eyes watering. "What is that?"

"Tanturian ale, best in this galaxy." Raven smiled slightly. "It tends to be potent."

"Aye." Beckett inhaled deeply. "It does pack a punch, but I'll wager Alban ale tastes better."

"I'll take your word for that." She took another short swallow of her drink, then leaned across the small table. "Do you know the name of the merchant ship your daughter left on?"

"The *Batista*."

"One of the Galacta line." She nodded, her brow furrowed. "I need to talk to the *Batista*'s captain." She jumped to her feet, pausing only briefly to glance back at Beckett. "If you plan to come with me, you'd better keep up."

Beckett leapt beside her in an instant. "I can keep up." He kept his voice low, the challenge in it barely hidden. "Dinna worry about me."

She had to be out of her mind. As she signaled for a shuttle, Raven darted a quick glance at the man by her side. Why had she agreed to look for his daughter? Children made her feel uncomfortable. They were always so . . . needy.

So, why? Because she needed the money. Simple. The thruster was failing on her ship and a long list of other things needed repair. A tracker without a ship couldn't track. If she didn't get her ship fixed soon, she'd find herself stranded . . . probably somewhere she didn't want to be.

And his gold medallion had to be worth a fortune. Gold was one of the scarcest ores in the universe. She only knew of three planets where it could be found.

The shrill whistle of a shuttle pierced her ears and she waited for the glide car to hover to a stop before her. As the hatch opened, she swung inside and waited for Beckett.

He stared at the shuttle as if it were a menacing beast, then slowly climbed onto the seat opposite her. The door slid into place with a gentle hiss.

"Merchants' Guild," Raven said. She noticed how

Beckett's muscles tightened when the vehicle began to move.

"What's happening?" he asked. His gaze searched the closed interior as if looking for an escape route.

"It's all right." She couldn't fault him for his trepidation. This had to be new to him. The dark interior and fluid movement of the craft still unnerved her, and she'd been in one many times. She much preferred to be the pilot and not trust Cirian technology, but a shuttle was the quickest method of ground transportation on the planet.

"What is this thing?"

"It's called a shuttle. It's programmed to take us anywhere on the surface."

"But there are nae windows. How do you see?"

"It knows where it's going. Besides, there's not much to see on Cirius. It's a pretty dismal place. If not for the Merchants' Guild, this planet would have nothing of value." Raven didn't mind not having windows; she preferred to look at Beckett. This Alban man intrigued her.
. He stood taller than she—something she didn't experience often when with humans. But the rugged planes of his face and his sculpted muscles interested her more. She rarely saw a humanoid in such condition. Most of them were paler, thinner, and definitely a lot less . . . solid. Maybe there was something to be said for the primitive lifestyle on Alba if it created such fascinating specimens.

His hair, the color of sim-coffee with lightener, fell to the base of his neck in wild disarray. It looked clean, soft, begged for her touch.

Raven stiffened and forced her gaze away. She had no desire to touch any man, especially not this uncivilized one. She would find his daughter and send both of them back to their isolated planet at the edge of the galaxy.

"What do you hope to find at the Merchants' Guild?" Beckett's voice, with its lilting accent, interrupted her thoughts.

"The pilot from the *Batista* will probably be there.

He'll know where your daughter went." She mentally prepared for the conversation, hating any contact with merchant pilots. They thought they owned the space lanes. "I doubt she went far."

With luck, the child would still be with the merchants. None of them would risk their profits on some girl's wild talk of a legendary sword. They preferred their credits risk-free.

The shuttle slowed and Raven gripped the handrail in anticipation of the inevitable sudden stop. She's barely opened her mouth to warn Beckett when the vehicle jerked to a standstill, throwing him onto her.

He reacted quickly, bracing his weight on his arms, but couldn't stop his body from touching hers. Instant awareness flooded Raven as she grabbed his forearms to steady him. His solid chest pressed against hers, his narrow hips lodged over her knees, his face—his lips— hovered just a short distance away.

Raven's breath caught in her throat, her gaze locked with his as she noticed his brown eyes darken. An odd sensation, similar to one she'd experienced during her first nosedive in Devil's Canyon, fluttered in her stomach.

Raven forced her constricted vocal cords to work. "The . . . the shuttle stops quickly."

He blinked and pulled back, his expression hardening. "Aye."

She punched the hatch control and leapt from the shuttle as the door opened. Drawing a deep breath, she studied the entrance to the Merchants' Guild Hall. As she concentrated on the ornate exterior, with its towering columns and overdone sculptures, her mind regained its usual equilibrium. The sooner she rid herself of this man, the better. She hadn't been this rattled since her first space battle.

Beckett joined her, his eyes widening when he looked at the Guild Hall. Raven tried to see it as he would. The building had been designed to be imposing and it succeeded. In addition to its extravagance, iron gates sealed the entrance where two Gatorians stood guard.

Fortunately, Gatorians were as dumb as they were big. Raven sighed loudly and approached them, motioning for Beckett to follow.

As she expected, one of the oversized alligators blocked her path, his black eyes unblinking and his sharp teeth bared. He looked mean, Raven would credit him that.

He spoke, but she heard only gibberish. Frowning, she tapped the universal translator hanging over her right ear. It shouldn't need charging again already. After a few taps his speech became intelligible.

". . . your business here."

"I have an appointment with Guild Master Hatuna." Raven straightened to her full height, but the Gatorian still towered over her.

"Show me papers." His speech sounded guttural even in translation.

Raven fished her parking permit from her upper pocket and waved it before the creature, not allowing him enough time to see it clearly. Drawing on her most haughty manner, she met his stare. "Hatuna will not like it if we're delayed."

The beast hesitated.

"Very well. I'll leave." Raven turned to go and frowned at Beckett's glimmer of dismay. She winked at him and his face went bland instantly. Turning back to the Gatorian, she smiled. "May I have your name? I'll need to explain this to Hatuna."

The creature decoded the gates at once and Raven gave him a regal nod as she led Beckett inside. Thank her lucky star that Gatorians didn't have the sense to call in and check. Of course, most creatures desiring entry were intimidated by the Gatorians' appearance and didn't realize how easily the guards could be bluffed. The merchants counted on that.

But the merchants hadn't met Raven . . . yet.

If the exterior was imposing, the interior appeared less so. The walls were dark, the high ceiling illuminated by recessed lighting. The corridors were wide and straight, apparently leading nowhere.

21

Raven knew better. She'd managed to infiltrate this place before. Locating her position from a barely visible icon on the wall, she quickly started down a long corridor.

Beckett fell into step with her. "What is this place?"

"The all powerful Merchants' Guild." She grimaced. "At least, they like to think so."

"What does that mean?"

She paused, framing her answer. She'd always known about the Guild. How could she explain it to someone who'd never heard of it? "The merchants are a powerful force in the universe. Their ships have the fastest engines, the best quality magnicite. They can travel anywhere in a fraction of the time it takes a smaller ship. Because of this, they control the distribution of goods from one end of the galaxy to the other."

"Then they're wealthy?"

"Very. Because of their wealth they look down on everyone else. They consider themselves better than any species in existence. In fact, they're only afraid of one thing. . . ." She smiled slightly.

Beckett eyed her curiously. "And what's that?"

"The privateers."

"Pirates?"

"They prefer to be known as privateers," she replied. "They have the ability to board a merchant ship in hyperspace and lighten the load before the merchant even knows they're there."

His eyes gleamed with amusement. "I suppose the merchants dinna like that much."

"Not much at all."

A group of Salurians, the dominant merchant race, approached them. The species was short as a rule, rarely reaching Raven's height, and often as wide as they were tall. With their short arms and legs, Raven thought they resembled a ball. Only their large bald heads protruding from thick necks destroyed that illusion. Their facial features were basically humanoid with two large purple eyes, nasal slits, and a surprisingly small mouth lined with thick purple lips. Overall, they were disgusting in appearance and behavior, yet this race controlled much of the power in the known universe.

Raven touched Beckett's arm. "Just ignore them," she whispered.

She could see him struggle to turn his gaze from them before he nodded. Not that she blamed him for staring. If the Salurians hadn't become merchants, she doubted they'd be good for anything else.

The Salurian group ignored Raven and Beckett as they passed, and Raven breathed a sigh of relief. Turning sharply, she led Beckett down the short corridor into a tiny room.

A human, his back to them, stood behind a short counter, bent over a display terminal. Muttering to himself, he punched several keys, then threw up his hands, whirled around . . . and gasped. "Raven, what . . . what are *you* doing here?" He frowned at Beckett. "And who's that?"

"This is my latest client, Beckett MacLeod. Beckett, Nehemiah Evanston, the coordinator for the Guild here on Cirius."

"You shouldn't be here," Nehemiah said, his gaze darting to the doorway behind them. "You know unauthorized personnel aren't allowed in the Guild."

Raven smiled in what she hoped was a beguiling manner. "I'll be gone as soon as you answer a couple of questions for me."

Her smile must have worked for he sighed dramatically. "Fine. What do you need?"

"The captain of the *Batista;* who is it?"

Nehemiah lifted one eyebrow but turned to his terminal and keyed quickly. He replied without turning around. "It's a Salurian. Hau te Dur."

"Is he here?"

More tapping of keys followed. "He's in the lounge." Nehemiah glanced at her over his shoulder. "Surely you're not—"

Raven cut him off. "Does he have a little girl with him? A human girl?"

"No."

"Is she elsewhere in the Hall?"

"Don't ask for much, do you?" Nehemiah examined a lit screen, then shook his head. "No human children anywhere."

Raven sighed and met Beckett's stony gaze. "This may not be as easy as I thought," she said.

"If she's nae here, then where is she?" His face darkened beneath his frown.

Holding up her hand, she forced a smile. "I'll find her. Don't worry." She edged toward the door. "Hau te Dur. In the lounge. Thanks, Nehemiah."

"You can't—" he began, his anxiety evident in his voice.

Raven didn't wait for him to finish. Instead, she pivoted and hurried down the hallway, knowing instinctively from the way the back of her neck tingled that Beckett followed only one pace behind. She had to find the kid and get rid of this guy . . . soon.

He snagged her arm before they reached the main corridor and swung her around to face him. Her muscles tensed, her hand automatically flying to the butt of her laser. His thunderous expression wasn't reassuring.

"Where are we going?" he demanded. "How will we find Ciorstan?"

Raven held on to her temper, rationalizing that her racing heartbeat was due only to anger. Beckett came from Alba, a primitive planet, she reminded herself. It helped to remember that. "I plan to talk to the captain of the *Batista*. He'll know where he left your daughter."

"Then why did Nehemiah act like we're in danger?"

"Because we are." She refused to blink. "The Guild doesn't care for trespassers. They're a very . . . private group."

Beckett paused. Raven could almost see him thinking. "What will they do if they catch us?" he asked finally.

She shrugged. "They might throw us out with a warning or send us to labor in the Turellian vineyards or, more likely, they'll kill us."

"I see."

Surprisingly, Raven thought he did see. For a person from an ancient culture, he had a peculiar worldliness about him. "I can show you a way out of here if you want to wait beyond the walls."

"I'm going with you."

"Suit yourself." Raven tugged her arm free. Her skin felt warm where he'd held her and it was all she could do to keep from rubbing the spot.

She paused to regain her bearings, then turned in the direction of the lounge. With luck, she'd find Hau te Dur quickly, get the information she needed, and be gone before anyone realized she didn't belong there. After all, many members of the Guild were human. They couldn't possibly all know each other.

The loud roar of conversation reached them long before Raven and Beckett saw the entrance to the lounge. Raven hesitated outside the open arch doorway to let Beckett adjust to the sight inside.

Hovertables dotted the enormous room with most of them surrounded by groups of merchants. The non-humanoid species stood out easily. Raven skipped past them quickly as she searched the interior for her quarry.

The greater number of those remaining were Salurians. Raven had met Hau te Dur only once, but fortunately she had a good memory. If he was in the lounge, she'd find him—without using a scanner. That device would give her away in an instant.

Catching a glimpse of Beckett's stunned expression, she smiled. What she accepted as ordinary he obviously saw as extraordinary. She tried to imagine having spent her whole life on one planet, never traveling in space, but couldn't. Soaring among the stars was her life.

"All the languages blend together," Beckett said suddenly. "How do you understand them?"

Raven unhooked her translator from her ear and laid it in her open palm. "With this. It's a universal translator programmed to handle two hundred of the known languages."

He reached for it. "May I?" At her nod, he lifted the device and examined it, a frown creasing his brow. "What does it do?"

"It takes the language spoken and converts it to the chosen standard—in my case, Earth Basic. Want to try it?"

"Aye." Beckett tried unsuccessfully to loop it over his ear.

Raven interceded, then jerked her hand back when it collided with his. "Let me help," she murmured, disturbed by the quick shock that tingled up her arm. Reaching up, she adjusted the translator into a better fit. Though tailored for her ear, it settled into his with little difficulty.

"It feels . . . different." He turned his head back and forth, as if seeking a conversation.

"Wait until you've worn one for a few weeks. You'll forget you have it on." She grinned. "Unless the battery goes dead. That happened to me once in the middle of bartering with a Tanturian and caused massive problems."

He smiled slowly, his face changing as the tiredness faded and warmth entered his eyes. "I can imagine."

His handsomeness stunned her. A wave of heat washed over Raven, and she yanked her gaze away. "Come on. We have business inside."

She stopped midway into the room and surveyed the occupants again. There. In the corner. The Salurian sat at a table across from a Dweezle, probably his load master.

Unwilling to shout over the angry conversation erupting nearby, Raven touched Beckett's shoulder and pointed. He nodded. They'd only gone a few steps when fighting broke out around them. As Raven ducked to avoid flying flasks, she was surprised to feel Beckett's arm stretch protectively across her shoulders.

She stared at him, her eyes wide. No one had ever tried to protect her before.

As he met her gaze, he dropped his arm with an apologetic twist of his lips. Before Raven could speak he stretched his hand and snatched something out of the air. Bringing his hand down, he opened it to reveal a translator similar to her own and raised his eyebrows in a questioning gesture.

Raven grinned. This Alban might not be so bad after all. She wove a path through the tempest of thrown drinks and furniture, then stopped and glanced back. "I wonder what brought that on."

Amusement flickered in Beckett's eyes. "If I heard correctly, 'twas some dispute about credits."

"That's normal." She indicated the translator still clutched in his hand. "Would you like help with that?"

" 'Tis nae likely to be missed, is it?"

Raven shook her head. "By the time they recover from the drinking and the fighting they'll have a hard time remembering where they last had it." She took the device and hesitated over the setting. "Is Earth Basic good for you?"

"I can understand you," he replied.

"Earth Basic, then." Once she adjusted the new translator on his ear she restored her own to its usual position. "Is it working?"

He turned his head toward a nearby hovertable of Salurians. "I understand them."

"It's working. You think quick, Beckett," she admitted grudgingly.

"Some things remain the same no matter the culture."

"I agree." From the corner of her eye Raven saw the Dweezle pad away from Hau to Dur's table. With a jerk of her head she motioned to Beckett to follow and slid into the vacated seat just as the Salurian began to rise. "Hau te Dur, a moment of your time, please."

He fixed his purple gaze on her, then shifted it to Beckett before he sat again. "Who are you?"

Raven shook her head as she grabbed several credits from her pouch and laid the coins on the table. "My name's not important. I have a question for you."

The top of the Salurian's bald head pulsed with apparent eagerness and he slid one four-fingered hand across the table to retrieve the credits. "And it is?"

"You brought a girl with you from Alba."

His head pulse increased. "That was a mistake. A nuisance, that one. She demanded I take her on some ridiculous quest across the galaxy."

Beckett stiffened, and Raven laid a warning hand on his arm. "Where is the girl now?" she asked. With luck, Hau would say she was in personnel processing and this job would be finished.

"I have no idea. I left her at the terminal."

"You left her at the terminal?" Even though she didn't particularly care for children, Raven couldn't imagine leaving any child in the madhouse of creatures arriving and departing from Cirius. "What are you—a Neeban?"

Hau te Dur stood, indignation apparent in his round body. "I brought her here as requested. I had no responsibility for her."

"Sit down." Raven hardened her voice as she eased her laser from its holster and lifted it just high enough for the Salurian to see. "Sit down *now*."

Slowly Hau resumed his seat. "You're inside the Hall. You can't—"

"Where is the girl? She's been here for a month." Raven could sense Beckett's frustration mingling with her own. "I'm willing to bet you know what happened to every single passenger on your ship."

"And if I don't?" Hau's manner screamed defiance.

"Everyone is still watching the fight over there. I could probably make a small hole right through your middle and no one would even know." Raven leaned across the table to meet his gaze, daring him to doubt her sincerity.

His large head wobbled. "She pestered merchants and passengers for many days with her insistent demands. Finally I . . . she hired someone to take her on her foolish journey."

"Who?"

"A Beta-human known as Slade." His disgust centered on the name.

Slade.

Raven fell back into her seat, hot and cold alternating beneath her skin, her stomach churning. *Neptune's Rings, not Slade.*

Dark memories returned in a rush, filled with sensations of horror, fear, helplessness. She couldn't speak through her constricted throat, but she heard, as if in the distance, Beckett speaking.

"Who is this Slade?"

"A privateer. A killer with no morals, no conscience."

Beckett flew at the Salurian, wrapping his hands around the thick neck. "You let my daughter leave with such a man?"

Jerked out of her isolation by new terror, Raven hurried to pull Beckett off Hau te Dur. "Stop it. You'll get us killed."

He was strong. His muscles rippled beneath her grasp, but he finally released his hold and staggered backward, his breathing uneven. Raven released a sigh of relief. Now, if they could get out of there before anyone noticed them . . .

Aware of the abrupt silence, she searched the room. Too late.

Four regulators were approaching with their lasers drawn.

Raven's heart sank. "Shibit."

Chapter Two

"I assume this isna good," Beckett murmured.

Raven tightened her fingers around the butt of her gun as she sent him a quelling glance. "I hope you have a weapon with you."

His eyes darkened. "Aye."

Hau te Dur leapt unsteadily to his feet and waved at the regulators to hurry. "These . . . these humans tried to kill me."

The thick-bodied, well-armored guards were almost upon them. Raven's stomach knotted as all her muscles coiled in readiness. As the regulators stopped, their weapons aimed at Raven and Beckett, she drew back her legs and kicked the hovertable with all her strength.

It slammed into the regulators, knocking them back. Raven catapulted up, firing her laser at the ceiling. Bits of it fell on the creatures below as she started for the entrance. "Come on, Beckett."

She trusted him to follow. A laser blast reduced a nearby table into rubble. She flinched and dove behind another table. Beckett slid in beside her.

Aiming carefully, she squeezed off several blasts designed to hit near the regulators but not on them. She preferred not to kill if she could help it, especially since killing a regulator would not earn her any good marks in the star lanes.

More shots erupted around them. Raven grimaced. They had to get out of there—fast. Scanning the room, she spotted the door to the kitchen. That would have to do.

She touched Beckett's shoulder. "Keep them busy until I get to that door; then you follow."

He nodded, his expression grave. "Get on with you, then."

The regulators fired off more blasts amid the protests of fleeing patrons. A chair careened over Raven and Beckett's heads before smashing against the wall.

We're outta here.

Raven darted toward the door, but skidded to a stop, whirling around as she heard Beckett release a primeval yell. He stood behind the table, brandishing a long sword.

A sword?

They were going to die, no doubt about it.

As she turned back to help him, she suddenly noticed the quiet in the room. Everyone stared at the Alban man, magnificent in his ancient stance. Even the regulators looked dumbfounded.

Maybe this wasn't all bad.

She slid to a stop by the doorway as one guard emerged from his trance. "Beckett, come on," she shouted. Firing steadily above the heads in the room, she kept her attention focused on the merchant guards, pausing only to nod at Beckett as he joined her. "Through here," she ordered.

He dove through the door without question. Laser blasts ricocheted off the walls. Raven ducked inside after him, the near misses almost scorching her.

The kitchen staff huddled together in one corner of the large room, jabbering in a variety of languages. Beckett stood by the door, his sword flourished in a challenging pose. "There's another door over there." Using his weapon, he pointed toward the back.

"Hurry." Raven heard loud footsteps approaching. Running past Beckett, she grabbed his arm to pull him with her.

He took the lead, his long strides carrying him past her and through the door into the sunlight. Raven raced outside in time to see him parrying blasts from a Gatorian guard's laser. Reacting instinctively, she fired. The creature's gun—and hand—fell to the ground as it roared in pain.

With a groan, she motioned for Beckett to follow. This was not going the way she'd planned. Darting a quick glance at the handsome Alban, she decided nothing was likely to go as she expected until she sent Beckett MacLeod on his way. Her own illogical reaction to him was only exacerbated by his ancient set of standards.

She maneuvered through the complex twists and turns of the Guild Hall's grounds until she finally reached the pathways.

Her chest burned from the reduced oxygen in Cirius's atmosphere. Placing her hands on her knees, Raven bent double to ease the pain in her side as she inhaled deeply.

Beckett's breathing sounded strained as well, but he paused to touch her shoulder. "Are you all right?"

She nodded. "We have to get to my ship." Hearing loud voices approach, she straightened. "It's still a distance from here."

He nodded grimly. "Lead on."

They ran again, Beckett close beside Raven as she stayed in the shadows along the narrow pathways. She concentrated on placing one foot before the other and tried to ignore her lungs screaming for more air. She'd never liked Cirius much—its gravity was heavy and air thin. Just as well. After today she probably wouldn't be too welcome around the spaceport.

Finally she spotted the spirals of the transport center,

towering over the crowded buildings. Not much farther.

The high-pitched hum of an approaching shuttle caught her attention. Quickly surveying the area, Raven pointed to several crates stacked against a building. Beckett reached the spot at the same time she did.

They crouched, forced close together in the small space. Raven's breathing suddenly became even more difficult. Surely it was just lack of oxygen. She tried to listen for the shuttle, but only heard her own heart hammering. Beckett's body heat enveloped her, stirring her senses. Her thoughts wandered. How could any creature smell as wonderful as Beckett MacLeod?

The shuttle's rapid pass caught her unaware. She stiffened, her hand tightening around her gun, and was surprised to feel Beckett's arm fall around her shoulders.

He was trying to protect her again. Raven looked at him. His expression was forbidding as he watched the pathway. What kind of man was he? Though armed with only an ancient sword, he'd been ready to face the regulators. He was either very brave . . . or very foolish.

Somehow, he didn't seem to fit the latter.

Once she ascertained that the shuttle had passed, Raven touched the ship-link band around her wrist. "Mac, activate."

He replied immediately. "Status ready."

"Run through preflight. Be ready for an immediate liftoff."

"Affirmative."

Closing the link, Raven looked at Beckett. At any other time his quizzical expression would have been humorous. "Just getting my ship ready."

"I see." He didn't sound convinced.

"Let's go." Raven stepped from behind the garbage and froze. A regulator, yellow eyes gleaming beneath his black helmet, waited for her, his gun pointed at her chest.

Raven swallowed . . . hard. Not good. Not good at all.

She plotted escape maneuvers quickly, but before she

Karen Fox

could move Beckett appeared at her side, his sword swinging. His blade flashed and the regulator fell to the ground, his mouth open in a soundless scream.

Raven's eyes widened. She'd barely seen Beckett move. "G-good job," she said finally.

Beckett gave her a tight nod. "I dinna see another option."

"That's because there wasn't one." Raven glanced at the fallen guard and inhaled sharply. A dead regulator; she would *definitely* not be welcome on Cirius again. In fact, she'd do well to avoid this entire sector for a while . . . if she lived to get off the planet.

She pointed to the spirals in the distance. "My ship's there—at the spaceport. We'd better hurry."

Beckett recognized the worry in her gaze before she looked away. He'd obviously added to their troubles. Sheathing his sword, he fell into a run behind her. It went against his upbringing to let a woman lead into danger, but on this planet he had little choice. She knew the territory; he didn't. Surveying the surrounding area, he realized the threat could come from any direction. He touched the hilt of his sword. He'd be ready for them.

He only hoped he and Raven reached her ship before his aching lungs gave out. He'd been warned about this planet's atmosphere but hadn't noticed much difference—until he started running. Another note to add to his growing list of knowledge about life off Alba . . . a list already too long of strange creatures, unusual habits, and a very different woman.

Watching Raven's buttocks move as she ran provided a brief respite from the agony in his chest. She did things for her jumpsuit that would no doubt be illegal on Alba.

A strange woman, that one. He wasn't sure if he liked her, but she intrigued him. More than that, she attracted him. He hadn't wanted a woman since his wife died, but this one . . . this one stirred his desire.

He shook his head to chase away the heat rising in his blood. He hadn't left Alba to find a woman, espe-

34

cially one so completely opposite from Nessa. Ciorstan was what mattered, not an alien tracker named Raven.

After all, he knew naught about her, though he had noticed the way she'd avoided killing anyone during their escape, had seen the brief flash of despair in her eyes when he'd slain the guard. Despite her tough exterior, Beckett suspected Raven had a heart.

And he needed a tracker with a heart to find Ciorstan.

Beckett refused to let panic overwhelm him. His daughter, only nine years old, had already been among these aliens for a month. Even though Ciorstan harangued him often about adapting to more modern times, she was ill prepared for this lifestyle. Then to learn she'd left with a privateer—a pirate. He shuddered.

He had to find her.

Raven slowed as they left the security of the shadows and approached the large open area known as a spaceport. Ships of varied shapes and sizes filled parking slots along one side. An odd assortment of creatures, some human, most alien, bustled through checkpoints in and out.

As Raven stopped, Beckett noticed her staring at one gate in particular—the checkpoint into the terminal. He scanned the area. No sign of the guards; nothing looked out of the ordinary. But then, he didn't know what ordinary was here.

" 'Tis a problem?" he asked.

"I don't think so. It doesn't look like the regulators have reached here yet." She pulled a slim silver card from her pocket. "Do you have your entry pass?"

Remembering the odd metallic device he'd been given upon arrival, Beckett retrieved it from his belt. "Is this it?"

"That's it." Raven inhaled sharply, straightening her shoulders. "Let's go. Don't say a word."

As they approached the checkpoint, Beckett could sense her nervousness. She walked stiffly, held her head erect. Reaching the entrance, Raven passed her card through a shining beam. A bell rang once and the gate swung open. She gave Beckett an encouraging smile, a smile that made him catch his breath; then she hurried through.

Following her lead, he swiped his card over the light. For a moment nothing happened, and Beckett's stomach contracted. Had he done something wrong? They didn't need to call attention to themselves.

He was ready to back away when a ding sounded and the gate opened to allow him through. Not given to wasting time, he walked quickly to Raven's side.

Her expression brightened slightly, but she gave him only a terse nod. "My ship's parked at twelve-G. Hurry."

They walked quickly, trying not to be obvious in their hurry, covering the open terminal with long strides until they finally reached the ships' parking area. Raven didn't slow her pace in the narrow aisles, dodging up one lane and down another.

She stopped suddenly and turned to face Beckett, her expression wary. "This is it. My ship, the *TrackStar*. No comments, please."

Her defensive tone made Beckett study the craft. The vehicle wasn't very big. Fat at one end, narrowing at the front, it resembled a teardrop in shape. It might have once been silver but now consisted of patches in several colors, emphasizing the dents and gouges. This ship had seen better days. Could it fly? Two large engines protruded from the back. Beckett heard a distinct humming emitting from them. At least the thing sounded like it worked. "It's . . . good."

Her gaze focused on him, as if she expected more. What else could he say? He had no experience with spaceships.

"Does it work?" he added.

She frowned. "It'll get us anywhere in the universe," she replied, indignation in her voice.

"Good. Can we leave now?" Beckett glanced over his shoulder. No sign of regulators . . . yet.

Placing her hand against the side of the ship, Raven stated her name. At once, a panel slid up and she stepped inside. Before Beckett could follow she held out her hand to stop him. "Just a minute." She spoke into the air. "Mac, scan one guest, name Beckett MacLeod." She motioned Beckett into the doorway. "Stand there for a moment."

The hairs on his neck prickled, but he did as she asked. She meant him no harm, he felt certain of that. He sensed rather than saw someone . . . something looking at him. All his muscles tightened and he fought the urge to leap from the doorway. He jumped when a voice spoke close by.

"Beckett MacLeod. Scanned. Mass calculated for lift-off."

"Good." Raven waved Beckett inside the spacecraft. "Close hatch."

The door slid into place and Beckett hesitated, waiting for his eyes to adjust to the dim interior. He couldn't make out much of anything and half expected someone else to emerge from the shadows. "Who spoke?" he asked finally.

"My computer."

"A computer?" He'd read about those devices—intelligent machines that had taken over many of the mundane jobs on Earth. The thought of them made him uneasy, especially when confronted with one that talked. Where was it? He could make out two seats situated before a wide console but saw nothing he thought had spoken.

Raven slid into one seat and immediately flicked several switches in front of her. The defensive note returned to her voice. "A Macintosh V3000. Any problem with that?"

"Nae." One brand was the same as the other where he was concerned. Letting a machine act in the place of a human seemed wrong somehow, but he knew they were an integral part of this culture—a culture his ancestors had fled.

"Sit down. Strap yourself in." As Raven pressed a button, the cover retracted from the window before them, revealing the night sky. "Mac, everything ready to go?"

"All conditions go." The mechanical voice filled the

spacecraft, apparently everywhere at once. Beckett shuddered. He preferred to see who was speaking.

Raven hesitated, her hand hovering over a switch. "Let's hope word hasn't reached the tower yet."

She flipped the switch and spoke. "Tower, this is *TrackStar* requesting permission to depart landing bay twelve-G."

Though her tone remained calm, he noticed her hand clenching into a fist. What would happen if the regulators had reached the tower?

"TrackStar, this is Tower. You're cleared for departure on star lane Gamma Six."

Relief flickered across her face. "Affirmative, Tower." She flipped the switch again and released an audible sigh. "Mac, power up the engines. Let's get out of here."

A loud roar reverberated through the craft, jostling Beckett. Though he knew spacecraft were normal for this culture, he couldn't stop himself from tensing. The merchant ship he'd ridden to Cirius had been loud, but nothing like this.

"Port thruster is at fifty percent," the computer said.

Raven frowned and quickly unfastened her straps. "Don't fail me now, ship."

"What is it?" Beckett started to reach for his straps, but she shook her head.

"Just need to make an adjustment. It'll only take a moment." She added her next words under her breath, but Beckett still heard them. "I hope."

Moving to the rear of the craft, she opened a panel. The roaring sound increased. She buried her head and arms into the opening. What was she doing?

The speaker on the console squawked and Beckett whirled back to face it. "Raven . . ."

She pulled her head out of the panel as words sounded. *"TrackStar*, this is Tower. Delay departure. Repeat. Delay departure."

"Shibit." She scowled at Beckett. "They're onto us. Flick the switch, there, back and forth several times. Don't say anything." Diving back into the panel, she continued to work.

Beckett snapped the switch, destroying the incoming words with bursts of static. This would only delay things for a short time. They needed to go. For the first time he wanted to find himself in space.

Abruptly, the engine sound evened to almost bearable proportions and Raven slapped the panel back into place. Sliding into her seat, she strapped herself in and grasped a lever in the front panel. She gave Beckett a wry smile. "Hang on. We're making a quick departure."

As she pulled on the lever, the ship thrust forward, throwing Beckett back against the seat. A heavy weight sat on his chest, a feeling he knew was normal, but that didn't stop his rapid heartbeat.

The lights of the spaceport flickered past in an instant until blackness filled the window—blackness broken only by blurred bright dots. Alba was one of those dots.

Beckett closed his eyes against an onslaught of home-sickness. He couldn't wait to find Ciorstan and return to Alba. This universe held nothing for him.

The pressure on his chest eased. His eyes flew open as Raven spoke to her computer. "Mac, stabilize life support. Initiate short-range scanning."

"Affirmative."

She turned to Beckett. "We're off-planet now. Once we're far enough away I'll take us into hyperspace. They'll never catch me there. I know how to maneuver better than they do."

"Hyperspace?" He hated not knowing the words she tossed around with such casual ease.

"It's . . . ah . . . a way to travel faster than light, to reach a destination in days and weeks rather than years or centuries."

He paused. Should he ask how it worked? Did he really want to know? Would he understand if she told him?

"Warning." Mac disrupted Beckett's thoughts. "Warning. Merchant Guild ship approaching with lasers on active."

Raven groaned. "This is not my day." She studied the

console. "Push the thrusters, Mac. We need launch location now."

"Port thruster may not withstand push."

"Do it, Mac."

Beckett felt the surge of power from behind him. The planet below diminished into a small globe in the blackness. Scanning the space, he spotted a ship in the distance and pointed to it as a steady beam of light shot from its nose. "Raven, there."

She reacted instantly, dipping the ship to allow the beam to explode over them. The craft shook from the blast. "Neptune's Rings."

Her face was taut, her lips set in a firm line. Beckett didn't need to be told they were in serious trouble. "Can I do anything?" He didn't like being in this situation. Normally, he was the one in charge, the one giving orders. To sit idle grated on his nerves. "Can we shoot back?"

"The *TrackStar*'s weaponry is slim to none," she replied grimly. Glancing again at the console, she leaned forward. "Mac, prepare for hyperspeed."

"We're not in optimum launch position."

"Mac, we're going." Another blast exploded nearby, tossing the ship.

"State hyperspeed route."

"Jenese Trade Route." Raven danced her fingers across the panel, setting numbers and flicking switches. With a glance at Beckett, she inhaled sharply and pulled a lever down.

Immediately the sound of the engines changed, became quieter, more a hum than a roar, and the view outside the window blurred as the blackness deepened and the stars faded into bright streaks. Beckett released his breath, unaware until that moment that he'd been holding it.

"Hyperspeed achieved. Final course objective?"

Beckett turned to Raven, curious to hear her reply to the computer's question. Where *were* they going?

She hesitated and avoided his gaze. "Final destination is Station Six."

"Coordinates set."

"Is that where we'll find this Slade character?" he asked.

Raven tensed visibly. Instead of replying, she unfastened her straps, jumped from her seat and moved away from him.

It only took Beckett a moment to follow her, all his senses on edge. Something was wrong, but what?

"Will we find Slade there?" he repeated.

Slowly she met his gaze. "No, I'm taking you to another tracker I know. He's human, too—not as good as I am, but almost."

His stomach lurched as panic rose in his throat. He'd reached the point where he trusted Raven. She'd been willing to risk her life in the Merchant's Guild Hall. If anyone could find Cirostan, it would be this feisty lass. "Why?"

"I . . . I . . . Slade and I have a bad history." Her words came with obvious reluctance. "It would be better if we didn't meet again."

"Is he an old lover?" Even as he asked, Beckett hoped it wasn't so. He didn't want to imagine Raven with a dangerous privateer. He wanted to imagine her . . . with him.

No, he couldn't allow himself to lose sight of what was important—Ciorstan. Yet something about Raven assured him she could locate his daughter. If only she'd agree.

Raven's expression hardened. "No, he's not my lover. Slade doesn't know what love is."

A sliver of relief seeped through Beckett. "Do you fear him then?"

She didn't speak. She didn't have to. A flash of alarm crossed her face, then was carefully hidden.

Beckett gripped her shoulders. "Is he truly heartless?"

"He . . ." Raven hesitated. "He has no heart, no soul."

Trying to fight a rush of terror, Beckett drew Raven closer until her body was just centimeters from his. "But he does have my daughter, a nine-year-old who's nae been off Alba in her life."

41

As Raven's eyes widened, he knew he'd reached her, but was it enough? "She needs *your* help, Raven," he added quietly. "I'll nae be wanting second best."

Her slim form trembled beneath his hands. When she looked at him, her guard dropped, allowing him a glimpse into her well-disguised vulnerability. "I can't," she murmured. "I can't face him again." She tried to pull away, but he tightened his hold, forcing her to face him.

"Torvik is a good tracker. He'll find your daughter." She spoke with a hint of panic.

"I don't want another tracker. I want *you*." As Raven tensed, he quickly finished his statement. "To find Ciorstan. I know you can do it." Raven had to agree with him. He couldn't trust anyone else.

"I . . . I'll think about it."

Beckett controlled his elation. She would find Ciorstan. He knew it. "Thank you," he murmured.

Her defiant gaze met his. "I haven't said I'd do it."

"I know." *But you will.* Already he understood a little of how this woman thought. But not enough . . . not nearly enough. He suspected Raven held many secrets.

Watching her swallow, Beckett found the movement of her slim throat strangely erotic. Despite his concern for Ciorstan, Raven affected him more than any woman he'd met. His body responded to her nearness, to her wide eyes, to her full lips. He lifted his hand to trace the line of her face. She stared at him, her gaze confused. "I trust you, Raven. I need you."

Her eyes widened, but she didn't pull away. He moved his hand beneath her curls to clasp the back of her neck. Leaning toward her lips, Beckett wondered at the rightness of kissing this woman, of the vulnerability hidden beneath her toughness. Wanting a kiss had never done this to him before—made his blood boil, his heart hammer, his desire peak. He trembled, she trembled, everything around them shook.

He didn't hear the computer until Raven suddenly whirled around. With a start he realized everything *was* shaking, the entire ship vibrating as if caught by an unseen force.

"What—?" He grabbed onto a nearby rail.

She flung herself at her seat as the computer spoke again. "Warning. Warning. Approaching hyperwave. Evasive maneuvers required."

"I got it. Give me control," Raven ordered, reaching for the console lever.

"Evasive maneuvers required."

The ship lurched abruptly, almost knocking Beckett off his feet. "What the hell's going on?" he demanded. From passion to confusion—would he ever find his way in this universe?

Raven ignored him, directing her ire at the invisible voice. "Neptune's Rings. I'm going to reprogram you, I swear. Mac, give me control."

"Control relinquished."

The ship continued to buck and Raven yelled to Beckett over her shoulder. "Get in your seat quick and strap in tight. This could be rough."

Beckett staggered toward his chair and threw himself into it. As he fastened his straps, he watched Raven struggle with the controls. "What is it?"

"A hyperwave. Blasted merchants." Glancing out the window, her expression changed, hardened, her jaw tight.

Following her gaze, Beckett peered at the blackness. With rising horror he realized something—something invisible yet seen in a disturbance among the stars—created a wave through space.

A wave headed straight for them.

Chapter Three

"Shibit." Raven stretched toward the thruster controls. If she'd been paying attention instead of melting in Beckett's arms, she could've avoided this. Now she had no choice but to push her already failing thrusters.

The wave swept quickly toward them. Now . . . or never. Inhaling sharply, she increased the power to meet the disturbance.

"Damnation," Beckett exclaimed as the ship shuddered beneath the first blow.

Raven wanted to reassure him but couldn't afford the distraction. Committed now, she had to hold her vehicle steady and continue to surf the onslaught.

The intense vibration shook her entire body and filled the ship with creaks and groans. She recognized each noise. Everything was holding . . . so far.

" 'Tis safe?"

Raven darted a glance at Beckett. Though he gripped the console tightly, he gave no other sign of alarm. The barbarian had courage—she'd allow that. She'd ridden waves before yet her heart still pounded.

"We'll make it. Don't worry." Even as she spoke, one of the thrusters sputtered, then started again. Raven frowned. She definitely needed to find Beckett's daughter soon or her next encounter with a hyperwave might end in disaster.

The shaking eased and Raven leaned forward to scan the vast blackness ahead of her. Usually a lessening meant . . . there; she spotted the merchant starship. The distant dot grew quickly as Raven's craft approached.

Beckett straightened, his gaze focused on it. "What's that?"

"A merchant ship. It's what created this hyperwave." Raven glanced at her trajectory. "Mac, are we still in the Jenese Star Route?"

"Confirmed."

"Mac, calculate the route for the merchant ahead of us."

"Salurian merchant *Grinval* is also following the Jenese Star Route."

"Convenient." Raven smiled, experiencing a sudden surge of anticipation. She hadn't ridden a starship in a long time, but she hadn't forgotten how.

She throttled the power and gauged her next move. Though it would be difficult, she could tear her ship from this hyperwave. Or she could ride the merchant ship. With the current condition of her engines she could be taking a big chance. Why did she feel it necessary to prove her skills as a pilot to Beckett MacLeod? No one else's opinion should matter . . . but his did.

Making a quick decision, she applied full power and guided her ship forward over the wave released by the merchant's engines. She sensed rather than felt the disappearance of the hyperwave and immediately cut her thrusters.

"Is that wise?" Beckett asked.

"You'll see." She eased her craft down in a glide, leveling only a short distance above the merchant's hull. Spotting the upper portals, she grinned. This would test her skill.

She fired her forward thrusters in short bursts until

the *TrackStar* slowed and bumped gently onto the hull. In a few rapid movements she disengaged hyperspeed and cut all power. Sudden silence filled the cabin, disrupted only by Beckett's loud exhalation.

"You could've warned me, lass. 'Twas unnerving," he said with a glare.

Shrugging, she unfastened her seat belt. "There wasn't time. I thought since the merchant disrupted our path the least it could do was offer us a ride."

Beckett followed her lead and stood to face her. "Do they know we're here?"

She waved her arm at the vast expanse of hull stretching as far as she could see. "Look at the size of it. We're nothing more than a microscopic nit to them. Riding in on the wave as we did, we avoided their sensors. I'm certain they're unaware of us."

"Where will they take us?"

"If we stayed with them, we'd probably reach some of the more populated planets along this route." But she didn't plan to stay with the merchant ship long.

Anxious to see how close she came to the portal, Raven approached the floor hatch near the rear of her ship.

"Mac, deploy anchors; then seal lower hatch to hull."

Recognizing the gentle hiss of the seal, she smiled. How long had it been since she'd heard that sound? "Mac, unlock lower hatch and open."

Beckett joined her as the hatch lifted slowly to reveal an opening to the hull beneath. " 'Tis safe?"

Bending to peer down, Raven nodded. "I just want to see how close I came."

"To what?" He glanced down, then back at her. "I dinna see anything."

She pointed to the slightly off-center circle cut in the merchant's hull. "That's an emergency exit for the merchants. If I'd landed a little more to the right, we'd be able to enter their ship."

"I dinna think they'd care for that."

"You're right, but if we had the right equipment, we'd be in and out before they even knew we were here."

"For what purpose?"

"The privateers use it to remove a merchant's cargo." Looking inside once more, she studied her match to the portal. For someone who hadn't surfed a hyperwave in years, she hadn't done half bad. "Mac, close hatch and remove seal to hull."

Catching sight of Beckett's quizzical gaze, Raven turned away to check the engines. She'd do better to concentrate on what was really important. Without the thrusters she might never find Beckett's daughter. Worse yet, she could end up adrift in space with him . . . forever.

She cast him a covert glance. *Things could be worse.*

She stopped abruptly, stunned by her thoughts. He'd almost kissed her and fool that she was, she hadn't tried to stop him. Okay, so he looked like a dream and actually treated her like she had some intelligence, but she wasn't about to let any man into her life. From her experience men only wanted women for their enjoyment, and she had no intentions of giving in to lust. She knew better than that.

"Where are we going now?"

Startled by Beckett's proximity behind her, Raven whirled around. "I . . . ah . . . I'll take off from the merchant ship when we reach the right coordinates." She stepped back, hating the sudden jump in her pulse. "Mac, how long until turn point for Station Six?"

"Eight point four hours."

"Check flight records to determine if Torvik is still there."

"I don't want the other tracker, Raven." Beckett spoke quietly, his lilt soothing. "Please."

His concern reached inside her. Raven closed her eyes briefly against a rush of sympathy. She had to remember what she'd be facing. "I can't. Slade . . ."

"What did he do to frighten you so badly?"

An immediate objection leapt to Raven's lips, but she bit it back. Slade did frighten her—she'd be a fool to deny it. "I'd rather not talk about it." Unwilling to meet

47

Beckett's gaze, she turned again to the rear of the ship and yanked open the panel.

He joined her. "If 'twas that bad, what is he likely to do to my daughter?"

She heard his barely restrained fear. Justified fear. His daughter was only nine. For a fleeting moment Raven recalled her life at nine and how drastically it'd changed—one moment loved, the next discarded. Could she turn her back on a child whose father obviously loved her? Even if it meant facing Slade? She hesitated. Though Torvik was good, he didn't have her knowledge of privateers. As much as she hated to admit it, she had the best chance of locating Ciorstan.

Raven's shoulders fell as she looked at Beckett. "Very well. I'll do it."

His slow smile added a sensuousness to his face that instantly made Raven regret her words. He touched her shoulder. "Thank you."

She steeled herself against the urge to step closer, to accept the warm invitation in his eyes. "I want to get one thing clear right now. This is a business relationship—nothing more."

He dropped his hand. "Aye, as you say." Stepping back, he nodded his head in an expression of courtesy. "Excuse me for imposing before. I was out of place."

"Just . . . just don't let it happen again." Immediate remorse raised its nasty head, and Raven leaned inside the thruster chamber in an attempt to squash the emotion. Did the Alban have to sound so sincere? She'd learned long ago that men didn't apologize for anything, yet this man constantly surprised her . . . and intrigued her.

Forcing her attention to the equipment, she examined their connections and stability. One fuel line sputtered dangerously. With a muttered oath, Raven grabbed tools from a nearby panel to make an adjustment. She couldn't wait much longer to get some extensive repairs. Maybe Beckett could be persuaded to advance her a portion of her credits. After all, his gold medallion could buy her a new ship.

48

As she closed the panel, she found him studying the cabin walls. "Yes?"

He smiled. "Is this all there is?"

"It's all I need. *TrackStar* may be old, but she's served my purposes."

"But where do you eat . . . sleep?"

Sleep. The thought of sleeping anywhere within the same galaxy as this man made Raven uneasy, but food she could handle.

Accessing another panel, she activated the meal replicator and removed two narrow bars. "Here's something to eat if you're hungry."

Beckett accepted a bar warily. Holding it before him, he studied it. "What is this?"

"A protein bar. It has all the nutrients you need." Raven bit into hers to prove its safety.

Cautiously he nibbled at a corner, then frowned. " 'Tis lacking in flavor."

She shrugged. "You get used to it."

He took a larger bite. "I prefer roasted leg of lamb."

Leg of lamb? She gaped at him. "You have real meat on your planet?"

"Aye, we have sheep, cattle and chickens." He sobered. "Though less now since the drought."

"Real meat," she murmured, trying to imagine the taste. "I've never had anything but synthetic, and that rarely."

The warmth of his smile surrounded her. "When you return Ciorstan and me to Alba I'll be glad to offer you a meal from our meager stores."

Raven returned his grin. "I think I'd like that."

His gaze caught hers and darkened. Her stomach knotted in response.

"Tell me about your daughter," she said quickly. "Do you have a holo of her?"

"A holo?"

"A picture."

"Aye." He reached beneath his sash and brought out a small oval-shaped portrait. "I had this miniature done at her last birthday."

49

Raven studied it, surprised by the vivacity captured in the painting. The girl looked older than nine, her face in the midst of transforming from a child's to a young woman's. Her coloring resembled Beckett's in her long brown hair and dark eyes, but her delicate features had to be from her mother. With Ciorstan's high cheekbones and fair complexion, she would be a beauty once she matured.

A beauty Slade wouldn't ignore.

Raven's throat constricted. She'd been nine once and believed in love, in family, in a future. A belief quickly shattered. She concentrated on Ciorstan's eyes in the painting and recognized a brief glimmer of what she herself had once been.

She tightened her jaw. Ciorstan MacLeod had a father who loved her. If Raven acted quickly, she could restore this family before it was destroyed. Though still terrifying, finding Slade took on a new importance.

"Mac, how long until turn point for Erebus?"

"Six point five hours."

Six long hours.

Raven handed Beckett the miniature. "We'll find her." He met her gaze. "I know."

Though he didn't touch her physically, his quiet voice sent a tremor rippling through Raven. Neptune's Rings, what was it with this man?

"We—ah—we have several hours. I think I'll sleep while I can." Hurrying to the port side of the cabin, Raven pressed a button to extract her bunk. Sleep did sound good if she could manage to close her eyes with the Alban so near.

"That isna very big." Beckett spoke at Raven's shoulder, startling her. He moved too quietly for such a large man.

"It's big enough." She had to swallow hard before she could continue. "There's another bunk on the lee side." Moving quickly, she activated the bed. "You can sleep here."

He studied it with a wry twist of his lips. "I'm nae certain I'll fit."

Raven measured his height with her gaze. "Most humans aren't built like you."

Surprise etched his features. "My structure isna strange on Alba."

"Then apparently your gravity is different." Though gravity didn't explain the uncommon breadth of his shoulders, or the sharply defined muscles barely disguised by his clothing.

"I'm thinking 'tis space travel that does it. My bones feel smashed every time I leave a planet."

Raven bit back a retort. He might have a point. She'd spent most of her life in space and barely noticed the acceleration pressure anymore. "Maybe," she said.

Extending his hand, Beckett grasped Raven's. "Thank you for what you're doing, Raven. I'll nae forget it."

Static shock raced up her arm, but Raven didn't pull away. "I . . . I haven't found Ciorstan yet."

"Nae, but you will." His gaze confirmed his belief, startling Raven with its intensity.

No one had ever trusted her so wholeheartedly before. Clients usually voiced their doubt in her abilities, showing surprise when she succeeded. Obviously Alba was a different world . . . a very different world. Or he was a very different man.

She withdrew her hand and forced a smile. "Rest while you can." Sinking onto her bunk, she drew a deep breath, her lungs suddenly short of air. A quick glance at the oxygen meter assured her that the air supply was fine. Her breathlessness obviously had another—more human—cause.

As she watched, Beckett stretched out on the bed. His feet dangled off the end and he shot her a grin. Turning onto her side, he drew in his legs. "Good night, Raven," he murmured.

Good night? She barely remembered the last time someone had said that to her. " 'Night," she replied quietly. Reclining, she stared at the ship's ceiling. "Mac, notify me when we reach the turn point for Erebus."

"Affirmative."

"Mac, dim lights."

In the darkened interior she tried to find a comfortable position despite her bulky laser and snug clothing. This was ridiculous.

Unfastening her laser belt, she hung it on the corner of the bed. She doubted Beckett would attack her in the middle of the night. After all, he needed her to find his daughter.

Her pulse quickened as images of Beckett's earlier touch flickered through her mind. Maybe an attack wouldn't be all bad. . . .

Forget it. Ripping open the Stic-Tite closures of her flight suit, she peeled down to her underwear and hung the garment on a nearby fixture. The cool air felt refreshing against her skin. Maybe now she could relax.

Lying supine again, she listened to Beckett's breathing. His masculine presence dominated the small space. At this rate she'd never get to sleep. She should never have brought him along. Something about him turned her into a total Neeban. If she intended to confront Slade, she'd need every bit of her wits.

Still, knowing Beckett would be there when she faced Slade offered some comfort . . . just a little.

Beckett didn't remember when he finally fell asleep. But he did remember what felt like hours of intense awareness of Raven sleeping across the small cabin. However, a shrill whistle and Mac's monotone voice awakened him with a start.

Bolting upright, his heart pounding, he heard Mac repeat the message.

"Turn point for Erebus approaching in ten minutes."

"Mac, raise lights." Raven jumped from her bed as the cabin's lights gradually increased. Catching a glimpse of pale skin, Beckett blinked, then stared. She wore only a sleeveless, low-cut T-shirt and a pair of close-cut underwear that caressed her feminine curves.

Fire flashed to his groin, and he suppressed a groan. He'd promised her that he'd maintain a business relationship, but his body didn't want to comply. As he watched, she stepped into her one-piece suit and tugged it up until she could slide her arms into the sleeves.

Shrugging the garment on, she hurried to the console and claimed her seat. "Mac, initiate warm-up sequence. Ready hyperspeed. Prepare for ninety-degree turn."

"Warm up sequence initiated."

Beckett drew a deep breath before he spoke. "What are you doing?"

She threw a surprised glance over her shoulder, as if she'd just remembered his presence. "Strap in now."

Her serious tone spurred him into action. Not bothering to put on his boots or sash, he hurried into place. He fastened the restraining belts, then watched as Raven's fingers flew over the panel.

"All engines are on-line. Hyperspeed on standby."

At Mac's voice, Beckett glanced upward. He would never get used to that infernal machine. "Can I help?" he asked.

"Sit still and stay quiet," she replied sharply. She focused her attention on the lights and switches before her, a frown creasing her forehead.

Beckett stiffened at her reply. No one spoke to him in that manner.

Before he could reply, Raven glanced back at the rear of the ship. "Don't fail me now, ship."

He heard the plea in her voice and suddenly recognized the danger in what she intended to do. Her ship rested on another ship traveling at a tremendous speed. He didn't need to understand space travel to know what would happen to them if she didn't lift off correctly. It would be the same if he tried to jump from a stationary horse to a moving one. Failure could be a wee bit painful.

Looking out the front window, he studied the blurring stars. Probably more than a wee bit at that.

He knew it had taken skill for her to land on the merchant's ship. If she could land, she could leave. Couldn't she?

"Okay, Mac, stay with me on this," Raven said. She gripped a lever, her knuckles white. "Set hyperspeed coordinates for Erebus. Initiate liftoff . . . now."

The engines roared to life, sending a shudder through the ship. A now familiar pressure wrapped itself around Beckett, but before he could acknowledge it, the craft lifted and swung sharply around. Raven pulled the lever toward her and they soared away from the merchant ship, the stars blurring into one bright light.

The *TrackStar* rocked from side to side, accompanied by a vibration so intense it jangled Beckett's teeth. Then, just as suddenly, the vibration disappeared, leaving an ominous stillness. He realized they were out of danger when Raven's shoulders relaxed and the tightness left her face.

"If leaving was hazardous, why did you land there in the first place?" he asked.

She grimaced. "Good question. Because I'm a Neeban, I guess."

"And what is a Neeban?"

She looked at him in amazement, then smiled sheepishly. "It's a small feathery creature on Tarcus Four that's so lacking in brains, it'll walk off the edge of a cliff rather than change its path."

"I see. Neeban." He grinned. "I like that."

"Yeah, well . . ." Raven returned her attention to the console, her cheeks pink.

As she leaned forward, engrossed in the controls, Beckett noticed she'd only closed her suit from the waist down. The edges gaped open, allowing him full view of her thin white shirt, plainly revealing rose-tipped breasts through the worn material.

Beckett swallowed and averted his gaze, but it returned unbidden to the tantalizing sight. Against all rational thought he ached to caress those peaks, to taste their sweetness, to hear Raven moan beneath his touch.

He closed his eyes. Dear Lord, he had other priorities—beginning with his daughter. He should be thinking of her, not drooling with lust. With luck they'd find Ciorstan at this planet Erebus, so he could return home. He had to remember Raven was his hired tracker, nothing else.

Why did she attract him anyway? Perhaps it was only

curiosity. After all, he'd never met anyone like her; she was as unlike Nessa as a woman could be. That had to be it. He obviously had nothing in common with Raven.

But he still wanted her.

"Mac, hold course to Erebus. Notify me when we enter its star system."

"Affirmative."

Beckett opened his eyes to see Raven sink back in her chair and sigh. As she turned to smile at him, he couldn't stop his gaze from lingering on her barely hidden nipples.

Following the direction of his gaze, she jumped to her feet and pulled her suit closed, fury blazing in her eyes. "I think I'll visit the lav, now," she said icily.

He nodded. "I . . ."

She didn't stay to hear him, but stalked to the rear of the cabin and slammed her palm against a luminous square. A door slid open and she vanished inside.

Damnation; all he needed was to anger the one person who could find Ciorstan for him. He unfastened his restraints and stood. If he didn't learn to control himself, she might leave him stranded on this Erebus and he'd never see Ciorstan or Alba again.

No, Raven wouldn't do that. She might be tempted to leave him, but she'd honor her word, just as he'd honor his.

Strange, he'd met Raven less than a day ago, yet he felt as if he'd known her much longer. Already he realized her tough exterior hid a passionate interior—a passion he wanted to unleash.

With a groan, he plopped onto his bed and put on his boots. He should've stayed on Alba where he belonged. At least there he knew what to expect from a woman. Among the stars with Raven, he found himself constantly surprised.

When she finally emerged from the lav, he gestured toward it. "May I wash up?"

"Of course." Her tone was civil, but the glitter in her eyes told him he wasn't yet forgiven. "If you need to, you may use the mister to cleanse yourself, but don't take long."

He nodded and entered the small room. He recognized the various implements, except for a narrow stall at one end. The mister?

Cautiously he waved his hand past a long strip of small holes, then jerked it back as warm mist sprayed out. With less hesitation, he tried it again and smiled. No doubt this stall provided a way to bathe.

Stripping off his clothes, he stepped inside. Tiny bursts of mist hit his body from all sides, almost as caressing as a woman's touch. He was going to enjoy this.

By the time he'd finished his bath and had dressed, he'd managed to regain some semblance of control. He needed to concentrate on Ciorstan. Her safe return was all that mattered.

Returning to the cabin, he found the beds gone and Raven sitting at a small table. She waved him over to a chair. Once he sat, she motioned to a drink and another of the awful food sticks set before him.

"I thought you might be hungry."

"I am, thank you." Beckett lifted the food stick and eyed it with resignation. Another reason to make a quick return to Alba.

"I'd like to hear more about Ciorstan and this sword she's searching for. You said something yesterday about a riddle?"

Surprised she remembered that conversation, Beckett fumbled to retrieve a paper tucked in his belt. Opening it, he laid it on the table. "Here's the riddle. 'Tis mostly nonsense."

Raven skimmed it quickly. "You're right. It doesn't make much sense."

"Ciorstan insisted she'd solved it." Beckett silently chastised himself as he recalled his arrogant dismissal of his daughter's claims. "She mentioned a new planet, but I dinna remember anything else. If it involved leaving Alba, I wanted nae part of it."

"Yet here you are."

"Aye, in a place I swore I'd never be." He grimaced.

"My ancestors fled Earth and settled Alba to escape from all this technology."

"But why would anyone want to escape it?" Raven's gaze swept the interior of the cabin. "I can't imagine never traveling among the stars, never visiting all the wonderful planets throughout the universe."

"Our records say Earth's people had become lazy, angry and violent. The Scots were losing their customs, their language. My ancestors wanted to create a world where people worked together and our heritage could survive."

"And you had to hide yourselves away to do that?"

"Aye, 'twas the only way. As long as technology ruled, the Scots could never regain their pride."

Raven shook her head, as if discarding his words. "Did you succeed? Is Alba a nonviolent planet?"

He smiled ruefully. "I wouldna say that. The clans do fight each other occasionally, but 'tis the Highland way. In desperate times, as with our drought, all the clans band together to fight a common enemy."

Her expression softened. "Is it that bad?"

His heart sank in despair as he thought of his planet's barren fields. "It worsens as each day passes without rain. 'Tis one reason I canna afford to be away for long."

She shifted uneasily. "With luck, Slade will be there with Ciorstan and we'll be able to steal her away."

"What if she isna there?"

"Then it means Slade believes her story and I'll find out where they went." Raven dropped her gaze to the tabletop and Beckett frowned.

She wasn't telling him everything. "And if Slade dinna believe her story?" he asked.

Slowly she looked at him, her face solemn. Beckett's stomach twisted, his chest suddenly tight. He knew instinctively he didn't want to hear her response.

"He'll kill her."

Chapter Four

Raven watched emotions cross quickly over Beckett's face . . . disbelief, horror, anger. Crushing his food bar in one fist, he jumped to his feet. "He'll kill me first."

"If necessary." She hated shattering his hopes, but he had to understand the type of man Slade was . . . or wasn't. Though Slade claimed to be Beta-human, Raven had long ago decided his similarity to humans was purely coincidental. If not for his appearance, he could be one of the warrior race of Thordons—heartless, killing beasts, who lived for profit and thought nothing of dying for that cause.

Beckett paced across the cabin. "Why would Ciorstan go off with such a man?"

"She must've been desperate for someone to believe her." Raven tried to reason like a nine-year-old but failed. She'd long ago lost any ties to such youth and innocence.

Groaning, Beckett returned to his chair and dropped his head onto his hands. "Because I wouldna believe her. If I had . . ."

"It's too late for that now." Raven fought the urge to touch him and assure him it wasn't his fault. Beckett had done what he thought best . . . for his world. "We need to work out a plan of action for when we land on Erebus."

Beckett raised his head to look at her, his gaze filled with despair. "Tell me about this planet. What should I expect?"

"Erebus." Raven grimaced. "Erebus is a hellhole. It's hot, it's dry, it's dangerous. No one in their right mind would choose to live there, which is exactly why the privateers do."

"What about the air, the gravity?"

Good questions, especially from someone who'd never left his own planet until now. "How was it for you on Cirius?"

He hesitated. "I felt somewhat heavier, but it dinna bother me until we ran. 'Twas hard to breathe then too."

"The air has a somewhat different mixture on Erebus. There's more oxygen, but you'll probably experience some initial nausea from the sulfur. On the plus side, the gravity's lighter. You'll feel like you can jump anything, but be careful. That's not always the case."

"Will I need to jump anything?" Some of the anguish left Beckett's eyes as his interest caught.

"Definitely. Erebus is volcanic and very rocky. I'm planning to land in Divider Canyon. It offers the best concealment along the route to the privateers' quarters, but it's a rough hike." Raven pictured the spot. Though good for landing the *TrackStar*, it would be a long trek for them, especially if they had Beckett's daughter in tow.

Of course, with Beckett's highly toned muscles and the planet's lighter gravity, he shouldn't have any problems carrying Ciorstan, if necessary.

"Will the privateers have guards? Will they be armed with weapons like yours?" He fired off questions as he leaned over the table. "What's their camp like?"

"Yes, they have guards with lasers like mine. In fact, some of their weapons make mine look puny." Though it had been a long time since she'd dealt with any privateers, she doubted things had changed much. They liked their sordid routine too much. "Their quarters are underground."

"Underground?"

"It's too difficult to live on the planet's surface. They've managed to locate an underground lake and use that to survive on the otherwise barren planet."

"Is it possible to avoid their defenses? Do you know of a safe route?"

"Yes to both. If I can land the *TrackStar* in the canyon without detection, we should be able to infiltrate the caverns without their knowledge."

Beckett narrowed his eyes. "Without detection? What do you mean by that?"

"They're privateers, Beckett. Naturally they have scanning devices. The last thing they want is to be surprised."

Tightening his fists, he frowned. "If they've hurt Ciorstan, I'll surprise them all right."

Raven nodded. She hoped Slade wouldn't harm the girl, but she knew him better than that. "I wish I had another laser you could use. Your sword—"

He grasped his weapon's hilt. " 'Tis all I need. I dinna want one of your weapons."

"It's no match for a laser."

" 'Twill do fine."

"Entering Erebus star system." Mac's toneless voice filled the cabin.

Raven hesitated. If she went to Erebus, she'd be committed. She'd have to face Slade. Stealing a glance at Beckett's tortured expression, she frowned. She was already committed.

"Mac, prepare to leave hyperspeed. Set coordinates for Erebus but stay outside of scanner range."

"Affirmative."

She moved to her seat before the console and studied the instruments. Years had passed since she'd been on Erebus. Could she remember the way to Divider

Canyon? They couldn't afford to be detected during their landing.

Beckett slid into his chair and tightened the restraining straps. Raven tossed him a slight smile. A quick learner, that one.

Grasping the hyperspeed lever, she brought *Track-Star* into normal space. Familiar constellations greeted her.

Dark swirls of clouds, filled with ash and dust from constant volcanic eruptions, covered most of the planet, giving it a sinister appearance. She wouldn't see much until just before her ship reached the surface.

With a calmness she didn't expect to feel, she readjusted her instruments and guided her ship toward the planet. "This may be a bit bumpy," she warned Beckett.

He raised one eyebrow. "I'd expect as much."

"Why?"

"It's been a rough journey ever since I stepped on this ship," he said dryly.

She grimaced. He did have a point. "It'll be better from now on."

The ship entered the atmosphere smoothly as Raven kept the speed even to avoid detection. Catching a thermal current to mask her ship's heat signature, she glided the craft along it toward the canyon. So far, so good.

A sharp sputter and pop from the thrusters shattered that illusion. Smoke poured from the rear panel. The engine's roar died. "Fardpissle." Raven cast an anxious glance over her shoulder, then turned to Beckett.

"Here, slide into my seat and hold this." She moved out of the way and he obeyed without question, closing his fingers around the lever. "Mac, guide him down and keep it steady."

Beckett stiffened. "I canna—"

Raven hurried to the rear of the cabin. "You have to." Some choice. She could let her ship crash or burn. Or both.

Before she reached the thrusters the extinguisher activated, sending even larger clouds of smoke into the cabin. Raven waved her hand to clear a path through it. "Mac, vent this stuff out through the air lock."

As the smoke cleared, she yanked open the panel door and studied the damage. Bad . . . very bad.

"Um, Raven . . ."

She glanced around at Beckett's uncertain voice. Her throat closed at seeing they'd broken through the cloud covering and were rapidly approaching the ground.

"Pull back on the lever, Beckett. Try to hold it level." She almost lost her footing as the ship's nose raised suddenly. "Easy. Get the feel of it. Mac, lock lower sensors on planet's surface. Find us a safe place to land . . . now."

Diving into the thruster cabinet again, Raven exhaled sharply. One thruster was dead, no doubt about it. The other had some life left in it . . . if she could just give it enough power so they could land without leaving *TrackStar* in pieces strewn across the planet's surface.

She ignored the hot cables as she rigged a sloppy fix. *This has to work.* "Come on, ship," she murmured.

The craft jumped abruptly, tossing Raven to the floor. "What was that?"

Beckett didn't look around. " 'Twas an eruption below. What are you doing?"

"Trying to fix this. You're doing good. Keep it steady." She hurried to complete the makeshift repair. "Mac, increase power gradually to port thruster."

The noise increased as the thruster roared to life. Raven watched the equipment anxiously. Would it hold?

The engine sputtered but continued to pulse in regular intervals.

She slammed the door and ran for the controls. Beckett's determined expression didn't waver as he stared out the front window. The ground was definitely much closer than the last time she looked.

Raven leaned over and placed her hand alongside Beckett's on the lever. "We're going to land now while we can. The engine's still unstable and we're at half power on the thruster. Mac, what did you find?"

"Rocky plains ahead one thousand meters."

"I see them." Raven felt Beckett's rapid breathing on her neck as she crouched next to him. When he released his hold she shook her head. "Don't let go. I think we'll need both of us to do this."

She quickly set coordinates and headed the *TrackStar* toward the uneven opening ahead. The lever vibrated within her grasp, fighting her as she struggled to slide it forward. Beckett added his strength until it moved. The ship dipped.

The landing gear descended in a loud rumble. The engine ceased for a moment, bringing Raven's heart to her throat, then resumed its unsteady roar.

They touched the rocky surface much faster than she'd intended and the ship bounced erratically over the uneven ground. "Pull back, Beckett. Now." Letting him struggle with the rebellious lever, Raven stretched across Beckett to fire the forward thrusters to slow the craft.

The ship's wild leap tossed Raven onto his lap. He wrapped one arm around her protectively but continued to slow the craft. The ship bounced, shuddered, then stopped.

Raven and Beckett released their breaths simultaneously. He tightened his hold on her in a reassuring gesture and Raven rested her head against his shoulder. For a moment it felt right to lean on this man and share his strength.

At a feather-light touch on her hair, she looked up. Though Beckett's face was pale, he gave her a smile. " 'Twas close."

"More than close." Raven drew a shaky breath and rose to her feet. "My thruster finally died. I'd hoped it would last until you paid me."

"I dinna know your ship needed repair. You should've said."

"Why do you think I took this job? My ship has to be repaired. Without it, I'll be stranded."

His expression hardened. "I see. 'Twas only for money."

Raven almost flinched at his sudden coldness. "You knew that from the beginning. It takes credits to survive out here."

"Aye, I see. Credits and every man for himself."

"Exactly." Unwilling to acknowledge a nagging twinge of guilt, Raven focused her attention on the damaged ship and hurried to seize her tools. Tiny wisps of smoke still trailed from the closed panel.

"Mac, lower the thruster section to the ground and open air lock."

Heavy, hot air blasted into the cabin as soon as the hatch opened. Scorching sunlight blinded Raven. No wonder she didn't miss this place.

With a sigh, she went outside and breathed slowly, allowing her lungs to adjust to the heated atmosphere. She turned to warn Beckett, but he'd followed too closely behind her.

His face grew red as he burst into tight coughs, almost doubling over. He brought his hand to his throat in a frantic gesture.

Raven ran to grab an oxygen mask from inside the doorway and held it to Beckett's face. "Breathe slowly," she ordered. "Take it easy. You're all right."

His natural color gradually returned as his breathing settled into a more even rhythm. "I thought . . . you said . . ." His voice sounded muffled through the mask.

She nodded. "You *can* breathe this air. You're just not used to it." Studying him intently, she touched his shoulder for reassurance. "I want you to remove the mask and draw in slow, short breaths. It'll burn. Breath out just as slowly. Once your lungs adjust it won't seem so bad."

His gaze met hers. In a deliberate motion he lifted the mask from his face. For a moment he didn't breathe at all, then his chest moved slightly—up, then down.

Raven tightened her grip on his shoulder, watching him closely, her heart pounding against her ribs. He'd never been off his planet before. Though breathable for limited periods of time, she couldn't be certain this atmosphere wouldn't incapacitate him.

After several short breaths Beckett's tension eased and he smiled slightly. "I think I'll live after all."

"Good." Caught in the warmth of his smile, Raven wondered for a moment if *she* was having trouble with the air. Her chest felt suddenly tight and her palm against his shoulder tingled.

Jerking her hand away, she picked up her tools and turned to the lowered thruster section. With luck, the damage wouldn't be as bad as it first appeared. She studied the mangled cables and burned units.

No such luck. It was worse.

"What are you doing?" Beckett joined her beside the smoldering wreckage. "We need to look for Ciorstan."

"I agree." Raven could sympathize with his concern. "But we'll probably need to leave in a hurry and I want to repair this first, if possible."

Beckett watched her sort through the mess. " 'Tis bad."

"Oh, yeah, 'tis very bad." She mocked his gentle lilt, needing an outlet for her anger and frustration.

"Can I be of help?"

His offer surprised her and she stopped her automatic head shake in midmotion. "Actually, yes. We need to remove this thruster. It'll never work again."

Together they unhooked the cables and hoisted the heavy metal cylinder to the ground. Raven looked at it in despair. She'd lived so long in this ship, she felt as if she was throwing away a part of herself.

Forcing herself back to the repairs, she returned to the remaining thruster. "Can you hand me that melder, Beckett?" She indicated the short, angular tool.

"Will the ship fly again?"

"I hope so." She concentrated on rerouting the wires and cables to make the best use of the remaining thruster's power. If this worked . . . when this worked . . . the fix would be temporary at best.

Uncomfortably aware of Beckett's nearness each time she stepped back, she faced him with a forced smile. "Would you mind searching the perimeter? I doubt our wild landing went unnoticed."

"Aye." His boots crunched against the rocks as he moved away. "What am I looking for?"

"You'll know them if you see them." *But we'd better see them first.*

Raven wanted to hurry but forced herself to work methodically. She couldn't afford any mistakes. Not now.

Nothing had gone right on this mission from the beginning. If she were superstitious, she'd take it as an omen to lift out of there immediately. But she couldn't leave the girl. Not with Slade. Raven owed it to herself as much as Ciorstan . . . and Ciorstan's father.

As she finished the makeshift repairs, Raven wiped the sweat from her forehead and ordered Mac to raise the unit. Now to test it.

That would definitely alert the privateers if their crash landing hadn't already. Raven started for the hatch. "After that farce of a landing I'm sure they're having a good laugh," she muttered.

"I dinna think they're laughing," Beckett replied, his voice oddly constrained.

Raven turned. Following the direction of his gaze, she spied a group of men circling her ship, their weapons held ready, their faces half-hidden by thin veils. Despite the planet's intense heat, her blood chilled.

Privateers!

"Mac, security alert one," Raven yelled. The air lock slid shut behind them.

Catching sight of the flash of alarm on Raven's face, Beckett drew his sword. At last, a situation he could handle. He'd fought in more than one battle on Alba and come away the winner.

"What is your business here?" he demanded, edging himself between Raven and the men.

"I'm asking the questions." One of the men stepped forward, aiming a large metal weapon at Beckett. "Drop your weapon or die."

Beckett tensed, every muscle ready for action. After Raven's warnings he knew these men to be dangerous. But he couldn't let anything happen to Raven. Without her, he'd be lost. "Hold," he ordered, hoisting his well-honed blade. "Dinna come any closer."

The privateer paused only to steady his weapon. Ready to leap aside, Beckett jumped when Raven caught his raised arm and pulled it down.

"Don't be foolish, Beckett." She threw her laser on the ground and motioned for him to do the same.

His pride rebelled. Give up? Without a fight? Obviously, no Scottish blood flowed in her.

"Nae."

Anger flashed in her eyes. "If he fires, there won't be enough left of you to fill a cup." She spoke from between clenched teeth. "Do you understand?"

"I'll nae let him harm you."

Her expression softened. "If you're dead, you'll have little to say about that. Drop the sword. We'll think of something else."

He hesitated, glancing from her to the armed privateer. If she spoke of another plan, then he had to trust her. She'd brought him this far. Reluctantly, he tossed his sword to the black-red dirt and aimed a defiant glare at their captor.

The man, obviously the leader, waved at another privateer, who gathered their weapons and returned to the group. The leader moved to confront Beckett, his eyes cold and dark above the thin veil.

"State your business." His voice sounded equally cold.

Beckett's stomach clenched. He wanted no dealings with these people. Yet Ciorstan was here . . . somewhere. "We're looking for a little girl—nine years old. Her hair's long, brown. She—"

"Enough!" The man slashed his hand through the air. "There are no children here."

Anger and sudden fear for Ciorstan created a hard knot in Beckett's chest. He seized the man's arm. "I know she's on this planet. I demand to see her."

The privateer swung the base of his weapon against Beckett's jaw. Thrown off-balance by the sudden attack, pain reverberating through his head, Beckett staggered back, his hand flying reflexively to his bloodied chin. Intense agony jangled along his spine. For a moment he couldn't even think.

Raven stepped toward him, her hand outstretched; then she whirled to face the privateer. "I've heard Slade has the girl," she said, her voice tight. "I'd like to speak with him. We can . . . make it worth his while to release the girl to us."

"Can you?" The man eyed her closely, his gaze lingering on her soft curves.

Panic appeared briefly on Raven's face. Despite his pounding head, Beckett moved to her side, issuing a silent challenge.

Amusement flickered in the leader's eyes as he nodded. "We can always kill you later." He raised his voice. "Take them to the fortress."

Instantly, the others surrounded Beckett and Raven and fastened their hands behind them with a metal set of bands that tightened but didn't actually touch the skin. Using their weapons, the privateers prodded Beckett and Raven into motion.

Beckett tried to stay close to Raven as they crossed uneven ground strewn with boulders. While climbing ridges he noticed the lighter gravity required less effort. Good; he had to conserve his strength. He'd probably need it later.

Raven covered the path easily, though her clenched jaw and frown warned him she wasn't pleased by the turn of events. He knew she feared this Slade creature. Did that cause her brief flashes of panic?

All too often the leader fell into step beside Raven, his lascivious gaze resting on her chest.

Indignation mingled with frustration as Beckett pulled against the braces on his wrists. His efforts gained him only a continuous burning against his skin. His code of honor demanded that he protect Raven, but something more than that whispered in his mind—this had become personal.

"Don't hurt yourself," Raven said, making her way over to him. "We'll be out of these soon enough."

"How can you let him look at you that way?"

She scowled. "I don't have much choice at the moment. Don't worry. I'm tougher than he thinks."

But not as tough as you think. Already Beckett knew a softness existed beneath her defensive exterior—a softness that could be easily destroyed by these men.

"Do you know where they're taking us?"

"I think so." Raven tripped over a stone, then gave Beckett a halfhearted grin as she regained her balance. "The entrance to their fortress should be over the next ridge at the base of the hill."

"What will happen there?"

Her grin faded. "If Slade's here, I'm sure we'll get to see him. We'll probably have to act quickly, so be ready."

"Aye." His muscles ached from his tenseness and adrenaline raced through his veins. He'd be ready.

At the base of the next ridge they stopped. Beckett searched the rocky surroundings for an entrance but found naught. He aimed a curious glance at Raven.

She nodded her head toward the leader. "Watch."

The leader stalked to the solid base of a mountain and placed his palm against a flat rock. Instantly, rumbling resounded as a massive boulder slid inside the hill.

Beckett caught himself staring in amazement. Would he ever adjust to this modern technology?

Once the boulder stopped, the privateers pushed Raven and Beckett inside. Darkness—blacker than a moonless night—greeted them. Beckett blinked, willing his eyes to adjust quickly.

A scraping noise behind him signaled the movement of the boulder into its original position. If possible, the darkness became even blacker.

He wanted to reach out for Raven, to know she was near . . . and safe. "Raven?"

"Close your eyes," she said quickly, her voice close by.

As Beckett obeyed, he heard the leader speak. "Activate lights, Tessie."

Even with his eyes closed, Beckett sensed overhead

lights snapping into full brilliance. Slowly, he lifted his eyelids, blinking his vision into focus as another door opened.

"Damnation." Outside the small antechamber, the size of the cavern overwhelmed him. His entire village—and some—could fit comfortably in its massive length and width. He saw people moving in the distance. How many lived here?

Before he could wonder further, his captors pushed him into movement again. Beckett quickly located Raven only two steps away.

She gave him a quick smile, but not enough to disguise the worry in her gaze. Beckett frowned. If not for him and his inexperience in this culture, she'd have found Ciorstan already. Perhaps he should've waited at Cirius for Raven to return with her.

Nae. As much as he trusted Raven, he needed to see his daughter for himself . . . soon.

Eyeing his surroundings, Beckett started in surprise at seeing several spaceships, many of them larger than Raven's, sitting inside the cavern.

"Wha . . . ?"

"They have to hide their ships somewhere," Raven said quietly.

"How many people are here?"

She hesitated. "I'm not sure. Around a hundred, I think."

"Where will they take us?"

"To the central chamber. We'll turn just up ahead."

"There's more than this?" Had these people burrowed out the entire mountain?

"A lot more than this. A person could spend days wandering the corridors in this place." Her jaw tightened as she paused. "This is only the entry chamber for ships and supplies."

She obviously knew a lot about these privateers and their fortress. How had she learned the details regarding the inside of this place? He frowned as a moment of doubt nagged him; then he shook his head to dismiss it. Raven had risked her life to bring him here. Her

70

knowledge probably came from her thorough preparation and previous missions as a tracker.

As they left the enormous cavern and entered a narrow tunnel, Raven turned to him, her expression concerned. "Beckett, there's something I need to tell you."

" 'Tis all right." He knew she feared meeting Slade. "We'll find Ciorstan safe."

"No, I—"

She broke off on their arrival at a big room, much smaller than the previous cavern, though still large enough to hold fifty people. Beckett searched the rock walls for a way to escape. Another tunnel led in the opposite direction, but two men stood beside it, cleaning their weapons with a small piece of cloth.

More privateers filled the room, some reclining in the odd floating chairs while others sat on the edge of a long table centered in the room. They looked up, curiosity on their faces as Beckett and Raven entered.

These men lacked the odd headgear that covered half their faces, and Beckett saw that a majority of them were human. Though they displayed a mismatched array of clothing and a variety of ungroomed haircuts and beards, he felt for the first time that he might be able to reason with them. Maybe they could tell him where he'd find Ciorstan.

The leader jerked off his veil and hood to reveal long curly black hair and an equally bushy beard. With his thick eyebrows and long, angled nose, he fit Beckett's image of a villain perfectly. Was this Slade?

Though Raven watched the leader intently, she displayed no apparent sign of alarm, so Beckett concluded it wasn't. The man motioned to a nearby privateer, who removed the restraints from Beckett and Raven's wrists. Despite the burning sensation on his skin, Beckett resisted rubbing it.

"Tessie, scan our visitors," the leader ordered.

"With pleasure." A woman's voice emerged from everywhere and Beckett searched the corners of the room. Another computer?

He sensed rather than felt a touch and stiffened.

"Hmmm, I'll keep this one, Jagger."

This didn't sound like a computer.

"Give me the details, Tessie." The leader—Jagger—snapped his hand in an impatient movement.

"Yes, boss." It . . . she . . . almost purred. "Human male. Definitely male. I can't determine planet origin. No diseases. In fact, no problems at all. And he's carrying the largest piece of gold I've ever seen."

Jagger whirled around and approached Beckett immediately. "Give it to me."

Beckett refused to cower before the man's dark gaze. " 'Tis a family heirloom and I'll nae be giving it to the likes of you."

With surprising swiftness, Jagger drew a smaller laser-type weapon from his belt and pressed it against Beckett's chest. "It doesn't matter to me if you're dead or alive, I'll have that gold."

"Please, Beckett, give him the medallion." Raven looked as if she wanted to touch him but didn't dare. "It's not worth your life."

Without the gold he'd have no bargaining power to find Ciorstan. Beckett hesitated. Then again, if he died, he'd never find her.

Anger mixed with his frustration as he reached inside his shirt and removed the MacLeod medallion. He'd barely held it out when Jagger snatched the gold from his palm and held it up to the light.

A collective exclamation came from the others in the room. Jagger smiled, a narrow stretching of his lips across his thin face. "Slade will be pleased."

"Where is Slade?" Beckett demanded. He curled his hands into fists, fighting the urge to smash them against Jagger's face. "Bring me my daughter."

Jagger lifted his dark gaze. "State your name."

"Beckett MacLeod, chieftain of the clan MacLeod." He straightened, allowing his native pride to swell. Even two hundred years behind in technology, the Scots were second to none.

"And your home planet?"

"Alba."

"Interesting." Tessie's voice surrounded him again. "I've never had an Alban specimen before. Are all the men like you?"

Beckett's muscles tightened. He refused to answer this . . . machine—no matter how human it sounded. He felt violated enough by Jagger's interrogation.

"Do bring me more, Jagger."

"Enough, Tessie. Scan the woman now."

Raven tensed, surprising Beckett. Surely she was used to these scans by now.

"Human female. Healthy. She's carrying a few credits. Wait." The computer paused. "No wonder the pattern looked familiar. Welcome home, Raven."

"Raven?" Jagger gripped her chin with his fingers and gazed at her, his expression dark. His lips lifted in a dry smile. "It *is* Raven." He turned to the others. "Raven's back."

The words crept into Beckett's consciousness as several privateers surrounded Raven in a flurry of greetings. Raven . . . home . . . back. A crimson haze blurred his vision.

He'd been tricked . . . betrayed. Ciorstan wasn't here. The whole story of Slade had been a lie. Sudden panic gripped Beckett's heart and squeezed. Where was his daughter? Was she even alive?

Raven emerged from the crowd, watching him intently. "Beckett . . ."

He forced words through his clenched teeth. "Do you know these people?" A part of him wanted her to deny it.

"I . . . ah . . . yes, but—"

Rage drove him. This had all been for nothing. She didn't know where Ciorstan was. She'd led him into a trap . . . for his gold. He leapt at her, aching to encircle her slender throat with his hands. "Damn you to hell, woman. You betrayed me!"

The others pulled him away before he could touch her. She stepped toward him. "Beckett." Her voice sounded raspy. "I can explain."

"I want naught of your lies." He glared at her, enjoying the trepidation on her face. After trusting her with all he held dear she'd brought him to this.

"Take him to a restraining cell," Jagger ordered. "We'll deal with him later."

Beckett struggled in vain against the men who held him. His sense of betrayal grew, fueling his anger. He would have his revenge.

He flexed his fingers, needing to hit something. As the men dragged him from the chamber, he kept his gaze fastened on Raven's pale face. Somehow he'd free himself.

Then Raven would pay for her deceit.

Chapter Five

Raven started for Beckett as Gordo and Madde dragged him from the chamber. She had to make him understand.

The accusing anger in his eyes brought her to a stop. Now was not the time. Maybe after he cooled down he'd listen to reason. She swallowed. At least she hoped he'd listen.

She knew how this appeared to him. Shibit, she'd tried to tell him about her life with the privateers. *Too late now, Raven.* After years of keeping her past a secret she'd waited too long to reveal it. Now he'd never trust her again.

Surprisingly, that thought hurt.

"Where did you find him?"

She turned toward Jagger and grimaced. "It's a long story." Inhaling sharply to gather her courage, she continued. "Where's Slade? I need to talk to him."

"Be thankful he's not here." A corner of Jagger's mouth lifted in a sneer. "He's never forgiven you for leaving."

"I don't plan to ask for his forgiveness. This is business."

He held up the medallion, turning it to reflect the light. "Once he sees this, he may be more lenient."

"Consider it payment for the safe return of the girl."

"Girl?" Jagger lifted one eyebrow. "What girl?"

"The girl looking for a magic sword—that girl," Raven snapped.

"Oh, yes, the magic sword. None of us believed her, although she was very convincing. Very pretty, too." He looked at Raven. "Prettier than you at that age, but look how you turned out." He didn't bother to hide his appreciation of her curves, his gaze sliding over her like Kellrissian oil.

Raven's stomach clenched. She didn't need this, especially not here and now. Her anger building, she curled her hands into fists.

Jagger moved closer, reaching out with one hand to caress her cheek. "Women are still in short supply here. I can protect you if . . . you make it worth my while."

Jerking away from his touch, Raven lifted her chin defiantly. "I can protect myself."

"Can you?" His voice held a threat as he dropped his hand. "We'll see." Glancing in the direction that Beckett had been taken, Jagger frowned. "Is the Alban your lover?"

"That's none of your business." Unbidden, a strange tingling swept through her at the thought of Beckett making love to her. She immediately banished it. In his current mood he was more likely to kill her than love her. "We came for the girl. Keep the medallion, give us the girl and we'll leave."

"You know the rules, Raven. They haven't changed." Jagger smiled at her mockingly. "Either you join us or . . . you don't."

A chill traveled along her spine. Yes, she knew the rules. What few prisoners the privateers took were given the same choice—they could either join their captors or take their chance at freedom on the planet's surface.

Raven only remembered one man who'd ever elected freedom. He'd been released above ground, certain he would find a way off the planet. Erebus decreed otherwise. The combination of a toxic atmosphere and intense solar radiation killed him in two days. Within three, his bones had been picked clean by tiny paramites, a voracious insect native to the dry soil.

There was no real choice.

"So we'll stay. I'll give Beckett a day to calm down and speak to him." Let Jagger believe that. She'd escaped once; she could do it again.

"He'll be given the allegiance test. As will you."

They'd be required to kill during the next raid on a merchant ship. Her stomach tightened into knots. With an effort she stopped herself from giving an impulsive negative answer. "Fine." Raven spat out the word from between clenched teeth. She'd be gone before a test could ever happen.

Before she could react Jagger seized the top of her suit and peeled it open to reveal her white T-shirt. "*Your* test will be different." His gaze rested on her breasts.

Anger fought with her panic as she pulled free and sealed her suit. "Think again, Jagger."

"Raven here?" A quiet voice interrupted them.

She looked around, recognizing the unusual accent, and smiled. "Naldo." Flinging her arms around his neck, she greeted the only person on Erebus she'd ever cared about.

"Good to see you, *lielan.*" Naldo's smile eased her tension and she paused to study him.

He had gotten older. The hair ringing his crested head had changed from a copper color to brown—a definite sign of aging on a Terellian. His square-shaped face, pointed ears and sculpted nose contained deep-embedded wrinkles.

He'd shrunk, too. Though she'd been taller than him when she left Erebus, his brown-skinned body looked smaller, now—thinner. Regret rolled over her. She should've taken him with her.

77

"Come Central." He turned his gold gaze on Jagger. "She with me."

Scowling, Jagger opened his mouth as if to protest, then closed it with a snap when Naldo raised his eyebrows. Raven grinned and fell into step with her old friend.

As the door to Command Central sealed after them, Raven skidded to a halt in surprise. A man, not much younger than her, sat in the command chair . . . and he was human.

She darted a questioning glance at Naldo, who went to touch the man's shoulder. He raised the controller device from his head and turned to face Raven.

Young. He was too young and too good looking to be trapped as a controller. And human. Raven struggled to hide her distaste. Had the privateers figured out a way to give humans the needed abilities for that position?

"Tristan, Raven. Raven, Tristan."

She nodded in acknowledgment of his short bow. "You're a controller?"

"Naldo is training me for the position." Tristan's voice held quiet bitterness.

Naldo frowned. "I resume control now. I need talk Raven . . . alone."

"As you wish." Tristan slipped from the room beneath Raven's incredulous stare.

Naldo slid into the command chair and brought down the controller device. As the helmet hovered over his head, he shuddered once and closed his eyes.

Immediately Raven crossed to his side. "Are you all right?"

"*Ti.*" He inhaled deeply, then opened his eyes to smile at her. "Getting old. Require more work. Need Tristan's help."

"But Tristan is human," she said. "How can he possibly replace you?"

"Telekinesis strong. Almost like Terellian." Concern flickered across Naldo's face. "He human outcast. Slade find. Slade bring to help."

Her sympathy swelled. She knew immediately that Slade had used the young man's ostracism among humans to manipulate him. Slade probably made it sound like a wonderful opportunity to the young man when all Slade wanted was to use Tristan's unique abilities to control the complex.

No doubt Naldo had befriended the human as he once had a lonely little girl. She knelt to grasp Naldo's hands, hidden in the folds of his robe, but only found one. His left arm ended in a stump.

Anger quickly followed her disbelief. She jumped to her feet. "Slade did that to you."

Naldo hesitated. *"Ti."*

She didn't want to voice her fear but had to. "Because you helped me escape."

His eyes, solid gold slits, flickered, and he looked toward the multiple view screens filling the wall before him. Instantly they revealed views of many rooms and corridors throughout the complex. Close-ups of the power and water gauges appeared in the center screens.

Raven moved in front of him to block his view. "Look at me, Naldo. He hurt you because of me, didn't he?"

"Slade angry when you go. Fire laser. Jagger try stop." Naldo's lips twisted in a wry smile. "Only lost hand, not life."

Her heart sank to her stomach, where it lodged like a stone. "You said he wouldn't hurt you, that he knew this place would die without you to control it."

The Terellian telekinetic powers enabled Naldo to mentally control all the necessary utilities to maintain the privateer hideout. He'd spent most of his life in a command chair, using the controller device to enhance his mental talents. With a single thought he could adjust water pressure, measure the oxygen, or raise the mountain entrance for departing ships.

Without his help, Raven never would've escaped from the privateers. And he'd paid for her freedom with his hand.

Naldo shrugged. "Slade angry lose you. I lucky Jagger remember my importance."

79

Tears stung her eyes as she hugged him. "I'm sorry, Naldo. If I'd known . . ."

"Na." He held up his hand to forestall her. "No choice. You had to go."

"Couldn't you have received a transplant?"

"*Ti.* Didn't want." He grinned. "Remind Slade this way." As if remembering, his smile faded. "Why you come? Dangerous."

"I know, I know." Raven paced across the small room. "Beckett hired me to find his daughter. Slade has her." She looked around. "Doesn't he?"

"Young girl. Like you. Very strong, very brave."

"Where is she, Naldo? Is she here?"

He shook his head. "*Na.* Slade take to sword."

"There is no sword. It's only a legend." Raven sighed. "And he'll kill her when he discovers that." She wanted to curl up next to Naldo as she had during her childhood, when he'd assured her everything would be all right. She knew better now. "Where has Slade taken her?"

A view screen flickered and changed to show a far reaching star chart. A light at the extreme edge flashed in a steady pulse. Naldo pointed. "There."

Raven moved closer to study it. "There's no planet there." She knew the star charts. After all, she'd used her many long, boring flights to memorize them.

"Is now." Naldo focused the screen in closer to view the planet's galaxy. "New discovery. Named Saladan."

"Saladan." Raven examined the chart. She recognized some of the stars, but not all. "How far is it?"

"Tessie estimate six-day journey. Top hyperspeed."

Six days? Raven's throat closed so that she could barely force her next words out. "When did they leave?"

"Two days past."

She sagged against the panels. With her ship in its present condition she had no chance of catching Slade before he reached Saladan and discovered for himself that the sword only existed in Alban tales.

"You go after Slade?"

"I don't know." Running her fingers through her hair,

Raven glanced at the other screens. "First, I need to find my weapon and free Beckett."

As she spoke, Naldo switched one of the central screens to show Beckett stalking across the small confines of his cell. His dark glower sent shivers along Raven's nerves. When he threw himself against the laser light barrier she jumped back with a gasp. He bounced off with a cry of frustration and glared at it.

Obviously he didn't understand how mere beams of light could keep him imprisoned. Circling his cell again, he stopped to hammer his fists against one of the solid rock walls.

"Angry that one," Naldo said.

Raven grimaced. "I think he's beyond angry. That's rage." And she had no doubt where it was directed.

What a fool. A tight-fitting suit, luscious breasts, and gently rounded hips had led him astray. How could he have forgotten his daughter? Where was Ciorstan? Was she even alive?

Beckett pounded his fists against the rough walls. Raven had lied to him. She'd made up her entire story of Slade taking Ciorstan in order to lure him to this desolate planet and steal his gold.

Why hadn't he checked on her instead of believing some alien creature's claim that she was the best tracker in the galaxy? He should've realized she had ulterior motives when he saw the way she looked at his medallion. She'd agreed to work for him fast enough then.

Closing his eyes, he threw back his head and roared—a cry of frustration and anger. Where was his daughter?

The tightness in his chest threatened to choke him. Fear enveloped him with an almost tangible presence. Everything had been a lie. Ciorstan wasn't here—had never been here. She could be injured, lost, frightened . . . or worse.

Beckett groaned. He'd fallen for Raven's trap. Somehow she'd managed to set this up so that the privateers would wind up with his medallion and he'd end up with nothing. All he wanted was his daughter.

No wonder Raven knew the privateers' ways so intimately. He should've expected this when she warned him to close his eyes in the antechamber. How could she have known that unless she'd been here before?

Scowling, he recalled her expertise at landing on a merchant ship. Further evidence of her pirate life. Damnation; he prided himself on his ability to determine a person's character. It had saved him in more than one instance.

But not this time.

He'd trusted her—not only with his life, but with Ciorstan's. Raven had appeared sincere. Obviously she had a lot of experience in this game of deceit. Fool that he was, he'd actually felt an attraction for her. No doubt she used that to manipulate him too.

Beckett paced across the front of his rock-hewn cell. Several brilliant beams of light shone from small disks on one side to similar disks on the other. They didn't look capable of holding anyone prisoner—especially Beckett MacLeod.

But they did.

Rubbing his shoulder, he reviewed his dash against the bright barrier only to be knocked back by a burning thrust of energy. His arm still tingled. This modern technology contained devices he'd never seen before, but that didn't mean he couldn't fight them.

Crossing from one end to the other, he examined the beam's circular outputs. Somehow that continuous ray of light generated enough energy to block the entire entrance. If he could somehow disrupt it . . .

He smiled wryly as he drew his dagger from his boot. The pirates might have taken his sword, but that didn't leave him unarmed. Those fools judged him against their modern standards—to his advantage.

Using the dagger, he dug at the edges of the disk. The well-honed blade slowly chipped the surrounding rock. Tiny pebbles formed a growing pile on the floor. When he reached the back of the device and revealed the first few strands of wire he paused and stood upright.

He didn't know much about non-Alban power sources. In theory, he should be able to cut through the wire and disable the jailing beam. Or he could kill himself trying. What did he have to lose?

Ciorstan . . . his freedom . . . his life.

He'd never find his daughter by remaining locked inside this mountain fortress. Instinctively he knew the privateers had no intention of allowing him to leave— alive. His only option was escape.

Clenching his jaw, Beckett crouched again beside the disk. He could barely make out the thin pieces of wire attached to it. One of them had to provide the energy.

Not allowing himself to think further, he ran his blade across the wires.

Shock. Pain. Fire.

Searing agony shot up his arm with power so strong it thrust him away from the wall to land on his rear. Small rocks showered about him. The room swung in a circle and he closed his eyes to fight off the dizziness as he held his throbbing arm. His head pounded in a rhythmic pulse and his ears rang, blurring any other sounds.

Time lost meaning as he huddled there for minutes . . . hours. Eventually the spinning stopped and the sizzling sensation in his arm ebbed. He opened his eyes to examine his wound.

A red streak lined with singed body hair traced a path along the back of his hand and up his arm. His fingertips looked almost black. Beckett touched them with his other hand and cringed at the onslaught of pain.

So much for that idea. He'd have to think of something else.

Glancing toward the light barrier, he started and stared. The beams were gone.

"Damnation." He snatched his dagger off the floor as he climbed to his feet and cautiously approached the entrance. No light emerged from the disks. Reaching out with his good hand, he swung it through where the barrier had been.

Nothing.

He smiled and stepped through. He'd done it.

As he started down a corridor, he suddenly realized a loud noise filled the hallway. It was a voice . . . Tessie's voice.

"Power surge in cell three. Power surge in cell . . ."

Her voice stopped abruptly. Beckett scanned the nearby area. Was anyone coming? He'd not be taken prisoner so easily again.

Hearing no noises to herald anyone's approach, he hurried away from the cell only to find himself lost in the maze of corridors. He kept moving.

Somehow . . . some way . . . he'd find Raven and force her to take him off this planet. If he could control his anger, he might even make her find Ciorstan.

No. He'd never trust her again.

He'd get to a safe place and then . . . then Raven would pay for her deceit.

As Raven entered the corridor leading to the weapons room, she recalled Naldo's words: "I talk Tessie."

If he didn't distract the computer, Raven could find herself in even more trouble.

Fortunately, many of Naldo's duties meshed with Tessie's, so that she considered him an equal despite his mortal shell. If anyone could persuade the surveillance computer to ignore alarms, it was Naldo.

Refusing to admit that fear caused her racing heartbeat and trembling hand, Raven scanned the area outside the weapons storage room. No one. She had to do this . . . now.

She placed her palm against the rectangular plate beside the door. "Raven DuPrés."

"Access denied." Tessie's soft voice dashed Raven's hopes. "Sorry, Raven, but you were removed a long time ago."

Naldo was supposed to have reinstalled her. "My access has been reinstated," Raven said with false assurance. "Check the logs again." *Hurry up, Naldo.*

"Checking."

Raven swallowed hard during the ensuing silence.

Regaining her weapon was the first step of her escape plan. Without it, she'd never be able to free Beckett.

"There it is. Access reinstated." The door slid open as Tessie spoke again. "Naldo has requested a game of Jungsa." She spoke with indulgent amusement. "The silly mortal has never won a game with me. Well, almost once."

Raven smiled. This contest had been going on as long as she could remember. "Good luck, Tessie."

"He's the one who needs luck. Call if you need me."

"I will." Releasing a shaky breath, Raven slipped inside the room and closed the door. Thank the stars for Naldo and a computer that couldn't resist a challenge.

Her eyes widened as she surveyed the arms supply. The stock had improved a lot since she'd last seen it. No wonder privateers had become a force feared throughout the universe.

Where was her laser? It might not equal the larger guns' power, but she'd feel better with it in her holster. *Ah, there.* Grabbing her weapon, she returned it to her belt and felt immediate reassurance at the familiar weight. Now to get herself and Beckett out of this mountain.

She turned to leave, then froze as she spotted Beckett's sword leaning against the wall. Light reflected off the blade, almost calling Raven, and automatically she went to grab it.

Shibit, it was heavy. Lifting the sword, she studied the engraved scrolling on the handle and the sleek deadliness of the edge. It fit Beckett MacLeod.

Without effort, she remembered his defensive posture in the Merchants' Guild Hall. He had to have known his sword couldn't match the regulators' weapons, yet he'd been ready to fight . . . to die.

She grasped the hilt even tighter. The least she could do was return this sword to its rightful owner.

Then he'll probably use it to cut off my head.

She had no doubts of his anger. He had to think she'd betrayed him and led him here to steal his medallion. As a caring father, he was probably frantic with worry over his daughter—a daughter Raven still intended to find.

She slid the sword through her belt and nearly fell from the off-balanced weight. How did Beckett ever run wearing this thing? She smiled slightly. Actually he ran well. Very well.

After checking that no one lingered outside, Raven slipped from the room and hurried down the corridor to her next destination. The only way to prove her innocence would be to return the gold . . . if she lived through her attempt to regain it.

Naldo had located the medallion in Jagger's quarters. Why couldn't it be in the vault with the other valuables? That she could break into, but Jagger's room . . . ?

If he captured her, she knew he'd either rape or kill her . . . probably both. Was regaining Beckett's trust worth that price?

Raven hesitated. The betrayed expression she'd seen in Beckett's eyes still brought an ache to her chest. Yes, she had to do this.

Though her movements were awkward due to the heavy sword, she managed to avoid meeting anyone as she hurried through the intertwining passages and silently thanked Naldo for making her review a map of the fortress hallways. As she neared Jagger's quarters, she forced down her nervousness. She was a tracker. Unpleasant duties were part of her job. She could do this.

Naldo had assured her that Jagger was busy in the antechamber, but she still needed to move quickly. At his doorway she unrolled the clear scan Naldo had helped her make of Jagger's palm and placed it over the rectangular screen. Pressing a button on a small recorder, she played back Jagger saying his name and held her breath.

Would it work? How alert were Tessie's scanners while she was engaged in Jungsa?

It worked. The door slid open and Raven darted inside.

She scanned the room, surprised to find it neat and

uncluttered. The order didn't fit with what she knew of Jagger. Star charts spread across a table were the only sign anyone even lived there. The single decoration was a large holo of a naked woman displayed on a three-dimensional screen that covered an entire wall. Raven rolled her eyes. Now *that* was more like it.

She turned away. Where would Jagger store the medallion? In his safe, no doubt. So, where was that? She quickly searched his bedframe and cabinets. Not there.

Placing her hands on her hips, she pivoted to examine the walls but found nothing. It had to be behind the projection. She approached the large screen with trepidation. Could she even move it?

She discovered a small space between the holo display and the wall—just wide enough for her to slide through. In the dim lighting she needed a moment for her eyes to adjust, but she spotted the safe mounted in the wall.

Good; it had a digital combination.

Raven removed her modified decoder from her pocket and attached the ends to the push-button pad. This tiny device had opened more than one lock for her.

After starting the random access program for locating the combination she waited. Numbers flashed on the device faster than she could read, but the search for the correct sequence seemed to take forever.

Hurry. Her hammering heart hurt her chest. *Hurry.*

The sound of the door sliding open brought her heart into her throat.

Jagger!

She stiffened. The screen hid her from his view . . . for the moment. If he decided to access his safe, she'd be trapped.

Unfortunately, the screen also blocked him from her view, and she listened intently. What was he doing? She heard something—his laser?—clatter against the table, followed by the ripping noise of Stic-Tite being opened.

He was undressing?

Fardpissle. Raven tensed.

His bed sighed as he laid on it, and Raven closed her

eyes in silent misery. Would he go to sleep? How would she know? She took a short step closer to the edge of the screen. If she could just see . . .

Her decoder trilled as it solved the combination—a quiet noise, yet it sounded amplified in the quiet room. She quickly silenced it, but not soon enough.

Jagger rose to his feet stealthily. Raven heard him grab his weapon from the table. She dropped her hand to her laser and silently withdrew it from the holster. She'd hoped to avoid this.

"Alert. Alert." Tessie's voice stopped Jagger's approach.

"What is it?" he snapped.

"There has been a major power surge in the holding cells. Two alarms have been triggered."

"It's that Alban." Jagger's footsteps now headed for the exit door. "With luck he's saved us the trouble of killing him."

The door slid open, then closed. Silence descended, but Raven refused to move, afraid Jagger might still return. After several minutes she returned her laser to its holster and examined the safe.

The decoder had activated the combination and the door hung slightly open. Raven looked inside and smiled triumphantly when she spotted the medallion amid a pile of stolen jewelry. After placing it around her neck so that it hung inside her suit she closed the safe and edged her way out.

As she slid from behind the screen, she paused. Hearing nothing, she moved to the door and activated it. Once she ascertained that no one waited in the corridor, she darted outside and hurried away from the room.

Now to rescue Beckett.

The Alban.

She froze, recalling Tessie's message. Beckett had somehow caused a power surge and set off the alarms. Was he hurt? Alive?

She refused to consider his death. He could be injured, which would change her plans considerably.

With Beckett immobile, their chance of escape dropped from slim to none.

She reexamined her options. She had her weapon and the gold. She also knew the way out. If she left now . . . alone . . . she would probably succeed.

No. She discarded the idea immediately. Beckett had hired her. He'd trusted her and she intended to fulfill that trust, whether he still believed in her or not.

She refused to ask Naldo to locate Beckett. This time she'd leave no clue pointing to Naldo's aid in her escape.

Grabbing her laser, she switched to an alternate route. Too many privateers would be in the cell hallways right now. She'd try to approach from the back and discover Beckett's condition. Then she could revise her plans, if necessary.

Eluding others proved more difficult than she'd thought, and Raven ended up dodging down several out-of-the-way corridors before she finally made her way to the cells. She approached silently, then had to bite back a gasp at seeing the condition of Beckett's cell.

The barrier was down. Small stones littered the floor and scorch marks blackened the rock walls.

For a moment Raven forgot to breathe. Beckett was dead. He had to be. How could anyone survive a blast like that?

She edged closer, unable to see the entire cell. Only two privateers stood inside, looking down at something. Beckett's body? Tears pricked at Raven's eyes and she blinked them away furiously. She'd sworn never to waste tears on a man—especially one she barely knew.

But it was what she did know about him that made the difference. She'd never met such an honorable, courageous man as Beckett MacLeod before.

As she sidled away from the holding area, grief constricted her chest. Now she'd never know if his kisses were as wonderful as his appearance.

Where did that come from?

She hadn't wanted him to kiss her. Involvement with a man only led to trouble, and she found enough of that on her own.

Yet, now that he was dead, she did admit to an attraction to him, to a curiosity about his kisses. She'd finally found someone who'd interested her and he was gone.

Raven exhaled and swiped angrily at a tear trickling down her cheek. *Enough.* She could still escape, and once away from Erebus, she'd continue to search for Beckett's daughter. Raven owed him that, at least.

As she rounded a corner, someone grabbed her, reaching one arm across her front to grasp her other shoulder and jerk her back against a solid bulk. Before she could open her mouth she felt the prick of a knife against her throat.

"Dinna say a word."

Raven almost fell from relief at hearing the familiar brogue. *Beckett. He's alive.*

She tried to look at him, but he held her firmly in place.

And the knife pressed closer.

Chapter Six

Beckett struggled to contain his anger. As much as he wanted Raven to pay for her betrayal, he didn't intend to harm her. Though when he thought about Ciorstan . . .

"You're going to take me off this planet," he said with a deep growl.

"Exactly."

Her reply stunned him, but it wasn't until she held his sword out for him that he lowered his dagger in amazement.

"You probably want this," Raven added. As he loosened his grip, she turned to face him, a hint of a smile playing about her lips. She offered the sword again. "Come on; take it. It weighs too much for me to handle."

He grasped the hilt. New determination flooded his veins as he gripped the familiar blade. Now he could face any enemy . . . even an attractive one. He focused his gaze on Raven. "Get me out of here."

She nodded. "Follow me." She darted down the hallway and he hurried to catch up with her.

"I'll nae be led into another trap."

"Don't worry." She tossed the words over her shoulder. "I want out of here even more than you do."

Despite his vow never to trust her again, Beckett wanted to believe her. She sounded sincere, but he'd learned how deceiving that could be. "Where are you going?"

"There's a back door into the complex. It's been locked for ages and forgotten about. I discovered it years ago when I was examining some old floor plans. I kept it in mind, figuring I could use it to escape someday."

"Escape?" Was this another of her lies?

She gave him a quelling look. "Not everyone who lives with the privateers *wants* to, Beckett."

Before he could question her further he heard voices nearby. He shifted his sword. They'd have a fight before they took him prisoner again.

Raven touched his arm. "This way."

He heard the urgency in her voice and followed her into a dark corridor. The voices faded.

Though she wasn't running, Raven set a brisk pace that made Beckett thankful for his years of running over the hills at home. At least inside this mountain he didn't find it nearly as difficult to breathe as he had outside.

She led him through a series of twists and turns that would have confused him more if he hadn't been confused to start with. They had to be going deeper into the mountain. He'd seen no sign of life for some time, and his keen hearing confirmed that no one followed them.

As they traveled farther, the hallways became darker, barely lit by the internal glow emitted from the ceiling.

At one crossroads Raven paused, frowning. She opened her mouth as if to speak, then closed it again and pressed her face close to the walls instead.

"What are you looking for?"

"A directional marker. I think we go right, but I want to be sure." She almost pressed her nose to the rock before she straightened. "Right it is."

"Is there a way to make more light?"

"I could ask Te . . . the computer, but then she'd know our location. As it is, I'm hoping Naldo's kept her too busy to track us."

"Can it do that?"

"Easily."

Beckett examined the dimly lit corridors closely. He hadn't thought about the computer once it quit shouting its warning.

"Could others be waiting ahead?"

"It's possible." Raven hesitated, apparently considering his question. "Though I'd hope we'd get a warning from Naldo first."

"A privateer would warn us?"

She grinned quickly, a brief flicker that brightened the darkness. "Naldo's my friend."

"A pirate?"

Instead of replying she resumed walking. Beckett stayed by her side, watching her. Who was Raven . . . really?

She stopped abruptly before a large metal door buried in the mountain rock. "This is it." Frowning, she examined the thick bolt holding it closed. "If I use my laser on this, it might bring down the whole tunnel."

"Let me try." Beckett had used his sword against many obstacles. What was one more?

He hoisted the blade above his head and swung it against the bolt with a fierce cry. The force of the impact sent a jangle up his arms, but the bolt held.

"Damnation." These modern metals were different and obviously stronger than the few he'd encountered on Alba. He glanced at Raven. "You might need your weapon after all."

She withdrew her laser but hesitated at aiming it. Motioning with her head, she directed Beckett to move away. "Go down the corridor a ways. I don't want you to get hurt by mistake."

"Wouldna that solve all your problems?"

"Not even half of them," she snapped. "I'm trying to

rescue you, Beckett. You don't have to be grateful, but you could cooperate."

Rescue him? That wasn't the way he saw it. And he wasn't about to let her get too far away—he'd learned his lesson.

Raven scowled. "Take your chances, then." Raising her laser, she took careful aim.

"That exit is forbidden, Raven."

At Tessie's voice, Raven stiffened, her eyes widening. She glanced at the dimly lit ceiling. "We have to get out of here, Tessie."

"No one is allowed to leave this complex without permission."

"This is an exception." Clenching her jaw, Raven fired at the door. Though the door glowed brilliantly as her laser beam hit it, the surrounding rock held firm.

The bolt fell to the ground and Beckett hurried over to yank the door open. The searing heat and suffocating atmosphere poured into the corridor.

He remembered his earlier lesson and breathed slowly until his lungs adjusted. Glancing outside, he saw the door stood on a narrow ledge cut into the mountainside. They'd have to follow it to get to the ground.

Raven joined him. "We'll have to hurry."

"Raven, I must sound an alarm," Tessie said calmly.

"Please, don't."

"I can't ignore my primary mission."

Closing her eyes briefly, Raven bit her lip. Finally she spoke again. "Then delay the alarm. Please."

"Hmm, delay the alarm." The computer appeared to consider the notion.

Beckett stared in amazement. What kind of machine was this?

"Yes, I can do that, but not for long. Take care, Raven."

"You, too, Tessie." Raven smiled slightly, then turned to touch Beckett's arm. "Go, quickly."

The ledge had barely enough width for them to stand. Though not frightened by heights, Beckett preferred not to look down and concentrated on the path instead.

Raven followed his example, her face determined. As they neared the bottom, she spoke again. "We'll have to run. Be ready to follow me."

"I'll have naught of your tricks." Beckett didn't know what to expect from this woman.

She gave him an exasperated look but said nothing. Instead, she leapt the short distance to the ground and started running. Beckett followed immediately.

The trail she took contained even more rocks than the one they'd traveled to the fortress. Thankful for the lighter gravity, Beckett leapt over them in a single stride. He only noticed the air scorching inside his chest when he climbed the hills, and he struggled not to breathe deeply. Raven appeared completely unaffected; but then, she'd lived here before.

A blast fell near them, jarring Beckett to a stop. Smoke rose in a column behind him

Raven snagged his sleeve. "Hurry. They know we've escaped. We have to reach the *TrackStar* before they do."

"Is that possible?"

"Not if we stand here yakking. Come on."

More explosions erupted—each one drawing closer—but Beckett didn't stop again. He marveled at Raven's ability to keep running, though she showed signs of weariness now. His legs and his chest ached from the strain.

Topping a ridge, he exhaled in relief. The ship sat where they'd left it, the hatch sealed tightly. He'd never thought a beat-up slab of metal could look so good.

They skidded down the hillside, rocks sliding beneath their feet. Raven dashed to the hatch and laid her hand against the rectangular patch. "Raven," she said. "Cancel security alert one."

The hatch opened at once and she darted inside. Beckett hurried after her, brushing past the computer's quick scan. He knew the routine by now and slid into the chair in front of the console.

Raven was already flipping switches as she called out

to her computer. "Mac, we need a quick liftoff. Ignore preflight check and begin engine prep."

"Ship is down to one thruster. Recommend testing prior to departure."

She froze, a startled expression on her face, as if she'd forgotten. Beckett didn't blame her. Their repair job on her thruster felt like days instead of only hours ago.

"Mac, no testing. Begin engine prep."

"Chances of successful liftoff are . . ."

"I don't want to hear it." Raven studied the control panel, then looked at Beckett, her face grim. "You know if we stay here, they'll kill us."

"I'm certain they'll kill me." He doubted she'd be harmed.

Her lips tightened. "We also have a pretty good chance of exploding when we take off. Do you have a preference?"

She meant it. He didn't doubt the serious glimmer in her eyes. "Do you?" She knew this ship better than he did.

"I'd rather die trying to find your daughter than wait to be slaughtered by privateers." She met his gaze with a defiant tilt to her chin.

He almost smiled. There might be a bit of Scottish blood in her after all. "Then get us out of here."

"Okay. Mac, apply power to the thruster—slowly. Let me know if it approaches critical."

The ship trembled as a roar came from the rear. Beckett eyed the back panel warily, expecting to see flames at any moment.

An explosion hit the ridge and he swung around to look out the front window. Rocks rumbled down the hill in a gigantic slide.

"They've caught up to us." Raven grasped the lever firmly. "We have to go. Mac, liftoff."

She applied more power until the ship shuddered and rose into the air. As it moved forward, it wavered, barely missing the side of the hill.

Beckett could only grip his armrests and apply every bit of his willpower into raising the vehicle higher.

More explosions burst close by. He could see men on the ground growing smaller as the ship climbed toward the blackness of space.

The engine sputtered and he whirled to look back, as did Raven. The panel appeared normal—normal as far as he knew. At least no smoke escaped from it.

The roar settled into a more even rhythm. Beckett exchanged a wry grin with Raven before turning forward again. The colors faded around them until the window revealed nothing but endless darkness broken only by tiny specks of light.

They'd made it.

Releasing his breath, he glanced at Raven. She still looked grave, her gaze darting between the control panel and the sky before them. Why?

The answer dawned immediately. "Will they come after us?"

"They'll try."

Her clipped reply renewed his tension. He wished for a rear window to check behind them.

"Mac, prepare for hyperspeed."

"Hyperspeed jump not recommended in ship's current condition."

"Mac, we don't have an option. Prepare for hyperspeed." She frowned at a circular screen on her panel and Beckett noticed small dots at its edge. Privateers.

Raven wrapped her fingers around the hyperspeed control. "Mac, set course for Lyra Station." She turned to Beckett. "If you know any ancient prayers, now is a good time to say them."

Before he could recall even one she pulled back, and the stars melded into streaks. The ship shuddered, but held together. Raven kept her hand on the control, her gaze darting from the control panel to the rear of the ship to the window.

Finally she released her grip and settled back in her seat, her tension visibly eased. Only then did Beckett inhale deeply to loosen his muscles.

"Can they follow us now?" he asked.

She shook her head. "Only if they have our exact co-

ordinates." Leaving her seat, she went to check on the
back panel. "*TrackStar* may be old, but it's gotten me
out of more than one tough situation."

Beckett stood. "And where are we going? Lyra Station?"

"Right. It's a space station between here and the system where Slade took your daughter. I know you don't
trust me any longer so I'll make arrangements for another tracker to take you the rest of the way. Torvik can
be trusted."

Another tracker? Could he trust someone else to find
Ciorstan? "I dinna know what to think," he admitted.
"You betrayed me, Raven." He drew nearer. When
Raven turned to face him, he gripped her shoulders. "I
hired you to find my daughter. Why did you take me to
those pirates?"

"I didn't betray you," she protested. Her gaze flashed
with anger as it met his. "I only went to Erebus because
I thought Ciorstan might be there. Believe me, it's the
last place I wanted to go."

She sounded sincere. For an instant he almost weakened and believed her, until he remembered Ciorstan
alone somewhere in this vast universe. He tightened his
hold and shook her. "I want naught of your lies. Tell
me where to find my daughter. I want the truth—now!"

Though she tilted her chin defiantly, he felt her trem-
ble beneath his hands. "The truth?" she asked.

"The entire truth. You owe me that."

She blanched and looked down, but Beckett refused
to let her loose. He would know all before he finished
with her.

Raven drew in several shallow breaths to cover the
hammering of her heart. Tell him the truth? She'd never
spoken a word of her past to anyone since she'd left
Erebus.

Hesitantly she met his gaze and recognized the
banked fury burning there. If anyone deserved to know
her story, this man did. His daughter's life depended on
defeating Slade. And in order to understand Slade,
Beckett had to know her past.

"Very well." She began slowly, forcing the words through dry lips. "My father was a wanderer. Because of that, my family never stayed in one place very long. I'm not even sure what planet I was born on."

"Are you human?"

"Of course," she snapped. "I'm a Beta-human. I'm born of human parents, but not on Earth itself. You'll discover Beta-humans are more common than humans now. You're one, too."

"I see. Continue."

"When I was six we crashed on Erebus. Naturally, privateers met us and took us to their fortress. Slade was only a young man at the time and Morgan was the leader. He was much more . . . compassionate than Slade, but the same rules applied. No one can leave Erebus alive except as a privateer. My father had no choice—he joined them."

"But you were a child." Beckett sounded amazed.

Raven shrugged, his hands rising and falling with her shoulders. "My brother, Gregor, and I had a good time at first. Everyone treated us well. Gregor was five years older than me and he enjoyed learning to fly and handle a weapon."

"But Mere hated it," she continued. "Women have always been scarce there, but they were even more so then. I was too young—I never paid attention—so I don't know what happened, but she cried a lot and begged Pere to leave." She paused, recalling her futile attempts to assuage her mother's tears. "But he couldn't.

"When I was nine—"

"Ciorstan's age."

Raven nodded, dropping her gaze, and shifted uneasily beneath Beckett's grasp. "When I was nine Slade came to tell me my parents and Gregor had died."

The scene, still so vivid after all those years, played in her mind. She closed her eyes in a futile attempt to blot it out.

"How?" Beckett spoke gently. "How did they die?"

"Their ship exploded. Pere had stolen a privateer vessel and tried to escape in it. Maybe it was shot down or maybe the reactor exploded, like Slade said. Either way it was the same."

Her lip trembled and she blinked furiously to keep tears from sliding down her cheeks. "They left me." Swallowing the lump in her throat, she looked at Beckett. "My parents left me behind."

"My God." He dropped his hands, his expression stunned, and Raven turned away, ashamed at revealing this vulnerability.

Nearly choking on a rising sob, she could still hear Slade's mocking words. "Good thing they didn't care about you. You lived."

But she hadn't wanted to live. For months, years, even now, she felt guilty for being alive.

"There must be some other explanation," Beckett said quietly.

"They didn't want me. That's explanation enough." She refused to look around. "I liked to go my own way and usually failed to heed my mother's warnings. I remember her telling me the day before that she wouldn't take much more of my willfulness." Raven tried to keep her voice from wavering and failed. "I didn't believe her at the time."

"Nae." Beckett tried to deny it.

"Not all parents are like you." She drew in a shuddering breath and faced him again. "After that I became close to Naldo, a Terellian. I was . . . upset. I wouldn't talk or eat, so they took me to him."

At Beckett's questioning glance she continued. "Terellians are known for their psi abilities. Morgan thought Naldo's telepathy might help me. It did."

Naldo's ability to know her feelings better than she did enabled him to guide her back to living again. Though no one ever put it in words, he became her guardian. How much better off would he have been without her? Because of her, he'd lost his hand. And if she hadn't covered her trail well enough, he could pay for her recent escape, too.

"So you became a pirate?"

"Yes." She refused to flinch beneath his censure. "By age ten they began teaching me how to fly. By twelve I was accompanying them on merchant raids. By fourteen I was one of the better pilots. By fifteen Slade noticed I was becoming a woman."

Beckett's gaze darkened. "Did he . . . harm you?"

"Yes. No." Beckett's concern on her behalf warmed Raven, but not enough to remove the chill of remembering those days. "Morgan died suspiciously when I was fourteen. Many of us suspected Slade, but no one could prove it. Though he was still fairly young, Slade took over the privateers. They changed after that—became more ruthless, more likely to kill than take prisoners."

"Dinna anyone try to stop him?"

"A few. They died. Slade has no qualms about killing anyone who gets in his way. He takes what he wants."

Beckett touched her face, cupping her cheek in his palm. "And he wanted you?"

She grimaced. "I don't know that he really wanted me. As I said before, women were scarce and I was there." She wanted to lean into the strength of his touch. Instead, she turned her face away, unable to meet his eyes. "Fortunately Slade had a woman, Cristela, so most of the time he ignored me. But one day he stopped me in a corridor. He'd had a fight with Cristela. He . . . he put his hands on me and told me what he planned to do to me."

Her stomach churned at the memory. "I kicked him, ran away and threw up. After that, whenever he came near me, he'd . . . touch me or whisper something lurid."

"The bastard." The barely controlled anger in Beckett's voice told Raven he was upset about more than just her.

"I knew I'd have to get out of there somehow. That's when I learned about the rear door, but I never had a chance to use it. One night, after we returned from a raid, Slade found Cristela with another man. He killed them both on sight."

He'd continued firing long after Cristela and her lover were dead. Raven had skirted to the edge of the crowd to see what had happened, but when she tried to slink away Slade had grabbed her arm.

"Then he told me I would be his woman. He gave me an hour to make myself presentable and appear in his chamber."

Beckett's eyes glowed with rage. "And he raped you?" His words came from between clenched teeth.

"No. I ran to Naldo and begged him to help me escape. We both knew we were taking a big risk, but the alternative was unacceptable. I stole a small ship and Naldo opened the hatch so I could launch."

"Did they come after you?"

"Not right away. Naldo made the launch look routine, so Tessie didn't sound any alarms. Frightened as I was, I just put the ship on top speed and jetted off to no particular destination."

And almost lost her bearings, but Beckett didn't need to know that. "I met a scrap freighter and swapped them my ship for a ride."

"You've been on your own since you were fifteen?" Beckett's face mirrored the disbelief in his voice.

"I've more or less been on my own since I was nine."

"Nine." He looked at her as if seeing her for the first time.

"Exactly." Raven watched his expressions change from doubt to concern to anger. Did he think this was another story? If only it *was* a tale.

He extended his hand. "I—"

A sharp sputter from the remaining thruster cut him off. Raven hurried to check on the equipment, uncertain whether her trembling resulted from her emotional upheaval or the fear of explosion.

The thruster held . . . for the moment.

"Mac, what's the engine status? Will we make Lyra Station?"

"If thruster maintains current output, this vehicle will arrive Lyra Station at predicted time."

"And if it doesn't maintain current output?"

"Unknown. Trip could take from twelve hours to six months."

They didn't have that kind of time—not if Beckett was to reach his daughter before Slade discovered there was no magic sword.

Raven leaned inside the panel once more to verify the connections. She'd done all she could. The rest depended on *TrackStar*.

As she straightened, an unfamiliar object bumped against her chest, and she remembered the medallion. Pulling it over her head, she handed it to Beckett.

His stunned reaction made her terror in obtaining it worthwhile. "Wha—?"

"It's your gold."

"But the pirate took it."

Raven smiled wryly. "I stole it back."

He glanced from the medallion in his palm to her, his confusion obvious. "Why?"

"You'll need it to pay Torvik." She turned to the control panel, trying to distance herself from him. Telling her tale had shattered her internal barriers, and she didn't dare spend any more time with Beckett than necessary. He made her aware of emotions she'd buried for years.

And she wasn't at all certain she liked that.

Beckett watched the approaching space station fill the front screen. Despite some shudders and ominous crackling from the ship, the *TrackStar* managed to come out of hyperspeed in one piece.

They were traveling toward Lyra Station at what Raven called standard speed, but he knew from her glowers and low mutters that they still weren't out of danger. After the time he'd spent with her, he expected as much. Things hadn't gone right from the beginning, so why was he reluctant to use another tracker?

Because he believed her.

He'd felt her pain when she spoke of her parents' death. His mind still refused to accept that they'd abandoned her. It would be the same as if he were to leave Ciorstan. Unthinkable!

As he'd listened to Raven's tale, he'd wanted to pull her into his arms and assure her that everything would be all right. But he hadn't. He'd seen beneath her tough shell to the frightened, isolated woman inside and knew—at that point—that she wouldn't have appreciated his embrace.

Though he understood Raven better now, his primary focus had to be on finding Ciorstan. If Slade was even half as bad as Raven said, Beckett wanted to kill the man. He would, too, if he discovered Slade had laid so much as a finger on his daughter.

"Strap yourself in."

Raven's sudden words cut into Beckett's musings, and he fastened the straps. The space station had grown in size, filling the front window. Though he had difficulty judging the size of objects in space, he knew this had to be larger than the merchant ships. And he'd thought those were enormous.

"*TrackStar* calling Lyra Station. Request permission to dock."

"Permission granted for docking at gate twenty-three. File copy of manifest upon landing."

"Will do."

"Manifest?" Beckett asked.

"My listing of passengers and cargo." She gave him a quick smile. "I have no cargo and only one passenger, so it's pretty short." She maneuvered the ship around the outside of the station.

Raven pointed toward a dark opening in the station's side. "There's our gate."

"Is it big enough?"

"It'll look bigger when we're closer."

The opening grew in size until it looked large enough to swallow two ships the size of Raven's. Beckett gulped as the *TrackStar* approached it and entered.

Lights lined the entry tunnel, allowing him to see the rear wall in the distance, with a landing pad before it. A long ramp led to it.

Raven guided her ship onto the ramp and leaned forward to flip a switch.

Nothing happened.

"Fardpissle." She snapped the switch back and forth several times.

Beckett didn't need to be told that they were in trouble . . . again. The flash of alarm on Raven's face had become all too familiar. In addition, they were approaching the rear wall at an alarming speed.

"Can I help?" he asked.

"Hold on," she snapped. Quickly flicking several switches, she grabbed a lever and pulled.

Sharp, grinding noises filled the ship, and for a moment Beckett thought he smelled something burning. A glance at the rear panel assured him that they weren't on fire . . . yet.

The ship slowed, but not enough to make Beckett feel secure. The wall looked very close. Too close.

Without asking, he lunged across the panel to add his strength to Raven's on the lever. He could feel the ship's resistance in the lever's vibration. They weren't going to stop in time.

"Damnation." He jerked hard on the lever and the ship slowed more, almost to a halt. As he glanced out the window, he realized it didn't matter anymore. They'd reached the wall.

The *TrackStar* skidded into it, tossing Beckett back into his seat, but amazingly the ship didn't penetrate. Instead, it bounced back and stopped.

Raven moved first, cutting all power, then turned to look at Beckett. Despite her pale face, she managed a dry smile. "We're here."

Beckett nodded in reply. It might not be such a bad thing to go with Torvik. *His* ship had to be better than this one.

They waited for confirmation of an air lock before leaving the *TrackStar*. Raven paused by the entrance to the station to stare at her ship. Her eyes watered and shoulders bowed as she looked at the damage.

And it *was* damaged. Even Beckett knew the black

smoke rising from beneath the vehicle wasn't good. "What happened?"

"My forward thrusters quit."

He heard the quaver in her voice, but before he could speak another voice cut in.

"I always told you that ship was a piece of junk."

Beckett turned to see a stocky man, a little older than himself, lounging in the doorway. His short red hair stood up like a brush and his face looked as if it had been in more than its share of fights, with its twisted nose and uneven lips. But he did look human.

Raven stiffened as she faced the man. "Hander, always on the lookout for a way to line your pockets."

Hander shrugged. "When I hear a ship has problems coming in it's my duty to meet the owner. You can't go back into space until you get it fixed, and since I run the best repair station you'll find, well . . ."

"This may be broken beyond my ability to fix." Raven sighed. "My main thrusters are shot and I lost the forward thrusters on landing."

Hander whistled. "I'm surprised you're still in one piece." He motioned toward the *TrackStar*. "May I?"

"Go ahead. Mac, Hander coming aboard." As she watched the man enter her ship, an expression of pain crossed her face.

"Who's he?" Beckett asked.

"Hander Thompson, the best ship repairman in the galaxy. We've done business before."

"You dinna look too pleased to see him."

"I know what he's going to tell me."

Hander emerged from *TrackStar* shaking his head. "This baby is shot, Raven. I told you when you bought it you were getting an antique. Jeez, the computer is eight versions behind the standard."

"Mac's always worked for me," she replied defensively. "So, how much to fix it?"

"You'd be throwing your money away. Sell it to me as scrap and get yourself a newer model. I know a guy . . ."

"How much, Hander?"

"Not counting all the other work it needs—like an overhaul of the hyperspeed—just replacing the blown thrusters will run around ten thousand credits."

Raven flinched. "Ten thousand?"

"Sorry, Rave, but that's the best I can offer." He raised one eyebrow. "The scrap deal is still open. I'll give you two thousand credits for her, and that's only 'cause I consider you a friend."

Though Raven's frozen expression revealed nothing, Beckett could see despair in her eyes. He raised an arm to touch her shoulder, then dropped it when she spoke. "Fine."

Hander nodded, his face sympathetic. "Stop by my bay and we'll do the paperwork."

"Just let me get Beckett situated first."

"Beckett?" Hander looked at him with open curiosity. "You a client of Raven's? You'll not find a better tracker."

"So I've heard," Beckett replied.

"I won't be tracking much without a ship," Raven said, bitterness in her voice. "Let's go, Beckett. We can contact Torvik on the intergalactic comm line inside."

As Beckett followed her, he again found himself reluctant to switch trackers. He'd felt from the beginning that Raven would find Ciorstan. Despite all reason, he still felt that. If anyone could, she'd find his daughter—even if she had to face Slade to do it.

But she didn't have a ship and her response to Hander told Beckett she didn't have much money.

Beckett paused, touching his medallion through his shirt. If what she'd told him was true, he had money. But was it enough?

"Raven, wait." He called her, then hesitated. Some inner instinct told him he was doing the right thing.

She turned to look at him, her expression wary, reminding him of their first meeting. "What?"

"I dinna want Torvik. I want you."

Chapter Seven

Raven's breath caught in her throat. She couldn't have heard correctly. "What?"

"I want you to find Ciorstan."

He trusts me. Unaccustomed joy flowed through her veins as she smiled broadly. After all she'd put him through, he still wanted her to track for him.

Her joy plummeted as reality intruded. "I have no ship," she said, every word painful. "I can't."

Beckett pulled his medallion from beneath his shirt as he approached. The gold glittered in the artificial light. "I have money."

Temptation wove its tendrils around Raven. For a moment she saw herself piloting a new ship, traveling through the galaxies at amazing speed. Then she met Beckett's gaze.

"I can't accept that. I haven't found Ciorstan yet." She started to turn away, unwilling to let him see her distress.

He caught her shoulder, halting her movement. "You *will* find her."

To Raven's dismay, her eyes watered and she quickly blinked away the dampness. Why could this man so easily touch her emotions? When she tried to speak she couldn't. The thickness in her throat held back any words.

"Will it be enough?" Beckett asked.

She nodded and gave him an uneven smile. "It's more than enough."

"Then we need to hurry. Can your friend help us?"

Hander. "Yes. Come with me." Propelled by her rising excitement, Raven ran through the wide corridors, Beckett close on her heels. For the first time in many years she saw hope in her future.

They paused in Hander's doorway, their breathing rapid. As Beckett stared in wonder, Raven searched for Hander among the ships and workers. An enormous bay housed the successful repair business, and a flurry of activity. Men hung over the sides and beneath a wide assortment of spaceships ranging from a tiny one-passenger speedster to a large merchant runner.

She finally spotted Hander, easily identifiable by his unruly shock of red hair and animated discourse. With a smile, she waved to catch his attention.

Acknowledging her presence with a nod, he didn't hide his surprise. He quickly concluded his conversation and hopped off the platform, using his anti-grav belt to lower himself to the floor.

"I just sent some people over to get your ship, Raven. You're not reneging on me, are you?"

"I wouldn't do that, Hander. I need to buy a new ship."

Hander, his gaze questioning, glanced from Raven to Beckett standing behind her. "What did you have in mind?" he asked.

"Can you get the new Orion model with the hyper-speed overdrive? It's very important we get that drive."

"Come with me." Hander led them to a terminal and keyed in several short commands until a list appeared on the view screen. "Hmm. I don't have one here, but I can get an Orion delivered within two to three days."

Raven's hopes sank. "We can't wait that long. I need a ship by tomorrow."

"That's impossible, Rave. We're too far from the central galaxy."

"There has to be a way," she insisted.

Beckett laid his hand on her shoulder. "What about your ship?"

"My ship?" Even as she echoed his words, realization dawned. "He's right, Hander. We can remodel the *TrackStar*."

He scowled at her. "Get serious."

"I am serious." Her words tumbled over each other. "You said it needed the hyperdrive completely redone. Just yank it out and put in an overdrive system. It's possible."

For several minutes Hander didn't speak and his eyes glazed over. His fingers seemed to move of their own accord as he brought up a schematic of the *TrackStar*. Finally he nodded. "I can do it."

Raven exchanged grins with Beckett, the warmth in his gaze triggering a strange tingling in her stomach. Unnerved, she forced her attention back to Hander.

"This is going to be expensive," he added.

"How much?" Raven knew the approximate worth of Beckett's medallion. Unless Hander charged an exorbitant amount, they should have plenty.

"We're talking twenty, maybe thirty thousand credits."

Beckett's fingers tightened on Raven's shoulder as she nodded. "We have it covered. One more thing: We need the ship by tomorrow morning."

"Raven—"

She cut off Hander's warning tone. "It's urgent." Darting a quick glance at Beckett, she continued. "Beckett's daughter has been kidnapped. They're already three days ahead of us. Without an overdrive ship by tomorrow I have no chance of catching them."

"A daughter?" Hander's eyes misted, and Raven stomped down any remorse at playing on the man's sympathies. Everyone knew Hander had a daughter whom he adored but rarely saw.

"She's nine years old," Beckett said. "I *have* to find her."

"It'll cost more if I put two crews on this project," Hander growled.

Despite his gruffness, Raven knew he'd already decided to do whatever it took. "We'll pay it," she assured him. "Just so long as the ship is ready by morning."

Hander's excitement showed as he snapped orders to his crew and a working bay emptied immediately. "I'll have to modify the onboard computer, too," he added as he hurried away.

"Oh no you don't." Raven said each word distinctly. "I do *not* want Mac humanized."

Her only reply was a soft shrug just before Hander vanished into a work area.

"Shibit." She grimaced and turned to lead Beckett outside.

"What is he planning for the computer?" he asked as he fell into step with her.

"The overdrive system requires an upgrade to my computer. All the newer models have the humanization chip in them."

"Humanization chip?"

"It makes them more like Tessie."

Remembering his unease with that computer, Beckett hesitated. "Is that a bad thing?"

"I just don't want a computer messing with my life." Raven led them into a lift and pressed the button for the city level.

Beckett's eyes widened only slightly as the doors slid closed and they began to move. Raven had to admire his courage and intelligence—he adapted quickly.

"Why do we need this overdrive?" he asked casually, as if he'd ridden in lifts every day of his life.

"It's a fairly new technology that allows ships to break all previous hyperspeed barriers and cuts travel time in half. What will take Slade six days will only take us about three."

He smiled. "Good idea."

111

Raven's breath caught in her throat. The man's smile made him truly devastating. As much as she enjoyed seeing it, she also feared its power. Never before had any smile—any man—caused this unsettling fluttering inside. With an effort, she looked away.

The lift signaled its arrival and the doors slid open. Allowing time for Beckett to adjust, Raven stepped onto the platform overlooking the city.

One of the larger space station cities, Lyra Station looked impressive even to Raven's jaded eyes. Contained beneath a clear dome that revealed the dotted darkness of space outside, the city stretched from one side of the station to the other and was dissected by narrow corridors.

"All this 'tis inside the station?" Beckett's awe sounded in his voice.

"This is a major outpost. You'd be surprised at how much business is conducted here." Raven touched his arm, her palm warming at the contact. "Come on. We need to get to the Credit Exchange."

"What's that?"

"The place where we can turn your gold into credits." Feeling Beckett's forearm tighten, she paused. "Have you changed your mind?" Her voice remained calm despite the sudden drop of her heart. Had he changed his mind about the ship? About her?

He met her gaze, his expression solemn. To her surprise, his lips lifted in a half smile and he gently touched her cheek. "I willna change my mind. Dinna worry about that."

For a moment Raven could only stare, her pulse racing. Though she hated to admit it, his trust meant a lot to her. And his touch affected her unlike any other man's.

With a jerk of her head she stepped back, and his hand fell to his side. Something indefinable flickered in his eyes, then disappeared.

"Let's go to this Credit Exchange," he said quietly.

Raven led them to the first of several moving glideways that took them to their destination. She located the Credit Exchange close to the towering complex that housed the slumber units.

The Credit Exchange building was small but busy, crowded with individuals exchanging their planetary currency for intergalactic credits. Spotting an open cubicle, Raven ushered Beckett over to it and into the chairs before the computerized exchanger.

"State your business."

As Beckett eyed the computer suspiciously, Raven spoke. "We wish to exchange gold for credits." She nudged Beckett. "Put the medallion on this plate."

He slowly removed the ornament from around his neck, his reluctance obvious. After running his fingers over the engraved surface he placed it on the flat pad.

Immediately, the scanner activated, displaying the weight and density on the screen. Raven inhaled sharply. Almost one hundred percent pure.

The computer paused while it collected bids for the medallion via the intergalactic network; then it posted the winning sum. When Raven saw the value in credits she gasped aloud. Her haphazard computations hadn't even come close.

Beckett glanced at her. "Is that good?"

"It's unbelievable. I can't accept all of that even when I do find Ciorstan."

Beckett broke into a stunning smile and Raven gaped at him. "Wh . . . what is it?" she stammered, suddenly aware of a roaring in her chest.

"You said *when,* not if."

Suddenly facing Slade again didn't seem nearly so bad. In fact, finding Ciorstan took on even more importance . . . even more so than maintaining her professional reputation. She had to locate Beckett's daughter just so she could experience that breathtaking smile again.

When the medallion slid inside the wall a small square lit up on the screen. "Please place your right thumb or equivalent digit on the illuminated space," the computer said.

Beckett complied, then reached for the palm-sized

rectangular card that emerged from a slot. " 'Tis this my money?"

Raven grinned. "Your credits and thumbprint are encoded on there and in the intergalactic system. The card is good everywhere."

"And I have enough to pay for your ship?"

"More than enough."

Confused, Beckett continued to examine the card as they went to the large building where Raven said they could get rooms for the night. Even after he used the card to pay for their rooms, he fingered it quizzically.

He found it difficult to believe any money was available with this small item, let alone the vast amount Raven insisted was there. She showed him how to slide it into available slots to check the available credits, but the numbers seemed too large to be real.

Just as the rooms they obtained appeared unreal. His chamber sat beside Raven's on an upper floor. When he slid open the door his spirits sank. He'd accepted that quarters on spaceships had to be spartan, but on this enormous station he had expected more than a plain narrow bed, a built-in terminal for some sort of computer, and a sterile bathing unit. The room embodied loneliness.

Unbidden, the image of his bedroom on Alba sprang into his mind. Recalling the plushness of his large wooden bed, the bright tapestries and ornaments and the mammoth fireplace, he succumbed to intense longing. God, he couldn't wait to leave all this technology and return home. From what he'd seen there was nothing he'd trade for his life on Alba. His ancestors had made the right decision.

However, the emptiness of his bed reminded Beckett of his own loneliness. Though he'd been surrounded by friends, family, and comrades, he hadn't found that special someone. After Nessa died he'd avoided any close relationships, concentrating on the welfare of his people instead.

He had to admit that since he'd left Alba to find Ciorstan he'd felt a new surge of life, and his constant despair had eased. Whether that was due to Raven or to the constant peril she kept putting them in, he couldn't say.

However, he could attribute his recurring desire to Raven. Beckett looked down at the small bed and grimaced. He'd rather discover the passion hidden inside one certain intriguing tracker than spend a long night on that uncomfortable bed.

Lately he'd found himself thinking too much about whether her hair was as soft as it looked, her lips as sweet, her curves as smooth. But Raven represented his only chance of locating his daughter. He had to remember that.

"I know it's not much."

He whirled around to see Raven standing in his doorway, her expression oddly apologetic. "Transients don't require anything more than a place to clean up and sleep," she continued.

"What about the people who live here?"

"They have quarters near their businesses." She tilted her head toward the hallway. "There's a place we can eat down the way, if you're hungry."

His expression must have revealed his opinion of Raven's food sticks for she grinned suddenly. "It'll have real food, Beckett. They have hydroponics here."

"Real food?" His stomach growled in response. "I'm suddenly very hungry."

They walked toward the lifts. "You can come back to your room after we eat," Raven said, her tone casual.

Beckett glanced at her sharply. "Where are you going?"

"To the galactorium."

"What's that?"

Frowning, she bit her lip. "I'm not sure how to explain it. It's a place with star maps and information on the galaxy."

"May I come along?"

"Sure. I just thought you might be bored."

Bored? Never with Raven. Beckett smiled. "I dinna think so."

*   *   *

It did look boring.

As they entered the galactorium, Beckett expected to see stars. Instead he saw nothing but booths similar to the ones in the Credit Exchange. When Raven slid into the chair before a computer terminal he followed her example. Though the view screen was larger than the previous one, Beckett failed to see how the machine would help them.

Raven pushed several buttons, then spoke. "Computer, display Andromeda Sector to include new discoveries."

Instantly the screen erupted into a mass of stars. One spot shone much brighter than the others and Raven tapped on it. "That's the central heat source—the sun—for this system. Computer, distinguish planet Saladan and show orbit."

A small light flared as did its odd elliptical path around the sun. Raven leaned forward. "So small. No wonder it stayed hidden so long."

"Is that where we'll find Ciorstan?" Beckett found it hard to associate that flashing dot with an actual planet.

"According to Naldo." Raven rapidly moved her fingers over the keyboard. "Computer, display all information on planet Saladan."

Moving images appeared showing scenes of wilderness, deep canyons and desert. Beckett blinked once. He'd heard of these pictures called holovids but hadn't expected them to look so lifelike.

As he watched the changing terrain appear on the view screen, a sudden chill gripped the back of his neck. Beckett reached up to massage the spot, staring at the rocky mountains and vast woodlands. Was the Sword of MacLeod actually on that planet?

No, it didn't exist. The sword was nothing but a legend. The important thing was Ciorstan.

Raven used her card to purchase prints of the sector and planet. After examining the copies she smiled wryly at Beckett. "Would you mind paying for some time in the astral dome? I don't have enough credits left."

"What's that?"

"It gives me a three-dimensional look at the galaxy so I'll know what to expect when we come out of hyperspeed."

Beckett nodded, his curiosity piqued. How could a person have a feeling of being in space when they weren't? Trusting Raven's need for this, he accompanied her to a panel across the room.

Sliding Beckett's card into a slot on the panel, Raven pressed several commands and a door slid open in the wall. She returned his card and led him inside.

They walked along a narrow path, bordered by waist-high rails on both sides. Beckett examined his surroundings. The whiteness of the room was almost blinding in its totality. The room was circular with white walls, ceiling, even the floor far below the ramp. What did Raven expect to see here?

The ramp ended abruptly in the middle of the room in a small round platform also surrounded by railings. Raven stopped and glanced at Beckett.

"You may want to hang on. This can be unnerving at first." She followed her own advice so Beckett grasped a nearby railing. "Computer, initiate program," she said.

The brightness changed instantly to blackness and tiny points of light peeked through. "My God." For a moment, Beckett felt as if he were falling and he tightened his hold. "Are we moving?"

"No, the stars are adjusting to simulate our approach into the Andromeda Sector." Raven touched his arm, her warmth reassuring. "It makes everyone woozy at first." She removed her hand to point at a distant light. "There's Saladan."

How could she tell one speck from another? Beckett had always known other worlds existed, but he'd never been able to distinguish between a planet or a star. Seeing tiny fragments near Saladan, he frowned.

"What's that?" he asked, indicating the fragments.

Raven hesitated. "Asteroids, I think. Good eyes, Beckett." She grinned at him. "Are you sure you haven't done this before?"

He gave her a wry smile.

"Computer, show path of asteroids in Andromeda Sector," Raven said.

A partial line wove its way among the blackness, erratic in its curve. "Orbit of asteroids has not been completely plotted at this time. Path shown is subject to change."

"Great." Raven leaned forward. "I'll have to make sure we exit hyperspeed at the edge of the system."

"Why?"

"The last thing we need is a meteor shower. Once the *TrackStar* is fixed, I'd like to keep it that way for a while."

"Aye." Beckett searched the darkness again, looking for something—anything—familiar. "Where are we now?"

As Raven twisted around, she teetered slightly, and Beckett caught her from behind, grasping her shoulders with his hands. To his surprise, she didn't pull away and even moved closer so that the warmth of her body added to the flaring heat of his. Whether her movement was conscious or not, Beckett enjoyed the feel of her slick suit beneath his palms.

"The station's there."

Beckett thought he detected a tremor in her voice as she pointed to a distant light. It shone slightly different from the rest.

"And Alba? Where's my home?" Beckett's throat thickened as he remembered the hills and fields surrounding Dunvegan.

Raven hesitated. "Computer, feature Meridian Sector, Scot System."

The stars changed and Beckett recognized some patterns. A planet orbited a yellow sun—his sun . . . his planet. He could almost see the vast expanses of Alba's two oceans and rugged mountains.

"Home." The name sounded rough even to his ears.

Raven stiffened suddenly, but Beckett only tightened

his hold on her shoulders. "Is your . . . wife still there? Ciorstan's mother?"

"She died when Ciorstan was five years old. I've nae married again."

She turned to face him, her expression clearly puzzled. "Why not?"

"I'm nae in a hurry. I dinna want to make another mistake."

"And Ciorstan's mother was?" Raven met his gaze, her voice soft.

"The marriage was arranged to unite Hamilton lands with mine. Nessa was beautiful but still a child herself. She . . . feared me."

"Feared you?"

"I can be fearsome when riled."

"So I've noticed." Raven gave him a quick grin.

"You are very different from Nessa." Cupping her face with his palm, he lightly brushed his thumb across her cheek. Her eyes widened. "Another reason I dinna remarry was that I couldna find a woman I desired and wanted to know better . . . 'til now."

"Now?"

He barely heard her whisper as he ran his thumb over her parted lips. "Now I find myself thinking of you and wondering what your kiss is like."

As he spoke, he drew her nearer until he could touch her lips with his . . . lightly, gently. Her body trembled in response and he kissed her with more force, caressing her mouth, drinking her sweetness.

She moaned, the sound spiking his desire. Running his hand along her back, he pulled her closer, molding her supple softness against his firmness. He deepened the kiss, teasing her mouth with his tongue. She gripped his tunic with both hands, as if wanting to keep him close.

Damnation, she excited him. When she responded her tongue tentatively stroking his, his chest tightened, his lung capacity suddenly too small. What was it about this woman?

Abruptly the lights switched on, reaching Beckett

through his closed eyelids. When Raven tensed and pushed away from him, he opened them.

Her lips looked well kissed, her eyes hazy, but her expression hardened as she turned toward the exit. "Our time's over," she said, her double meaning clear.

Beckett followed, unable to hide his satisfied smile. Over? After that response? "It's only just beginning."

Chapter Eight

Unable to sleep for long, Raven roamed her room. Her heart still pulsed erratically, her hands shook, and her body ached with a need she'd never wanted. She'd come out of laser battles calmer than she'd emerged from Beckett's kiss.

She'd wondered how he kissed. Now she knew . . . wonderful . . . fantastic . . . dangerous. Her uncontrolled response and the onslaught of desire terrified her. Especially since she'd vowed never to care for a man. Men couldn't be trusted—sooner or later they'd leave. Her father had proven that.

She didn't need a man. She didn't *want* a man. But her restless urgings said otherwise.

Angry at her rebellious body, Raven yanked on her suit and hurried for Hander's sector. Maybe he'd let her help with *TrackStar*. After all, she knew that ship better than anyone else.

She didn't see her ship in any of the working bays when she arrived. How did Hander expect to get it done in time? To her disgust, he couldn't be found either.

Karen Fox

Before she could invade his personal quarters, she heard the warning alarm of an air lock seal. Pivoting, she saw the *TrackStar* land in a bay and the inner seal slide open. Was Hander just starting on it?

She glanced at a chronometer. The time they'd agreed on for delivery was only a couple of hours away. Frowning, she hurried for the bay and met Hander as he stepped out of the craft.

Before she could speak he gave her a dazzling grin. "Even if I have to say so, I'm proud of myself. We turned a ship you couldn't give away on the Exchange into a high-speed, unbeatable machine."

"You're finished already?"

"Almost. Only a few adjustments to make." Hander stroked the outer hull. "I just tested the overdrive—flew to the Excelsior Nebula and back in two hours. Impressive, eh?"

She emitted a low whistle. "Very. Can I check it out?"

"Not yet. I'll let you know when." He guided her away from the *TrackStar*, waving to his men with his free hand. Issuing a command for her to stay put, Hander went to join them.

Frustrated, Raven resumed pacing, her hands itching to test the improvements to her ship. At least she'd nearly forgotten her earlier, more physical frustration.

Until Beckett walked in.

Instantly her heart jumped into her throat. The way his gaze roved over her implied ownership and Raven frowned. She belonged to no man.

Lifting her chin, she met his gaze defiantly, but Beckett only smiled and turned to look at the *TrackStar*. "I thought I'd find you here. Is it finished?"

"Almost." She bit off the word. This ownership issue needed to be settled, but not with Hander's workers surrounding them. She'd have several long days enroute to Saladan to set Beckett straight.

Her stomach clenched. Several . . . long . . . days. "Shibit."

Beckett glanced at her. "Anything wrong?"

"No." Nothing that leaving him behind wouldn't cure.

122

Raven grimaced. To be fair, it wasn't entirely Beckett's fault. If her body hadn't responded like a love-starved fiend, he wouldn't be grinning with such smugness.

Once they left the space station she'd tell him she didn't desire him.

And hope he believed her.

When Hander signaled from the open hatch, Raven ran to her ship, then hesitated at the entrance. *TrackStar* had seen her through many altercations. Would this remodeled ship still feel like the old one?

Her steps tentative, Raven slipped inside. Nothing looked different. She breathed a quiet sigh of relief and went to examine the thruster panel. New equipment glimmered inside.

"The overdrive unit is here," Hander said from further back. Opening a new panel, he quickly explained the basics of the unit.

Though listening intently, Raven knew when Beckett stood behind her by the tingling along her neck. She refused to look around.

" 'Tis that the thing that will take us at super speeds?" Beckett asked.

Hander turned. "That's it. Top of the line."

Beckett glanced at it, then quirked his lips. "Do you guarantee it willna explode?"

"I guarantee it." Hander waved his hand toward the exit. "Let's you and I talk credits while Raven looks things over."

Raven whirled around. What was Hander trying to pull? True, Beckett had the credits, but he wouldn't understand most of Hander's charges. "I'll come too."

"Stay and get the ship ready," Beckett said. "I want to leave as soon as I've paid."

She gave him a quelling stare, but he merely smiled, his gaze so warm it brought a flush to her cheeks. "Fine," she snapped. Let him give all his credits to Hander. With her ship fixed, she had all the payment she needed.

Once Beckett and Hander left, she concentrated on the new controls. They were different enough that she had to recalculate to set the hyperspeed coordinates for Saladan. At least her magnicite fuel level was good—plenty to get across the galaxy and back.

She'd just finished a preflight check when Beckett returned and automatically slid into the chair next to hers.

"Ready to leave when you are," he said.

"Good." Raven sealed the hatch and radioed for an air lock. "Computer on vocal. You ready, Mac?"

"All systems ready, Raven. Coordinates are set for Saladan system. Overdrive is off-line but thrusters are ready at your command."

"Shibit." Raven glared at the speakers. It might sound like Mac, but it didn't speak like Mac. "Hander messed with you, didn't he?"

"A complete motherboard swap was required for the upgraded equipment, but you'll find I retained all my previous programs."

"Great."

"It *is* different." Beckett nodded toward the ceiling.

"Hander humanized it after I told him not to."

"Why do you object to a humanized one? I thought you liked Tessie."

"I do. I just . . ." She trailed off, unable to put her misgivings into words.

"You're afraid you might become attached to it, aren't you?"

"What?" She exhaled sharply.

"I think you're afraid to let yourself care for anything . . . or anyone." Beckett spoke quietly, but Raven felt each word as a blow.

"You don't know me," she said icily.

"I'm beginning to." He faced the front window. "Let's go find Ciorstan."

Her lips compressed, Raven verified her permission to depart and fired the forward thrusters. The ship eased backward into space. Swinging it around, she used the rear thrusters to propel them away from the station. The man-made structure soon became nothing but a glimmer in the distance.

"Mac, prepare for hyperspeed overdrive."

"Overdrive is on-line and awaiting command."

Raven glanced at Beckett. "This is it. Hold on." Gripping the lever, she pushed it forward.

The screen went black. The ship's ride felt so smooth, Raven would've sworn they weren't moving at all, but the controls said otherwise. According to them, her craft was on course at fantastic speeds.

Raven stared at the window. Seeing nothing but darkness bothered her. "Shi—"

"Bit," Beckett finished. They exchanged quick smiles. "How long until we reach Saladan?"

"A little over three days. With luck we should arrive at the same time as Slade."

Beckett's expression darkened. "When I get my hands on him . . ."

"Just so we see him first."

"What do we do in the meantime?"

Raven tightened her hand around the arm of her chair. "I plan to study the star charts and information on Saladan."

He raised his eyebrows. "For three days?"

"I usually find lots to do on a long journey."

"I can think of other . . . more interesting activities." He leaned forward, his smile disarming.

Raven bolted from her chair to as far away as the small confines of the ship would allow. "Just because you kissed me doesn't mean you own me, Beckett."

"No one owns you," he replied. "But your kiss gave me every reason to want more."

She shook her head, her heart racing. "What we have is business." Though she tried to be firm, her words didn't sound convincing even to herself.

Never dropping his gaze, Beckett stood and moved toward her. "It could be more, Raven. I want you and I think you want me too."

Despite her rolling stomach, Raven held her ground. "I *don't* want you."

Before she could react, Beckett leaned forward and seized her lips in a quick kiss that left her trembling inside. Only when he drew back did she realize he hadn't touched her with anything but his lips. But they had caressed, soothed, teased, all in that brief moment.

Shaken, Raven could only stare at him.

Beckett inhaled sharply, then smiled. "We'll see."

By the next morning every nerve Raven possessed tingled at Beckett's nearness. She never knew if this time he would steal a kiss, caress her face or merely give her his warm, intimate smile.

Worst of all—she liked it. Despite telling herself she needed . . . wanted no man, she found herself looking forward to his next approach.

Ridiculous. She had to shake these feelings.

Planning to ignore Beckett's presence, Raven gathered her information on Saladan and spread it on the table to study. Anything she could learn about this new planet would prove useful at some time. With luck, she'd locate Slade at the colony, but she couldn't plan on it.

Beckett emerged from the mister, clad only in his tight pants, drops still glistening on his broad chest, and Raven's resolve to remain unaffected evaporated. With his physique and handsomeness, he should be on display somewhere. No other man of Raven's acquaintance could begin to compare. With an effort she forced her gaze back to the holos in front of her.

The newly developed colony at Saladan existed on some good farm land, a vast prairie fed by an enormous lake. Past the prairie sprawled a wide expanse of desert with few plants and even less water. High craggy mountains loomed in the distance on the holos.

Switching to the next holo, Raven examined the deep canyon along the mountains' base, obviously carved by the river running through it. Though she studied several views, she didn't see any visible way across.

Beckett pressed a quick kiss on the top of her head, then took the chair opposite her. Trying to deny the ripple of delight caused by his touch, Raven aimed a glare at him.

As usual, nothing bothered the Alban. He twisted his lips in a half-grin and reached for Raven's discarded holos. "May I?"

She nodded and returned to her perusal of the rugged mountains. Several odd formations dotted the foothills, reminding Raven of various creatures.

One vaguely resembled a Tanturian warseal, another a slumbering bear, another a protective dog, another a nirvani in flight. The detail was amazing. The dog looked as if it had been carved.

The dog . . .

Raven drew back, trying to recall the phrase. "Beckett, do you have that riddle?"

He looked at her in surprise but reached inside his belt to pull out the crumpled piece of paper. As he handed it to her, he raised his eyebrows questioningly.

In reply, Raven pushed the mountain holophoto across the table. He must have seen the image immediately, for he bent to read the line of the riddle with her.

" 'Journey far and seek the guardian who points the way.' "

Raven tapped on the dog formation. "A dog is a type of guardian. It looks like it's pointing toward something, doesn't it?"

"Yes, but—"

" 'Linger not at the bottomless depths,' " she continued, her excitement rising. "That could be the canyon. 'Nor tarry amidst the burning sand.' That's the desert." She gazed at him in awe. "I think your daughter *did* solve the riddle."

"But it's a legend. The sword isna real." Beckett looked as if he'd been punched.

"How do you know? Where did this riddle come from?"

"My ancestor found a paper tucked into one of the Clan MacLeod books that had been brought by the original colonists. 'Twas so old at that point, the writing was barely legible. He transcribed the words and mounted the paper in a hall at Dunvegan."

"Dunvegan? What's that?"

"My home. 'Tis a castle named after my clan's ancestral home in Scotland."

"A castle?" Raven gaped at him. He lived in a castle? Their worlds were even farther apart than she originally thought. "Isn't it possible for the sword to be real?"

" 'Tis possible," he admitted. "But I dinna believe in magic, so even if it does exist, it willna solve our problems on Alba."

He did have a point. "Magic won't help, but technology will. You have enough credits to purchase some waterseekers to take back to Alba."

"No!" Beckett looked at her as if she'd suggested shooting Ciorstan. " 'Twould violate the reasons why my ancestors left Earth."

"It will save your people, Beckett." Could he really be so afraid of modern technology that he'd let his people suffer more?

"Nae." He pushed away from the table. "The early settlers only brought those tools they considered necessary. The whole idea was to escape the horrible life created by technology."

"I don't think there's anything wrong with my life." Raven straightened, clenching her fists. "I'd never be able to be on my own and roam the stars if I lived on your world."

"You wouldna want to roam if you lived on Alba. You'd have a husband who'd keep you very satisfied." A definite twinkle appeared in Beckett's eyes, which only irritated Raven further.

"And barefoot and pregnant." She leapt to her feet. "Just what I'd expect from someone from your backward planet. I *like* flying and visiting new planets and I definitely *don't* want a husband and a pack of crying children."

Beckett's twinkle changed to an angry gleam as he stood. "My culture values its heritage. Without the chaos of your world families still have meaning. We care about each other."

As opposed to Raven's family, who left her behind.

Hurt, she reacted without thinking. "Which is why your daughter ran away."

She immediately regretted her words as Beckett's face paled, then flushed.

"Ciorstan left because she was willing to sacrifice herself in order for everyone to survive. How many in your culture would be willing to do the same?"

Raven knew of no one and bit her lip. "I'm sorry. I shouldn't have said that."

"Aye." Though his expression remained forbidding, he returned to his seat. "Apology accepted."

Unwilling to face him, Raven went to her control chair. She peered unseeingly at the panel as Beckett's words echoed in her mind. Her family had loved her . . . once. She still didn't know what she'd done to make them leave her behind. True, she'd always been headstrong, but her father had teased her about that—not condemned her.

When Beckett touched her shoulder she looked around. He knelt beside her, sliding his hand behind her neck. Easing closer, he kissed her gently—so gently Raven wanted to cry.

She blinked furiously and refused to meet his gaze as he drew back. Catching her chin with his thumb and finger, he lifted her head up.

"On Alba, men respect women. We treat them as equals, not property. They share in everything." He spoke quietly, his eyes searching Raven's. "When a woman gives birth to a man's child she's giving him the greatest gift she can—out of love."

"What about Nessa?"

He grimaced. "Though I dinna love her, I did care about her. And I dinna force myself on her. Though timid, she came to me willingly. When she carried Ciorstan in her womb she was radiant."

Raven couldn't resist stroking his bristled cheek. "That life isn't for me, Beckett. I like what I do. I've never wanted to share it with anyone. Can't you understand?"

Dropping his hand, he rocked back on his heels, his

129

face solemn. "Aye, I ken." Without another word he stood and returned to the table.

Raven forced herself to do her regular check of the controls, but barely registered any meaning from the readings. Why did she feel as if she'd just lost something precious?

"Where will we find Slade after we land?" Beckett looked up from the maps of Saladan.

Though he'd remained polite, his manner had become distant. His kisses and gentle teasing touches had stopped. To Raven's chagrin, she missed them.

As Beckett spoke, she left her laser recharging and joined him at the table. Scanning the map, she pointed to the spaceport located near the new colony.

"If we're very lucky, we'll arrive before Slade, but I'm not going to count on that. If he's already landed, then I want to meet him while we're in the colony." Noting the absence of details on the map, she hesitated. "If he's left the colony, then we'll follow."

"Across the desert?"

"If Ciorstan translates the riddle the same way we do, then that's the way they'll go. I doubt Slade knows we're following, so I should find their trail easily."

"Will it take long to catch them?"

Raven shrugged. "It depends on how far ahead of us they are."

"We will emerge from hyperspeed in four point two hours," Mac said in his usual periodic update.

After verifying the controls Raven glanced at Beckett. "We might as well get some rest while we can. I doubt we'll get much after we land."

Beckett nodded and went to activate his bed. For someone who hated technology, he'd sure learned his way around her ship quickly.

Raven dimmed the lights and climbed onto her bunk. Knowing Mac would notify her before they left hyperspeed, she closed her eyes and willed herself to sleep. She was tired—so tired. Lately she'd slept fitfully, never waking rested, only depressed.

Soon Beckett MacLeod would be out of her life forever. That was what she wanted . . . wasn't it?

Trying to relax, Raven stared into the darkness. She needed to concentrate on facing Slade. Strangely, that thought no longer terrified her. Just knowing Beckett would be with her gave her courage . . . and determination. She wouldn't let herself be Slade's victim ever again.

But she did need to remember the danger. Slade didn't follow any rules and had no compulsions against killing. He'd shoot Raven—and Beckett—on sight.

Raven's stomach clenched. She'd have to be very careful and keep Beckett from taking the lead. His safety mattered to her. She closed her eyes. How long had it been since she'd cared about anyone's safety but Naldo's? And why did it have to be that of this backward Alban?

After what felt like hours of uneasy rest Raven slid quietly from her bunk and shrugged into her pantsuit. Padding to the control panel, she examined the readings. Less than an hour to hyperspeed termination.

She'd programmed coordinates so they'd emerge at the outer edge of the star system on a course that provided easy access to Saladan. Since her information was sketchy at best, she wanted to be at the controls when they left hyperspeed.

Another wave of despair washed over her as she watched the blackness outside the window. In an hour this could all be over. Slade could be defeated, Ciorstan recovered and Beckett united with his errant daughter. All Raven would have to do then was deliver him to Alba—mission accomplished.

A small sob tore from her throat. She didn't want it to be over—not yet.

"Raven?" Beckett turned her to face him. His bare chest gleamed in the diminished lighting and Raven swallowed the sudden lump in her throat. "I know we come from different worlds," he said quietly.

He captured her head between his hands and caressed her cheeks with his thumbs. "I know we dinna have a future. But I canna stop thinking of you."

As he traced her lower lip with his thumb, Raven trembled. "Beckett." Unable to recall any objection that made sense at that moment, she raised her lips and eagerly met his.

He groaned, tightening his arms around her, and kissed her deeply, his mouth molded to hers. When Raven parted her lips, he slipped his tongue inside, stroking her mouth, dancing with her tongue.

A growing fire burned low in her belly and she found herself rubbing against the hardness in Beckett's pants. With a moan, he ended the kiss. Raven cried out in disappointment and he bent to kiss her face, the line of her neck, the rapid pulse at the base of her throat.

"Warning, Raven. Your heart rate has increased to—"

The computer startled her. This must be one of its new capabilities. "Mac, vocal off," she said sharply. Before Beckett could draw back, Raven kissed him, entwining her hands in his hair to hold him close. When she slipped her tongue into his mouth he sucked on it, and all her muscles clenched in response.

As his tongue mated with hers, Beckett eased Raven's suit off her shoulders and down her sides until it fell in a pile at her feet. He gently held her away from him and looked at her.

Raven's body tingled under his heated gaze. Beneath her T-shirt her breasts swelled, the nipples hardening. Lower, her insides moistened in anticipation . . . of what?

"Beautiful." Beckett pulled her close to his heat again and seized her lips. With one hand he tested the weight of her breast, then caressed the nipple.

Raven gasped. It had never felt like this when Slade touched her—never. Now she wanted more, she . . .

"I . . . I want . . ." she whispered against Beckett's mouth.

In reply he used both hands to push her shirt up so that he could cradle both her breasts and gently roll the pebbled tips between his fingers.

Agony . . . ecstasy. Raven pressed against Beckett's erection with her hips, wanting release from her inner tension. As he kissed a path down her throat, she leaned back and he continued along the curve of her breast.

When he drew one tip into his mouth she cried out, her insides threatening to explode. Sliding his hand between them, Beckett's fingers delved into her moist womanhood, searching, then finding.

His touch sent tremors of delight through Raven. Nothing had ever felt this good. Even her first solo flight paled in comparison.

Beckett moved to her other breast and suckled there, too, using his tongue to tease her already sensitized nipple while his fingers maintained their rhythmic caress. Raven's knees threatened to buckle.

Her insides churned, spun, then coiled into a knot so tight it threatened to tear her apart. She was going to die, to explode, to . . .

Suddenly her body dissolved into spasms of pleasure, the sensation so overwhelming, so wonderful, Raven lost herself in it.

Slowly, she opened her eyes to see Beckett grinning at her. "I . . . I never . . ." she began, trying to speak with a chest that felt too small to allow breathing.

Beckett kissed her carefully, thoroughly. "That's just the beginning of what I want to share with you," he murmured. To Raven's surprise, he swung her into his arms and approached his bunk. "But let's get more comfortable."

Suddenly the floor tilted. Beckett fell to one knee and Raven rolled from his arms. Dashing toward the control panel, she gaped at the window in horror.

They'd emerged from hyperspeed so smoothly she hadn't even felt it. But instead of arriving at the edge of Saladan's system, they'd appeared in the middle of it.

Directly in the path of the asteroid cluster.

Chapter Nine

The ship tilted wildly again. Beckett tumbled across the floor, crashing into his bed. Pain sliced through his arm and he knew from the damp feel that he'd cut it on the sharp edge. "Damnation."

"Mac, terminate the avoidance system and give control to me." He dimly registered Raven's voice as he staggered to his feet and made his way to his seat. As he strapped himself in, he glanced out the window. It took him a moment to register the objects outside the ship—rocks, thousands of them.

A smaller one passed close to the window and Beckett flinched. This didn't look good. What would happen to the *TrackStar* if it was hit?

He glanced at Raven and noticed she'd tugged her shirt down, but otherwise appeared totally engrossed in navigating her ship.

As if sensing his gaze, she grinned at him. "Buckle in. We're in for a wild ride."

Only his faith in her flying abilities kept Beckett in his seat. His instinct told him to duck as asteroids flew toward them. As the ship began to turn, he gripped the arms of his seat. They flew sideways, even upside down, as Raven maneuvered the craft between, over and around the rocks.

Thankful for his tough stomach, Beckett could only watch while his appreciation for her talent grew. They dodged so quickly, she barely had time to make adjustments. Her decisions had to be instantaneous.

When they finally reached clear space again he remained frozen, his heart thumping in his chest. He couldn't believe they'd survived. Slowly he turned to look at her.

"Is it over?" he asked.

"I think we're out of it. That's Saladan ahead." She indicated a bright dot that grew larger as they approached. Turning, her smile faded quickly. "Neptune's Rings, what happened to you?"

Following her gaze, Beckett noticed the blood trickling down his arm. His earlier adrenaline had dimmed the pain, but now it returned afresh with piercing agony. "I cut it on the bed."

Raven threw off her belt and whirled out of her seat. "Let me get the medtech unit. It'll heal you in no time."

He was slower to release his belt. "What's that?"

"This." She pushed a lever and a large, rectangular, man-sized box emerged from the wall of the craft. Though clear, it seemed to pulsate as if alive. "Just put your arm through this opening and I'll set the controls."

Though his wound throbbed, Beckett looked at the machine with distaste. "I willna use that."

"Beckett, it'll heal you."

"No. I dinna need your modern technology. A bandage will suffice."

"I don't have a bandage." She glowered at him, her eyes lit with angry sparks. "Will you quit being a fool and put your arm in?"

"Nae. I dinna need it." He grabbed his shirt from the bed and tore it into strips. Though he struggled to wind them around his wound, they kept sliding down his arm.

With a heavy sigh, Raven yanked the material from his hand and proceeded to wrap it about his upper arm. "I can't believe you're willing to suffer with this when it could be healed in a matter of minutes."

" 'Twill heal on its own."

"I suppose you'd let someone die rather than use my equipment," she said dryly.

" 'Tis nae for Alba."

She finished tying the bandage and stepped back. "Maybe it should be."

He refused to respond to her anger. She looked too magnificent with her hair tousled, her eyes flashing, her breasts heaving beneath her thin T-shirt, the peaks clearly visible. Beckett's desire returned full force as he remembered when they had been were interrupted.

Reaching out, he caressed her cheek with the back of his fingers. Raven inhaled sharply, her eyes darkening, then drew away from his touch.

"You need to clean up," she said, her voice not completely even. "We'll be landing soon."

Glancing at the window, Beckett could see Saladan more clearly now, its features becoming more detailed as they drew closer. He nodded in resignation and turned toward the mister.

By the time he returned Raven had dressed and was sitting in her customary seat in front of the control panel. He paused to watch her. God, he wanted her now more than ever. If she returned him and Ciorstan to Alba, he knew he'd never see her again. Blast those asteroids!

"I thought we were supposed to miss the asteroids," he said as he took his chair.

"So did I," she replied. "Mac, why didn't you warn me?"

"As I recall, you ordered me into vocal off. I flashed warning lights, but apparently you didn't notice them." The computer sounded upset and Raven shook her head.

"This is what I meant by a humanized computer," she

muttered. "Get over it, Mac, and locate the spaceport on Saladan."

"Spaceport located. I've set the coordinates for landing."

Beckett couldn't stop his grin. The disembodied voice still held a hint of pique. Raven shot him a sharp glance, then flicked the switch for communications.

"Saladan Spaceport, this is *TrackStar* requesting permission to land."

The reply crackled back within moments. "Permission granted. Dock in landing bay twenty."

"Acknowledged. Estimate time to touch down is ten minutes."

The planet grew in size until it filled, then surpassed the ship's window. Beckett could make out the large lake that supplied the colony as well as the vast expanse of desert in the distance. The riddle ran through his memory, but he immediately discarded it. The sword didn't exist . . . but his daughter did. And she was somewhere on this planet.

As Raven took her ship into the atmosphere, his muscles tightened. This time her thrusters worked flawlessly and Beckett barely felt the gentle bump that indicated their arrival on Saladan. She coasted into the landing bay and brought the *TrackStar* to a stop.

Beckett glanced around in amazement. "So, that's what a landing should be."

Raven whirled to look at him, her eyes narrowed, but he grinned in response. Finally her lips lifted in a wry smile. "It helps to have everything working," she replied.

Leaping from her chair, she went to grab her laser from the charger and fasten the belt around her hips. She glanced at Beckett as he approached. "I wish I had another laser for you."

He shook his head and buckled his belt. "I have my sword. 'Tis enough."

She paused before him, searching his gaze with her own. "Be careful, Beckett. Slade is a very dangerous man."

Her concern warmed Beckett. His hardened tracker was mellowing . . . bit by bit. Cradling her head in his hand, he kissed her, his lips lingering until her own moved in response. "I'll be fine," he murmured.

She blinked once, then pulled away and pressed the button to open the hatch. "Mac, seal the hatch after us. Respond to my command only."

"Acknowledged."

As she stepped from the craft, Beckett noticed her hand hovering near her laser. He gripped the hilt of his sword, empowered by the familiar feel against his palm. His weapon might not be as fast as Raven's, but it was equally as lethal. If Slade had harmed Ciorstan in any way, he would know Beckett's wrath.

A building stood at the end of the landing bays and they walked in that direction. Beckett hadn't expected the planet to be so well developed. "How can there be so many buildings already? Wasna this planet just discovered?"

"Not really. Explorers first located it nearly a year ago, but word didn't spread until after the preliminary scouts opened it for colonization. It doesn't take long to set up an initial settlement, and the spaceport is always one of the first things put together."

"Will the people there be able to tell us if Slade is here?" Beckett asked.

"He should've registered, just as we need to do." Raven scanned the other bays as they passed. "If he's here, they might know where . . ."

She stopped abruptly, the color draining from her face. Beckett followed the direction of her gaze. A ship, easily twice the size of *TrackStar*, sat in a bay. Painted a solid black, it looked sleek, fast, and dangerous.

"Slade's ship," he said, surprised at his calmness.

"Yes." Her voice sounded strained. Before Beckett realized her intentions, Raven slid her laser from its holster and approached the ship. His heart leapt into his throat as he ran to join her. She'd not face this villain on her own.

Approaching stealthily, Raven edged her way to the

closed hatch. Using her laser, she rapped twice on the door, then pressed against the side. Beckett quickly took a position on the opposite side of the hatch, his sword ready. The hammering of his heart echoed in his ears as they waited.

Nothing.

Raven pounded again. "Slade, you there?" She hesitated. "Slade, it's Raven."

Silence.

"He's not here." Raven pushed away from the ship, her expression haggard. Keeping her gaze on the hatch, she started toward the terminal again. "Stay alert, Beckett. He could be anywhere."

The stiffness of her back and neck indicated her tension. Beckett ached to massage it away. She was searching for her greatest enemy—facing her biggest fear—for him. Was it only because her job required it?

Falling into step with Raven, Beckett kept a constant surveillance on his surroundings. Two other men—humans—stood beside a ship, but they paid little attention to Raven and Beckett, other than a short nod of their heads. Raven ignored them, so Beckett did the same.

"It would help if I knew what Slade looked like," he said.

When she turned to look at him the terror in her eyes touched something deep inside him and he impulsively wrapped his arms around her. For a moment she relaxed against him, and he breathed in the fresh scent of her short curls. She was so soft, so vulnerable.

"Tell me who to look for and you can stay here," he murmured.

She jerked away, her body stiff with indignation. "I'm the tracker. I'll find him . . . and Ciorstan." She stalked toward the building, not even glancing back to see if he followed.

Damn her stubbornness. He was trying to help, didn't she see that? Beckett caught up with her as she entered through sliding doors. They paused, searching the interior.

There was little activity. Three men stood in one corner, discussing a newly arrived shipment. A large screen in the center displayed ships arriving and departing, and Raven went to stand before it.

"There's his ship," she said, pointing at the screen. "The *Raider*. They arrived yesterday."

"Then they're still a whole day ahead of us." Beckett's hopes sank. He'd imagined hugging his daughter by this point.

She nodded curtly. "And knowing Slade, they're already on their way to find the sword." Pivoting, she headed for the exit. "We need to visit the colony and see what we can find out."

Beckett grimaced. Somehow, he didn't expect good news.

"What is that thing?"

Raven rolled her eyes. If Beckett would quit asking questions and leave her alone to make preparations, they might actually get on their way today. Tension pulled at the muscles in her neck. "It's a skimmer. We'll be able to cross the desert with it."

"I dinna think it'll hold both of us."

"It's designed to carry two people and some gear. It'll go a long way quickly on a small amount of fuel. That's what we want. If we travel day and night, we should be able to catch Slade." Since the colonists had confirmed Slade and Ciorstan's departure on a similar skimmer yesterday afternoon, Raven had hurried to gather the gear she and Beckett would need to follow.

"How will we find them? Being told they went out over the desert isna enough." Beckett's face reflected his worry—well-founded worry—over his daughter.

Raven sighed, her irritation fading. "I'll find them." Though this planet offered new challenges, she was confident in her tracking skills. If it was humanly possible, she'd locate Ciorstan. "Let's get this stuff loaded on here."

As they packed their supplies, Raven verified the contents. She didn't expect to be gone long, but she'd learned to be prepared for anything. Food, water, sleeping bags, and a portable medtech unit.

The skimmer had two seats, one in back of the other. Raven climbed into the front seat before the controls as Beckett took the rear seat. As she powered on the unit, it rose to hover over the ground.

"Damnation. It flies." Beckett's warm breath fanned the back of her neck.

"Hang on." Easing a lever forward, Raven sent the skimmer into action.

As they passed by the large, newly planted fields, she studied the sinking sun. There weren't many more hours of daylight left, and the nebulous warnings she'd received about traveling the desert at night didn't offer any comfort.

Beckett touched her shoulder, then spoke, his lips close to her ear. "What's that?"

She turned to look and grimaced. A large bulblike tank jutted out of the ground. "It's what you won't buy—a waterseeker."

"A waterseeker?" He sounded stunned.

"Yes. What's wrong?" She glanced at him over her shoulder.

"We have several of those on Alba."

"What?" Raven almost lost her hold on the skimmer's guidance control. "You have waterseekers and you're not using them?"

"They nae work. They've sat idle for as long as I can remember."

"What's wrong with them?"

"I dinna know."

The skimmer left the fields behind and soared over the endless horizon of gleaming white sand as Raven considered Beckett's revelation. "If you have watermakers on Alba, then your ancestors didn't totally give up technology, you know."

Even without looking around, she felt him stiffen. "We have managed to survive without these things."

"Until now." She couldn't resist poking holes in his almost religious belief in evil technology. "At least you can take one back with you."

141

"Nae."

She gave him an icy glare. "You're a stubborn man, Beckett MacLeod."

"No more so than you."

That didn't deserve an answer. Instead, Raven concentrated on the uneven hills before her, her gaze sweeping the ground for signs of Slade's passing. Her present coordinates should take them to the mountains. Slade should've gone the same way.

Finally she found it—the circular tracks left by the propulsion system of a skimmer. With a yell, she pointed them out to Beckett. "There's his trail. We've got him now, Beckett."

He squeezed her shoulder in reply, his touch sending warm tendrils to her middle. Raven inhaled, her breathing suddenly uneven. What was she to do about Beckett? She didn't want to care about him. She didn't want to remember the pleasure of his touch.

Her body dictated differently. Already her breasts swelled as she recalled the magic performed by his mouth and hands.

Shaking her head, she forced away that memory. She had no time for that now. Tracking Slade had to take precedence. She'd affirm Beckett's belief in her by returning his daughter safely.

The skimmer continued its path over the sand as darkness fell with the swiftness of a dropped lamp. One moment daylight lingered at the horizon, then suddenly blackness reigned, as thick and impenetrable as the deepest black hole.

The temperature fell, too, reaching Raven through the insulated protection of her suit. She shivered, then jumped as something soft fell around her shoulders.

Glancing around, she saw Beckett had removed the cloaks they'd brought with them and placed one over her. He paused in fastening his own cloak to give her a slow smile.

Raven returned it, knowing the sudden warmth in her chest had nothing to do with the cloak. "Why don't you try to get some sleep?" she suggested.

Beckett squirmed in the small seat and grimaced. " 'Twill be difficult in this thing."

"I know, but we have to keep going."

"Aye, keep going. Tell me when you wish to rest and I'll steer."

"Will you?" That she'd like to see.

"I've been watching you. 'Tis nae difficult."

Raven raised an eyebrow. "We'll see." Actually there wasn't much to controlling the skimmer at that point. Their coordinates were set, though she had adjusted them after finding Slade's trail. Aside from monitoring the speed or slight changes in direction, she had little to do but watch the monotonous sand stretch before them.

As hours passed, her eyelids drooped. After several nights with little sleep, weariness tugged at her. When her chin dropped to her chest she felt Beckett's hand gently shake her shoulder.

"Let me sit there now."

Shaking herself alert, Raven hesitated. They still had several hours to travel before they reached the canyons. Beckett should be perfectly capable of controlling the craft for a short while. "Promise not to crash it?" she asked with a smile.

"I promise." His voice, husky in her ear, sent shivers down her spine.

Settling the skimmer onto the sand, Raven slid from her seat and stretched. Before she could lower her arms, Beckett wrapped his arms around her waist and pulled her closer. She dropped her hands on his shoulders and stared at him in surprise.

"Get some rest," he ordered. He ran one hand along her back, massaging her tense muscles with strong fingers.

Her bones melting beneath his touch, Raven pressed nearer to him, using her hands to ease the tension in his shoulders. However, her own inner pressure grew as her breasts swelled against the hardness of his chest and her throat tightened.

Beckett pressed a kiss into her hair. "If this keeps up,

we'll never find Slade." Though his voice was light, he couldn't hide the unevenness of his breathing.

Startled back to reality, Raven quickly climbed into the rear seat. Neeban, she berated herself. Why did her body constantly betray her?

When Beckett swung into the front she stood up, careful not to touch him, and explained the control panel. "That switch controls power. When it's on we lift, off, we fall. That lever is for the speed and that one changes direction. Just keep that arrow pointed in that direction."

"I ken." Beckett switched on the power and jerked the acceleration lever forward with such abruptness that Raven flew back into her seat. He threw her an apologetic glance. "Sorry."

The skimmer went into motion, flying over the sand. If not for Beckett's distaste for technology, Raven would've sworn he was enjoying himself. As the craft reached an even speed, she settled back into the chair, her eyelids heavy. It wouldn't hurt if she closed her eyes for just a moment.

She must've fallen asleep for Beckett's tense voice woke her abruptly. "Raven, 'tis nae right here."

As she pulled herself upright, something reared in the darkness, towering above the skimmer. Raven had a brief view of an enormous mouth and rows of dagger-like teeth before it bumped the craft, tossing her off onto the sand.

Rolling to a stop, she leapt to her feet. Beckett had managed to stay with the skimmer and she waved at him. "Get away." A blast from her laser would take care of this creature—whatever it was. She didn't want Beckett in the way.

Sand exploded into the air beside her and Raven stumbled back as the beast roared at her. For a moment she could only stare. It was huge, easily big enough to swallow her with one bite. The head resembled that of a mythical dragon, the snout elongated and rough, only there were no eyes. The body, however, looked more like a snake, though it was large enough across the middle to hold her entire ship. It tapered to a long, thin tail that snapped in the darkness.

Drawing her laser, Raven shook off the clinging sand and fired. The weapon crackled, but no beam emerged. Panic rising, she hit her palm against it and tried again. Still nothing.

With another ear-piercing roar, the creature dove at Raven. She threw herself out of the way, watching with terrified fascination as it buried itself beneath the sand. Scrambling to her feet, she examined her laser. The sand had somehow worked its way into the firing mechanism and kept it from working.

"Fardpissle."

The ground suddenly rumbled beneath her. Raven's heart filled her throat as she tried to escape the moving sand. Again the creature burst from below, throwing her backward with its emerging body.

She'd just climbed to her knees when the beast dove at her, its mouth open. Her throat closed. She couldn't even scream. Teeth, nearly as tall as she, came closer.

The creature roared, the sound different than before. To Raven's surprise, it twisted away from her. Then she saw why.

Beckett had his sword buried in the monster's neck. As it whipped toward him, he withdrew his weapon and plunged it in again. Another agonizing roar pierced the night.

He leapt aside to avoid being crushed by the attacking beast. With a yell, he sliced his sword across the rough hide. Blood, black ooze in the night, poured onto the sand.

As the creature thrashed, its cries deafening, Raven ran to grab Beckett's arm. She only had to tug once for him to follow her. Together they ran toward the skimmer.

Jumping into the front, Raven didn't wait to sit. She ignited the power immediately, lifting the craft from the ground. "Hold on," she warned Beckett. She accelerated dangerously to full speed and the craft sailed over the sand. The howls continued in the distance.

When the sounds faded Raven finally allowed herself to relax in the seat. Beckett touched her shoulder. "Are you all right?"

Looking around, she nodded, then gasped in alarm. "Are you?" Blood stained his new shirt.

He glanced down at it and grimaced. " 'Tis nae mine."

Swallowing hard, Raven brushed her cheek against his hand. "Thank you." Her voice trembled. Without Beckett and his sword, she would've died.

He said nothing, but looked at her, the warmth of his gaze so intense she felt it as a physical touch. Her stomach coiled into a knot and her heart suddenly felt too big for her chest. Forcing herself to look away, she couldn't as easily erase the tingling from her body.

The sun cleared the horizon, flooding the skies with light, at the same time as plants began to appear in the sand. The greenery increased as the sand thinned, disguising signs of Slade's trail, but the appearance of the canyon still caught Raven by surprise. It filled the entire landscape, looking bottomless from a distance.

Raven landed the skimmer close to its edge and stepped off. Looking over the side, she could see the bottom far below, the river a thin blue-gray line running through the middle.

"My God, it's fantastic." Beckett joined her and they both stared in awe at the immense gorge.

Scraggly trees, no taller than Raven's knee, dotted the landscape and jutted out from the cliff walls. The sand had given way to a red, rocky soil that crunched beneath her boots. The canyon itself looked rough, jagged, as if dug from the earth with a dull knife. With the depth making her dizzy, Raven sat down and examined the surrounding area.

The canyon stretched as far as she could see in both directions, with a thick expanse of trees and rising mountains on the other side. Somehow they had to get over there.

The skimmer wouldn't work. It hovered only a short distance above the ground and would fall if she took it over that tremendous depth. Even an anti-grav belt—

not that she had one—would be limited. It wasn't designed to cross so wide a gulf. "How do we get across?" she asked aloud.

Beckett turned from the edge, surprised. "With our hands and feet."

"What?"

"Look." When Raven joined him, he pointed out a narrow ledge protruding from the cliff. "It looks like it winds all the way down."

"But it'll take a whole day to climb down and back up."

"We dinna have any other options." He turned toward the skimmer. "Let's pack what we need and go."

Dividing their supplies into two backpacks, Raven and Beckett pulled them on and began their descent. The limited space on the ledge reminded Raven of their escape from Erebus—only now they had fifty times the distance to fall.

Beckett insisted on leading. To Raven's amazement, he found footholds and natural paths where she saw nothing but craggy rocks. Slowly, one step at a time, they descended the cliff.

By the time they'd gone halfway Raven's shoulders ached so badly, she doubted she could continue. Sweat trickled down her face, drops plopping off the end of her nose. Her tracking duties normally kept her in space or spaceports. She'd never tackled an unexplored planet before and wasn't sure she wanted to continue on this one.

But she couldn't quit now. She had to find Ciorstan.

Though moisture beaded on Beckett's forehead, he showed no signs of fatigue and kept his voice encouraging as he guided Raven after him. If he could do it, so could she. After all, he was only a primitive man.

But what a man.

The sun had long ago crossed its zenith by the time Raven stepped onto solid ground again. Still clinging to the rock wall, she looked around, unable to believe she'd finally reached bottom. Narrow, flat expanses of

147

a rugged grass littered with rocks lined both sides of the raging river.

The river looked much bigger now, the current swift and angry as water tumbled over large rocks in its path. It looked deep and spanned wider than any person could jump across. Raven shivered. How were they to cross that?

Beckett smiled at her as he eased his pack to the ground. "Let's take a break here before we tackle the river."

"Agreed." Raven sank down to sit on a boulder and shrugged out of her pack. Her shoulder muscles screamed in protest and she rotated her neck to loosen the kinks.

Coming to stand behind her, Beckett massaged her shoulders. Raven dropped her head forward, reveling in his strong, soothing touch. The tightness of her muscles ebbed, to be replaced by a growing warmth. "You're very good at that," she murmured.

"And other things."

Hearing the smile in his voice, she briefly considered surrendering to the pleasure he sent through her body. With an effort, she raised her head and slid out from his hands. "Why don't you sit and I'll return the favor."

He took her place on the boulder, but when she placed her hands on his shoulders he gripped her wrist and swung her around onto his lap. His arms held her firmly in place as she made a weak effort to push away. " 'Tis not the favor I had in mine," he said softly.

She opened her mouth to protest but he covered it with a kiss, more heated, more passionate than any she'd previously experienced. Fire erupted in her middle and flowed to the farthest reaches of her body. With a sigh, she wrapped her arms around his neck, pulling him even closer.

As his tongue stroked the roof of her mouth, her insides knotted, the coils tightening in her lower belly. His hands traced a path along her arms and down her sides. Her earlier aches faded. This felt good . . . right somehow.

Releasing her lips, Beckett lifted his head and gazed at her. "You frightened me earlier. I thought that beast would have you for supper."

She managed a tremulous smile. "So did I."

"What happened to your weapon?"

"I think the sand fouled it up. I'll have to clean it."

"Aye." His lips lifted in a smile. "Or get yourself a reliable sword."

Shaking her head, Raven pushed away from him. *Score one for the Alban.* She searched her pack for nourishment. "Are you hungry?"

"Aye." His gaze lingered on her. "But 'tis nae for food."

Her cheeks warmed as she pulled out the large rolls and thick slices of cheese she'd procured in the colony and waved them before his face. "Not even real food?"

He snatched it from her hand. " 'Tis always an exception."

Once they finished their meal Beckett scouted the edge of the river while Raven cleaned her laser. Sand had permeated every tiny crevice on the weapon. Reassembling it, she used a nearby tree as a test target. The gnarled wood burst into flame immediately and she nodded her satisfaction.

Beckett's head jerked up at the blast and he ran to throw water over the fire. "We dinna need to be trapped here by fire," he said sharply.

"Sorry." Raven returned her laser to its holster. "At least it's working again." She joined him by the river. "Is there a way across?"

"These trees are nae big enough to use as a bridge and the current's too swift to swim across. We'll have to use the rocks as stepping stones."

Raven's breath caught in her throat. The stones varied from large to small as they decorated the riverbed, but many had wide gaps between them, and water flowed over some. "Isn't there another way?"

"I dinna see one." He grinned and went to retrieve his backpack. "Have you nae crossed a stream before?"

"No." She reluctantly tugged on her pack.

"Just follow me. 'Tis easy." He leapt to the first rock, then the second, and turned back to Raven. "Come on. Stay close and I'll catch you if you slip."

Trying to ignore the thudding of her pulse, Raven jumped to the first rock. Water swirled around her feet and she watched it with trepidation. It looked cold . . . and dangerous.

As Beckett moved from one stone to another, he held out his hand for Raven, encouraging her to follow. Focusing on the safety of his hand, she followed him despite the trembling of her limbs.

He'd nearly reached the other bank when a surge of water washed over Raven's feet, knocking her off-balance. She wavered, struggling to regain her footing, but the backpack proved her undoing. With a cry, she fell into the rushing river.

She sank immediately, the pack weighing her down. Splashing her way to the surface, she saw she was already some distance from where Beckett stood. "Beckett!" Waves washed over her again.

Sputtering, she flailed her way up again. The current drove her into a boulder and she gasped, swallowing a mouthful of water. Beckett had reached the shore and ran toward her, shedding his backpack.

"Let the pack go," he yelled. "Try to swim with the current."

Choking, she bounced off another rock as the coldness numbed her body. She struggled to grab hold of something . . . anything . . . but her hands slipped away. "I . . . I can't swim."

Chapter Ten

Beckett dove immediately into the rushing water. Raven disappeared beneath the surface and his panic spiked. With all her other capabilities he never imagined she couldn't swim.

Working with the current, he struggled to reach her. She reappeared briefly, then sank again. He stroked faster, ignoring the rocks that scraped and tore at his body. He couldn't get close—the flow carried her away too swiftly.

Suddenly he spotted her pressed against a boulder. Drawing on the last reserves of his strength, he strained to get to her. As the water threatened to claim her again, he lashed out and caught her wrist. Refusing to yield to the water's suction, he dragged her closer until he could wrap his arm beneath hers.

Her face was pale, her eyes closed, and blood trickled from a wound at her temple.

Fear gripped Beckett. His stomach knotted. He tugged off her backpack and let the river have it. Clenching his jaw, he turned toward shore. He tried to

Karen Fox

cut across the current, but it fought him for control. His body ached from the cold.

He smashed against a boulder, almost losing his hold on Raven. With an oath, he tightened his grip and continued. His muscles protested the strain. Sudden weariness flooded his veins.

Just as Beckett feared the river would win, he realized he could touch the bottom. Staggering to his feet, he carried Raven to the shore and gently laid her on the ground. He fell to his knees beside her. "Raven!"

He rolled her to her stomach. Panic seized him when she didn't move. He thumped her back and she began coughing. Water sputtered from her lips as she racked her body to clear her lungs.

Aching for her, Beckett lifted her and cradled her in his arms until her breathing became more normal. Slowly she raised her head from his shoulder, her eyes fluttering open.

"I knew that wasn't a good idea," she muttered.

He stroked her damp curls and dabbed at her wound. Fortunately, the bleeding had already stopped. "I thought everyone could swim."

Her lips twisted in a half-smile. "I grew up on Erebus. Where would I have learned?"

Remembering her dry, arid planet, he grimaced. "Are you all right?"

"I . . . I think so. Just cold." She shivered within his arms, and he noticed the purplish cast to her lips.

He set her on her feet and placed his arm firmly around her shoulders to lead her along the shore toward his discarded backpack. Kneeling, he rummaged through it for his sleeping bag. "Take off your clothes."

"Now there's an original line," Raven said dryly, but Beckett heard the fastening on her suit rip open.

Locating the small square of silver material that Raven had assured him was a full-sized sleeping bag, he looked at it dubiously. He opened the packet, then shook it as directed. To his amazement, the material rolled out, softening as it formed a man-sized bag.

He turned to hand it to Raven, then froze and swallowed hard, unable to stop staring. She'd removed her suit but remained clad in her wet T-shirt and underwear—for all the good it did. The material clung to her skin, clearly revealing her puckered nipples and dark curls of womanhood. Desire hit Beckett like a hammer against his chest.

Clearing his throat, he found it hard to speak. "You're soaked clear through." His words came out as a husky whisper. "Take everything off, Raven, then get in the bag." He gave it to her, knowing from her sharp inhalation that she'd seen his longing. With an effort he turned his back to her. "Now, Raven, or I'll do it for you."

She said nothing, but he heard the slight sounds of her movements. Closing his eyes, he pictured her pulling the T-shirt over her head, fully revealing her perfect breasts, the pink tips crinkled, begging for his touch. He held in a groan caused by the ache in his loins. His sex swelled painfully.

Still, he continued to fantasize about her removing her underwear. As she stepped out of them, she would stand naked, the curves of her woman's body made to fit his. He wanted to touch the smooth curve of her buttocks, to kiss the inner softness of her thighs, to bury himself in her hidden womanhood.

"What now?"

Her voice broke through his fantasy and he clenched his fists, trying to regain control of his body. Reluctantly he turned. Despite his best efforts a quiet moan escaped. Though she was covered, it didn't help his desire.

Though she held the edges of the sleeping bag to her chin, the smoothness of her bare shoulders peeked through, alluding to the treasure buried inside.

Tearing his gaze away, he scooped up her discarded clothing and went to spread it on some rocks to dry. "Make yourself comfortable. We'll stay the night here."

"But we have to keep going," she protested, though her enthusiasm was weak.

" 'Twill be dark before we're halfway up the cliff,"

Beckett said. " 'Tis best to wait. May I use your laser to make a fire?"

She shifted to the ground. "You can try, but I doubt if it'll work. It's not designed to handle water."

As she predicted, the weapon failed to emit so much as a spark. With a sigh he discarded it and searched for two sticks to rub together. Despite multiple attempts, he couldn't get a fire generated. He cursed the unusual wood.

The cold penetrated to his bones. He shivered and tugged off his wet shirt, then laid it to dry beside Raven's clothing. Darkness overtook the land with the same surprising swiftness as the previous night, bringing a sudden drop in the temperature. With no fire and Raven's sleeping bag lost in the river, he resigned himself to a frigid night.

His damp pants clung to him as he huddled beneath his cloak. The cloth around his shoulders offered some warmth but not enough to keep his teeth from chattering. To make matters worse, a chilling wind blasted through the canyon, whipping the edges of the cloak in its passing.

"Damnation." Beckett pushed to his feet and paced the shore, searching for some pocket of shelter.

"Beckett."

He barely heard Raven's voice, she spoke so softly. Peering through the night, he could make out her form tucked against the foot of the cliff. "Get some sleep," he said sharply, knowing there'd be naught for him that night. "You'll need your strength in the morning."

"You're soaked too. You must be freezing."

" 'Twill pass in time." Perhaps when the sun rose again.

She hesitated. "This bag is big enough for two. I . . . I'll share."

Beckett froze in place, his fists tight at his side. His longing returned full force. "Raven." He spoke through clenched teeth. "If I join you, I'll nae be able to stop from making love to you."

"I know."

Her words floated on the wind to his ears. He stared in disbelief, then approached the spot where she sat. As she watched, he removed his boots and peeled off his pants. His shaft, already swollen with desire for her, sprang free of its constraint.

Raven gasped. He forced himself to stand there, though his blood boiled with his need, his want, for this woman. " 'Tis your last chance to say nae."

In reply, she unfastened the bag and held open the top covering, allowing a brief glimpse of her breasts, the nipples pebbled by the cold air. He quickly slid in beside her and sealed the bag closed.

The heat from her body warmed his . . . in every way. Her breasts tickled his chest while his manhood pressed against her curly mound. Though desperate to take her, Beckett caressed her face and searched her eyes.

Her gaze shone back at him, full of trust, with only a tiny bit of fear. After living among the privateers she probably only knew violence. To be made love to with tenderness would be a new experience for her. He vowed to make it a pleasant one.

Leaning forward, he kissed her lips, lingering a moment. When she whimpered he traced the outline of her lips with the tip of his tongue. Her mouth opened and he sealed their lips together, using his tongue to explore and entice.

As her tongue met his, he groaned. Lowering his hands to caress her breasts, he gathered the flesh in his palms, teasing the peaks into rigidity until Raven moved against him in an age-old rhythm.

"Not yet," he murmured against her lips. His erection throbbed in protest.

He left her mouth and blazed a trail with his lips along the satiny curve of her throat to her taut nipple. Teasing the tip with his tongue, he waited until she gasped aloud before he drew it into his mouth.

Sweet, so sweet. He suckled greedily as Raven buried her hands in his hair, as if to hold him in place. Moving his ministrations to her other breast, he caressed her deserted peak with his hand.

Karen Fox

Her moans grew louder as her undulations increased, her body begging for release—a release he was anxious to share. But not yet . . . not yet.

Continuing his attentions to her breast, he slid his hand over the soft skin of her abdomen and through her tight curls to the moistness of her inner warmth. He located her hidden bud and gently stroked it until Raven arched against the ground.

"Beckett, I . . . I need . . ."

"Aye, me too," he whispered. His fingers confirmed her readiness and he pressed her onto her back and knelt over her, his arousal poised at her opening.

He returned to her lips, trailing his fingers over the silkiness of her inner leg, across her belly and to her breast. She raised her hips in a pleading gesture and broke off their kiss to gasp for air. "Beckett," she cried, her voice ragged.

"Aye, sweet Raven, aye." He entered her carefully, then froze, stunned to find a barrier in his way. After her years among the privateers he hadn't expected to find her a virgin. Irrationally pleased to be her first lover, he thrust forward quickly and swallowed her cry with his mouth.

Despite the fires tormenting his body, he held still, his shaft buried deep within her tightness. She was so snug, so hot that he almost lost control.

Instead he turned his attention again to her breasts, teasing until she writhed beneath him. He withdrew then, almost fully out. At her cry of alarm he slid forward, trying to keep his movements slow.

She would have none of it. Grasping his shoulders, she wrapped her legs around his waist and thrust her hips against his.

Beckett needed no encouragement. He increased his pace, his desire threatening to explode. *Not yet.*

Her head thrown back, Raven's breathing intensified, her hold almost painful as she clenched his shoulders. Sensing her approaching satisfaction, Beckett cupped her buttocks in his hands and drove deep.

She shuddered around him, torturing him further.

With a groan he finally allowed his essence to pour into her.

He'd never experienced such ecstasy before. Raven's tough innocence touched his heart, heightening his desire, his need for her. 'Twas not a need he would lose soon.

His chest heaving, he searched her face for some sign of regret. Instead she looked at him with awe and reached up to caress his cheek. "Beckett, that was wonderful."

He grinned. "Aye." He stole a quick kiss, then gently eased himself away from her and rolled onto his side.

Raven traced idle designs on his chest as she pressed closer. Their combined heat dispelled any chill brought by the now-howling wind. Smiling, Beckett pressed a kiss against her forehead, her nose, then paused to drink from her lips. She'd been everything he'd imagined and more.

"I never knew it could be like that," Raven murmured, continuing to explore the contours of his chest.

"Perhaps now you'll nae run from me." Beckett ran one hand lightly along her side, over the dip of her waist and the gentle swell of her hip. Her body trembled.

"Perhaps," she said, her voice shaky. She ran her hands over his abdomen and he inhaled sharply as desire shot through him. Immediately she pulled back. "Should I stop?"

"Nae." He kissed her softly. "Explore as you will, but there may be . . . consequences."

She reached for him again, running her hands lower until she grasped his manhood. It swelled to attention within her palm and she ran her fingers along it gently. "Consequences?"

Even in the darkness he caught the twinkle in her gaze. "Aye, only this time 'twill be better."

"Better?" She sounded stunned.

"Aye, 'twill be slower and I'll raise your pleasure higher." As she continued to touch him, his longing spread throughout him like liquid fire. "You'll beg me to take you," he promised.

She paused to meet his gaze. "I beg for nothing."

He just smiled and bent to draw her breast into his mouth. This time he would teach her more about passion.

Before long she begged.

Raven awakened to find her head cradled on Beckett's shoulder and his arm wrapped around her torso. The sun had risen, flooding the ravine with brightness. Stretching, she acknowledged the aches of her body but dwelled instead on the warm tingling that lingered still.

Most other men had groped for her, trying to take, but Beckett gave . . . and gave. As far as she was concerned, he didn't need a sword to give him magic; he dispensed it with his body. Her skin warmed just remembering the pleasure brought by his hands and mouth and the feeling of him pulsing inside her. And she'd gone all her life never knowing this existed.

Pushing herself up on one elbow, she watched Beckett sleeping. His face looked strong even in slumber, the sculptured lines adding to his handsomeness. Only the strands of his brown hair falling over his face gave the illusion of youth.

Smiling, Raven gently pushed the strands back. This was no boy, but a man—a very unique man. His eyes fluttered open and a slow grin stretched across his lips. "Good morning, lass," he said softly.

"We have to go." As much as Raven preferred to linger, she still had a mission to complete. With even more conviction than before, she vowed to locate Ciorstan. And to do that she had to scale a cliff.

"Aye." Beckett didn't sound any more pleased than she was, but he sat up and slid from the sleeping bag in one smooth movement.

Raven watched unabashed as he crossed over to the stream and cleansed himself quickly with the cold water, verifying with her eyes the splendor of his body that she'd explored with her hands in the darkness. Every inch of him contained sleek muscle, his skin taut, his stature tall and proud. She inhaled sharply, suddenly wanting to touch him again.

No, she had work to do.

Emerging from the bag, she suffered a moment of insecurity. Would he find her as appealing in the daylight as he had at night?

Obviously he did, for he watched her steadily, his expression resembling that of a starving man at a banquet. He shifted uncomfortably in fastening his pants, and Raven noticed the bulge that had formed. Hot desire sprang to life in her belly and she turned away to wash swiftly, then pull on her stiff but dry clothes.

Unable to locate her backpack, she realized the river must have claimed it. "Most of the food was in my pack," she said quietly.

" 'Twill be all right. I have some here."

They shared a chunk of cheese and repackaged the sleeping bag, then turned to face the cliff. It looked even taller than the one they'd descended. Raven searched the side for signs of an obvious path but saw only occasional footholds. How could they possibly climb that?

Beckett reached up to grab an outcropping. "Let me find the way, then you follow. Stay close." He hopped up, ascending quickly.

As Raven emulated his footholds, she gave silent thanks that she didn't have to carry a backpack. Already her muscles ached, their burning increasing as she pulled herself up. She didn't dare look down, though Beckett glanced back at her constantly.

His primitive background obviously had some merit. He scrambled up the cliff with little effort that she could see while she struggled for each breath.

If only she could've landed her ship in this wilderness, she could've avoided all the discomfort of the climb and river—but not the night in Beckett's arms. That she preferred to remember.

Even now his gaze held concern each time he looked her way. Despite the circumstances, Raven found it heartwarming. It had been so long since anyone but Naldo had cared about her.

Her foot slipped suddenly and Beckett's hand closed around her wrist before she could complete her gasp. Gripping her handholds tighter, she probed with her feet until she found a solid surface again. Only then did Beckett's grip ease.

"All right?" he asked.

She nodded, unable to speak. Apparently satisfied, he resumed climbing. Glancing up, she sighed. At least the top appeared closer.

Beckett rolled over it first, then knelt and reached down for her. As soon as Raven came within reach, he grabbed her wrists and pulled her the rest of the way. Together, they flopped back on the rocky ground, their breathing erratic.

"I never want to do that again," Raven muttered. Sitting up, she glanced over the edge. The river appeared as a thin rivulet through the basin. "Never."

"We'll have to return to our craft," Beckett said calmly.

Shaking her head, Raven moved away from the canyon. "Your daughter will never make it." The picture she'd seen of Ciorstan showed a young girl, beautiful and obviously pampered.

He hurried to join her. "Dinna underestimate her."

Raven didn't answer as she studied the rocky foothills looming over the trees. She recognized the nirvani in flight, but no dog. Where was it? She scanned the mountains until realization dawned.

"Shibit. This is all wrong." Whirling around, she wanted to throw something.

"What?"

"I am such a Neeban." She pointed an accusing finger at Beckett. "This is all your fault. You make me so crazy I can't think straight."

"Is that so?" He looked absurdly pleased with himself, and Raven scowled in response. His expression immediately sobered. "What is it?"

Indicating their skimmer, parked on the far edge of the canyon, she rolled her fingers into a fist. "We have to find the dog formation. It's nowhere near here. We should've stayed on the skimmer and followed the canyon until we saw it."

His features tightened. "Aye."

"We're not going back for it, so now we walk."

"Which direction?"

Raven shrugged. Although Slade's skimmer trail disappeared when it reached the rocky soil, she thought she'd kept on the same path. Obviously she'd miscalculated or they'd have seen his craft parked beside the canyon.

Neptune's Rings, where was her brain? Lost in the clouds of desire, no doubt.

Stalking along the forest boundary, Raven refused to look at Beckett. "Don't talk to me, don't kiss me, don't touch me, don't even come near me, do you understand?"

He remained silent and she turned to glare at him. "Well?"

"You said nae to talk," he replied.

She clenched her hands into fists. "I'll take that as a yes." Pivoting, she studied the rocks towering in the distance. The one formation was the nirvani, she'd swear to it.

Recalling the maps of the mountain range, she pointed to her right. "That way." She started in that direction, unwilling to share her uncertainty with Beckett. The last thing they needed was to waste any more time.

She kicked at a boulder in her path, then winced as the pain traveled through her foot. *What a Neeban.* And to think, she was supposed to be the best tracker in the universe.

They walked for some time, the canyon narrowing beside them, before Raven finally spotted the dog formation in the rocks. As they drew equal to it, she saw Slade's skimmer on the opposite side of the canyon. Even more frustrating to see was a natural rock bridge that spanned the chasm's narrowed width. They could've walked across.

Her shoulders sagged beneath sudden invisible

161

weights. Raven dropped her head, unwilling to look at Beckett. "I'm sorry. I should've done better than this."

" 'Twill make it easier to return." His voice was filled with encouragement, rather than the condemnation Raven expected. She glanced at him in surprise. "Dinna worry, Raven. We will find Ciorstan," he said firmly.

He approached her, his intention of claiming a kiss obvious, and Raven held out her hand to forestall him. "Stay away." Now that her brain was finally functioning she didn't need any diversions.

Taking the opportunity to study the dog, she made note of the direction in which it pointed. Though she couldn't determine the exact spot the dog indicated, she knew they'd have to enter the forest to get to it. She searched the boundary until she found signs of Slade's passing in a snapped twig and crushed bush, and she went to kneel beside them.

Now she could do what she was hired to do—find Beckett's daughter.

He stood beside her when she rose to her feet and she gave him a sharp look. "I'm nae touching you," he said, though a smile played at the corners of his lips.

He didn't have to touch her to play havoc with her senses. Raven edged away, then plunged into the forest. She had a trail to follow.

The trees grew taller in this area, their limbs and trunks twisted in grotesque arrangements. Leaves as large as Raven's head fluttered from their branches, creating a loud flapping sound when the wind passed. Equally warped bushes lined the path, their branches lined with sharp, knifelike greenery that made Raven appreciate her thick boots.

The ground felt spongy, as if it was rotting beneath her feet, the sensation sending quivers of unease along her spine. She saw no animals or traces of any, for which she was secretly glad. After meeting the desert creature she had no desire to encounter any more of this planet's native inhabitants.

They'd only gone a short distance when she found the remnants of a camp in a small glade. Indentations from two sleeping bags flattened the earth near the still smoldering embers of a circular fire. Kneeling beside the fire, Raven discovered the torn wrappers from several food sticks. That fit the Slade she knew. He wouldn't bother with obtaining real food if it would slow him down.

"They spent the night here," she told Beckett, wiping her hands against her legs. "I doubt if they're too far ahead."

Beckett's eyes glowed with an inner light. "Then let's go."

She found Slade's trail again easily. As she'd predicted, he didn't know they were searching for him so he made no attempt to hide his path. Beckett pressed ahead as one possessed, using his sword to slash the tree limbs out of his way. His concern for Ciorstan became a palpable presence amid the wilderness.

Though Raven appreciated his concern, she also knew it meant the end of any relationship with Beckett. She had no love for children. In fact, she usually felt awkward around them. They needed . . . wanted everything from a person, and she wasn't willing to give it. She *couldn't* give it. Her heart had been cold for too long . . . until Beckett.

At least now she knew the pleasures that could be shared between a man and woman, but the thought of sharing them with anyone but Beckett made her stomach hurt.

A sudden wailing noise made them both freeze in place. Raven drew her weapon and searched the area. Only the thick foliage surrounded them.

"What is that?" Beckett asked, his sword held ready.

"I don't know. It can't be human. An animal maybe?"

He glanced at her laser. "Does that work now?"

She'd grabbed it without thinking. Aiming at the ground, she fired. Nothing. "Nope." Just what she needed—a useless laser. With a sigh she returned it to her holster.

Though neither of them said anything, they closed the space between them and continued to advance.

Karen Fox

Once Raven thought she'd lost the trail, but Beckett moved ahead without hesitation and, to her surprise, she found it again.

"Do you know where you're going?" she asked. He hadn't faltered once since they'd left the camp.

He paused then, as if considering her question. "I . . . feel like this is the right way to go. I can't explain it."

Raven nodded and resumed walking. Ciorstan and Slade's trail was equally sure. She'd found no sign of them changing direction.

The wail echoed through the forest again, but this time Raven ran toward it. Bursting from the trees, she found herself beside a small lagoon fed by a tall waterfall. As the drops cascaded from above, the sun created an array of vivid color—red, yellow, blue, purple. It was the closest thing to a rainbow she'd ever seen.

"It's beautiful," she said in awe.

Beckett stood unmoving as he watched the falling water; then he smiled. "The riddle," he exclaimed. " 'Bow before the rainbows pouring from heaven.' "

The sword had to be there. Raven searched the area. Aside from the rocks lining both sides of the waterfall, trees formed a barrier around the lagoon. But where?

She stepped closer to the edge of the water, then grinned. "I know where to go."

Chapter Eleven

Beckett followed the direction of Raven's gaze. The waterfalls? "Where—?"

"This way." She went to the rocks surrounding the falls and scrambled over them, heading for the falling water.

When she darted a nervous glance at the lagoon Beckett tensed. If she fell in, he'd be right behind her. He hurried to join her on the large boulders.

The roar of the falling water made it difficult to hear, so Beckett was surprised when Raven put a finger to her lips and motioned toward an opening ahead of them. Between the waterfalls and rock wall was a ledge—big enough for them to stand on.

As the wind passed, the strange howling sounded again—very close. Beckett studied the opening. Somehow the wind blowing through the tunnel caused the noise . . . or there was something besides Slade and Ciorstan inside there.

Beckett's heart hammered against his ribs as he fought back an urge to run in and find his daughter.

Raven laid a restraining hand on his arm as she drew her laser.

He raised his eyebrows. Her laser didn't work. Did she still intend to face Slade?

Obviously she did, for she clambered over the rocks to the opening and slipped inside. Cursing her courage, Beckett followed her. Without an operable weapon, she should let him handle this.

As he entered the hollow, the roar faded and he noticed that the space went deeper than he'd first guessed. Raven grabbed his hand and pulled him into a crouch beside her.

Before Beckett could question her, he heard voices and stiffened.

"Are you sure this is the spot?"

"Aye, I'm positive. Can you reach in there for me, please?"

Ciorstan! She was alive. Beckett bowed his head as relief mingled with joy.

When he glanced at Raven, she returned his smile, then motioned him forward. Creeping along the slippery ledge, they finally reached a position where they could see the speakers.

Beckett recognized Ciorstan at once. Though she only reached Slade's shoulder, her erect bearing made her seem the taller of the two. All he could see of Slade was his back. The man stood shorter than Beckett and was much thinner. He wore a raggedy black coat that hung to his feet, but it did nothing to disguise his bony shoulders. Surprisingly, Slade's hair was white and long, falling to the middle of his back. He looked nothing like Beckett expected.

This was the man who'd terrorized Raven?

Turning toward her, Beckett instantly felt her fear. She barely moved—only her chest rose and fell with shallow breaths—and her expression had tightened.

He touched her shoulder and she jumped. When she looked at him, he could see the panic in her eyes. Squeezing her shoulder, he tried to tell her without words that it would be all right, that he'd never allow Slade to touch her again.

Her only response was a wan smile before she focused again on the man and girl.

"There *is* something here." Slade's voice sounded deep and dark in contrast to his appearance. He removed a long, narrow object from a crevice in the rock wall and held it before him.

"The sword!" Ciorstan said eagerly. She reached for it, but he moved it above her head.

Removing the wrapping, a yellowish cloth, Slade dropped it on the ground and gazed at the sword. As Slade turned toward the water, Beckett could see the ornate hilt and glittering blade.

The Sword of MacLeod. It did exist.

Beckett stared. Was it magic also? At this point he'd believe anything.

"Give me the sword," Ciorstan ordered. " 'Tis mine."

"Oh, I'll give it to you all right." Slade pointed the blade toward her and Beckett's throat nearly closed.

Without thinking, he jumped from the shadows. " 'Tis best you remember who that sword belongs to."

Ciorstan's face lit up with joy. "Da!"

Before she could run to Beckett, Slade grabbed her arm and yanked her back. Beckett drew his sword, his anger mixing with caution, and approached.

Slade placed the sword against Ciorstan's throat and she gasped, the sound echoing in the chamber. "Should I test the sharpness of this edge?" Slade asked. His lips twisted in a warped smile.

Looking at Slade's face, Beckett could see that evil permeated this man. It radiated from every line in the narrow visage and glittered in the black eyes. "Dinna harm her."

"Then drop your sword." Slade fingered Ciorstan's long hair. "I'd intended to keep this one. She'll be good in bed when she's older. But I will kill her if you so much as move a muscle."

Beckett lowered his blade to the floor, then stood, his fists clenched, every muscle aching for action. He was going to kill Slade. For Raven . . . for Ciorstan . . . for himself. But first he had to get his daughter away from this madman.

Slade edged toward the exit. "Now we're going to leave, this sweet, young thing and I, and if you try to follow, why then, I'll have to kill her."

"Stop right there, Slade." Raven stepped in front of him, pointing her disabled laser at his head. "Lose the sword."

A cold chill raced down Beckett's spine. If Slade decided to call Raven's bluff, she could be killed.

Slade's eyes narrowed as he looked at Raven, but he lowered the sword. Ciorstan immediately pulled away and ran to Beckett.

As he wrapped his arms around her, Beckett inhaled sharply. His daughter alive . . . unharmed. He'd been afraid to think otherwise, but doubts had plagued him from the moment he'd found her note. He held her back to study her face and noticed the dark circles beneath her eyes.

"Ciorstan, are you all right? Did he . . . ?"

She shook her head. "I'm fine, Da. I'm so glad you came. I dinna think you would."

He frowned. "We'll talk about that later."

"Raven." Slade suddenly spoke. "It's my little Raven all grown up." His gaze lingered on her breasts, and Beckett's muscles tensed.

"Da." Ciorstan squirmed within his hold and Beckett realized that he'd unknowingly tightened his grasp.

He pulled her to his side and bent to retrieve his sword. He tensed, ready to pierce Slade, but Raven stood between them. Reluctantly, Beckett returned the sword to his scabbard. For now, her ruse had fooled Slade, but Beckett kept his hand near his side—just in case.

Glancing at Raven, he noticed the strain on her had intensified with Slade's words. She kept her spine ramrod straight, but her hand trembled, her laser wavering slightly.

Slade must have seen her fear, for he moved closer,

168

a deadly smile creasing his face. "I was going to make you someone special, Raven, and you ran away. What kind of thanks is that?"

Beckett stepped toward him, touching the hilt of his sword. "Stay away from her."

"Get Ciorstan out of here now." Raven shot him an angry look despite her terror.

Unwilling to leave her with Slade, Beckett hesitated. How could he get his daughter to safety and still protect Raven?

Moving with lethal speed, Slade leapt at Raven. She fired her weapon, but it only sputtered. With a deep-throated laugh, Slade knocked her laser from her grasp and brought his hand across her face. Raven tumbled back to the ground.

Beckett started for Slade, then froze when the man turned, his laser drawn. Slade fired and Beckett dodged, feeling the heat of the beam as it passed. Ciorstan cried out in alarm. More blasts followed.

Whirling around, Beckett seized Ciorstan by the hand and dove into the falling water. Buried deep by the water's force, Beckett struggled to the surface, dragging his daughter with him. At least she knew how to swim. Upon breaking through the water, they gasped for breath.

Beckett pushed her toward the shore. "Get away from here. Hide."

"Da, where are—?"

"I canna leave Raven with him." Beckett slashed through the water, then halted when he saw Slade and Raven emerge from behind the falls.

Slade had the Sword of MacLeod tucked into his belt. He had twisted Raven's arm behind her and pushed her in front of him, his laser held to her head. A large bruise highlighted her cheek.

Hot rage filled Beckett. Locating the solid bottom of the lagoon, he thrust himself out of the water. "Let her go."

Mild surprise flickered across Slade's face before he lowered his weapon and fired. Beckett threw himself into the water to avoid the blast. As he surfaced, he saw Raven twist away from Slade and aim her fist at his jaw.

Slade calmly stepped back and shot again. The beam hit Raven in the middle. She cried out, her eyes wide, then fell to the ground.

"No!" For a moment Beckett could only stare in disbelief. Not Raven. His heart filled with terror. With a cry of anguish, he drew his sword and raised it high above his head. This weapon worked despite sand or water.

As Slade fired at him, Beckett used the blade of his sword to deflect any beams that came near and made his way closer. Once he reached land, he ran. Slade would die.

Panic filled Slade's expression. Firing wildly, he plunged into the surrounding forest.

Beckett paused at the edge of the trees and turned back. Kneeling beside Raven, he felt her neck for a pulse—the same pulse he'd kissed so tenderly only the night before. Though erratic, it continued to beat.

"Is she alive, Da?" Ciorstan joined him, her brow wrinkled with concern.

"Barely." Blast marks surrounded a small circle on Raven's suit. Ripping it open, Beckett searched for her injury. He found it easily. Blood oozed from a wound on her side just below her rib cage. "Damnation."

He removed his shirt and placed it against the wound, pressing hard to staunch the flow of blood. Scanning the surrounding area, he searched for something to tie the shirt in place.

Ciorstan leapt to her feet. "I know." She hurried into the chamber behind the waterfalls and returned with the discarded yellow cloth in her hand. "Will this work?"

"Aye. Thanks, daughter." He gently lifted Raven to wrap the material around her and secured his makeshift bandage in place. As he lowered her to the ground, her eyes fluttered open. Though she looked straight at him, he wasn't sure she saw him.

He ran his fingers along her cheek. "Raven." He

couldn't stop a tremor from entering his voice.

"M-m-med t-tech," she whispered.

"What?" Her words made no sense.

She tried to speak again but failed, her eyes closing as she lost consciousness.

His stomach twisted. He'd failed her. Unable to hide his despair, he glanced at Ciorstan, kneeling across from him.

"Who is she, Da?" she asked.

"Her name's Raven. She's the tracker I hired to find you."

His daughter smiled at him sadly, her eyes too wise for a child her age. "She's more than that, isn't she?"

Beckett sighed. "Aye, lass. She's more than that." He studied Raven's pale face. Damnation, he hated being powerless. There had to be some way to help.

He crossed to where he'd left his backpack and rummaged through it. Tossing aside the food remnants, he removed a large rectangular box. Unable to make out any identifiable markings, he set it beside the food and continued his search. He located the sleeping bag and quickly activated it. At least he could keep her warm.

"The colony should have something to help her," Ciorstan said as she helped him ease Raven into the bag. "If we can get her there."

Remembering their perilous journey over the planet, Beckett hesitated. He could kill Raven trying to make that trek. But what choice did he have? He couldn't leave her here either.

"Let's go." He scooped Raven into his arms, then glanced at his daughter. "Can you make it?"

"Aye." She hurried to reload the pack and fastened it onto her own back.

Pleased by her initiative, Beckett gave her a tight smile. With his daughter alive and obviously more competent than he gave her credit for, he should be a very happy man. He glanced at Raven's pale face. Some part of him would never be happy again if he lost this woman.

Tightening his grip, he made his way into the trees,

Karen Fox

Ciorstan close at his heels. With his experience tracking animals on Alba, he had no problem retracing the path through the forest. For one of the few moments since he'd ventured into space he'd encountered a situation where he felt somewhat proficient.

Raven's slight moans reassured him that she still lived, but also spurred him to increase his pace. Ciorstan managed to keep up without complaint and Beckett's heart swelled with pride. He had underestimated her; he wouldn't do that again.

They reached the canyon in good time. His heart pounding, his chest tight, Beckett gently lowered Raven to the ground and studied the natural bridge. Though it crossed the entire cavern, it wasn't very wide—barely enough for a man to cross. But a man with a burden . . . ?

"Is there any water, Da?" Ciorstan sat on the ground and swiped her arm across her brow.

"Aye, lass." He helped her remove the backpack and pulled out the narrow metallic container that held the liquid. As Ciorstan drank, he located the remaining food and offered it to her. She ate with enthusiasm as he returned to studying the bridge.

"Did you cross over on this bridge?" he asked.

"Aye; 'twas frightening. I think if nae for the lure of the sword, Slade would nae have crossed at all." She looked up at him. "Dinna you come that way?"

"Nae, we took a . . . different route." Finding the bridge would have made the trip easier, but Beckett doubted he'd have shared the wonderful night with Raven if they had. And their lovemaking more than made up for any additional hardship.

Remembering Raven's passion made his chest ache. He couldn't lose her. He knelt beside her to verify her thready pulse. Weak . . . much weaker than before. A sheen of perspiration highlighted her white face. Fear tied his stomach into knots.

"We have to hurry. I'll go first." He turned to Ciorstan and ran his hand over her hair. "Be careful, lass."

She smiled. "Dinna worry, Da."

172

He lifted Raven in his arms again and approached the bridge. He cautiously tested his weight on the structure. Once satisfied, he proceeded carefully.

Despite his good coordination, Raven's weight threatened to knock him off balance. Moisture beaded on his forehead as he made his way across. He didn't dare look down.

He'd almost reached the other side when his foot slid on some crumbling rock. With a strength he didn't know he possessed, he jumped for the edge and made it, falling to his knees at the force of his landing.

Settling Raven on the ground, he bent over her, his breathing rapid, his stomach churning. He didn't want to do that again.

"I'm almost there, Da."

At Ciorstan's voice, he jerked around, his heart filling his throat. He could see blast marks near the edge of the bridge. *Slade's doing.* Only a narrow piece of rock remained attached to the side.

"Nae, Ciorstan." He forced the words out through his closed throat.

Too late.

As she approached the edge, the rock crumpled, the bridge falling toward the bottom. Ciorstan screamed, her arms flailing.

Beckett threw himself flat, extending his arms, seizing her arm. Though she cried out in pain, she said nothing else, her eyes reflecting her panic.

With only the lower part of his body on solid ground, Beckett's muscles burned from the strain of holding Ciorstan. Only his grip kept her from plunging to her death. He'd not fail her.

Slowly he squirmed backward until his chest lay on the ground. With an effort, he lifted Ciorstan, drawing her up to where he could seize her waist and drag her onto the ground.

They stretched out on their backs, their breathing equally strained. Ciorstan crawled over and wrapped her arms around him as tears streamed down her cheeks. Beckett sat up, cradling her in his embrace, bur-

Karen Fox

ying his face in her hair. Finally her sobs eased and she pulled away from him.

" 'Twas fine before," she said, looking at the remnants of the bridge.

"I think Slade did something to it. I saw black marks on the rock before it fell."

"He also took our skimmer." Ciorstan met Beckett's gaze in despair. "We canna walk across this desert. 'Tis too big."

Grateful now that Raven hadn't taken them directly to the dog rock, Beckett smiled. "Raven's skimmer is down further." He playfully tugged on the ends of Ciorstan's hair. "Can you make it?"

"Aye." She scrambled to her feet. "I want to get out of here."

The walk to the skimmer seemed to take less time than Beckett's earlier trek along the canyon. To his relief, it sat where they'd left it—apparently undisturbed. But how to travel on it?

Raven was easily a head taller than Ciorstan. With the additional burden of the sleeping bag, she was too bulky for Ciorstan to hold in the rear seat. Yet Beckett couldn't control the skimmer and hold her as well.

Before he could voice his worries, Ciorstan climbed into the front seat and examined the controls. She glanced at Beckett over her shoulder. "You can hold Raven in the back."

"Can you fly this?"

"Aye. 'Tis easy."

Beckett looked toward the horizon. Their daylight hours were limited and he dreaded meeting another desert creature in the dark. Yet they couldn't linger; Raven needed help now.

He swung into the seat and situated Raven across his lap. Immediately Ciorstan powered up the skimmer and it rose a short distance off the ground. She fiddled with the controls for some time before they started moving.

"It has a homing device built in," she explained. "It'll take us back to the colony."

174

"How do you know that?"

"A man at the colony showed me how to work this." She handled the craft with competence and Beckett relaxed. He should've known Ciorstan would welcome learning any new technology. They'd had many an angry discussion over it.

As darkness fell, he scanned the sand with rising trepidation. "Did you travel over the desert at night?" he asked.

"Very little."

"There's a creature that lives beneath the sand. It's dangerous. Watch for a strange movement like waves. If you see that, veer away and increase the speed."

Ciorstan's back straightened and she nodded. Beckett didn't doubt she watched the surrounding area as intently as he did. Her head only nodded once during the night and she jerked it upright when he touched her shoulder. He wished he could relieve her, but cradling Raven strained his muscles. Ciorstan would never be able to handle the load.

She spotted the odd undulations in the sand first and pointed them out to him. Beckett's muscles tensed. "Change direction. Hurry."

They darted to the side just as the monster burst from below—directly beneath their previous position. Ciorstan gasped and increased their speed. The skimmer sailed over the sand, sending tiny particles into the air to prick at Beckett, but the creature didn't follow.

Dawn illuminated the sky when they arrived at the colony. Ciorstan landed their craft before a building designated as the medical center and a man came to meet them. He took one look at Raven and ushered them inside.

Sterile, white walls surrounded a surprisingly small room. Aside from two computer terminals, the only other furniture was five of the clear, boxlike devices Beckett had seen on Raven's ship. The man opened the top of one.

"Take her from the bag and put her in here," he ordered.

175

Karen Fox

Beckett hesitated. This box could heal her?

"Get moving. She may be too far gone to be healed as it is."

He still hesitated. " 'Tis unnatural for a device to do this. Where are your doctors?"

With a frustrated exclamation, the man seized Raven from Beckett's arms. "Get out of here now." When Beckett didn't move the man raised his voice. "Security, remove these individuals."

Two guards appeared beside Beckett, but he barely glanced at them, his attention focused on Raven as the man slid her from the bag into the box. "What are you doing to her?" Beckett demanded.

"Out. Now." The man waved at the guards, who urged Beckett and Ciorstan toward the door. "If it was up to you, you'd let her die." He glared at Beckett. "Barbarian."

Ushered none too gently outside, Beckett paced before the door. " 'Tis unnatural," he repeated. "It goes against what's right to use a machine."

Ciorstan placed her hand on his arm. "Da, this is their way. Do you want Raven to die?"

"Nae." He looked at her in horror. Lose Raven? When he'd just found her? "Nae."

"Then be patient. I suspect even a healing in their box will take some time."

Beckett couldn't stop a slow grin from crossing his lips. "You sound as if you are mothering me, Ciorstan MacLeod."

She smiled, illuminating her young face. "I've always been told I'm too old for my age."

"Aye." Beckett had heard the same thing from many in his family, but he'd discounted it. Though he never doubted his daughter's intelligence, he saw her only as a child—albeit a very willful one. "You did solve the riddle, lass."

Her eyes sparkled. "I found it, Da. The Sword of MacLeod." Her excitement quickly gave way to disappointment. "And Slade took it. 'Twas our destiny. It dinna belong to him."

176

"At least you're alive. 'Twas wrong to leave as you did." Beckett kept his voice even.

"I'm sorry." She hung her head. "But you wouldna believe me. We'll die without the sword, Da."

"You could've died trying to find it. What then?" His voice rose despite his efforts to keep calm. "Dinna you know what type of man Slade is?"

"I suspected, but no one else would bring me here." Her lips pursed in a pout. "They laughed at me."

"Ah, lass." With a sigh, Beckett drew her into his arms, torn between the urge to shake her or hug her. "You willna be allowed near the merchant ships again—if I allow them to return."

She looked up at him, her eyes wide. "They have to keep coming. We canna live without their supplies."

"The drought willna last forever. Soon we'll be self-sufficient again."

Ciorstan's eyes reflected her doubt, but she remained silent and rested her head against his chest. Idly, Beckett stroked her long hair. They *would* be self-sufficient again. Once he returned to Alba he wanted nothing more to do with this modern technology. It went against all his ancestors' plans for the Scot future.

Except for Raven.

She warmed his soul, stirred his desire, and touched his heart. He thought he'd never find the woman with whom he felt complete. One night with Raven shattered that illusion. With her by his side, he knew he could meet any challenges the future held.

'Twas impossible.

She harbored no more love for his lifestyle than he did for hers. If she lived. . . .

He glanced at the door, but it remained closed. Clenching his fists, he fought back the need to burst through and check on her. No man in his right mind would trust a . . . a box to heal her wound.

As if sensing the direction of his thoughts, Ciorstan slipped from his hold and walked to the door. She paused and turned back to him. "How did you find this Raven person?"

Karen Fox

"I hired her on Cirius. An alien said she was the best tracker in the universe, and that's what I wanted."

"But how did you pay her?"

He hesitated. "With my medallion."

"Oh, Da." The sympathy in her voice also appeared on her face. " 'Twas Papaw's medallion."

" 'Twas worth it. We found you."

"How long have you been looking for me?"

"Over a week now."

"Over a week," she repeated in awe. Her eyes narrowed. "How close *are* you to her?"

"We're . . ." What? Friends? Lovers? Business partners? All, and yet none of those. Raven fell into a category of her own—one he couldn't put a name to. "She's . . ."

"I see." Ciorstan turned away, but not before Beckett caught a glimpse of her disappointment. She'd never shown any interest in obtaining a new mother—possibly because of Nessa's frailty. Not that Beckett intended to make Raven Ciorstan's new mother. He just . . . What *did* he intend to do?

At the sound of the door opening, he whirled around to see the first man standing there. "You're a fool," the man said flatly.

Startled, Beckett didn't react right away. "What?"

The man slid the pack from Ciorstan's back and opened it. Rummaging inside, he removed the boxlike container that had defied explanation and waved it before Beckett. "All this time you had a portable medtech unit with you. You could've saved her without causing her the additional pain of that trip."

Beckett looked at the box blankly. He hadn't known, and even if he had, would he have used it? "Is she . . . is she dead?" He swallowed the thick lump in his throat.

Glaring at him, the man turned to go back inside. "You're far luckier than you deserve to be."

He entered the building and Beckett started to follow. "Where's Raven?"

"I'm here." She appeared in the doorway and Beckett stopped abruptly. "Fit and ready to fly." Glancing at the

178

scorch mark on her jumpsuit, she grimaced. "Well, almost ready."

Unable to stop staring, Beckett feasted on the sight. Her face still looked drawn and pale, her hair tousled, but she stood with no apparent sign of pain or injury. He stepped closer. "Raven?" Extending his hand, he cupped the curve of her face. " 'Tis possible?"

She swallowed and smiled slightly. "You can't kill me that easily."

With a groan, he enveloped her in his grasp and claimed her lips, tasting the sweetness he thought he'd lost forever. She responded instantly, her body molding to his, her arms circling his neck. Hot desire bubbled to life, robbing Beckett of any conscious thought but of the woman in his arms.

"Da. Da." Ciorstan tugged on his sleeve. Realization dawned, and Beckett drew away from Raven. Glancing at his daughter, he saw that she carefully kept any expression from her face. He smiled wryly.

"She'll nae be alive long if you dinna let her breathe," Ciorstan said calmly.

Raven stiffened, her gaze focused on the girl. Beckett stepped back farther, watching them both. "Raven, this is my daughter, Ciorstan. Ciorstan, Raven."

Ciorstan offered no form of greeting. "Are you healed?" she asked abruptly.

"Yes." Raven replied slowly, her expression puzzled.

"Do you have a ship?"

"Yes."

"Good." Ciorstan whirled around and started for the spaceport. "Then let's get going."

"Aye." Beckett prepared to follow her. "I'm anxious to return to Alba myself."

"Alba?" Ciorstan looked at him in surprise. "Nae Alba."

Beckett exchanged a confused glance with Raven. "Where then?"

"To get the sword back from Slade, of course."

Chapter Twelve

"We're nae going after Slade," Beckett said emphatically.

Raven released her breath. Just the thought of facing Slade again brought her heart into her throat. "That's good. Finding the sword wasn't part of our deal. I found your daughter as agreed."

"We *have* to get the sword back," Ciorstan exclaimed. She stomped her foot on the ground, and Raven pressed her lips together.

Children. What did she expect? Little adults? "Fine. Get your sword back," Raven said. "But don't expect me to take you there."

"We're nae going after the sword." Beckett frowned at Ciorstan, then glanced at Raven. "Dinna worry. You never have to see Slade again."

Something warm trickled through Raven's veins at Beckett's insight, and she smiled until she caught Ciorstan's angry glower.

"We'll die without the sword, Da." She tugged on his arm until he looked at her. "We need the magic."

Beckett's expression softened. " 'Tis nae magic, lass. 'Twas just a sword."

"The riddle wouldna show us the way there if the magic dinna exist."

Raven had to admit to a certain logic in that reasoning. "But Slade has the magic sword now," she said. "What makes you think he won't use it against us?"

Ciorstan hesitated, apparently considering Raven's words. "Still, we—"

"Enough, lass." Beckett laid his hand on her shoulder. "I have you safe. 'Tis all that's important to me. We'll return to Alba. I've been away too long as it is."

"Da." Ciorstan's voice held a whine that grated on Raven's nerves.

"Dinna say any more, lass." He urged her into motion. "Let's go."

"Wait." Raven held out the strange-looking cloth used to bind her wound. She'd grabbed it, thinking they'd have at least something of the sword. "There's this."

Ciorstan's sullen expression didn't change as she accepted the cloth. She gave it only a cursory glance, then stuffed it in her pocket. "Thank you," she muttered and continued walking.

Exchanging glances with Beckett, Raven grimaced. Well, she'd tried. Her spirits lifted at seeing the *TrackStar* in the landing bay. She'd had more than enough of this planet. Glancing down at her scorched jumpsuit, she grimaced. She'd come a lot closer to dying than she ever wanted to again.

She placed her palm against the verification plate and stated her name. Instead of the hatch opening, she received a shock that knocked her back. Holding her hand to her chest, she searched the exterior of the ship. "Wha—?" The answer came immediately. "Slade."

"What's wrong?" Beckett joined her.

"Slade's done something to my ship." She stretched her fingers until the tingling left her palm, then approached the craft warily. Any touch against the hull produced the same sharp shock. "Great."

Bending low, she moved underneath the ship until

181

she located the wiring's outer panel. The small piece of tape she'd adhered to the square opening had been torn, indicating tampering. Silently calling Slade every name she could think of, she inhaled deeply, then pushed on the two latches despite the steady shocks. The panel swung open and Raven cradled her hands close to her body until the pain ebbed.

"Can I help?" Beckett asked.

"Stay there and let me know when the hatch opens." Raven saw at once where Slade had rewired her ship's defense system and fixed it quickly. Triggering the hatch, she nodded with satisfaction when Beckett indicated that the door had opened.

She joined him in time to see Ciorstan hurrying up the ramp and put out her hand in alarm. "No, wait."

Too late.

Ciorstan hit the inner force field and bounced off, landing on her rear. To her credit, she didn't cry, though her eyes watered suspiciously as she climbed to her feet. She glared at Raven. "I thought you fixed it."

"I returned the wiring to normal, but my security is still in place." Raven placed her palm on the panel again. "Raven. Mac, cancel security."

"Security canceled. Defenses lowered."

Ciorstan's face lit up at Mac's voice. "You have a talking computer. May I see it?"

"There's nothing to see. It's built in." Raven cautiously entered the ship and looked around. Everything looked normal, but she doubted Slade would tamper only with her security system. "Mac, scan guest Ciorstan MacLeod; then I want you to do a complete diagnostic."

"Confirmed."

Raven motioned Ciorstan into the doorway and held up a hand to keep her there.

"Ciorstan MacLeod scanned. Mass calculated for liftoff. Beginning diagnostic."

Beckett followed his daughter inside. "Where will Ciorstan sit?"

"This ship is only designed to hold two comfortably.

Sword of MacLeod

She'll have to use the jump seat." Raven pulled a lever and a narrow chair slid into place at the rear. "She's small enough that she won't be uncomfortable."

"You'll sit here, lass." Beckett waved his hand at her seat, but Ciorstan only nodded and continued her exploration of the ship. She kept her hands entwined behind her back as she studied each button, lever and display within the cabin.

When she reached the control panel she pointed to the hyperdrive lever. "What's that?"

Raven hurried to the front. "Don't touch anything."

Ciorstan gave her a dry look. "I willna. I'm nae a nimnul."

Raven raised her eyebrows in surprise. "A what?"

"A nim . . . na . . . nee . . ." As the girl struggled to find the word, Raven suddenly grinned.

"A Neeban," she said.

"Aye, a Neeban." Ciorstan smiled, a hint of laughter in her eyes.

Perhaps the child wasn't entirely awful. Raven indicated the lever. "That's the hyperdrive control."

"What's hyperdrive? Is that when the stars blur?"

"Yes. It's a faster way of traveling from point to point in space. I would've thought you'd learned that already."

A dark shadow crossed Ciorstan's face and she lowered her gaze. "I did ask Slade some questions, but he usually dinna answer."

Sudden sympathy swelled within Raven. "Feel free to ask all the questions you like," she offered.

As she turned from the controls, she found Beckett smiling at her warmly. Though her stomach automatically flip-flopped, a sudden little chill raced along her spine. She wasn't playing mother for any child . . . no matter whose it was.

"Mac, any progress?"

"Diagnostic almost completed. No discrepancies found at this point."

She still found it hard to believe Slade hadn't done more damage. A sudden fear clutched at her chest and

183

Karen Fox

she ran to check the thrusters and overdrive. They looked fine—just as she'd left them. She eased out a sigh of relief.

"Diagnostic complete. No problems to report."

Raven looked around at Mac's voice. No problems. Perhaps Slade had been in a hurry to depart and only took the time to fiddle with her security system.

Well, of course. He didn't expect her to be alive, and Beckett certainly wouldn't have known how to repair the damage Slade did to her security system.

"Okay, Mac. Run preflight and plot the overdrive course to the planet Alba in the Scot system." Raven swung into her chair and began her configurations. "Beckett, Ciorstan, you need to strap in now."

She heard Beckett quietly reassuring his daughter as he helped her fasten her straps. He'd switched to father mode upon locating Ciorstan . . . which was just as well. They had no future together; Raven had known that from the beginning.

But that didn't stop her from remembering the passion of his kiss or the pleasure of his lovemaking.

"Preflight completed and I've plotted the overdrive course," Mac said.

As Beckett took his seat beside her, Raven requested permission to depart from the tower. Once she received it, she ignited her engines. If Slade had done anything more, now would be when it happened.

Her engines roared to life, all the gauges indicating perfect operation. Raven released a breath she'd just realized she was holding. Glancing at Beckett, she smiled slightly. "Let's go."

Her ship lifted from the planet flawlessly and soared into the darkness of space. After verifying the position of the asteroids, Raven gripped the hyperspeed lever. "Are you ready?" she asked.

"I canna wait to be home," Beckett replied.

She pulled and the screen went black.

"Is it supposed to do that?" Ciorstan's shaky voice came from behind her.

"It is. I have a new hyperspeed system." Raven double-checked her coordinates, then removed her straps.

"How long will it take to get there?" Beckett asked, his enthusiasm obvious.

"About five days. You'll soon be home, Beckett MacLeod." Raven met his gaze, then wished she hadn't. Desire shone in his eyes, igniting tiny flames in her blood.

Inhaling sharply, she pushed herself from her seat and went to lower the bunks. "I only have two beds, but the sleeping bag will work on the floor."

"You're going to sleep?" Ciorstan managed to undo her bindings and stood in the middle of the cabin. "It's morning." In defiance of her words, she yawned.

"As you'll recall, neither of us got much sleep last night," Beckett said. "And I'm certain Raven could use more rest."

"I *am* worn out." She caught herself, surprised that she'd admitted it, and shrugged sheepishly. "All I want is an hour or two."

"That sounds good." Beckett steered Ciorstan to the other bunk. "You sleep here, lass. The floor will work for me."

With everyone settled, Raven dimmed the lights and removed her jumpsuit. It had definitely seen better days. She'd get a clean one when she awakened.

Closing her eyes, she willed the tension to leave her body. Though her wound had healed completely with no residual pain, an ache still permeated her chest. Unfortunately, this ache wouldn't be nearly as easy to heal.

When Raven awakened the cabin was quiet, the only disruption Beckett's rhythmic breathing. After dressing in the half light she made her way to her chair and settled into it. A quick check of the chronometer signified that she'd slept at least twice as long as she'd expected.

That wasn't all bad; sleep might be the best way to pass this journey. Now that she knew the joy obtained through Beckett's touch, she longed for more, her body tightening with nothing more than a glance from him.

If Ciorstan hadn't been along, Raven knew the trip

could've passed very quickly. As it was, she was trapped in a small space with a man she desired and his child.

His child.

Raven leaned forward, propping her chin in her hands. She tried. She honestly tried, but every time Ciorstan came near, something inside Raven tightened into a tense knot. Part of her problem was not knowing what to say to the girl. Raven had dealt with adults for as long as she could remember. Her lone interaction with children had been with her brother, and she preferred not to remember that.

"Hi."

Ciorstan's quiet voice startled Raven and she jerked upright, turning to see the girl slide into the other chair.

"May I sit here? I willna touch anything," she added in a rush. "Da's still asleep."

Raven shrugged. Despite her unease, she couldn't send Ciorstan away. Where else was there to go?

Ciorstan stared at the blackness outside the window before speaking again. "This is fantastic. I always wanted to go into space, but Da would hear naught of it."

"I wouldn't think your people even knew about space travel."

"Some dinna, until the merchant ships came." Ciorstan studied the control panel. "But I'd read all the old books—trying to solve the riddle, y'ken—and I knew what it had been like when our ancestors left Earth and came to Alba." She aimed her piercing gaze at Raven. "Will you teach me to fly?"

"Beckett won't like it." Raven could imagine his fury if she taught his daughter the ways of modern technology.

"Aye, but as his only heir . . ." She frowned. "Are you going to wed my father?"

Raven replied automatically, her heart clenching. "No."

"As his only heir, I'll one day be Chieftain of Clan MacLeod, and I'll allow other aliens to visit. I think we

186

should know how to fly space ships. How else can we protect ourselves?"

That young exterior held an intelligent mind. Raven agreed with Ciorstan's reasoning. "You sound as if you've thought about this a lot."

"I have." She looked back toward the window. "When I left on the merchant ship I was afraid, but I was excited, too. I loved seeing the stars and ships and other planets. Even the aliens are interesting." She paused, as if remembering. "Most of them," she added.

Raven understood Ciorstan's enthusiasm. She still felt that same excitement each time she traveled through space. "It is wonderful," she said. "Did you know there's a planet near the Orion Nebula where the native life form resembles a rock? The creature requires neither water nor oxygen, yet it has a low level intelligence."

"Teach me to fly." Ciorstan's eyes gleamed as she touched Raven's hand. "Please. Teach me."

The warmth of her touch seared Raven, the tan hand looking small atop Raven's pale one. Raven glanced from the hand to Ciorstan's expectant face. Why shouldn't she help the girl? Maybe then Beckett would accept modern technology.

"I'll do what I can," Raven said quietly. "When your father sleeps."

Ciorstan's smile nearly engulfed her face. "Aye."

Though their sessions were often short and hurried, Ciorstan impressed Raven with her quick grasp of the ship's instruments and their functions. Her ability to understand the reasoning behind each function took more time, but at least she tried. Sometimes Raven forgot Ciorstan was a child.

If only it was as easy to forget Beckett's presence. Every moment near him tugged at Raven's nerves. His eyes clearly telegraphed his desire, tamed temporarily, but lurking just beneath his constrained behavior. When Ciorstan wasn't looking he'd run his finger along Raven's cheek or trace the outline of her lips.

But they were never alone.

By the fifth day Raven couldn't wait to escape the confines of her small ship. With her patience waning, she counted the minutes until they emerged from hyperspeed. As she paced the limited floor space, Raven decided to quickly deliver Beckett and Ciorstan to their home and leave.

And go where?

She paused. A destination had never been a problem before. Yet now all she could think of was Beckett. Unless he changed his mind about alien interaction, she'd never see him again.

"May I sit here, Raven?" Ciorstan motioned toward Raven's chair before the console. "I want to see us come out of hyperspeed."

Raven nodded.

"Are you sure?" Beckett asked, coming to stand before her.

"She won't touch anything and Mac can bring us out of hyperspeed easily enough." She smiled slightly. "There are no asteroids here."

Beckett gently touched her shoulders and ran his hands along her arms. Raven's skin tingled, her breasts swelling in anticipation of his touch. A touch that would never come again. She groaned with frustration.

Tucking her close to him so that Raven could feel his burgeoning hardness, Beckett skimmed his hands along her sides, his thumbs just barely grazing the edges of her breasts.

She couldn't take much more of this. Smothering a moan, Raven gripped Beckett's shirt and pulled his lips down to hers. His mouth molded to hers, his tongue slipping inside to tease, then quickly withdrawing.

Raven rubbed her pelvis against his erection, wanting to feel him inside her again, to feel the smoothness of his skin against hers. "Beckett . . ." His name sounded like a plea.

"Stay on Alba, Raven," he murmured against her lips. "Let me make love to you in comfort."

Stay on Alba? She briefly considered the idea as her

desire fought for control. "I . . . I can't," she said finally. "I don't belong there."

He kissed her with more force, running his hands along her sides again, this time allowing his thumbs to pass over her pebbled nipples.

Raven wanted to rip open her suit and make love right there, but Ciorstan's voice brought her back to reality.

"We're coming out of hyperspeed now." She turned in the chair to look at them. "Are you two all right?"

Beckett didn't release his hold on Raven. "Aye." He spoke through clenched teeth in an obvious effort to control his breathing.

Rolling her eyes, the girl faced forward again.

"Stay for just a while," he said quietly. "Let me show you my planet."

Tempting. Almost as tempting as Beckett. Raven started to disagree, then stopped. She enjoyed visiting new planets and her need for Beckett threatened to overwhelm her. Why not stay . . . for a while?

As she studied his rugged features, a small voice of reason worked its way into her mind. In the midst of making love to Beckett she could very well agree to stay with him forever. Give up her ship? Give up the ability to soar among the stars? Never.

Placing her palms against his chest, she pushed away. "No. I can't." When he reached for her, she stepped back, eyeing him suspiciously. "Has this all been a ploy to make me want you so much I'll agree to anything?"

He grinned, the warmth of his gaze a caress. "Aye. Is it working?"

She couldn't stop her answering smile. "Almost." A wave of sadness washed over her. "Beckett, we don't belong together. I can't give up my life in space and you won't give up your traditions."

"You haven't even seen Alba. How do you know you wouldn't like it?"

"You won't even allow waterseekers, the most basic of technology; that's how I know."

"Warning. Warning. Fuel level is dangerously low."

At Mac's voice, Raven looked around in alarm.

"There's a light flashing here, Raven," Ciorstan said. " 'Tis a fuel warning, but the gauge shows nearly full."

"Verify we're on course to Alba and stop engines." Raven made her way forward even as she spoke. At least they'd made it out of hyperspeed already.

Ciorstan hurried to comply. "I think the course setting is right. Engines off . . . now."

A tiny tremor ran through the ship as the engines stopped, and Raven gripped the back of her chair to maintain her balance. She motioned to the other seat with her head. "Scoot over."

As Ciorstan moved, Raven slid into her chair and examined the control panel. What was going on? She had plenty of fuel. Magnicite recycled itself during its production of energy.

Unless someone had damaged her fuel cell.

Slade!

The fuel gauge still showed full. Frowning, Raven managed to work it from the panel and glanced at the bottom. Disconnected. "Fardpissle."

"What is it?" Beckett stood behind them, his hands holding the back of the chairs.

"I think Slade did something to my fuel cell. The gauge was disconnected so it still showed full, but I'm willing to bet I haven't been recycling since we hit hyperspeed."

"But you said you only needed a little bit of magnicite to go for a long time," Ciorstan said, a frown creasing her forehead.

"That's true, but if my magnicite has been leaking out of the ship instead of recycling, then I'm most likely down to nothing by this point."

The girl paused. "Dinna you say there is a backup cell? Can you transfer what's left into there?"

"I can try." Raven quickly went through the procedures for the transfer and studied the auxiliary gauge as it rose slowly, then stopped. "That's all?"

Ciorstan leaned forward to look and her eyes grew big. " 'Tis bad, Raven."

"I know." Raven stared at the panel, her heart rising in her throat. If she hadn't had the new hyperspeed drive, they would've run out of fuel in the middle of their journey here—light years from any well-traveled space lane. Then it would've been just a matter of which ran out first . . . the oxygen or the food. No doubt that had been Slade's intention. As it was, she only had enough left for a couple of short bursts of her thrusters.

"Can we get to Alba?" Beckett asked.

Raven glanced at the blue and green planet rapidly swelling to fill the window. "If I can coast in almost to the atmosphere, we might be able to land. But it'll be rough."

Placing his hand on her shoulder, Beckett gave Raven a tight smile. "You can do it. After all, you've landed without thrusters."

"More or less."

"How can you land without thrusters? Dinna you have to use forward thrusters to stop?" Ciorstan asked in surprise.

Beckett looked at his daughter with a frown, and Raven felt a sudden chill of trepidation. "How you do know so much about flying a spaceship, lass?" he asked.

"I . . . ah . . . I . . ." Ciorstan looked at Raven, her gaze pleading for help.

"I taught her," Raven said calmly, but inwardly she winced, waiting for the explosion.

"And why did you do that?" Beckett's voice still sounded even, but his hand tightened painfully on Raven's shoulder.

"Because she wanted to learn."

" 'Tis nae reason to learn." He stalked across the small interior. "We need naught of this technology on Alba."

"But Da—"

"Then you're a fool," Raven replied. She'd had enough of his ravings against her way of life. Pushing out of her chair, she went to face him. "Your planet is not going to survive without adapting to some technology."

" 'Tis nae our ancestors' wish."

"Your ancestors aren't here. You are. I'm not saying

191

you have to build a fleet of spaceships, but when you refuse something as basic as a waterseeker . . . something that can help, then you're sentencing your planet to an early death."

"We've survived this long." Beckett's dark gaze bored holes through Raven, but she only tilted her chin defiantly.

"And you won't survive much longer." She wrapped her fingers into fists. "Is that what you want? If not for Ciorstan, would you have allowed the merchant ships to stop?"

"Da. Raven." Ciorstan ran over and put a restraining hand on each of them.

Raven pressed a finger into Beckett's chest. "This is exactly why I can't stay with you. You're the most stubborn, backward human I've ever met. You won't give—even a little."

"I won't give?" His face flushed red. "I don't see you bending either. You say it has to be your way or naught at all. My people like their lifestyle."

"Of course," Raven said mockingly. "Who doesn't enjoy starving to death?"

Beckett gripped Raven's arms, nearly lifting her off her feet, but she refused to back down, aiming her glare at him.

"Da. Raven. Stop it." Ciorstan tugged on their clothing with no results. She raised her voice. "Stop it!" Lashing out, she kicked them each in the leg.

Raven looked at the girl in surprise as Beckett released his hold.

"Stop it," Ciorstan repeated. "Da, I asked Raven to teach me and she agreed. I dinna know how to build a ship, but if something happened to Raven, I might be able to get us home. At least one of us should know that, y'ken?"

All the anger seemed to leave Beckett's body. His shoulders fell as he faced his daughter. "Your reasons are sound, lass, but you dinna ask me for permission."

"Because you—"

He held up a finger to stop her. " 'Tis twice now you've

gone off on your own. I'm your father and you're but nine, lass. I willna have any more of this."

"Aye." Ciorstan's chin dropped to her chest so that the word sounded muffled.

He lifted her chin. "Y'ken, lass?"

"I ken." She started to turn away, then stopped to look at them. "You're both right, but you're also both wrong." She whirled around, then stiffened abruptly. "Raven?"

Jerking around, Raven saw they'd nearly reached the outer atmosphere. With a muttered oath, she leapt into her chair and aligned the thrusters. She'd only have one chance to get this right.

As Beckett took his chair, she prepared to fire the thrusters. He pointed to a hilly region some distance from one of the major seas. "Dunvegan is there."

"I'll do the best I can." Raven tried to steady her rapid breathing. "At this point I'm more concerned with landing in one piece than where I land. Hold on."

The thrusters roared and they entered the atmosphere.

Chapter Thirteen

Beckett gripped the edges of his chair as the ship plowed through thick clouds. Catching a glimpse of blue water below, his muscles tensed. The oceans on Alba were vast. If they crashed in one of them, they'd receive no help.

The ship passed through the clouds as the water gave way to land. Somehow they were skimming across the surface as they landed. He studied Raven's tense face. Apparently she knew what she was doing.

He glanced over his shoulder at Ciorstan. Though her eyes were wide and her face pale, she gave him a half-hearted smile. He returned it, his chest tightening. After all they'd been through, they had to reach Dunvegan safely.

The land changed to rolling hills and thick forests as the ship descended even lower. Despite their rapid speed, Beckett doubted they'd reach his village before they touched the ground.

They passed over large lakes filled with clear water. Envious, Beckett tried to think of some way to carry that water back to his people.

The rolling hills became larger now, the slopes straighter, the peaks taller as the trees faded to brown shells. Water signs became practically nonexistent. Beckett stared at a small pond in the distance with desolation, then straightened as he recognized the surrounding territory.

"There's Dunvegan," he said, pointing to his castle at the edge of a deep indention. That indentation had once been a thriving lake. Now it was nothing more than a brackish puddle.

"Where can I land?"

The urgency in her voice touched him. Scanning the area, he indicated the empty fields beyond the castle. "There. Nothing's growing now."

"Hang on." Raven fired her thrusters once more and the ship angled toward the ground.

The land came to meet them quickly . . . too quickly. Beckett swallowed, unable to breathe. Before they touched ground, Raven ignited her forward thrusters and the ship slowed.

They hit the ground with a sharp thud, the craft skidding across the field. Abruptly the forward engines quit and Raven swiftly grabbed the braking lever.

The ship bounced along, dirt showering the window, blocking their view. They stopped with a suddenness that jerked Beckett forward, then back. As silence filled the craft, he hurriedly unfastened his straps and ran back to Ciorstan.

She'd already loosened her bindings and wrapped her arms around his neck in a tight hug. Beckett held her as he approached the hatch and tried to open it. As he glanced back, he noticed Raven still sat in her chair before the console.

"Raven, we need to get out of here. The ship could explode."

She stood and faced him with a bleakness in her eyes that tugged at him. "It won't explode. You need fuel for that." Her lips tightened. "Mac, open hatch."

The door slid open and Beckett inhaled deeply.

195

Home. The last smells of winter lingered in the brisk wind and crisp air. He stepped into the doorway and paused. Empty fields and brown trees stretched as far as he could see. He sighed. Home.

A jangling noise caught his attention and he looked around to see Raven fastening her gun belt. "You dinna need that," he said sharply.

She continued in her motions. "I didn't spend the entire trip fixing it to leave it behind."

" 'Tis unnecessary on Alba." His people would be frightened to see her with a weapon.

"Where I go, it goes." She joined him at the opening. "You carry a sword. What's the difference?"

" 'Tis nae . . . women dinna . . ."

Her eyes grew cold and she pushed past him. Jumping to the ground, she surveyed the area. "It's pretty barren, isn't it?"

" 'Tis winter," Ciorstan said as she jumped down. " 'Twill be spring soon though. 'Tis beautiful then, with flowers and grass and trees all blooming." She hesitated. "If we get rain."

" 'Twill rain." Beckett had to believe that.

"Are those your people?" Raven pointed to a crowd approaching across the vast fields.

"Aye." His heart swelled. His people. His home. He'd never leave again.

"They don't look very happy to see you." Raven stepped closer to Beckett, and he smiled at her unspoken nervousness.

"That's only because they dinna know it's me." He waved at the gathering, calling out names as he recognized the individuals. "Hamish. Duncan. 'Tis me—Beckett."

"MacLeod. 'Tis the MacLeod."

"Aye, and he has Ciorstan."

The voices rose and blended together as everyone talked at once. The men surrounded Beckett, each shaking his hand heartily, while the women drew Ciorstan into warm hugs. "We thought we might never see you again," Hamish said.

" 'Tis time you returned," William added.

"And *who* is that?" Duncan looked past Beckett at Raven. As one the men turned their gazes on her. The hungry expression on many faces caused Beckett to shift uncomfortably.

If only he had a blanket he could throw around Raven. That damned suit of hers revealed every curve, and he preferred to keep those curves for himself. Perhaps one of Shauna's gowns would fit her.

" 'Tis Raven." He motioned her closer. "She's the tracker who helped me find Ciorstan."

"She's an alien?" Duncan asked incredulously.

"I'm as human as you are," she retorted.

"You're from Earth?"

"No. Most humans don't live on Earth anymore."

Hamish pushed his way forward. "Are you planning to stay long?" he asked, his expression openly suspicious.

Raven cast a forlorn look at her ship, then shook her head. "My ship's out of fuel. I'll only stay until the next merchant ship arrives." She met Beckett's gaze, her own defiant.

" 'Tis two weeks away." Duncan pushed closer, his gaze dropping constantly to the thrust of Raven's breasts. "Where will you be staying?"

Beckett dropped his arm around Raven's shoulders. Duncan's lust bothered him more than Hamish's antagonism. "She'll stay at Dunvegan as my guest. I ask that you treat her as such."

Duncan apparently realized he was treading on forbidden territory for he backed away quickly. "Aye, Beckett. Of course."

"Now if you'll excuse us, we've been traveling a long time and I'm anxious to get home." Already the sun hovered around the mountain peaks. " 'Twill be dark soon." Beckett extended his hand for Ciorstan. "Ciorstan?" She left the women to take it.

The crowd parted and they walked through it undisturbed, though Beckett saw many gazes lingering on Raven. She obviously felt it, too, for she held herself stiff beneath Beckett's arm and hadn't yet shrugged him off.

"I feel like dinner," she muttered when they'd walked some distance. "You're not cannibals, are you?"

Beckett bit back a grin. "Nae. However, most women here dinna give the men so much to see."

They'd grown closer to the village and he indicated some of the women watching from a distance. "See, there."

Raven studied them, her expression bland. Only the twist of her lips revealed her distaste. "I wouldn't survive a minute in my line of work if I wore cumbersome garments like those."

"Perhaps." Beckett preferred her out of her line of work and, even better, out of her clothes entirely. He smiled broadly. Tonight . . . tonight she'd join him in his large hand-carved bed and he'd educate her further on the pleasures of passion.

Spotting his castle on the horizon, he enjoyed the warmth that flooded him. "There's Dunvegan."

Raven stopped abruptly, staring. "That's your home?"

"Aye."

"It's huge. It's . . . it's a castle."

He grinned. "Aye. 'Tis that."

Shauna met them at the door as he'd known she would. Throwing her arms around his neck, she hugged him enthusiastically. "Beckett, I've been constantly afraid for you."

In the next instant she was smothering Ciorstan with affection. "Lass, I have a gray hair because of you."

Raven had become very still, her face carefully masked. Jealous? Beckett could hope. Drawing her forward, he stood behind her, his hands on her shoulders as he introduced her.

"Shauna, this is Raven. She's the tracker who helped find Ciorstan."

The ever-impulsive Shauna immediately hugged Raven, who jumped and stiffened. "I canna thank you enough for finding that errant child. Och, she needs a mother, that one." Shauna aimed a telling gaze at Beckett, but he only raised his eyebrows in reply. She'd been trying to get him remarried ever since Nessa's death.

"Raven, this bundle of energy is my sister, Shauna MacInnes."

Raven glanced at him, her mouth falling open. "Your sister?"

"Aye. What did you think?" He grinned and squeezed her shoulders, sensing some of the tension leaving her body. "She lives here with her husband and children."

"Here you stand blathering while dinner boils over." Shauna urged them further inside. "Cook has prepared a soup." Her smile faltered for a moment. " 'Tis not much, but 'twill fill your bellies. Come along now."

Beckett enjoyed watching the amazement play over Raven's face as he led her through the vast halls of the castle. Perhaps now she knew a little of how he'd felt in her world.

A tantalizing aroma drifted from the hall and Beckett's stomach rumbled in reply. He'd not had anything but those tasteless food sticks for days.

Obviously Raven caught the scent, too, for she turned toward him with a questioning look.

"You'll like this, lass," he said as he pushed open the doors. A large table spanned the entire length of the great hall, but only the front portion was set for dinner.

Guiding Raven inside, he held out a chair and seated her. She touched everything—the plate, the bowl, the silverware, the crystal goblet, her eyes wide with awe. When Ciorstan giggled Raven suddenly dropped her hands to her lap.

Rory entered the room and Shauna greeted him with a kiss, then performed introductions. Even Rory, a man who Beckett knew adored his wife, stared at Raven. Beckett definitely had to find other clothes for her.

When a servant poured wine into her glass and another spooned soup into her bowl Raven sat upright. Catching her gaze on him, Beckett made a big flourish as he lifted his spoon and ate the soup. Potatoes, carrots and a tiny bit of meat swam in the too thin base, but it warmed his insides and tasted delicious.

Raven devoured her soup in moments. "This is wonderful," she exclaimed, her eyes shining. "I've never had anything like it."

"I only wish we had more," Shauna said softly. With hope in her gaze, she reached across the table to touch Beckett's hand. "And what of the fabled sword? Did you find it?"

The food lost its appeal. "Aye," Beckett muttered.

"I found it," Ciorstan added. "But 'twas stolen from us."

"Stolen?" Rory looked startled. "It truly exists and you dinna retrieve it?"

" 'Twas more important for me to return to Alba than traipse across the galaxy for a sword," Beckett said sharply.

"But if it had magic . . ." Shauna's expression revealed her disappointment.

" 'Twas nae magic. 'Twas only a sword." Beckett pushed back his chair, anxious to escape. "If you're finished, Raven, I'll show you where you can sleep."

She jumped to her feet. "I'm finished." She gave Shauna a dazzling smile. "Thank you very much."

As Beckett led her up the central staircase, she tripped, her gaze elsewhere. He caught her elbow and held her close to his side. "This place is immense," she exclaimed. "I don't know what to look at first."

"You'll have time." He reached the door of Nessa's old room and pushed it open. Servants had kept the chamber clean with its wide canopied bed and ornate decorations. Nessa had liked pink, so many of the tapestries adorning the walls contained that color.

Raven didn't seem to mind. She stood in the middle of the room, turning first one way, then the other. "All this?" she gasped. "For me?"

"Aye." Beckett crossed to the opposite door and opened it. "This leads to my room." Noticing his large bed, he recalled his fantasy of Raven naked upon it and his loins burned with sudden fire.

She came to stand behind him and peered inside. "Your room," she repeated quietly.

Beckett crushed her to him, seizing her lips with a fierce passion. "I canna wait any longer," he said finally. "I need you, Raven."

Her lips moved beneath his as he kissed her again, branding her his. His shaft swelled with desire and he pressed it against her feminine mound. To his surprise, she twisted her head away as her hands pushed ineffectively at his chest.

"Let me go," she ordered.

"Raven?"

"I won't make love to you, Beckett. I told you that already."

Hot need swirled within him. He could barely focus on her words. "But that was before . . ."

"I'm stranded here, but that doesn't change my position. I will leave when the merchants come. It's better if we call it quits now."

No. She couldn't be serious. He'd thought of nothing but this moment since they left Saladan. He dropped his arms. "Raven . . ."

Anguish quickly passed over her face as she stepped away from him. "I'm sorry, Beckett."

She still wanted him. He knew it. Then why . . . ? He stared at her intently until she turned her face away. "Please go," she whispered.

He'd broken her resistance once. He could do it again. She belonged with him. Without another word, Beckett stepped into his room and closed the door.

She had to do it.

Unable to sleep, Raven rolled onto her back in the too large bed and stared at the cloth covering overhead. When Beckett made love to her, her brain went on vacation. And without the ability to think she might agree to something she didn't really want to agree to.

She only had to make it for two weeks. With a groan, Raven threw her arm over her eyes. Two weeks? Already her body yearned for Beckett's touch, a steamy pool of desire lingering in her lower abdomen.

Rolling onto her side, Raven watched the closed door

between their rooms. If she were to go to him, he wouldn't turn her away. No. She had to remain strong. If she slept with him, she'd only find it harder to leave . . . and she had to leave.

But for a moment she had trouble remembering why.

Exhaustion finally claimed her, for the next thing she knew sunlight poured in through the tall, narrow windows cut into the wall. Sitting up, she searched the room for entry to a lav. All she could see were two doors—one to the hallway, the other to Beckett's room.

It had to be here somewhere. This chamber was larger than *TrackStar*'s interior. Raven climbed into her jumpsuit, but sealed it only to the waist. Her need for a lav was becoming urgent.

She went to the adjoining door and rapped on it sharply. She heard something suspiciously like a splash; then Beckett opened the door and poked his head through. "Can I do something for you?" he asked. Water dripped from his wet hair in rivulets down his face.

Swallowing, Raven fought back the urge to kiss them away. "I . . . ah . . . where's the lav?"

"Things are different here, Raven." He gave her a sheepish look and pointed across the room. "See that screen over there? Behind it you'll find a pot in a chair. That's your lav."

"You're not serious?" A pot in a chair?

"Aye, I'm serious."

Dubious, Raven headed for the screen, then paused. "Is there a mister available, too?"

"No, but I just finished my bath, such as it is. The bulk of our water is used for survival, but that which canna be drunk is used for bathing before 'tis given to the crops. We share to conserve water, but 'tis still fairly clean. Do you want me to bring it over?"

A bath? "Yes, please." Raven ducked behind the screen and found the chair as Beckett described it. Grimacing, she removed her suit and made quick use of the pot. "Barbarians," she muttered.

She heard the sound of water splashing as Beckett

pushed something into her room. "Here's your bath," he called.

"Thank you." Leaving her suit off, she left the screen, then froze in disbelief.

Her first image was of an odd-shaped tub partially filled with cloudy water. A bath? But her gaze didn't stay there long. Not far from the tub stood Beckett . . . gloriously naked.

The beams of sunlight highlighted the sculpted planes of his torso, the solid muscles of his hips and legs, and his erection, jutting proudly from his loins.

Instant longing sprang to life in Raven's belly as her nipples tightened. He was magnificent.

Finally raising her gaze to his face, she saw his undisguised desire, which only further heightened the craving inside her. Clearing her suddenly dry throat, she forced herself to speak. "Ah . . . shouldn't you be wearing something?"

"For what I have in mind I shouldna need any." He moved closer and she held out her hands to hold him back.

"Please go." She choked the words out.

"You dinna mean that." His husky voice wrapped around her like a caress.

"I do." With an effort she turned her back to him. "Please go."

"Very well."

Raven didn't move until she heard the door close; then slowly she made her way to the tub. She'd never seen this method of cleaning before but would try it. After removing her underwear she climbed into the semi-warm water, enjoying the silky feel as it cooled her flushed skin. Different, but not altogether unpleasant.

She'd almost completed her washing when the connecting door opened again and she paused, the cloth in her hand. Beckett came in, some clothing over his arm. At least he'd put on his pants, though their tight fit only accented his flat behind.

"What do you want?" she demanded, sinking low in the tub.

He placed the clothing on the bed. "Here are some new clothes for you. They belong to Shauna, but I think they'll fit."

"I'll wear my own suit, thank you," she replied coldly.

"I dinna think so." As Beckett talked, he picked up her T-shirt, jumpsuit, and laser and started from the room.

Alarmed, Raven stood up. "Put those back! I won't wear those bulky clothes."

Beckett glanced at her, his body tightening as his gaze lingered on her exposed breasts. "You'll wear these clothes or naught at all." He smiled. "I prefer naught."

He closed the door after him, and Raven sank back into the tub and beat her fists against the water. Who did he think he was? He couldn't force her to wear that clothing.

Maybe he could. After trying to open the connecting door she discovered it was locked and kicked it futilely. With a sigh she went to examine the articles on her bed. She had to wear something. Remembering the hungry stares from some of the men yesterday, Raven picked up a plain white shirt with puffy sleeves. Maybe she would do better to dress like one of them.

She pulled on the shirt and discovered that though she was somewhat taller than Beckett's sister, Shauna's chest was obviously larger, for the sleeves slid off her shoulders and the front dipped low, revealing the beginning swells of Raven's breasts. This was better?

Resigned to wearing something until she could locate her jumpsuit, Raven fastened the plaid skirt around her waist. It fell a hand's width above her knees, leaving the rest of her legs bare. Since it was loose around her waist, she had no trouble slipping the shirt inside.

The last piece confused Raven until she determined that it went over her head and the shirt. The soft blue material surrounded her torso. As she tightened the front lacing, the item molded to her waist, with the top of it cupping just beneath her breasts, thrusting them to prominence in the low-cut shirt.

As Raven went to pull on her boots that thankfully

Beckett had left, she wondered how this outfit would make her fit in better. She felt more revealed in this than in her jumpsuit.

Cool air swished against her legs as she made her way to the front staircase and the skirt flared around her hips, moving slightly with every step she took. Beckett waited for her at the bottom of the stairs and his eyes darkened when he saw her.

He extended his hand to her, but she brushed past him. "You'll pay for this, Beckett," she murmured.

"I thought it would help," he said, huskily. "But it dinna. I only want you more."

"Forget it." Raven kept her tone cold, but she didn't dare turn to look at him. "The only reason I'm here is because I need fuel for my ship. Do you understand?"

"I ken."

The sadness in his voice tore at Raven and she closed her eyes for a brief moment. "Where do I go now?" she asked with an effort.

"Breakfast is served in the hall where we ate last night. 'Tis only bread but should be sufficient." As he spoke, Beckett steered her through the hallways. "After that I thought I'd show you the village. If you're interested, of course."

What else was there for her to do? "I'd like that, thank you."

Though the bread looked strange, Raven found it every bit as delicious as the soup from the previous evening. No wonder Beckett had complained about her food sticks. They'd never taste the same to her after these meals.

However, she blamed the bread for her suddenly queasy stomach when Beckett led her outside. It couldn't be nerves. She'd faced Gatorians in battle and her stomach had never bothered her. It had to be the bread.

Beckett paused on the gentle slope leading down to the village and indicated the indentation in the ground beside the castle. It stretched from the castle to the distant fields, with a small puddle of brown water in the center and dried, broken dirt elsewhere. "This used to be our loch."

Hearing his despair, Raven gently touched his arm. "It will rain again. It has to."

He gave her a half-smile that never reached his eyes and resumed his descent. Raven cast one last look at the desolate loch. If this had supplied all their water, Beckett's village was in serious trouble.

"Do you have any wells?" she asked, running to catch up with him.

"A few, but most of them have run dry. This entire area hasna had but a few drops of moisture in the past two years."

"Have you considered moving?"

Beckett's glare brought her to a sudden stop and she lifted her chin. "It's a reasonable question," she added.

He sighed. "Aye. At first we thought the drought would end quickly. Each day we believed the rain would come. But it hasna. Before I left in search of Ciorstan we discussed relocating our village. 'Twould be a tremendous hardship on everyone. But we agreed if we dinna get spring rains, we'll be forced to move."

"You could use waterseekers."

"Nae."

"Beckett, they're nothing more than—"

"Nae. I dinna want to hear of it again."

"Fine. Be a Neeban. Destroy yourself." Raven turned her attention to the village ahead.

The buildings looked uniform in design, with stone walls and thatched roofs, most of them not any bigger than the room she had slept in last night. "People live in these?" she asked in amazement.

Beckett didn't meet her gaze. "Aye. Many of them have larger estates farther out on MacLeod lands, but with the drought they've all come together here in an attempt to survive."

A cacophony of sounds greeted Raven as they reached the main street—babies crying, children playing, men shouting, a strange whistling noise and an equally strange moaning. Villagers greeted Beckett warmly, their gazes curious when they fell on Raven.

He answered each of them by name, inquiring about that one's health or another's children. And he listened as if their replies mattered to him. He cared about these people. Then why didn't he accept the use of some minor technology to help them?

"MacLeod, MacLeod, I'd like to speak with you." A man approached them, his expression glowering. As he walked, he limped badly, using a carved stick to assist him. Raven recognized him from their brief meeting yesterday. He appeared quite a bit older than Beckett, with thinning gray hair that hung in limp strands to his shoulders and many lines creasing his weather-beaten face.

Beckett's smile flickered, but he had it firmly in place when he moved to greet the man. "Hamish, what is it?"

The man rested on his stick and pointed a shaky finger at Raven. "Dressing that one in our clothes isna going to change what she is. Her kind dinna belong here."

Startled, Raven looked at him in disbelief. "I have no intention of staying here. I'll leave with the next merchant ship."

"And until then she's my guest," Beckett added coldly. "Is that all you cared to discuss?" He put his hand against Raven's back, pushing her gently into movement again.

"Nae." Hamish blocked their path. "The food is nae likely to last until the next ship arrives and what with the sheep dropping left and right, 'tis unlikely we'll have many plaids to trade."

"I'll look into it."

"And the water is nearly gone. How do you plan for us to survive?"

"It'll rain soon." Beckett sounded as if he was trying to convince himself as well as Hamish.

Hamish snorted. "Ha. Been saying that for two years."

He hobbled away, and despair darkened Beckett's eyes. Impulsively, Raven laid her hand on his chest. "It will work out."

207

"It has to." He gave her a pale imitation of his regular smile. "The animals are over here."

"Animals? Is that what's making that strange moaning?"

"Moaning?"

"Yes." She waited until she heard it again. "There. That."

He glanced at her with a genuine grin. "That's a cow mooing."

Raven shrugged and headed for the noise. "How am I supposed to know? I've never heard a cow before."

"I imagine this will all be new to you. These are Earth creatures, not Salurians or sand monsters."

Several large structures stood just outside the village limits, many of them hemmed by fences. Raven recognized the listless creatures in the pens as cows, sheep and horses, with an occasional chicken scattered between. After all, she had seen holos of them. Each type had a distinctive call and she quickly matched the unusual sounds to the correct beast.

As they drew closer, she wrinkled her nose at the horrible smell. "Is that scent normal?"

"For a farm." Beckett leaned on a fence post and surveyed the animals. "They're dwindling fast. 'Tis almost the birthing season. Without more water, the newborns will never survive."

Though the pens were full, Raven made a quick estimate of their numbers. "Is this all you have for the entire village?"

"At one time they filled the pastures." He sighed. "And they will again. I have to believe that."

Raven remained silent. She couldn't promise him rain without access to the technology he hated.

"The fields are over here." His expression drawn, Beckett led her away.

Two men met them as they reached the vast areas of shriveled soil. One crushed the dirt in his hand and let it trickle through his fingers. "The frost is out of the ground now," he said. "We should be planting soon."

"Will it do any good?" the other asked. "We lost most of our crop last year."

"We plant," Beckett said firmly. "It'll rain."

The two men scanned the clear blue sky, their doubt obvious.

Raven could feel his desperation. Their survival came down to water. Without it, they'd all die. "Beckett, you have to let—"

Shouts cut her off and they whirled around to see a small group of men making their way across the brown fields, carrying something . . . someone.

Beckett ran toward them immediately. "What is it?" He glanced down. "My God."

Close on his heels, Raven followed his gaze and inhaled sharply. The group carried a man—at least she thought it was a man. He was badly mangled, covered with blood, flesh hanging from his arm.

"Is he alive?" Beckett asked.

"Barely. Sean has run ahead for the doctor."

"What happened?"

"We think he had a run in with Old Bess just past the fields. There were tracks all around him."

"Old Bess?" Raven glanced up at Beckett.

" 'Tis a mountain lion."

"A mountain lion? Here? Why would your ancestors bring something so dangerous with them?"

"They dinna. This creature is native to Alba, but since it closely resembles an Earth mountain lion, our ancestors gave it the name they were familiar with." He turned his attention back to the men. "Old Bess usually stays in the hills. Are you sure?"

"If we dinna have food and water, it stands to reason she dinna either. She's come close."

"Aye." Beckett frowned. "We'll have to keep the children in town. But, for now, let me help. He needs a doctor immediately."

Raven stiffened and glanced toward her ship. Surely Beckett couldn't turn down her assistance in this case. "Beckett, I'll be right back."

He caught her arm before she could turn. "Where are you going?"

"To get my portable medtech. It'll save him."

"Nae." Beckett released her arm and bent to help the injured man.

"He'll die, Beckett. I can help."

"Nae." He didn't look at her. "I'll have naught of your technology here."

Raven dropped her jaw in disbelief. He would let a man die rather than accept her modern help? "You're not the man I thought you were, Beckett MacLeod."

Without another word, she pivoted and ran toward the castle.

Chapter Fourteen

Raven stormed into the castle, her chest heaving with her outrage. How could a man be so unbelievably blind and stubborn? Why did he persist in seeing mechanical aids as tools of disaster?

Pausing in the front foyer, she looked from one hallway to another. Beckett had always guided her through this massive place. She didn't know what was where.

It didn't matter. Choosing a hallway, she hurried down it. She'd learned the maze of corridors in the privateer fortress—she could learn her way here too.

She found the ballroom empty and continued until she heard voices. High-pitched giggles brought an involuntary smile to her face. She paused before an open door and examined the interior. Large windows admitted the brilliant sunshine, flooding the room with light, glistening off the gold trim along the ceiling and the massive crystal chandelier hanging in the center. Several small couches and chairs lined the walls, separated by an occasional ornate table, but all the people sat on the floor.

Shauna looked up and beckoned at Raven to enter. Slowly, her gaze on the other occupants, Raven stepped inside. "Are those your children?" she asked, then groaned inwardly at the tenseness in her voice.

Beckett's sister didn't seem to notice. She hugged the larger of the two children, then released him to pursue his dizzying dance around the room. "That bundle of mischief is my son, Cullan. He's three." A silly smile crossed her face as the smaller one crawled across the floor toward her. With a laugh, she scooped him up and planted a kiss on his nose. "And this is Niall. He's eight months old."

Raven shifted uncomfortably, trying to swallow her unease. There was no doubt the two boys were brothers. They both possessed Rory's dark red hair and Shauna's lively green eyes. "They're good-looking boys," Raven said finally.

"They're tiring, is what they are." Shauna set the squirming Niall back on the floor and climbed to her feet. "But I enjoy them so much." She glanced at Raven. "Where's Beckett?"

"He stayed in town. A man was injured by a . . . a lion."

"Old Bess?" Shauna's eyes widened. "Dear Lord. Do you know who it was?"

Raven shook her head. "Why is Beckett so adamant against accepting help, Shauna? I can help this injured man and he won't let me."

"I suspect 'tis due to the histories."

"The what?"

"The histories. They're kept in the family library. They detail life on Earth when our ancestors left and what they hoped to obtain here. As chieftain of Clan MacLeod, Beckett is responsible for following their path."

"Even if it's wrong?"

Shauna met Raven's gaze, her own somber. "Wrong for whom, Raven? Wrong for you, perhaps, but nae for Alba."

Surprised by Shauna's defense, Raven hesitated.

Maybe she was wrong. "I don't understand."

"Ask Ciorstan to show you the library. The histories are nae secret. Read them for yourself. Perhaps then you'll understand." Shauna raced forward to grab her son from where he balanced precariously on the back of a chair. "No, Cullan."

Niall attempted to follow his mother, skittering on his hands and knees after her. He climbed up a table leg until he could snare the edge and pulled himself up to a standing position. Immediately the table teetered.

Reacting without forethought, Raven snatched the boy into her arms before the table toppled over. He felt warm and soft, with a distinct odor that touched something soft inside her. They stared at each other, each wary.

"Thank you, Raven."

At Shauna's voice, Niall turned to see her and broke into a lusty squall. Raven quickly deposited him in his mother's arms and backed toward the door.

"Where is Ciorstan?" she asked, anxious to get away from there.

Shauna smiled wryly. "You'll find her polishing silver near the kitchen."

"Polishing silver?"

" 'Tis punishment for her latest escapade."

"I see. Which way do I go?" Once pointed in the right direction, Raven hurried down the wide hallway, the baby's cries still echoing in her ears.

It was definitely going to be a long two weeks.

She found Ciorstan seated before a long table spread with an assortment of shiny objects. The girl held one tall slender object with a wide base in her hand and rubbed a cloth against it with the other. Scanning the table, Raven could tell which articles had been polished by their gleaming beauty. Ciorstan had over half the table length to go.

The girl sighed heavily as she set down her current item and lifted another. Raven twisted her lips in a dry smile. She remembered similar punishments issued by her mother when she'd gone off without permission.

"Do you need any help?" She surprised herself by actually saying the words.

Ciorstan jumped, then gave Raven a sheepish smile. " 'Tis *my* punishment," she said. "Da said I should think while I polish about the folly of what I did."

"It was very dangerous." Raven slid into a chair beside her and located another cloth. Without looking at Ciorstan, she lifted a wide bowl from the table and started rubbing it. "You could've easily been killed . . . or worse."

"Aye. Da told me what you went through to find me." Her eyes watered, but she didn't cry. "I dinna mean to cause trouble for anyone. I only wanted to help."

"I understand," Raven murmured. "You thought the Sword of MacLeod would save your people."

"And it would . . . if we had it." Her voice fell and she rubbed her goblet fiercely.

Should they have continued to track the sword? It would've meant facing Slade again, and Raven couldn't think of anything she wanted to do less. But after seeing how serious the drought was on Alba, she reconsidered. She didn't believe in magic any more than Beckett did, but what if the sword did have powers? It might've been one aid Beckett wouldn't have refused.

"Ciorstan, can you show me where the histories are kept? Shauna said it might help me understand why Beckett acts the way he does."

"You mean, why he refuses to believe anything good can come from anywhere but Alba?" Ciorstan stood and stretched. "Though you're nae from here and he likes you." She smiled. "I like you too. Come on. This way."

Raven didn't answer. She couldn't. Her throat had closed at the unexpected praise. Somewhere in teaching Ciorstan to fly the *TrackStar*, Raven had reached the point where she forgot Ciorstan was a child. The girl's current statement brought back that realization full force. The child liked her . . . and, surprisingly, that mattered.

When Ciorstan swung open the door to a large room Raven gasped. Aside from a floor-to-ceiling window and a massive fireplace, the walls were filled with shelves of books. Real books—not computer or audio versions, but open-up-and-turn-the-pages type of books.

As if caught in a spell, Raven went to touch the outer bindings. "These must be ancient," she murmured.

"Aye. Most of them came with our ancestors." Ciorstan moved to a glass case containing several thick volumes. "The histories are in here."

"Thank you." Taking the utmost care, Raven lifted the lid and removed the first book. The rough binding rubbed her palm as the pages fluttered loosely, whispering with hints of mystery. She placed the book on a small table and pulled a chair before it.

With reverence, she lifted the cover and began reading.

"I'll get back to my polishing now," Ciorstan said quietly.

Raven nodded, already ensnared by the faded text. Drawn into the plight of the Scot people, she suffered with them as the writer detailed the loss of their native Gaelic language, kept in use by only a few Highlanders. She had trouble breathing when she read of the polluted air that caused a myriad of diseases and killed without bias. When she learned that the poisons carelessly tossed into the ground produced equally poisonous crops, her stomach clenched.

Reading further, her heart pounded rapidly. Had murder really become that common on Earth? True, it existed now, but not with the casualness mentioned here . . . except for the privateers.

No wonder Beckett's ancestors had wanted to leave and start over. They didn't have much choice if they wanted to survive.

Their preparations and journey to the newly discovered planet of Alba filled a second volume. With surprise, Raven read that they had brought many mechanical tools with them, though the writer insisted over and over that the people intended to have no further contact with Earth once they left.

They left for the unknown and cut all their ties. She had to admire their courage as well as their foolishness. They had made nothing more than an initial survey of Alba when they'd left. What if it had turned volatile? Without maintaining some kind of contact, they could all have died.

Fortunately Alba had turned out to be very Earth-like despite its lower gravity, vast oceans, and native life forms, such as the drover, a cross between a rabbit and a beaver, which nearly destroyed the colonists' first crops. From the beginning the chieftain of Clan MacLeod had been the leader of the colonists. That first leader, Devlin MacLeod, had devised a way to keep the drovers from the crops and inadvertently discovered that the creatures made good eating as well.

The colonists thrived and prospered. In the beginning they were so intent on survival that clan rivalries fell aside and MacLeods, MacKinnons, Campbells and MacInnes all worked side by side. Even when the feuding returned, it never reached the bloody proportions of centuries past, usually involving a raid for livestock or crops. Land disputes were rare, since Alba had more than enough arable land for everyone.

Grudgingly, Raven had to admit that she admired these people. With nothing more than the most basic of tools, they'd forged new lives on an alien planet. But they had used the tools. She read references to water supplies divined by a waterseeker or fields tilled by a planter.

About ten years after the colonists reached Alba, all mention of mechanical tools disappeared. The people appeared to be suffering from an increase in deaths, so perhaps that took priority. Raven kept reading but found only one more mention of the mechanical aids when the writer proudly proclaimed the colonists as Albans, no more a part of Earth or having to do with any of its monstrosities. They had and would survive without the tools.

She looked up from the book and stared unseeingly out the window. What had happened ten years into colonization to bring about this reasoning? Nothing was detailed. And why did ten years ring a bell in her mind?

Of course; the power cells. The hand-sized cells that powered the tools only provided a ten-year life span. After that time they had to be replaced. Could the discontinuance of technology on Alba be as simple as the result of failing to bring fresh batteries?

Raven gave a short laugh. Beckett would never believe that. His ancestor wrote that they didn't need the tools; therefore, Beckett followed that creed even though it was a hundred and ninety years old.

Thoroughly hooked, Raven continued reading of the colonists' progress as they survived plagues, discontent, growing pains and clan feuds. As far as she could tell, there had never been a drought like the current one, and she wondered if this would be the disaster that destroyed the fierce Alban pride.

She didn't want to live here, but neither did she want to see these people destroyed. They'd worked hard for all that they had. It didn't seem fair for the lack of rain to negate all that.

"There you are. 'Tis almost time for supper."

Raven jerked her head up at Beckett's voice and spied him standing in the open doorway. Feeling as if she'd been trespassing, she closed the book and returned it to the glass case. "Shauna said it was all right. . . ."

" 'Tis fine. We have naught to hide here. I only ask that you handle the books carefully. They're very old." He came to meet her and she noticed the haggard lines drawn across his face.

"The man?" she asked quietly.

She thought at first that he wasn't going to answer; then, when he did, she had to strain to hear his words.

"He died."

Coldness flowed through Raven's veins. "I could've saved him."

" 'Tis nae our way."

He was suffering—she could see it in his eyes—yet he still clung to his traditions. Raven recalled what she'd just read, all overlaid with intense pride.

217

"I understand now why you act this way," she said with an effort. "And I'll try to do better in following your rules."

His expression lightened and he laid his hand on her bare shoulder, his touch kindling a fire deep inside. "Raven—"

She pulled away and forced herself to meet his gaze. "I said I understand, but I still don't necessarily agree. It's too barbaric for me."

Brushing past him, she hurried from the room before she broke down and gave him the hug he so desperately needed.

Beckett remained silent during the meal, yet Raven felt his gaze each time it lingered upon her. By the time they finished darkness had swallowed the daylight, and he insisted on escorting Raven to her room. He didn't speak until she opened her door.

"You know where I'll be if you need me." He turned to enter his room and Raven closed her door.

At first she could only pace, the visions created by her earlier reading filling her mind. Was she to be haunted forever by the history of these Albans?

When she finally decided to try sleeping she realized Beckett had taken her T-shirt along with her jumpsuit. She couldn't sleep in her present clothes. The coarse material scratched as it was. A quick search of the room turned up nothing more than another outfit similar to her current one.

"Shibit." Squaring her shoulders, Raven approached Beckett's door and rapped upon it.

"It's open."

She stepped inside and found Beckett standing before his open window, his back to her as he looked out into the night. He'd removed his shirt and Raven eyed the taut muscles in his back, remembering vividly how they felt beneath her palms.

Rolling her fingers into fists, she inhaled deeply. "I'd like you to return my clothing and laser."

"I'll return them when you leave." He didn't look around and she moved closer.

"You've taken my T-shirt. What am I supposed to sleep in?"

He turned at that, a slow grin crossing his face. "Sleep naked. I do."

Her skin warmed beneath his gaze. "Please, at least return my T-shirt."

"Nae."

The only time she'd ever slept naked had been with Beckett. To do so again would only ignite memories she wanted to stay buried. Drawing up straight, she whirled for her door. "Fine. Stay out of my room then."

"Dinna go."

He spoke quietly, but when she looked around he stood only an arm's length away, his eyes dark and his intent obvious. Her heart rate increased and her limbs felt suddenly shaky.

"Stay, Raven," he murmured.

"I . . . I can't."

"My blood boils for you." He gently gripped her shoulders and pulled her closer. "I need you."

Before she could reply he claimed her lips in a possessive kiss that proclaimed his desire even as it stirred hers. Despite her vow to resist him, Raven found herself softening, her body leaning into his hardness, her tongue mating with his.

As he kissed her, he lowered the sleeves along her arms, dropping the front of her shirt. When he lifted his head and stepped back she noticed that only the very tips of her breasts remained covered and that they tightened as a cool breeze played over her exposed flesh.

Beckett trailed kisses over her shoulders and down her chest even as he caressed her hidden nipples with his hand. Suddenly he tugged her shirt down to reveal her breasts. Before she could protest, he drew one rigid peak into the heat of his mouth. Raven's knees threatened to give way as moisture pooled between her thighs.

He wrapped one arm around her waist and tucked his swollen manhood into the juncture of her thighs. Without meaning to, she pressed against it, longing for

219

the release only he could give. Her breathing increased and a low moan escaped her lips.

As he turned his attention to her other breast, she ran her hands over his shoulders, entwining her fingers in his hair to hold him to her. Pressure built low in her belly until she thought she would burst.

When he finally raised his head he traced the outline of her lips with his tongue. "Ah, lass, I need you. I . . ." He faltered, then drew in a ragged breath. "I really need you."

The first quiet knock on the door didn't truly penetrate Raven's consciousness, but when the door started to open, followed by Ciorstan's small voice, she and Beckett jerked apart. Raven had barely succeeded in yanking her shirt over her swollen breasts when the girl entered the room.

"Da? I . . . oh, I'm sorry." Ciorstan hesitated, obviously ill at ease, but Raven knew the emotion couldn't compare with her own humiliation.

Raven hurried for the adjoining door. "I . . . I was just leaving."

"Raven . . ."

She closed the door on Beckett's plea and found the bolt to secure it. Her body still tense with yearning, she sank onto the bed and buried her head in her hands. She'd almost given in. If she made love to Beckett again, she might never want to leave.

Beckett would never allow her to travel in space again, and without that, a large part of her would die. She had no choice. She couldn't stay here.

If only his slightest touch didn't turn her hormones into dizzying whirlwinds, she could manage better. She'd have to avoid being alone with him . . . somehow.

Raven found only a small basin of water available for washing when she awakened, but she didn't complain. She wasn't about to ask Beckett to share his bath water again. With resignation, she dressed again in the restrictive clothing.

She tried staying in her room—that way she'd be sure

to avoid Beckett—but boredom drove her out by mid-day and she made her way to the hall. Shauna and Cior-stan sat at the table eating their noon meal, but Raven found no sign of Beckett. She relaxed slightly and took her seat.

Shauna passed some bread with an apologetic smile. "I'm sorry for the lack of a bath this morning, Raven, but Beckett decided to eliminate that luxury. Even though the water went through several uses, we need it more elsewhere."

"I understand." Now that she thought about it, Raven was surprised she'd been allowed any type of bath at all. No doubt yesterday had been a special occasion for Beckett's return home. "I can make do." She'd gone without daily mists before and survived. "Where is Beckett?"

"He and most of the men went hunting for the lion. 'Tis too dangerous to be roaming near the village."

"That's true." Raven recalled the mangled mess that had been a man and shuddered.

"I'm sorry I interrupted you and Da last night," Cior-stan said quietly. She didn't glance up from her plate.

Raven's cheeks warmed despite her efforts to control the flush. "Don't worry. We weren't discussing anything important."

Ciorstan looked at her then, her eyes too old for the childish body. "Are you truly going to leave when the merchant ship comes?"

Taken aback, Raven paused before replying. "Yes. I have to. Your life is here." She swept her arm across the room, then lifted it to the sky. "And mine is there."

"Will you visit us again?"

"I . . . I don't know." The idea of seeing Beckett on a recurring basis nudged Raven's heart rate up a notch. "I doubt your da would agree."

Ciorstan's face fell, and the sudden urge to give her a hug surprised Raven.

"We'll just cross that bridge later," Shauna said briskly.

Though Shauna had been nothing but friendly to her,

221

Raven suspected Beckett's sister wouldn't mind seeing her leave. Raven's ways were too radical for this group of colonists.

A servant appeared in the doorway from the kitchen. "Milady, the rations are ready."

Shauna nodded. "Thank you, Jean." She pushed back her chair. "Are you coming, Ciorstan?"

"Aye." The girl shoved the remaining bite of bread into her mouth and jumped to her feet.

"Where are you going?" Raven asked as Jean brought a large kettle into the room.

"As chieftain, Beckett receives the first ration of water, but usually I set aside only enough for the children and take the rest back to the villagers. Their need is much more desperate." Emotional pain glimmered in Shauna's eyes as she met Raven's gaze.

The last thing they needed was an extra mouth to feed. "May I help?" Raven left her food untouched as guilt welled up within her.

"If you wish."

With Jean carrying the half-filled kettle of water, they made their way down the slope to the village. The woman who opened the door at their first stop welcomed Shauna warmly.

"Come in, milady, please." She held open the door so they could enter.

From what Raven could see, the cottage consisted of only two or three rooms filled with a bare minimum of furniture, but the interior looked clean and well kept. Five children huddled in a corner of the main room, the tallest not even reaching Raven's waist. They looked surprisingly clean but thin, their clothes hanging as if on poles, their eyes overly large in their faces.

While Shauna ladled water into a pitcher, one of the boys ran his tongue over his cracked lips as if seeing a great delicacy. Raven's stomach twisted. She'd been thirsty before but never like that.

When they returned to the main street she touched Shauna's arm. "I hope you didn't save any water out for me," Raven said.

Shauna looked startled. "Actually, I did."

"I don't need it."

Shauna smiled and took the kettle from Jean. "Jean, return to the castle and get the ration I set aside for our guest. We'll continue on until you join us."

"Aye, milady." Jean hurried back to the castle and Shauna led them to the next small cottage.

" 'Tis sad, isn't it?" Ciorstan murmured. "I wish I could do something more to help."

Raven nodded and continued to watch the girl as they repeated the water dispersal for another family. For a nine-year-old, Beckett's daughter possessed a great deal of intelligence and maturity. All the other children Raven had the misfortune to come across had seemed concerned only with themselves. But not Cirostan MacLeod. Did Beckett realize how fortunate he was?

At the next home the woman answered the door with a nursing baby attached to her breast. With the way the woman's skin drew tight over her bones, Raven wondered how the child could obtain any nourishment.

This mother barely had enough strength to wave them inside before she sank into a well-worn rocking chair, her eyes wide and dry, as if she had no moisture left for tears. Two children played listlessly with a ball, rolling it back and forth from their sitting positions. When it went astray they watched it roll, but neither moved to chase it.

"Neptune's Rings," Raven muttered, her heart aching. How could children be like this? She fetched the ball and rolled it back to the older child, who let it bounce off her sticklike inner leg before she reached for it.

Shauna transferred water into a bowl. "How is Fia doing today?"

The mother lifted her arm only enough to indicate a cot tucked against a wall. As Raven moved closer, she could make out a tiny figure lying motionless on it. "Is she alive?" Raven went to feel for a pulse and the child jumped, her skin burning beneath Raven's touch. "She has a fever." Raven looked toward Shauna. "What can we do?"

"Here." Ciorstan brought over a cup of water. Raven lifted Fia to a sitting position and Ciorstan pressed the lip of the cup to the child's mouth.

The lips partly slightly and Ciorstan poured slowly, pausing when water dribbled down Fia's chin. The little girl swallowed as if it required great effort, but managed to drink half the cup before she turned her head away.

Raven laid her back down, the child weighing barely more than air in her arms. She had no substance, no life to her at all.

Fia moved her hand until she could touch Raven's arm. "Thank you, milady," she croaked.

"You're welcome." Raven didn't realize she was crying until a drop splashed against the back of her hand. Her insides twisted into a horrified knot and she struggled to hold back the sob that wanted to escape.

As she stood, she strengthened her resolve. It didn't have to be like this. "Shauna, I need to leave. There's something I have to do." She hurried for the door, not waiting for an answer. "May I borrow Ciorstan to help me?"

"Aye. What—?"

Raven burst from the cottage, nearly running toward where her ship rested. Ciorstan hurried to catch up to her. "What are we doing?" she asked.

"Something that will make your father very angry," Raven replied. "We're going to find water."

Chapter Fifteen

Once inside her ship, Raven paused. How many power cells would a waterseeker need? Knowing she only had a total of six onboard the *TrackStar*, Raven grabbed two and passed one to Ciorstan.

The girl required both hands to hold it. "What's this?"

"It's a power cell. If we're lucky, it'll power the waterseekers Beckett said are here."

"Waterseekers?"

"Have you seen any machines around here that are slightly taller than me but wide around the bottom? They look somewhat like a barrel."

Ciorstan's face brightened. "Aye. They sit in the back of the main barn. We've been told to nae touch them."

"I intend to touch them, Ciorstan." Raven left the ship and headed for the distant barns. "They're called waterseekers because that's what they do. If there's water left here, it'll find it."

"But . . . but that's wonderful. Why would Da be angry?" She paused only a second before she answered her own question. "Because 'tis technology, of course."

225

"Of course."

They were both panting by the time they reached the barn. Setting the power cells aside, they tugged on the large doors until they could prop them open.

Ciorstan led Raven inside and pointed out the shadows of the machinery, barely visible in the dim light. "There are three of them."

"I'll be happy to get one working." Raven approached carefully until she could make out the familiar design of a waterseeker—a very old waterseeker.

She circled it, noting the various controls. "This is older than any I've seen before."

"What can I do to help?" Ciorstan joined her.

"You should probably get out of here. I don't want to get you in trouble too."

"Nae. If this seeker can find water, it'll be worth polishing all the silver on Alba."

Raven smiled. "All right. I'll explain as I work." She located the power panel and managed to get it opened. "The power source is located in here." As she removed a battery, she released a sigh of relief. "Good, my power cells will work. I was afraid they might have changed."

She handed it to Ciorstan, who in turn gave Raven a new cell. "We'll need both of them," Raven added. She hooked up the first battery, then quickly swapped the second one.

Securing the panel, she noticed the straw on the floor around them. "Let's get this into the center before I try to start it. I'm not sure what's going to happen, so I want you to stay back."

The device weighed more than the waterseekers Raven had used before, but together they pushed it out of the straw and into the cleared center of the barn.

Raven hesitated as she studied the switches. "This should power it on," she explained. "Once I set it to seek, it should show us the direction to go on this display here." She indicated a small square screen located above the controls. "I'll use this lever to steer it in that direction. After I reach the indicated spot, I switch it to excavate."

"What then?"

"There's a laser tunnel built into the bottom of this. It'll use that to dig down and bring up the water." Raven drew in a deep breath. "If it works."

Ciorstan smiled. "We have naught to lose."

"Back off then." Raven waved Ciorstan away and waited until the girl stood at the entrance to the barn. As far as Raven could tell, the seeker appeared to be in good shape—one of the advantages of thilanium. It didn't rust like older metals.

She touched the power switch and swallowed the last of her doubts. If she didn't try this, she could never live with herself again. These people needed water—whether Beckett believed in technology or not. She triggered the power and the machine came to life with a tremendous roar.

Raven stepped back, surprised. She'd never heard such a loud seeker before. Slowly the initial noise diminished and she approached the controls again. Without hesitation, she turned a knob to seek. Would it work? Could it still locate water? A sudden horror gripped her. Was there water to find?

The screen lit up, defining the four basic directions but nothing more. Raven caught her breath, waiting. Finally a single blip appeared in what looked like a northwestern position.

"Is that water?"

At Ciorstan's excited voice, Raven turned to see the girl beside her. "I hope so. Once I get it outside, I'll be able to see how the directions work on this planet."

She played with the lever to get the waterseeker moving, then had to trot to keep up with it. As they emerged outside, she correlated the directions on the screen to the land. "It looks as if we need to go toward the village."

Ciorstan grinned. "This will be fun."

Screams greeted their appearance on the central road, and mothers ran to snatch their children inside. Raven glanced at Ciorstan and raised her eyebrows. They didn't want to alarm the village.

"Let me handle this." Ciorstan raced ahead and assumed a position, as if she were guiding the water-seeker. Almost instantly, the screams stopped, but people were slow to reappear on the street.

Raven adjusted the direction slightly. It didn't look as if she needed to go much farther. Just so long as the blip didn't locate in the middle of a cottage.

As she neared the bottom of the hill leading to the castle, a second blip appeared on the screen, and Raven wanted to shout with joy. Water! More water!

She followed the direction toward the remnants of the lake, then stopped with the first blip centralized beneath the seeker. Glancing around, she saw they sat just off the main road on the former lake shore.

"Is this the place?" Ciorstan joined her again.

"It says it is." They exchanged hopeful glances. "Let's try it." Raven rotated the knob to excavate and the device lowered its base to the ground as the roar changed to a gentle hum.

Ciorstan circled the seeker, her anticipation obvious. "How long will it take?"

"It's hard to say. It depends on how deep it has to go."

"Oh-oh."

Turning to follow Ciorstan's gaze, Raven sighed. The villagers had apparently overcome their fright and were approaching cautiously, alarm plastered across their faces. Raven could handle that. She expected some trepidation.

However, Hamish hobbled behind the group, his expression set in a dark glower. Him, she didn't want to face.

Ciorstan came to her side and tried to speak, but the cries of the crowd drowned out her small voice. Stiffening her spine, Raven stepped forward and held out her arms in an attempt for quiet.

"Listen," she cried. "Listen!"

The noise dimmed and she continued. "This machine will not hurt you. I swear it." Voices raised again and she signaled for silence. "It's called a waterseeker. It's designed to find water."

The villagers erupted into talk again, but this time

more quietly, with a sense of awe. Raven waved her hand at the seeker. "Right now it says it has found water beneath the ground, and I've started tunneling for it."

" 'Tis a lie." Hamish made his way to the front of the group and swung his cane in Raven's face. " 'Tis an alien machine to destroy us."

Raven shook her head. "This device was one your ancestors brought with them to Alba. It quit working because the power supply ran out. All I did was put in new batteries."

"Bah." From his stooped position Hamish had to look up to see into Raven's face. " 'Tis nae place for alien machinery or aliens here."

"Raven's nae alien." Ciorstan pointed her finger at the old man. "She's as human as you or I. All she's trying to do is help. If you—"

She stopped abruptly at hearing the seeker rumble as if ready to explode. As one the crowd stepped back. Raven turned to watch it, unable to quiet a small voice of alarm. Was it dangerous or was it . . . ?

Water exploded from the spouts located around the machine and poured into the deep troughs of the base. "Yes!" Raven fired her fist into the air in triumph. Behind her, the villagers cried out in surprise.

The seeker's analysis of the water showed it safe to drink. Knowing she had to lead the way, Raven scooped up the liquid in her hands and drank. Cool, refreshing water. At that moment it tasted better than the sweet dramberries on Dlaptha.

The women needed no other encouragement. They ran to the troughs and tasted for themselves. Raven spied tears on many cheeks as the women realized their good fortune. Her tension eased. These people would now have water. No matter how angry Beckett became, their hopeful faces made it worthwhile.

"Damnation, Raven. What have you done?"

As Beckett's voice thundered behind her, Raven winced and wondered about changing that opinion. Swallowing the sudden lump in her throat, she turned to face him. His blazing eyes and the set lines on his face indicated that he'd gone straight past mad into full-fledged rage.

"Your people needed water," she replied, lifting her chin. "The seeker found some."

"We dinna need mechanical tools on Alba." His cold tone turned her blood to ice.

"It's not—"

"Shut it down," he ordered.

Her mouth dropped open. Shut it down? Once the water had been found, she never thought he'd throw it away. "I—"

"Shut it down."

Her anger bubbled to the surface and she assumed as much of a fighting stance as her skirt would allow. "No. It stays on."

Beckett's hands opened and closed in rapid succession. Raven didn't doubt he wanted them around her neck. As he approached, she tensed, her mouth suddenly dry.

"Shut. It. Down."

"No."

He came close enough that she needed to tilt her head to meet his fiery gaze, but she refused to budge.

"She's right, Da." Ciorstan appeared at Raven's side, her eyes ablaze with the same anger. "We need this."

"Return to the castle, Ciorstan. Now."

When she didn't move he shifted his stare to her. "Now, Ciorstan."

Raven gently nudged the girl's shoulder. She didn't want Ciorstan to suffer on her behalf. Though Beckett's strength surpassed hers, Raven knew she could give him a good fight on her own . . . if it came to that.

With obvious reluctance, Ciorstan moved toward the castle. "She is right, Da," she called over her shoulder.

"Your people are dying, Beckett," Raven muttered between clenched teeth. "When's the last time you talked to any of the women or their children?"

He hesitated for only an instant. "I am the leader here, Raven. 'Tis nae your place." Extending his finger

toward the seeker, he spat out his words. "Turn off that
. . . that *machine* now."

Her insides trembled, but somehow Raven kept it
from showing. "No."

With a cry of rage, Beckett seized her shoulders, and
she clenched her fists, ready to fight.

"She's right, milord."

A timid voice interrupted them, and they turned to
see a woman step into place beside Raven. "Please,
dinna shut it down," she said quietly.

"We need it, milord." Another woman joined her,
then another and another. "It'll save our children."

One by one the women joined Raven in her stand,
many of them ignoring the outbursts of their husbands
to do so. Raven's heart swelled and new determination
filled her. "The seeker stays, Beckett," she said firmly.

The women had stunned him. She could see it in his
bewilderment and the fading of the fire in his eyes.
"Raven . . ." He seemed at a loss for words.

Behind him, Raven met the gaze of one of the few
women remaining with the men—Shauna. Surely she
knew better than anyone how desperately these people
needed water.

As if understanding Raven's silent plea, Shauna came
to her brother's side. "Beckett, there are children who
will die soon if we don't have this water."

Raven understood his internal struggle and wished
she didn't have to defy him for this to happen.

" 'Tis that bad?" he asked Shauna quietly.

"Aye. Two died while you were gone."

He closed his eyes, his agony evident. "Very well." He
finally opened them again. "The device can stay."

"Thank you, milord. Thank you." The woman surrounded him, touching his arm as they expressed their
gratitude. Beckett acknowledged them with a small
nod, but his icy gaze stayed locked on Raven. She
hadn't been forgiven yet, nor had she expected to be.

"To the castle now," he muttered, his words barely
loud enough for her to hear, though his anger came
through very clearly.

Raven bowed her head and turned toward the slope. The forthcoming argument would not be pleasant, but at least the children had their water. As she met Ciorstan on the path, they exchanged wry looks.

"So you're letting aliens tell you what to do, are you now, MacLeod?" Hamish's taunting voice made Raven look around.

Turning slowly, Beckett aimed his glare at the old man. To his credit, Hamish didn't falter but stared back defiantly.

"She's my alien, Hamish," Beckett snapped. "And I'll handle her."

"To be sure." Hamish shuffled away.

His alien? Raven bristled. She wasn't his, nor was she an alien. She treasured her humanness.

Yet when Beckett started up the slope, his expression glowering, she and Ciorstan increased their pace, neither anxious to confront him.

He caught up with them quickly and placed one hand on the back of Raven's neck. "Ciorstan, go to your room and stay there," he ordered.

She didn't argue, but shot Raven an apologetic look and dashed off. Using his hand, Beckett steered Raven toward the drawing room, not hurting her with his grip but using enough pressure to convey his displeasure.

Once inside the room he thrust her away from him, and Raven crossed the room before facing him. She needed as much distance as possible between them. "Beckett, I'm sorry. I honestly didn't want to confront you like that with everyone there."

"Nae." He paced the room restlessly. "Now the entire village thinks some shapely alien has become chieftain."

"It's not like that," she protested. "If you'd listened to me—"

He rounded on her, his fists clenched, his eyes wild, and she froze with a sharp breath. "I have always tried to do what's best for my people."

"But you didn't. You're letting your fear of technology blind you. You need the waterseeker."

232

"What I need is for you to remember who's chieftain here. I am the MacLeod. Just yesterday you said you understood; then today you openly defy me. Which is it, Raven?"

"I didn't think you'd order the seeker shut down once it found water. I honestly thought you weren't that heartless." A heavy sadness settled onto her chest. "I was wrong."

"Starting the machine began your defiance," he snapped.

"Your ancestors brought those machines with them, Beckett. I didn't. Go read your histories again. The only reason they quit using them was because the power cells died. Ask yourself why all of a sudden the colonists experienced such hardship at the ten-year mark. Power cells only have a ten-year life cycle."

He brought his face close to hers. "And what was so important *you* had to have water?"

Didn't he know how badly his people suffered? She started to speak, then stopped. Why bother defending herself? He wouldn't believe her anyhow. "I couldn't stand it not to have any more baths," she replied flippantly.

His face flushed an angry red and he drew back as if from something distasteful. "From now on you will restrict your movements to the castle. Better yet, to your room. Then you can have as many baths as you like."

His distrust hurt, but Raven held herself erect, refusing to show him her pain. "I'll do even better. I'll stay in my ship until the merchant vessel comes. Then I won't bother anyone."

She spun on her heel and hurried through the doorway. Shauna stood outside and placed her hand on Raven's arm.

"Raven—"

Raven shook her head and pulled away. She'd had it with Alba and their archaic ways. Two weeks alone in *TrackStar* had to be better than any time in Beckett's presence, especially when he obviously thought so little of her.

233

Bursting from the castle, she skirted the village as she made her way to the barren fields. When her path blurred she swiped her hand across her eyes, then stared at the dampness, surprised by her tears.

But she hurt—deep down inside where the pain burned worse than any laser blast. He had a right to be angry with her for the way she openly defied his authority before the village, but he'd brought it on himself. Then, for him to think she'd be so bold because she wanted a bath . . . he didn't know her any better than she knew him.

Worse yet, she'd begun to care about him. Otherwise, his opinion wouldn't matter as much as it did. He'd called her an alien and that cut deeper than any name Slade had ever used.

Raven resumed walking, slower now, and wiped again at her watering eyes. She'd made the right decision to leave. Alba held no future for her. Not now. Not ever.

Maybe, in time, she could look back at all of this as a distant memory and remember Beckett without longing for his touch. Maybe she'd forget his unreasonable anger and think only of his kisses.

She paused. Was his bitter anger unreasonable? As a tracker, she sometimes put herself in her quarry's place and tried to think as he or she did. She'd never done that with Beckett. Was it because she couldn't relate to his culture and thoughts because she never tried?

He had a good portion of pride. Probably all of the people here did, if the histories were any indicator. Beckett's pride occupied even more prominence due to his position as chieftain. He led these people and they obeyed him.

Until today.

From his point of view she'd blatantly used a modern device after saying she wouldn't. But he hadn't seen the children and adults dying in their small cottages. And he'd refused to see the waterseekers as anything but modern when they had been in existence for well over two hundred years.

Raven sighed. She'd tried to apologize, but he wouldn't hear it. His own anger made him deaf. What she needed to do was wait until the next day and try again when he'd lost the first flush of fury. Perhaps then he'd hear her and understand.

Glancing at the surrounding hills, Raven noticed shadows already creeping along the ground. Daylight kept short hours in this place. Before long darkness would cover the village.

TrackStar sat at the edge of the massive fields, its nose buried in the bark of a thick tree and its base covered with soil. As she approached, Raven experienced a momentary panic. Would it still be able to fly once she did get more fuel?

It had to. She'd run a complete diagnostic, both with the computer and by hand. After all, she'd have plenty of time.

A low growl caught her attention and she stopped abruptly to survey the area. She saw nothing, but the growl sounded again . . . closer.

Pivoting, she found herself trapped in the yellow gaze of . . . what? The creature had to be Beckett's mountain lion, but it didn't look like the holos she'd seen of that creature. She reached immediately for her laser, then cursed Beckett silently when she encountered the skirt.

This beast easily covered more ground from head to toe than Raven stood tall, its head as big as her torso, its teeth gleaming fangs the length of her hand. Each paw exceeded the size of her head and contained several protruding claws. Though the lean, tawny body and sculpted head resembled that of members of the cat family, the eyes were larger, the golden yellow rimmed with black, and the ears stood out like massive scoops.

It had a tail almost as long as the rest of its body that it cracked through the air like a whip. The agility with which it controlled its tail frightened Raven. The lion obviously had more than one weapon.

She froze, not daring to move. The *TrackStar* sat within running distance, but she knew the creature only needed two leaps to be upon her.

Swiftly reviewing her options, she decided she didn't have any. Beckett had her laser in the castle, which only left her her hands and feet for weapons. This beast had killed a man with little difficulty. Raven doubted she'd survive long beneath those teeth and claws.

Shibit. She didn't want to die this way, not with so much left undone. She wanted to make peace with Beckett. She wanted to see the village return to life. She wanted . . .

The cat growled again, edging nearer, its teeth prominently displayed.

And Raven trembled.

Beckett's anger ebbed as Raven dashed out the door. What had she said? Baths? Raven didn't care about baths. God, what was he thinking?

He started for the doorway, then paused when Shauna entered. His sister didn't often get irate with him, but she was now. Anger glimmered in her eyes.

"Beckett MacLeod, you're a fool."

"I've heard that before," he replied calmly. Surprised, he wondered why her words didn't stir his ire, while Raven only had to look at him to do so. Of course, everything Raven said or did fueled his passion—either in lust or in fury. He found it impossible to remain unaffected in her presence.

Shauna poked her finger against his chest to accent each word. "Do you honestly believe Raven brought out that waterseeker because she wanted a bath?"

He didn't want to believe it. "That's what she said."

"She only said that because you werena listening."

"I heard her."

"Nae." Shauna touched his ear. "You listened here." She moved her hand to cover his heart. "But nae here."

Chastised, Beckett recalled the sadness that had crossed Raven's face. She'd tried to explain, but he'd been too angry to hear her. The embarrassment he'd felt before his village consumed him. She'd defied him and made him to look like a fool whether he fought her or agreed.

"She did it for the children," Shauna added.

The children? Beckett looked up in surprise. Raven didn't like children.

"You've been gone for several weeks so you dinna know how serious things are now. Raven went with Ciorstan and me this afternoon when we dispensed our water ration."

"You what?" His own sister operated without his knowledge now.

"I kept enough of our ration for Niall and Cullan, but the rest I took to those in the village who needed it more than we. And there are many. Raven saw the families, the children who haven't energy to play, who want nothing more than a sip of water and a slice of bread. She saw little Fia Gordon, who will die shortly without more water, and perhaps even then."

Beckett's chest hurt as he listened to Shauna's vivid description and he dropped his head. Why hadn't he seen this?

"She ran out, Beckett, and brought the waterseeker. And it worked." Shauna squeezed his hand. "That's why the women stood with her. They'd do anything . . . anything to save their children."

When Beckett looked up he saw tears shimmering in her eyes. "Dear brother, 'tis only a machine that's sat in the barn for all my life. 'Twasna handled tactfully, I'll grant you that, but Raven meant nae harm. Surely you know that."

"Aye." He sighed. "I do know." After clasping her hands warmly he moved to the door.

"Where are you going?"

He gave her a dry smile. "I dinna intend to let her stay in her ship. 'Tis most uncomfortable."

Walking slowly from the castle, he tried to formulate his apology. This time he'd listen . . . with his ears *and* his heart.

He replayed their argument mentally and winced at recalling his brutal accusations. As much as he wanted

237

to blame Hamish for goading him into irrational anger, he couldn't. His pride drove him. He'd never been as humiliated as when he'd had to back down before the entire village.

Some chieftain. He snorted in disgust at himself. A true leader listened as well as led. Somehow Raven had made him forget that. To be honest, she made him forget a lot of things. Every time he looked at her, he longed for the sweetness of her kiss and the feel of her skin against his.

As he entered the fields, he saw her in the distance, a beacon against the gathering darkness. She stopped suddenly and he paused. Had she changed her mind?

A shadow detached itself from the trees lining the fields and Beckett's throat closed. He recognized the shape instantly. Old Bess. Damnation.

He started running. When Raven reached for her laser Beckett groaned aloud. She had no weapon. His foolish insistence that she follow his rules would get her killed. One swipe of that lion's paw could decapitate her.

Panic drove him. He pushed his legs to cover as much ground in a stride as possible. Dear Lord, he needed her—not just in his bed, but in his life. He couldn't lose her now.

He grew close enough to see the lion crouch into its jumping position. Raven tensed, her knees bent, her hands held out in front of her.

Beckett drew his sword and held it ready. Only a little farther. He couldn't be too late.

Then the lion leapt.

Chapter Sixteen

The creature flew through the air toward Raven. Her heart thumping wildly, she waited until the last possible second, then threw herself aside. The lion landed behind her with a loud roar. She cursed her skirt as it wrapped around her legs and she stumbled to her knees.

Raven hurried to stand again, but the lion swung out with its massive paw before she regained her balance. Though she pulled away, the claws shredded part of her skirt. "Shibit." She tugged her garment free and scrambled backward, not daring to drop her gaze from the advancing beast.

Feeling around the ground, she closed her fingers around a palm-sized rock. When the lion crouched again she threw the stone as hard as she could at the creature's head. A ferocious roar confirmed that she'd hit her target.

She staggered to her feet and whirled around to run. Her ship sat close by. It was her only chance. Before she could go even two steps, something snaked around her ankle. Jerked to a stop, she glanced down and gasped in horror. The lion had wrapped its long tail around her boot.

Trying not to give in to her rising panic, Raven fought back but couldn't loosen the hold. The beast's fetid breath reached her. Raven uttered a small cry of alarm and worked her foot free of the boot. As she scooted backward, she glanced up to see the lion leaping at her and raised her arms in an instinctive defensive gesture.

The creature fell short, dropping to the ground as she heard a strange war cry. Blinking, Raven recognized Beckett as he withdrew his sword from the beast's belly.

"Get out of here," he shouted. As he glanced at her, the lion swung its paw, knocking Beckett backward and sending the sword flying through the air.

Raven didn't hesitate. The beast had transferred its immediate attention to Beckett now and Raven ran to seize the sword. It remained as heavy and awkward as she remembered it, but she grasped the hilt firmly. This . . . this lion wasn't going to beat her.

It approached Beckett, blood dripping from the wound on its side. He'd managed to get to his knees before the creature attacked. With an angry yell, Raven swung the sword and separated the lion's head from its body.

Beckett jumped to his feet and ran to Raven as she lowered the sword. She stared at him, unable to believe the weapon had cut so cleanly.

They spoke together.

"Are you—?"

"Are you—?"

Cutting off, they exchanged dry grins. "God, Raven." Beckett wrapped his arms around her in a tight hug.

She could feel trembling but wasn't sure if it was hers or his. Entwining her arms around his neck, Raven pressed even closer to his strength. He smelled of sweat, dirt and blood, but she didn't care. Right now knowing they had survived unharmed transcended everything else.

"Where did you come from?" she murmured.

"I followed you." He caressed the side of her face, cupping her chin in his palm.

"Why?" She held her breath, half afraid to hear his answer.

"To apologize. I had—"

She didn't let him finish. Instead she pulled his head down and kissed him, reveling in the touch of his mouth against hers. Desire flashed through her, assurance that she lived despite her certainty of death.

When the kiss ended he ran his thumb gently over her parted lips. "Raven . . ." he said huskily.

The clamor of voices interrupted them and they turned to see villagers approaching over the vast fields. With a sigh, Raven dropped her arms and stepped away from Beckett to locate her boot.

The men surrounded the fallen lion, comparing its size and ferociousness. " 'Tis Old Bess," Duncan declared. "You killed her."

Beckett smiled at Raven. "We killed her."

"Are you all right?" Shauna pushed her way through the crowd. She glanced from Beckett to Raven, her eyes wide.

"Fine, just dirty." He glanced down at his clothing and grimaced. "Perhaps now that we have a fresh water supply you could arrange for a bath."

"Of course. I'll have the servants start it immediately." She touched Beckett's arm but included Raven in her warm smile. "I'm glad you're all right—both of you."

Once Shauna left, Raven let Beckett explain how they had defeated the massive lion. She couldn't believe it herself. Beckett's sword performed much more efficiently than she'd expected. There might be something to his method of fighting after all.

As reaction set in, her limbs trembled and she wrapped her arms around herself in an effort to control it. Beckett must've noticed for he turned from the men.

"I think we need to get back to the castle. Girard, Sean, would you dispose of the carcass?"

"Aye, MacLeod."

Beckett placed his arm around Raven's shoulders and

241

steered her toward the castle, leaving the men chattering among themselves.

Shauna met them in the main entry, her hands on her hips as she searched them up and down. "You're both a mess. I had the tub placed in your room, Beckett, but Raven needs a bath as much as you do."

He smiled. "Dinna worry. I'll take care of it."

Shauna raised her eyebrows but said nothing more. Raven could only think of basking in the warm water. Already her body ached from her falls and she longed to relieve the pain.

"Thank you," she murmured. She left Beckett's side to climb the staircase, but he followed close behind. When she approached her bedroom doorway he shook his head and pushed open his door.

Raven looked at him in surprise, recognizing the heat in his gaze. "I don't think—"

"The tub is here. You may use it first." He held open the door and indicated the large bath inside.

Though suspicious, Raven entered. The bath sat on a rug in the middle of the large room, steam curling up from it. As the door clicked shut behind her, she turned to see Beckett standing before it.

"This isn't just about a bath, is it?" she asked quietly, her pulse leaping at the hunger in his eyes.

"Nae. 'Tis more than that." He didn't move, as if giving Raven a chance to escape.

She glanced at the interconnecting door, knowing that if she went through it, he'd leave her alone, but suddenly she didn't want that. Having his arms around her earlier had felt right. She no longer wanted to fight her body's longing for him. Lifting her gaze to his, she smiled. "All right."

A quick look of surprise crossed his face. He came toward her slowly, the heat of his gaze almost enough to burn away her clothes.

He paused, cupping her face in his hands. "I thought I'd lost you. I . . . I need you, Raven."

Her stomach clenched at the sincerity of his words

and all her doubts disappeared. "Make love to me, Beckett."

Groaning, he bent to take her lips. She opened her mouth to receive him and moaned softly as his tongue stroked hers, triggering tight flashes of heat and moisture low inside her. He ran his hands over her back, gathering her buttocks to pull her tightly against him.

Raven's breasts swelled against his chest as she moved her hips to stroke his hardness. She ached deep inside, ached for him to fill her.

Beckett lifted his head, his breathing irregular, and brought his hands up to the ties on her vest. Once they were loosened, he lifted the clothing over her head. Tugging Raven's shirt free of her waistband, he slipped his warm hands beneath it to stroke the flatness of her stomach.

Raven squirmed, wanting his touch on her breasts, but he continued to run his fingers over her skin. He kissed her again, giving of his passion even as he drank of hers. With unbearable slowness he lifted his hands until he caressed the underside of her breasts with his thumbs.

Moaning into Beckett's mouth, Raven grasped his shoulders, then ran her hands over the taut muscles of his back. Her blood burned with need, longing tight in her belly.

In an abrupt movement Beckett yanked her shirt over her head, then stood back, looking at her. Raven could barely stand still, so great was her need.

But he didn't satisfy that need. Instead he unfastened her skirt and let it sink into a pile at her feet, then followed it with her underpants.

Still he watched, his gaze traveling over her at a leisurely pace. Raven's nipples peppled into tight buds of longing. She couldn't stand it.

Stepping toward him, she gripped the edges of his tunic and tugged it over his head. Able to feast on his bare torso, she ran her hands over the outlines of his muscles, teasing his nipples with her fingertips. His body stiffened in response and she smiled, moving closer, pressing her sensitive peaks into his chest hair.

His erection throbbed against her thigh and Raven lowered her hands to the fastening on his pants, working it open.

Instantly, Beckett lifted her in his arms and deposited her in the tub. Sputtering her way to the surface, Raven stared at him in surprise. "What the—?"

He grinned. "You need a bath." He removed his pants, allowing his manhood to burst free. "And so do I."

Before Raven could do more than gasp, he climbed into the tub with her, maneuvering so that she sat on his lap facing him. "Let me help you wash," he added. Lathering his hands with soap, he ran them over her body, the silky feel heightening Raven's desire.

Finally, with exaggerated care, he massaged her breasts, teasing her erect nipples with his fingers. Raven rose as need pierced her body from head to toe.

He resettled her on his lap and continued to lather her body, each passing touch on her breasts driving all coherent thought from her mind. In self-defense she located the soap and performed the same function for him, enjoying the way his muscles tightened beneath her palms.

Reaching beneath the water, she located his erection and caressed the hard length of it with a soapy palm. Beckett's eyes darkened. After rinsing Raven's breasts, he drew one taut peak into his mouth, his tongue tormenting Raven into unbearable need.

"Beckett." She gasped as he found her swollen cleft beneath the water and unerringly massaged that most sensitive spot with his fingers. Her hips rocked against his hand. She needed . . . "Beckett, please."

Releasing her breast, he gripped her waist and impaled her on his shaft. Her inner muscles contracted around him immediately. Beckett held her still, the effort to do so evident in the tautness of his body. He held her and reached out again with his mouth to devour her turgid nipples until Raven couldn't help but move in response.

The gentleness of the water combined with the hard

feel of him inside her only added to Raven's delight. Pressing her knees close to Beckett's hips, she slid up and down, the new sensations sending fresh quivers of desire throughout her body.

He guided her as the pace increased, her insides drawing so tight they threatened to snap. Her explosion began low but spread to every fiber of her being. Raven cried out, arching her body.

Beckett's hands tightened on her waist and he thrust her down, burying himself inside completely. With a groan he obtained his release, the tenseness leaving his body.

Raven held on to his shoulders, welcoming his reassuring kiss, then leaned her head atop his. "I think we're clean now," she said lightly.

He pressed his lips quickly against each of her nipples, sending a shudder through her insides. Meeting her gaze, his eyes dark, he smiled. "Then we can dry off."

Once out of the tub, he grabbed a large cloth and wrapped it around Raven. Before she could tuck in the ends, he took them and briskly rubbed the cloth back and forth over her body, teasing her already sensitized skin. Pulling the cloth closer, he pressed her against him, his heated flesh searing hers.

"I want you, Raven, beside me in my bed, beside me in the village." He spoke huskily, his words almost a growl.

Raven's heart rate quickened. After their rapturous lovemaking, she could no longer deny the pleasure he gave her. "I'll share your bed . . . until the merchant ship comes."

He opened his mouth, then closed it and nodded instead, but a flicker deep in his eyes warned Raven that he hadn't fully accepted her answer. Startling her, he dropped the towel and seized her lips, his mouth passionate, his tongue stroking hers in a familiar rhythm. Desire quickly flared to life and Raven responded without restraint.

Using his mouth and hands, he easily made her want

him again. He lifted her and laid her gently on his bed, then stood beside it, staring at her. She writhed beneath his gaze, her skin heated, her need threatening to overpower her.

He smiled. "This is where you belong," he murmured. He knelt over her but didn't provide the relief she required. Trailing his lips over her skin, he covered every pore, every bump, every crevice until she reached for him in desperation.

This joining shook her to her teeth, her body becoming one with his until they reached mutual satisfaction.

Afterward he cradled her within his arms, her head resting on his chest. She'd never felt so sated, so complete, as if Beckett filled a part of her long left empty. Despite the drought, despite the lion, despite Hamish's distrust, she'd found peace for the first time and it frightened her.

Even as she ran her hand idly over his chest, she knew she still had to leave. She didn't want to—at least, not right now—but if she didn't, she might never get another chance. She'd soared from one end of the heavens to the other. How could she ever be happy staying in one place? Especially one as backward as Alba.

"I am sorry about the waterseeker," she said, recalling their earlier argument. "I honestly never meant to defy you in front of the village."

A laugh rumbled through his chest, reverberating in her ear. She propped up on her elbow to look at his face. Laughing?

" 'Tis nae your defiance you're apologizing for, but for doing it in public?"

"Well, yes." She grimaced. "Your people needed that waterseeker and it was here. It's not as if I brought it with me."

His smile faded. "You're right."

"I am?" She couldn't have been more stunned.

He kissed her quickly. " 'Twas worse here than I thought, and as you said, my ancestors did bring the equipment. We'd become too proud of the fact that we'd succeeded without such devices."

"There were others. Will you let me set them up, too?"

He hesitated, and she could see him waging an inner war. Finally he sighed and nodded. "For as long as this drought lasts. Do you have enough power cells?"

"For now, but I'll have to replace them when the merchants come. Otherwise I won't have any water."

"You took the cells from your water unit, yet you planned to live in your ship?"

Raven grimaced. "I haven't taken them from the water unit yet."

"Then where?"

"From my food stick producer." She grinned. "After eating this food I didn't think I'd miss it."

His chest rumbled again. "Aye. Good choice, lass."

Returning her head to her previous position, Raven snuggled closer. "Will you let me help now?"

His arms tightened around her. "I willna have more of your technology, Raven. The waterseekers were here. 'Tis the only reason I agree to them."

"No. I want to help with what you do here. I have no idea how your village works and lives."

He relaxed. "Of course. I'll be glad to put you to work." He ran his hand over the length of her side. "But the nights belong to me."

Her body still humming with pleasure, Raven smiled. "Good."

A week flew by. As Raven looked out on the newly planted fields, she allowed herself to bask in satisfaction. The soil had been tilled, rocks removed and precious seed sown.

When she and Ciorstan set up the other waterseekers one discovered water in the middle of the fields. The position couldn't be better; Raven helped design a primitive but effective irrigation system fed by the seeker.

She rolled her shoulders, testing the ache there. Each day's work led her to discover new muscles unused to this type of labor, but she didn't mind. The women and men of the village worked together to plant and now planned to rebuild some of the homes.

The camaraderie warmed Raven's heart. She'd never been among a group of people who so obviously cared about one another. With the exception of Hamish, they'd all welcomed her in their midst, but Raven wondered if that came more from her position as Beckett's lover.

Certainly everyone knew they slept together. Beckett's hot looks and casual caresses couldn't have gone unnoticed when he worked beside her, and sometimes Raven's cries of passion echoed through the castle. Even Shauna had mentioned that, bringing a hot flush to Raven's cheeks.

Yet no one appeared to condemn Raven or Beckett for their relationship. If anything, the villagers became friendlier. One woman had told Raven she'd never seen Beckett look happier.

Of course, they trusted and respected Beckett. He made an exceptional leader. Raven knew of no man who would've apologized to the village and admitted he was wrong as he did regarding the waterseekers. Her own pride in him had swelled at that moment.

He triggered other emotions during their nights together. They fit so perfectly together. He only needed to look or touch her to stir her desire. Raven enjoyed her newly discovered peace and found—for a while—that she could forget everything in her past.

But it wouldn't last.

As she stood in the castle window, she watched darkness stretch across the sky and the first stars peek through. She knew people out there. A restless yearning worked its way free. Planets existed that she still hadn't seen.

She briefly considered returning to Saladan to help map and explore the new planet. Besides the challenge and excitement, such a mission usually paid very well. Raven sighed, unable to generate her usual enthusiasm. When she thought of Saladan now all she remembered was Beckett making love to her beside a roaring river. No, she couldn't go there.

"Making wishes on stars?" Beckett's low voice

growled in her ear just before his lips nuzzled the side of her neck.

Raven's breathing quickened instantly, her body coming to life. "Hmmm," she murmured, tilting her head to expose more of her throat. "I think one just came true."

He continued to plant hot kisses on her flesh as he brought his hands from behind to slip inside her shirt and cup her breasts, his thumbs brushing the nipples. Fiery need pierced Raven, and her insides tightened.

"What do you do to me?" she gasped, pressing back against him until she could feel the hardness of his arousal.

"Me? What do you do to me?" He nipped at the skin on her shoulder. "Every time I see you, I want you. It's taken all my willpower to keep from making love to you in the middle of the fields."

He turned her to face him. "Every time I saw a trickle of water slide down between your breasts, I wanted to follow it." Using his lips, he burned a trail down her chest, pausing at the exposed hollow of her cleavage.

The heat of his mouth and the expert teasing of his tongue made Raven's insides clench with need. She moaned softly, her knees suddenly weak, and gripped his shoulders.

"Beckett?" Shauna's voice drifted down the hallway. "Beckett?"

He straightened immediately and held Raven in front of him. "What is it?" he called over his shoulder.

Shauna rounded the corner, then stopped abruptly. Though Raven couldn't see her, she felt Shauna's knowing gaze. "Darce is here. He needs to talk to you."

"I'll be right there." Shauna's footsteps faded and Beckett gave Raven a wry smile. "Later."

"I'm counting on it." Raven inhaled deeply to regain control of her trembling limbs. "Shall we see what Darce wants?"

They found the young man pacing the front entrance, running his fingers through his tousled hair. He looked up sharply as they approached and came to meet Beckett. "MacLeod, we have a serious problem."

"What is it?" Beckett placed his hand on Darce's shoulder.

"I was visiting my betrothed at the Clan MacKinnon when a group of Campbells came in. They've heard about our waterseekers and are planning to come steal one."

Beckett stiffened. "Do you know when they're planning this?"

"I think this group was the advance party. I left immediately and rode hard, but I doubt if they're more than a few hours behind me."

"We need to meet them at the boundary . . . before they get to the village. Darce, gather the men. I'll be there shortly."

"Aye, MacLeod." He quickly left.

Beckett pivoted and headed for his chamber. Her heart pounding, Raven hurried after him. "What are you doing?" she asked. "We've shared our water with other clans. Surely this one will accept that."

"You dinna know the Campbells, lass. They prefer fighting over talking." Once inside his room, he gathered his gear—a thick leather tunic, his sword and a short knife.

"Then let me go with you." Raven couldn't stop the clenching of her stomach. "Give me my suit and I'll be able to fight as well as anyone else."

"Nae. You canna have your laser. 'Tis nae fair."

"Then I'll use a sword." She caught his arm. "Let me help."

He smiled at her softly. "Dinna worry. I'll be back soon. 'Tis nae the first time we've had dealings with the Campbells."

"Beckett, I'm not the type of person who can sit around and let others do the fighting."

Pausing in the doorway, he reached out to caress her cheek. "Fine, lass. If they somehow get past us, then you're responsible for guarding the waterseekers. How's that?" His indulgent tone told her he didn't expect that to happen.

Raven scowled. "Beckett—"

He cut her off with a quick kiss, then hurried away. Raven slammed the bedroom door, momentarily enjoying the resounding echo down the hallway. Whirling around, she searched Beckett's room with her gaze.

Her suit had to be here somewhere.

She frantically searched the room, every corner, every drawer, every wardrobe, all to no avail. What had he done with it? He wouldn't have destroyed her clothes and laser. After all, he knew she would need them when she left.

When she left.

A cold chill wrapped around her. What if he didn't intend to let her leave? More than once he'd mentioned never having enough of her. But would he keep her prisoner?

No. She knew Beckett and he was too honorable for that. Placing her hands on her hips, she surveyed the room again. However, he did hide things well.

As inspiration hit, she smiled. She was becoming too acclimated to this style of living. All she needed to do was visit her ship and retrieve her other jumpsuit.

She hurried outside, then froze on the gentle slope leading from the castle as she saw Beckett and the men of the village leaving on their horses. "Shibit." How dare he leave her behind? She needed to be there—to help, to fight, to watch over Beckett.

Her heart thumped erratically and she inhaled sharply. She cared about this man. His well-being mattered. With a frustrated sigh, she ran her fingers through her hair. She didn't want to care about him.

As a tracker, she had to remain detached to do a good job, but since she'd met Beckett nothing had gone as planned. She shouldn't have given in to her body's urging.

Raven twisted her lips in a wry smile. She could no more control her response to Beckett's caresses than she could stop breathing. And she still had a week before the merchant ship arrived. What kind of chaos would her emotions be in by then?

She walked toward her ship in no particular hurry. What could she do? She didn't want to be a part of this community, yet the people already treated her as one of them. Except for Hamish, and she didn't expect to change his mind. As far as he was concerned, she had arrived as an alien and nothing would change that. She'd do well to remember that. She belonged in space, not grounded on one planet.

As she climbed into her jumpsuit, she debated spending the remaining week in her ship, then instantly discarded the idea. All her power cells were running the waterseekers. She wouldn't survive long without food or water.

Still reluctant to return to the castle, she sat in her chair and idly studied some star charts. If she didn't find work soon after leaving Alba, maybe she could visit the outer barrier. The colonies settled on the larger asteroids were reputed to be exciting and provided an excellent jump-off point to unexplored territory. With the new drive on her ship she could travel farther and faster.

Her excitement built at that thought, but it lacked continued enthusiasm. Would she be exploring uncharted planets or running away from memories of Beckett?

The first rosy fingers of dawn stretched out from the horizon when she made her way back to the castle, her footsteps heavy. She hadn't resolved anything. As much as she cared about Beckett, she couldn't give up travel among the stars.

Glancing down at her jumpsuit, she wondered why she still wore it. Probably because it felt more natural. She'd given up her earlier idea of following Beckett. Since she'd never ridden a horse, she doubted her ability to control and guide one, especially in the dark.

A woman's scream in the village pierced Raven. She fell into a run, adrenaline pounding. What now? Had the Campbells defeated Beckett?

She refused to acknowledge the stabbing pain created by that thought and dashed between buildings until she reached a large crowd around the first waterseeker.

It was the Campbells. She didn't recognize their tartan, which was enough to know they didn't belong with Clan MacLeod. Mostly women remained in the village, the men having followed Beckett. The women hovered outside their cottages, many of them clutching their children close. Only a few older men had been left behind, and they stood between the dozen Campbells and the waterseeker. Hamish held a sword aloft despite his withered frame.

"You'll nae be taking our water," he said, his face red with anger.

"Who's going to stop us? 'Tis nae you, old man." The leader, a large man with unruly dark hair and an unkempt beard, swung his blade to meet Hamish's. It only took him two swipes to knock the sword from the old man's hand.

It spun through the air to land on the ground not far from where Raven stood in the shadows. The Campbells advanced on the old men, their swords gleaming in the first rays of the morning.

They couldn't take the waterseeker. Someone had to stop them. Knowing she was probably making a big mistake, Raven bent and lifted the sword.

Chapter Seventeen

Hefting the blade to familiarize herself with the weight, Raven inched forward. If only she had her laser. Since she didn't she needed every advantage and timed her first attack carefully.

She pierced one man's shoulder with the blade, grimacing at the feel of it. As he cried out, she drew back and kicked the man beside him in the stomach. Both men fell to the ground.

The rest of them turned on her. She reacted quickly, not giving them a chance to recover from their surprise at seeing her. She didn't have the skill to beat them with swords so she aimed her next kicks to break the men's wrists and release their weapons.

Two more down, but she'd lost her advantage. Holding the sword before her, Raven backed up until she found the waterseeker behind her. Her mouth dry, she tried to swallow but couldn't. Time for a stand.

"You're not taking this machine," she said calmly. "You might as well just go back the way you came."

The leader laughed, his gaze following the curves of

her suit. "The MacLeods use women to do their fighting?"

"You might be surprised." She swung at him hard, hoping that if the leader went down, the rest would give up.

"This one is mine." He met her sword with his. Shock waves reverberated down Raven's arms, but she only tightened her hold and swung again. He parried her thrusts with a skill she knew she lacked.

Her shoulders felt the strain, but she refused to back down. He advanced on her now. She bent her knees to absorb the blows. Her strength failing, she knew she couldn't last much longer.

When he thrust forward she dodged his sword and leapt nimbly onto the edge of the water trough. Lashing out with her foot, she caught his chin and knocked him backward.

Wiping blood from his chin, he growled as he came at her, his eyes glaring. Raven jumped from the side of the waterseeker and met his blade. Her palms burned. Pain screamed from all her muscles. She couldn't give up.

Moisture beaded on her forehead, but she didn't dare wipe it away. She hadn't time.

As he swung again, her grip loosened. Her sword fell to the ground. He aimed his blade at her. Struggling for breath, she watched him warily.

"Now you'll be mine," he said triumphantly. He reached out to grab her wrist.

Instead she snared his arm and used his forward momentum to flip him into the side of the waterseeker. "Think again, fur face." As he yowled in rage, she scrambled to grab her fallen sword.

Before she could reach it he seized her hair and jerked her back, placing his blade against her throat. "I'm thinking you're too much trouble to keep."

Raven couldn't move. The sharp edge pressed against her skin, threatening to cut if she so much as swallowed.

Suddenly the man stiffened and the sword dropped

from his hand. Raven jumped away and whirled to face him, but he collapsed on the ground. Blood oozed from his back where a knife protruded.

Glancing up, Raven met Hamish's satisfied smirk. He nodded at her as a roar went up from the remaining Campbells. Together, Hamish and Raven turned to face them.

There were too many of them and her sword still lay on the ground. "This is your last chance to get out of here." She drew herself as tall as possible, trying to bluff.

It didn't work. They came closer. "Or what?" one sneered.

"We'll be forced to kill you."

They obviously didn't take the threat seriously until several of them cried out in pain and fell. Raven saw some women jump back from where they'd buried knives into the intruders.

Taking advantage of the moment, the old men thrust forward with their swords and downed several more invaders. Only three Campbells remained, forming a tight group to face the villagers.

Raven advanced with more confidence. "Drop your weapons now and you'll live."

To her surprise, they obeyed, and she released her breath in a whoosh, releasing her fear. "Tie them up and keep them under guard until Beckett returns." She turned to the man beside her, half afraid to make her request. "Hamish, will you check the village to be sure none remain?"

"Aye, lass. I can do that." He gave her what she thought was a smile. "You did good, lass."

She couldn't stop her grin as she watched him limp away. Hamish actually had said something nice to her. Walking over, she picked up the sword despite her sore hands. Such a primitive but effective weapon. Despite her aching muscles, she considered asking Beckett for one of her own. Perhaps he would teach her how to use it better.

Beckett! She set the sword beside the waterseeker. As

she looked up, moisture dropped on her face, but she ignored it. Was Beckett all right? How had the men gotten past him? Surely he could have defeated this small group.

Her heart contracted. He had to be safe.

More drops fell on her head. Others left large splats on the dry soil. Impatiently, Raven swiped her face clear and made her way to the prisoners. She'd make them tell her what had happened.

Before she could take more than a few steps, the sky rumbled loudly and water fell in torrents, quickly soaking her. The excited cries of the women cut through Raven's concern and she glanced around in wonder. Women raised their hands to the sky, uncaring of their dampness. Children laughed and splashed in the growing puddles.

She looked up at the dark clouds in realization. It was raining!

A cry of joy escaped her. Raining . . . finally.

She spotted Hamish waving at her in the distance, but she couldn't her his words over the thunder.

Suddenly Beckett rode up and pulled his horse to a stop before her. In one fluid motion he dismounted and wrapped his arms around her.

"It's raining," she said unnecessarily, relieved to see him unharmed. She lifted her hands to touch the dampness of his hair.

He laughed and bent to claim her lips. "Aye, lass, 'tis raining."

His kiss warmed her to her toes, sharing his joy and passion until her body ached for him. When he raised his head he swung her around in an exuberant circle. "Ah, Raven, what need have I of magic when I have you?"

She met his gaze, her pulse leaping at the heated depths in his eyes. "I thought they'd defeated you when these men appeared."

"Nae. We met a larger portion of the clan. 'Twas a diversion so this group could get through while the village was defenseless. If I'd known, I—"

Karen Fox

Raven smiled. "We managed. No one was hurt except them."

He scanned the fallen bodies. "I can see that." He looked at her in amazement. "Did you . . . ?"

"No. We worked together."

"Da. Da." Ciorstan ran from the crowd and threw herself at her father. " 'Tis raining."

He caught her in a tight hug. "Aye, lass." He ran a teasing finger along her nose. "And it came without the Sword of MacLeod."

Ciorstan grimaced as he set her on her feet. "You should've seen Raven, Da. She fought so well with a sword. I ran back to get one, but it was finished before I returned."

"You fought with a sword?" He faced Raven, his expression stunned.

She shrugged. "I need some practice."

Before she could react Beckett gripped her hands and turned them over, revealing her red blistered palms. Ciorstan gasped, but Raven only grimaced. Beckett's gaze darkened and he lifted each palm to his mouth and pressed a gentle kiss against the tormented skin.

A pool of warmth formed in Raven's middle and spread throughout her body. She smiled at him. "They should heal rapidly now."

Ciorstan giggled. "Come on, Raven. We have some salve at the castle that will help."

Raven paused, hesitant to leave Beckett's side, but he dropped her hands and motioned toward the castle. "Go on. I need to clean up here."

Reluctantly, Raven accompanied Ciorstan up the slope, her feet slipping in the mud. At least Alba had rain again. She wouldn't have to feel guilty when she left.

Raven glanced over her shoulder. The last thing she wanted to do at that moment was leave.

Sunshine filtered through the heavy drapes in Beckett's bedroom and spilled over the sleeping woman in his arms. He smiled softly, enjoying the shine of Raven's hair in the light. It had grown since their first meeting and almost reached her shoulders.

Moving carefully, so as not to wake her, he ran his fingers through the soft curls. His heart swelled with unexpected warmth. He couldn't deny it any longer.

He loved her.

After despairing for years that he'd ever find a woman he could love he'd had to leave Alba to do it. He'd wanted a woman with intelligence and courage. Raven had that and much more. He hadn't expected this nor wanted it, but she'd become a part of him, as necessary as breathing.

And she still insisted on leaving.

He couldn't let her go, but neither could he stop her. How could he persuade her to stay? Ciorstan adored her and, once they had bypassed their initial hesitation, even his clan had accepted her. Most of them treated her as if she was already his wife.

His wife.

Beckett rolled the words over on his tongue. After Nessa's death he'd sworn never to marry again. Their marriage had been tepid at best, their lovemaking routine. He'd cared about her, but he'd never once experienced the toe-curling ecstasy that he did with Raven.

As she stirred slightly in his arms, he pressed a kiss to her forehead and held her closer. Life with this woman would never be boring or routine. If only she didn't long for the stars.

He'd seen her watching the night sky, her expression thoughtful, her eyes revealing her thirst for the heavens. Once she left Alba he'd never see her again. He knew that with dreaded certainty.

Could he convince her that his love would make up for adventures on new planets? That Alba held enough wonders to keep her occupied? That here she had a place to stay among friends?

She'd had so much upheaval in her life that love and trust didn't come easily. She'd shown her trust, and he suspected she did care for him, but she hadn't yet said the words. What could he do to overcome the horrors of her childhood?

All he could think of was to love her—more thoroughly, more consistently than she'd ever experienced. But was it enough?

Raven's eyes fluttered open and she smiled slowly. Beckett's loins tightened instantly. Easing his hands into motion, he changed her morning yawns into moans of desire, then used his body to bring her to cries of pleasure.

Leaving the bed, he called for his bath—another routine experience that had become infinitely more pleasurable with Raven's presence. He walked to the window. "Looks like a nice day," he murmured.

Raven sat up amid the disheveled bedclothes. "It's about time. After three days of rain I thought we'd never see the sun again."

The torrents of rain had triggered the advent of spring as green reigned supreme over the country. Beckett eyed the distant mountain slopes. "Would you like to go on a picnic?"

"A picnic?"

"A meal eaten outdoors." He turned to feast on her exposed beauty. "We could go to the mountains."

"All right."

As she slid from the bed, he glanced down at the simple gold band on his little finger, his mother's wedding ring. Today he would show Raven some of Alba's natural beauty, then . . . then he would ask her to marry him.

The bright sun illuminated the new blades of fresh grass and budding trees as Beckett rode his horse Aod into the hills. A cool breeze kept the day from becoming too warm, but Beckett burned from another heat.

Raven sat behind him, her arms wrapped around his waist, her breasts pressed into his back, her thighs wrapped tightly to his. Her slightest touch triggered waves of desire. His mind whirled with thoughts of making love to her. Thank God, he knew this territory well, or he'd have been lost by now.

As the gentle slopes gave way to more rugged mountains, Beckett steered Aod along a narrow path, forcing himself to pay attention. One misstep here could be fatal. High cliffs formed a barrier on one side of the path, while a sheer drop bordered the other side, the tops of trees visible in the distance.

Raven's grasp tightened and he gave her a quick glance. "All right?"

She smiled, her cheeks rosy. "I'm fine. This is beautiful. I've never seen anything like it, at least, not up close."

"Oh, we'll get a lot closer before we're through."

The path opened onto a wide, flat mesa, covered with tall grass and blooming flowers. Beckett grinned. If he didn't know better, he'd swear the mesa had planned to look its best for him. He inhaled the gentle fragrance, hoping Raven would notice it too. At this point he'd take any support he could get.

When he heard running water he nudged his horse into a gallop, stopping only when he reached the bank of a small stream. "We're here." He slid off and held up his arms to help Raven down.

She placed her hands on his shoulders, her eyes dancing as he held her against his body while he lowered her. Her softness only compounded his longing. When her feet finally touched the ground she pressed her lower body against his erection, then whirled from his grasp with a teasing smile.

He could barely walk, so he didn't try. Instead he watched her as she took in the landscape, her expression revealing her delight. He'd always loved the mountains. Something about their majesty and solitude soothed him. He'd come here often before he left Alba to find Ciorstan. Now he just wanted to share it with Raven.

"What do you think?" he asked.

She turned to smile at him, her face glowing. "It's wonderful. Why don't you live here?"

" 'Tis nae enough land for farming and the lake provided our water."

"There's water." She indicated the shallow stream.

" 'Twas dry the last time I was here." He held out his hand for her and she placed her palm in his. Closing his fingers around hers, he paused, letting a surge of pleasure fill him. He couldn't lose her.

He led her to the edge of the mesa and waved his arm to encompass the vast land below. "There's our village."

"Where?"

Wrapping his arm around her shoulders, he pulled her closer until their faces touched. He pointed again. "There."

"I see. Look, the loch is almost full." She glanced at him, her excitement plain, her lips parted.

He bent closer, needing just a taste of her sweetness, but she dodged and extended her arm. "What village is that? The one closer to here?"

With a sigh, he followed her gaze. "We passed it on the way. It belongs to the Clan Sutherland."

"Didn't we share water with them?"

"Aye. They're good neighbors."

"Where do the Campbells live?"

"You canna see it well from here, but their village is beyond the thick forest there. I dinna think they'll bother us again, especially since the rains came."

"They'd better not." Raven turned back toward the stream, then paused.

She wore another of Shauna's outfits, the sleeves of her blouse constantly sliding down her arms. As Raven bent to pluck a flower, the blouse gapped open, giving Beckett a tantalizing view of her cleavage.

He inhaled sharply and she looked up. His expression had to reveal his desire for she smiled mischievously and straightened up, holding the brilliant white flower to her nose. "This is beautiful and smells so sweet. What is it?"

"We call it a lilicup." He traced the oval-shaped petals with his finger. "Women here spread them on their marriage beds to ensure fertility."

"Interesting." She went to pick another flower. "What about this one? The blended purple color is so unusual."

"Ah, 'tis a moriana." Beckett grinned as he joined her. "That one is even more powerful."

She tilted her head, her expression dubious. "Is it put on marriage beds too?"

"Most definitely. It also fills vases in the bedroom."

"What's so wonderful about it?"

Gripping the stem, he inhaled deeply, then met Raven's curious gaze. " 'Tis said to enhance one's desire and heighten lovemaking."

With a laugh, Raven dropped the moriana and stepped back. "That's the last thing you need."

"Too late." He advanced on her. " 'Tis already working its magic."

She held up her hands in mock protest, but he encompassed her in his grasp and kissed her before she could speak. She opened her mouth to his probing tongue and he entered, stroking the roof of her mouth, dancing with her tongue, tracing the outline of her teeth and lips until she undulated against him with a low moan.

As he sucked gently on her lower lip, she entwined her hands in his hair and molded her body to his. Her breasts bored twin points of heat into his chest, and the softness of her pelvis surrounded his hardened manhood. He wanted to throw her to the ground and bury himself in her. She would welcome him; her need rose as quickly as his.

Instead he broke off the kiss to slowly unlace her vest, running his gaze over her reddened lips and swelling breasts. Her breathing became even more irregular and she moved her hands to pull at his tunic. Impatiently, he tugged off his shirt; then, with more control, he eased Raven's vest and blouse over her head.

Her bare shoulders moved with her uneven gasps for air and her rose-tipped peaks thrust out, begging for attention. Attention he was more than willing to give.

Running his hands over her sides, enjoying the feel

of her silky skin, he lowered her gently to the soft grass. She grasped his shoulders to pull him on top of her, then reached down to stroke his erection.

He gasped, nearly losing control. "Nae, lass." Straddling her waist, he grasped her wrists in one hand and pulled her arms over her head. "Dinna touch. 'Tis my turn."

Her eyes darkened, but she left her arms in place, watching him carefully. He kissed her lips first with light touches, then moved across her cheekbone to her chin and down the long line of her throat. As she swallowed, he ran his tongue along the base of her neck and she trembled, her fingers clenching in the grass.

He continued to press kisses over her torso, carefully ignoring her breasts despite her attempts to bring them to his attention. She tasted so good, her softness and unique smell fueling his inner fire.

He made his way around her breasts, cupping them in his hand to reach the tender flesh beneath. Raven twisted beneath him, rubbing against his already throbbing need. With deliberate slowness Beckett stroked his tongue over one of her puckered nipples. The flesh contracted even tighter and Raven whimpered as he repeated the action on her other breast.

She arched her back against the ground, thrusting her breasts higher. Continuing to hold them in his palms, Beckett ran his thumb over the taut peaks, allowing Raven's obvious desire to stoke his own. He teased her nipples, trying to maintain his control as her hips rose from the ground.

When she gasped his name he finally bent to draw one peak into his mouth and loved it thoroughly before devoting the same attention to its mate. Raven's moans grew louder, her body hotter.

His need became excruciatingly painful and Beckett left her breasts to kiss a trail over her abdomen to the waistband of her skirt. With one swift movement he had it unfastened and slid it and her underwear off. As he removed his pants, he watched her naked form, her hips still rocking slightly, her peaks sweetly swollen, her skin flushed with need, her hands pulling grass from the ground as they remained over her head.

It only took him a moment to reclaim his place between her thighs. Cupping her mound, he explored her inner heat with his fingers. Her moistness told him of her readiness. When he stroked her hidden bud of desire she rose off the ground with a cry.

"Beckett, you're killing me," she gasped.

" 'Tis nae pleasurable?" He teased her bud further with slow, gentle movements until her body stiffened. As he felt the first throes of her release, he entered her. Her muscles clenched around him and he forced himself to remain still in order to regain control.

Then he moved with long, hard thrusts, his heart hammering in his ears. Raven lifted her hips to meet him, wrapping her legs around him and grasping her hands—no longer over her head—around his arms.

She held him tight inside, stroking every inch of his length. As her breathing increased, so did his pace, until he again felt her ripple around him. With a groan, he permitted his release, then sank against her, supporting his weight on his arms.

" 'Tis nae pleasurable?" he repeated with a smile.

"If it was any more pleasurable, I would die." She stroked his cheek, then kissed him thoroughly.

Once she lowered her legs, he rolled to his side and gathered her in his arms. He needed to ask her now while her sated condition left her more vulnerable, but how? He swallowed the sudden lump in his throat.

"Raven, will you consider staying on Alba?"

She blinked, her gaze clearing, her defenses rising immediately. "I can't. I don't belong here."

" 'Tis nae true. If there's anywhere you do belong, 'tis here." Beckett propped himself up on his elbow. "In a short time you've become one of us. Even Hamish sings your praises."

"That's only because he likes nothing more than a good fight." Raven pulled free from his arms and started to dress.

She had distanced herself emotionally too. Beckett

could feel it. Panic rose in his belly. He couldn't lose something this important. "Marry me, Raven."

She froze in her movements but didn't look around. "You don't mean that."

"I want you for my wife."

"For how long?"

"Forever." He went to touch her shoulders. "Raven . . ."

As she turned to face him, her expression solemn, his hopes sank. "From my experience men take what they want for as long as they want it and then cast it aside."

Beckett tightened his hold, wanting to shake her. "I'm nae Slade."

"No, you're not." Pain glimmered in her eyes as she met his gaze. "But you're still a man."

How was he supposed to fight that? Damnation, she wasn't likely to believe anything he said. "What if you're pregnant?" he asked in a sudden burst of inspiration. She couldn't leave him then.

"What?" She stared at him, obviously stunned.

He gestured at the flowers surrounding them. "We just made love in a field of fertility. 'Tis possible, lass."

"No. It won't happen." Turning away, she finished dressing.

"You canna be sure of something like that. Stay, Raven. I—"

"I won't get pregnant. Don't worry." As he touched her again, she whirled around. "I take a shot every six months that prevents it from happening."

"A shot?" It was his turn to be stunned. "Why? I was your first. How could you have known?"

"I didn't know." Her voice softened. "I've never wanted children, Beckett, and in my line of business I knew there was always the chance I might be taken against my will. That would be bad enough; having a child as a result would be worse."

His stomach clenched. He loved Ciorstan and wanted more children . . . many more. After seeing Raven with his daughter he knew she could be a good mother. "When does this shot wear off?"

"Not for another two months. By that time I'll be able to visit Lumina and get another one."

He caressed her face. "Stay with me, Raven. Would it be so bad to have my child?"

She hesitated and her eyes watered before she blinked them clear. "I'm not mother material, Beckett. It's not you. I've never been good with children." Her chin wavered. "They're too needy and I have nothing to give."

"Raven, you've done naught but give since you came here." He cupped the back of her head and bent to touch her lips. "Please stay with me. I love you."

His words went unheard beneath a sudden explosion that jerked both of them around. Smoke blossomed from a spot near his village. Beckett ran to the mesa edge as something silver streaked from the sky, followed by another burst from the ground where it hit. Even from this distance he could see the resulting flames.

Glancing skyward, he saw more projectiles hurling toward the ground. "My God, what is it?" These things destroyed as much territory in one blast as days of clan fighting.

Raven joined him, her face so pale even the lilicups had more color. As another object impacted, she shuddered. "It's Slade."

Chapter Eighteen

Beckett turned to Raven in disbelief. "Slade? You canna know that."

"Who else would do this? No one has any reason to war with Alba except Slade."

Her words made sense. Beckett's stomach twisted with dread. "What does he want?"

"I don't know. Maybe me; maybe Ciorstan. Obviously the Sword of MacLeod wasn't enough." She spoke almost mechanically, and Beckett wrapped his arms around her.

He wanted to swear that Slade would never harm her again, but after seeing privateer's weapons Beckett wondered if he could defeat this man. "We have to get back," he murmured.

"I know." Raven left his arms and walked toward the horse. "I might have something on the *TrackStar* that can help."

"Nae." Anything she had would only delay the inevitable. "We will fight him on our own."

Her brow dropped in a frown. "Then you'll die."

"Then we'll die as Albans. Look at the assault he's launching. No matter what weapons you have, Raven, he's going to have something more."

She didn't reply, her lips pressed tightly together.

With a heavy sigh Beckett swung onto his horse and put down his hand for Raven. She tried to keep from touching him, but by the time they'd made it halfway down the narrow mountain trail, she'd molded herself to his back.

Beckett forced himself to concentrate on controlling Aod, who jumped at every distant explosion. Once they reached the gently rolling hills drifting smoke added to the horse's nervousness . . . and Beckett's.

He could barely see the ground in front of him. Grinding his teeth in frustration, he kept their progress slow despite his internal urging to get home . . . now . . . fast. Was Ciorstan all right? Shauna? Was Dunvegan still standing? The village? Though he didn't know what good he could do against these deadly missiles from the sky, he needed to be with his people.

A sharp whine pierced the smoke, ending with a sickening thud and a loud roar as the ground rolled beneath them. Dirt flew through the air, rocks pelting them.

With a terrified whinny Aod reared, and Beckett struggled to control him. Raven cried out, sliding back. Damnation. Beckett swung out his hand to reach for her, knowing she didn't have any horseback experience.

He grabbed only air. Raven called his name as she fell into the smoke. Beckett made another desperate grab as Aod slipped on the jostling ground. Cursing his lack of balance, Beckett tried to regain control and failed.

As if in slow motion, he slid from the saddle and somersaulted to the ground. Even as he winced at the hard impact, the breath knocked from his chest, he heard Aod gallop away. He quickly determined his injuries: nothing serious, only scrapes and cuts. Pushing to his knees, he searched the hazy landscape for Raven.

"Raven?" She should be close by.

"I'm here." Her voice sounded weary and he made his way toward it.

He found her climbing to her feet, shaking her skirt until it hung properly. "I'm fine," she said before he could say anything. "Now what?"

Beckett whistled, but received only the distant whine of another missile in reply. "Aod's probably halfway to Dunvegan by now. We'll have to walk."

"Do you know where we are?"

The haze shifted enough for Beckett to recognize the hills. "Aye, 'tis only a short distance to the Sutherland village. We may be able to find a fresh mount there."

They made their way with caution, but as they grew closer, the wind shifted, driving the smoke away from them. When they reached the edge of the village Beckett silently wished the mists would return to hide the horrifying carnage.

His chest ached to see the flattened cottages, the bodies littering the street, the flames devouring everything in sight. Rolling his fingers into tight fists, he vowed to make someone pay for this senseless killing.

Beside him, Raven inhaled sharply, her eyes wide in her pale face. "It has to be Slade," she murmured. "No one else is this heartless."

They advanced carefully, stepping around the fallen. Beckett saw one man, his arms wrapped around his wife and child, all of them dead. Beckett's insides tightened and he tried to swallow the lump lodged in his throat. What about Ciorstan? His resolve grew. Whoever had done this would die, and Beckett would ensure it wasn't quickly or painlessly.

"Is everyone dead?" Raven whispered, as if speaking aloud would offend the deceased.

"I canna believe that." Making his way to what had once been the town center, Beckett cupped his hands around his mouth. "Is anyone there? Can you hear me?"

"Here. Help me." Though faint, Beckett whirled at the voice.

"Keep talking. Where are you?"

"Here. Here. I'm trapped."

Raven ran toward the voice, then skidded to a halt beside a collapsed cottage. She glanced at Beckett, horror etching her features. "It came from under there."

He didn't hesitate, but grabbed the wood and rock and tossed it aside. Raven immediately joined him. Working in silence, the only noise that of their exertions, Beckett and Raven didn't pause until they'd revealed a woman, the lower portion of her body still buried beneath heavy beams, her arms and shoulders wrapped around a wooden cradle.

Her eyelids fluttered as Raven knelt beside her. "We have to get her uncovered," Raven said. She stroked the woman's hair away from her face. "It'll just be a little longer."

" 'Tis . . . 'tis too late for me." With obvious effort, the woman pushed herself off the cradle to reveal the still form of a baby inside. "Help Kerr. I . . ." She gasped for breath. "I give him to you."

The look Raven gave Beckett held pure panic. He strained to lift the thick wood pinning the woman, but couldn't budge it, the far end lodged firmly beneath more rubble. Gathering all his strength, he pushed again. This time the beam moved slightly.

"Just a little longer," he promised.

"Stop, Beckett." The sob in Raven's voice brought his head up to see her bent over the woman. "She's dead."

With a cry of anguish, Beckett pummeled his fists against the beam, wishing it was Slade. His shoulders heaving, he turned to Raven. "And the baby?"

She hesitated, her hands on the edges of the cradle. "He must be dead too. He's so quiet."

Placing her hand on the infant, she shook him gently, then jumped when he let out an angry scream.

"He sounds alive to me." Beckett stepped closer to peek over Raven's shoulder. The baby, five or six months old from the look of him, squalled lustily now, his arms and legs pumping, his face flushed crimson.

Raven's unease showed in the stiff line of her back, her reluctance to touch the infant. She drew back from the cradle. "Get him, Beckett."

271

"Nae." He prayed he was making the right choice. "She gave him to you, Raven. He's your responsibility now."

"No." She shook her head to reaffirm her words. "I don't know anything about babies."

" 'Tis time you learned then." He climbed out of the rubble. "I'll scout ahead to see if anyone else survived."

"No, Beckett." Raven jumped to her feet, but he kept moving. If he stopped, he'd give in. "I can't do this."

He tossed his parting words over his shoulder. "You have nae choice."

No choice? Of course she had a choice. Raven watched Beckett disappear down the street, seething inwardly. If she left the baby, Beckett would come back for him.

She glanced down at the infant, viewing it as she would any alien creature. He didn't look much longer than her arm and wore only a thick cloth around his bottom and a dirty brown shirt on his top. Though his cries weakened, he continued to swing his limbs in angry movements, his open mouth revealing no teeth, only smooth red gums. Atop his flushed face he had quite a bit of black hair; more than Shauna's baby, Niall, though Raven felt certain this child was younger. With his eyes squeezed shut, Raven couldn't determine their color.

His sobs eased in strength but still continued, interspersed with an occasional hiccup.

He looked so small, so helpless.

Raven considered the child's mother. She'd given her baby into Raven's care, trusting that she would care for him. Closing her eyes, Raven tried to control the panic bubbling inside her. What did she know about children, especially babies?

Absolutely nothing.

Yet she reached for the infant, grabbing him beneath his arms, and lifted him from the cradle. He swayed in the air as she held him in front of her and his cries increased again.

That didn't work. He felt too loose, too awkward.

Remembering how she'd seen Shauna carry Niall, Raven pressed the baby against her shoulder, cradling his bottom with her arm, her other hand holding his back. He buried his face into her neck, his distinctive scent, not altogether unpleasant, reaching Raven's nose.

She ran her hand over his head, surprised to find his hair soft, his skin warm. "It'll be all right," she said softly. She recalled the name his mother had mentioned. "Kerr. It'll be all right, Kerr."

To her amazement his sobs faded, though his hiccups continued, jerking his entire body with each one. Without any conscious thought she found herself patting his back as she swayed back and forth, shifting her weight from one foot to the other.

As soon as she realized it, she stopped. What made her do that? Fortunately it worked. Kerr calmed considerably and laid his head on her shoulder, his hands entwining in her hair. Only an intermittent hiccup disturbed him.

So far, so good. With one last glance at Kerr's mother Raven left the destroyed cottage and went in search of Beckett.

He met her at the outskirts of the village, his face grim, the anguish in his gaze tugging at Raven's heart. "I dinna find anyone else alive," he said.

Raven looked back at the smoking ruins. "Why?" It took her a moment to realize she'd spoken aloud. "What does Slade want?"

"I'd like the answer to that myself." He swallowed with visible effort, his hands curling into fists. "Why Sutherland? Why not just Dunvegan if he's after me or you?"

She could only think of one explanation and she didn't like it. "I think he's used the scanner to locate my ship and is targeting any life forms in a certain area. Sutherland's misfortune lies in being too close to the *TrackStar*."

"The ship." He scowled. " 'Tis another example of the evils of technology."

"Don't worry. I'll be out of here as soon as I can." Raven brushed past him, heading in what she hoped was the direction to their village.

"Raven . . ." He caught up with her easily. " 'Tis your ship; it isna you."

"My ship is part of who I am, Beckett." She hesitated long enough to meet his gaze. "That's what you can't seem to understand."

Kerr tugged on her hair, and she winced and gently uncurled his fingers. "Here, Beckett. I brought him; you can carry him now."

"You're doing a fine job." Beckett backed away. "I'll lead the way."

"I know what you're doing," she said. He couldn't be more obvious than if he placed the baby in her arms and told her to play mother.

He smiled slightly. "Good."

Before Raven could say another word he hurried away. She sighed and tried to shift Kerr's weight. Already her arms felt the strain of holding him against her shoulder.

Wanting his hands away from her hair, she fitted him into the crook of her waist and wrapped her arm around him. At least she shouldn't feel so lopsided while walking with this method.

"Dinna get lost," Beckett called.

"I'm coming." Raven made her way after him, noticing how he kept just far enough away that she couldn't talk to him. "He thinks he's being clever," she told Kerr. His eyes focused on her as if he understood. "He thinks that if I'm forced to take care of you, I'll lose my discomfort with children."

Kerr gurgled and Raven grinned. "As if I know what I'm doing now." She lurched as her foot came down in a small hole and fought to maintain her balance. The infant grabbed her shirt as she swayed. Finally she felt secure enough to continue.

"How do women do this?" she asked. "Already you weigh a lot more than you did when we started."

He blew bubbles, obviously charmed to discover he

could do so. Raven couldn't help but smile at his antics and swiped the drool off his chin.

"It's not you," she continued. "I'm just not the mother type. Children bother me."

And Beckett would want more children. Which was just another reason why she couldn't stay, despite her inner urge to do so. At some point, maybe after weeks, months, years, he'd tire of her and ask her to leave. She'd seen Slade do it often enough. Even her own parents had left her.

Then what would she do?

She was better off leaving now, before Beckett hurt her. He hadn't spoken of love, only of wanting her. But her heart already ached at refusing his proposal. The thought of spending many more days—and nights— with him appealed to her. He made her feel emotions she hadn't known she could. He made her believe in love.

But he would leave. They all left eventually.

She shifted Kerr to her opposite hip and rotated her stiff shoulder. "I don't know what to do, Kerr. A part of me wants to be in space, but another part wants to stay here."

As she glanced at him, he screwed up his face, his eyes closing, his complexion darkening, his mouth opening—all before any sound emerged. His cries exploded and Raven stared in amazement.

"What did I do?" She teased his lower lip. He'd liked that a moment ago. He only screamed louder. "Kerr, what . . . ?"

No wonder children drove her crazy. How was she supposed to know what set him off? She exhaled her exasperation.

Realization dawned as she felt the dampness of her shirt and skirt. "Oh." She held him away from her, her hands under his arms. His lower padding did look heavy and wet . . . very wet. "Ewww."

She searched the terrain. "Beckett! Come here. Quick."

He arrived out of breath, his sword drawn. "What?"

275

"It's him. He's . . . he's all wet."

Lowering his weapon, Beckett grinned. "Is that all? He just needs changing."

"Into what?"

Beckett pulled his shirt off in one easy motion and held it out. "You can use this for now."

"Here." She tried to give him the baby. "You do it."

He held up his hands in a defensive gesture. "I found some rubble ahead. I need to find a way through it. I'll be back." As swiftly as he appeared, he disappeared, leaving his shirt on the ground.

"Beckett." Raven resisted the urge to stomp her foot on the ground. With a grimace, she surveyed the crying child. "Great." She managed to find a patch of grass and laid him on it. Loosening the pins on either side of his padding, she opened it and wrinkled her nose in disgust. Even Gatorians smelled better than that.

Easing off the padding, she tossed it away. "Now what?" She grabbed Beckett's shirt and folded it into a manageable size. Kerr's sobs had eased by the time she slid the shirt beneath him. "I hope you know I'd rather be in a laser battle than do this."

He kicked his legs, unwrapping Raven's careful folds. "Stop that," she told him. He ignored her.

Locating a large pink rock, she waved it before him. "See the rock? Isn't it pretty?" His legs stilled as he reached for it, and she concentrated on fastening the shirt around him.

She surveyed her handiwork with immense satisfaction. It wasn't perfect, but it wouldn't fall off either. She glanced at Kerr to see him put the rock in his mouth. "Don't do that." She snatched it away. "It's dirty."

His face puckered and she panicked. "No more crying. No more." He'd found her hair amusing earlier. Bending over him, she dangled her curls in his face, then pulled back before he could latch on. The pucker vanished and he thrust his hands in the air.

Raven caught the tiny fists in her hands and he wrapped his fingers around her thumbs. To keep him occupied she moved his arms out, then in. "That's a boy," she murmured. "No crying now." His skin felt so smooth, so soft. She couldn't stop stroking the back of his hands.

He smiled at her, his large blue eyes filling his face, his entire body wiggling with the force of his pleasure. Raven found herself smiling back. He did have a certain appeal, she admitted, when he wasn't crying.

Scooping him up, she returned him to her hip and followed after Beckett. He joined her instantly, as if he'd been close by. Watching her, no doubt.

"That wasna bad, was it?" he asked.

Raven glared at him. "What do we do with him once we get back?"

"Shauna's still nursing Niall. 'Tis possible she'll agree to nurse this one, too. Else we can try to feed him cow's milk. 'Tis been done before."

"All that does is feed him." Raven pictured Kerr snuggled against Shauna's breast and her stomach clenched. "Where will he go?"

"We'll find someone to care for him." Beckett gave her a quick glance. "Dinna worry, Raven. 'Twillna be you."

"That's good." She meant those words. She did. But still a heaviness lingered in her chest. "Do we have much farther to go?"

"If we can pass this crater ahead, I think we'll be at the edge of the fields." He took her elbow. "Be careful."

He helped her over the upheaval—dirt and rock tossed aside as if they were toys, and through a deep ditch, no doubt produced from a missile's impact. Smoking remnants of burnt grass and trees lingered, making her eyes water.

They'd reached the edge of the fields when Kerr squirmed, throwing Raven off her stride. Her foot slipped and with a cry she stumbled backward into the ditch. She landed on her rear and slid down the slope, trying to wrap Kerr in her arms.

The crater, though wide, wasn't deep, and she rested at the bottom, wincing as she tested her limbs. Kerr screamed loudly and she tried to examine him. He didn't appear to be hurt.

Beckett reached her as she tried to stand and took Kerr from her. The empty feeling in her arms surprised her, but Raven regained her footing and climbed back to the fields.

Kerr continued to cry as Beckett brought him over. "I don't think he's hurt," Raven said. "Just scared."

"Aye." Beckett rubbed the baby's back in a circular motion and crooned soft sounds. Kerr wailed louder and Beckett patted faster.

Raven bit back a smile. Now Beckett could share her fun. He rocked from side to side, turning in place.

Suddenly Kerr spotted Raven. To her surprise, he extended his arms toward her. Without thinking, she took him from Beckett's arms and cradled him against her shoulder. His cries ceased as he wrapped his arms around her neck.

Beckett grinned. "I guess he prefers you."

"I guess." Raven held the baby close as they crossed the fields. When his grip loosened she peered into his face to check on him only to be rewarded by his sweet smile. With a sigh he nestled his head into the crook of her neck.

Her heart swelled as her chest constricted. He trusted her to take care of him, to stay with him. Moisture blurred her vision. And she would. She wouldn't leave him.

She came to an abrupt halt. Just because her parents left her didn't mean she would leave her child. Tears rolled down her cheeks. She'd been afraid of needy children because she'd needed so much for most of her life . . . love, laughter, hope—all the things Beckett gave her. All the things she *could* give. Sobs tore from her throat.

"Raven, what is it?" Beckett gripped her shoulders, but she couldn't speak through her closed throat and shook her head. He pulled her close, encompassing her in his strong arms. "I'm here, lass. I'm here."

She struggled to speak. "I . . . I've been such a Neeban."

"Sometimes, aye." He kissed the top of her head. "But

278

so have I. 'Tis that which causes these sobs?"

"I can love a child." She blinked the tears from her eyes as she met his gaze. "I won't leave one because my parents left me."

He jerked, obviously surprised. "I never thought you would."

She gave him a watery smile. "Children always frightened me because they depended on a person for everything and I didn't think I could give it. I've always wondered why my parents left me. I've never felt sure of myself before . . . of who I am. But I'm not like my parents. I can be trusted."

"Raven . . ." He kissed her softly, his lips lingering. "I've always known that." He wiped his broad thumb across her cheek to clear away the tears. "Be careful you don't drown the bairn."

Kerr didn't appear to mind his dampness. As Raven glanced at him, he reached out to pat her cheek, then clamped hold of her hair. She winced and extracted it.

Beckett let the baby snare his finger and smiled. When he looked at Raven his gaze held such warmth that she inhaled sharply. "It's about time you realized how special you are—to Ciorstan, to the village, to me—especially to me." He kissed her again, holding her as close as the infant would allow. "I love you, Raven."

Her eyes watered again. She couldn't remember anyone telling her that . . . ever. Did love cause this warm, shivery sensation that flooded her body? Did love make her heart thud so hard her chest hurt? "I—"

"MacLeod!"

They turned to see Duncan running over the war-torn ground. He skidded to a stop, his breathing ragged. "We're all in the castle," he said finally. "What's doing this? What can we do?"

"I dinna know," Beckett admitted. He met Raven's gaze. "But we'll figure out something."

As they entered the castle, Beckett noticed the inside looked intact, though one parapet had been destroyed outside. Ciorstan ran across the wide entry to meet them.

"Da, are you all right?"

He hugged her tightly, not realizing until he felt his breathing ease how afraid he'd been for her. "I'm fine. What about you and your aunt?"

"We're all fine." She looked at Raven. "Raven?"

Raven bent to hug her, obviously surprising Ciorstan. Despite her stunned expression, the girl returned the hug with fervor. "I couldn't be better," Raven said.

Ciorstan beamed and held out her hand toward Kerr. "And who's this? He's a right winning lad."

"His name is Kerr."

"He's the only survivor of Sutherland," Beckett added.

"All of Sutherland?" Ciorstan's expression grew solemn.

"Aye."

She turned again to Raven. "May I hold him?"

"Please." Raven eased Kerr into Ciorstan's arms. "Be careful."

The girl gave her a dry look. "I've taken care of Niall, you know."

"He'll probably be hungry soon," Beckett said. "See if you can find that nursing bottle and some warm milk."

"Aye, Da." As she departed, Ciorstan glanced over her shoulder. "Everyone's waiting in the great hall."

Duncan preceded them and threw open the doors to that room with a flourish. "The MacLeod is here."

The room erupted with shouts and cries. Beckett skimmed over the familiar faces, trying to assure himself that they were all accounted for. His heart sank. Many faces were missing.

He glanced at Shauna, standing beside the door with raised eyebrows. The sad shake of her head confirmed his fears and he inhaled deeply to ease the pain.

"MacLeod." "What do we do?" "What happened?" Villagers attacked him with questions from all sides. He couldn't afford to give into his grief now.

Holding up his arms, he shouted for silence and the

room stilled. "I believe the privateer who took the Sword of MacLeod has returned. For what, I dinna know. But we will find out. I think the explosions have stopped. I've heard naught since I left Sutherland. Duncan, take two men and check the perimeter."

He waited for them to depart, then continued. "The Clan Sutherland village has been destroyed. I couldna find any survivors."

Cries of outrage and soft sobs followed this and he paused. Some of these people had relatives in that village. Anger grew over the top of his grief.

"If 'twas Slade who did this, he'll be on the ground soon. Then we'll learn why he did it," he added.

"Then we'll make him pay," Hamish shouted, raising his fist.

"Aye, he will be destroyed." Beckett hoped he would be the one to mete out the punishment.

"Beckett." Raven caught his arm. "It won't be that easy."

He glanced at her, noticing her serious expression. "What is it?"

"Slade won't come alone. He's not a fool. From the extent of the bombings, I'd guess he's brought all the privateers with him. That's over sixty men, and they'll all have lasers."

Sixty men? With lasers? At best guess, he had only forty men with swords. He'd seen the power of Raven and Slade's weapons. What chance did his people have?

"I can help," Raven said quietly.

For a moment he considered her earlier offer of weapons. Even if he had time to teach his men to use them, they'd only feel comfortable with their claymores. "We willna use your weapons, Raven."

"I know." She gave him a wry smile. "But I can give you some tips on how to use your swords against the lasers."

Beckett nodded. "Thank you. All those able to fight, get your weapons if you dinna have them with you and meet out by the fields. Raven, come with me."

Despite her quizzical look, she accepted his hand and

went with him toward the front stairs. "Do you think this training will help?" he asked.

She grimaced. "It can't hurt."

He hesitated, needing to know but not wanting to hear the answer. "Are these privateers truly ruthless?"

"If Slade tells them to, they'll destroy everything—and everyone—here."

Beckett stiffened. He'd die before he let anyone harm his daughter, his sister or Raven. "Then we'll have to destroy them."

Raven opened her mouth to reply, then shut it again as the front doors were flung open. Duncan stalked into the room, dirty but exuberant. Seeing Beckett, he held his sword a loft.

"We caught an alien."

Chapter Nineteen

Duncan stepped aside, and his two companions thrust their captive forward, their swords placed at his throat. Raven gasped and rushed forward, waving their weapons down.

"Leave him alone." She glared at the villagers until they stepped back, their expressions stunned, then threw her arms around her friend's neck. "Naldo, what are you doing here?"

"Steal shuttle," he replied. "Must talk to you."

Raven sensed Beckett's presence behind her before he spoke. "Raven . . ."

She smiled. "Beckett, this is Naldo. I told you about him."

As Beckett studied the Terellian, Raven saw apprehension in his gaze. "Naldo," he repeated. Abruptly his head jerked up. "You're the one who took care of Raven."

"*Ti.*" Naldo bobbed his head. "Take care each other."

"Your accent is unusual." Beckett frowned. "I can barely understand you."

Naldo grinned, revealing his white, even teeth. "Earth Basic privateer language, not mine."

Raven touched Beckett's arm, wanting him to like her friend. "Naldo's language involves a lot of sounds our throats can't handle." Noticing the wild-eyed stares of Duncan and his companions, she leaned closer. "I think we should talk somewhere private."

To her relief, Beckett nodded. "Let's go up to my room. Duncan, continue to watch for intruders." He glanced at Raven. "Are you likely to have any more friends show up?"

"Naldo's my only friend," she said as she took his arm and led him to the stairs.

By the time they reached Beckett's chambers Naldo's breathing became more labored. Raven led him to a chair and knelt before it. "Are you all right?"

"Gravity strong," he replied.

Strong? Raven hadn't noticed much difference from her setting on *TrackStar*, but Erebus's gravity was very light. "How did you get off Erebus? Who's running the Command Center?"

"Tristan in charge." Naldo drew in a deep breath. "Helped me hide on fleet."

"Fleet? Slade's brought everyone?"

"*Ti.*"

Raven exchanged glances with Beckett. This didn't bode well.

"Hide to Alba. Steal shuttle. Come give warning."

Beckett moved closer. "Do you know what Slade has planned?"

"*Ti.* Short time till attack."

Beckett's hand moved to the hilt of his sword. "Then tell us . . . quickly."

"First talk Raven." Naldo gave her a sad smile. "More important."

"What could be more important than preventing this attack?" she asked. Stunned by Naldo's presence, she could only stare at him. He'd never left Erebus before—not for as long as she'd known him. Slade's attack,

284

though serious, didn't seem like a strong enough reason. What made him leave?

Naldo placed his hand over hers. "Have news. Overheard Slade. About your parents."

Icicles pierced Raven's veins and she stood slowly. Her throat tightened. "My parents?"

"Are they alive?" Beckett asked as he placed his hand on Raven's shoulder in a reassuring gesture. She barely felt his touch, her mind trying to comprehend his words.

"They're alive?" she echoed, hope rising.

"*Na.* Dead. Still dead."

The cold lump in her stomach expanded. Naldo studied her, obviously judging her emotional state, before he continued. He knew how talking of her parents affected her. "Slade killed."

She grimaced. "I always figured Slade had something to do with their ship's explosion. Did he shoot them down?"

"*Na.* Parents never leave."

Raven couldn't breathe. Tight, invisible bands wrapped around her chest. "Wh . . . what?"

"Slade want your mother." Naldo spoke with a solemn quietness. "He take. She fight. He kill."

Raven's knees threatened to give out, but Beckett wrapped his arm around her shoulders and held her tightly. She could picture Slade with her mother—her beautiful, petite mother—and Raven's stomach rolled.

"My . . . my father? Gregor?" The words nearly choked her.

Naldo lowered his yellow gaze, then raised it, an angry gleam shimmering in its depths. "Found Slade with mother. Big fight. Slade kill."

"But . . . but Slade said . . ." She stopped. She knew better than to believe anything Slade said . . . now. At nine she'd believed every word he told her. Her heart rate accelerated and her breath came in short gasps. "They didn't leave me."

Smiling softly, Naldo nodded. "No leave little girl."

Fresh tears filled her eyes. She glanced up at Beckett.

"They didn't leave me," she repeated, absorbing the impact of that statement.

The love in his expression enveloped her in its warmth. "I knew they couldn't," he murmured.

A heavy weight lifted from Raven. For the first time she experienced a sense of freedom. Freedom to believe in herself, freedom to love. As she gazed at Beckett her heart swelled. She did love this man.

With a happy sob, she pressed her head against his shoulder and linked her arms around his neck. Her parents hadn't left her behind. They had loved her. If they hadn't been killed . . . Her joy faded. But they had been killed . . . murdered . . . by Slade.

Angry now, she pushed away from Beckett. "Slade has to pay."

"Aye, lass. I mean to kill him for what he's done to Alba."

"No. I want to kill him."

"Raven." Naldo reached out to touch her, then waited until she faced him. "Revenge bad. Destroy self."

"But he murdered them, Naldo. He ruined my life." She curled her hands into tight fists.

"You found life," he said firmly. "By self." He raised his gaze to Beckett. "Maybe have help?"

"I did have help," she admitted. Without Beckett she'd still be searching for that elusive place—the right place—when all she needed was love. "But Slade deserves to die."

"*Ti.* Slade evil man. Will die. Maybe today. Maybe next year. You live for revenge. Linger in soul forever."

Raven dropped her gaze. She understood Naldo's point. Now that she'd finally found herself, devoting her life to Slade's destruction would only throw it away again. Beckett touched her arm gently and Raven smiled slightly. She had so much more than that to live for.

"You're right, Naldo. As usual." She bent to hug him, wincing at his thinness, the feel of his bones.

"Now tell Slade's plans."

"Aye. Tell me." Beckett crouched before him.

"Land in field by *TrackStar*. One point six hours from now. Sixty-two men. All have hand lasers. Six laser cannons. Ordered destroy all, kill all. Only leave you two and daughter."

"Ciorstan? And us?" Beckett frowned. "Why?"

"Unsure. Problem with magic sword."

"All these people have are swords, Naldo. Can we defeat them?" Raven's insides twisted with pain. Would all the people she'd come to know and care about be killed?

Naldo's gaze held hers. "You know answer."

Depression filtered through her, then stopped as she remembered. She'd seen these people practicing with their weapons. They had courage, wit, cunning and the ability to use a sword with deadly accuracy. Flinging away her despair, she straightened. "We can stop them—with training."

When she looked at Beckett he grinned. "Aye, lass. We can do it." Turning, he lifted the thick mattress on his bed and pulled out her jumpsuit and laser. "You'll need these."

"So, that's where they were." She smiled sheepishly as Beckett raised his eyebrows.

"I'll gather the men and meet you outside." He grabbed his battle shirt, then paused before Naldo. "Thank you."

Naldo bowed his head. "Am glad to help."

Once Beckett left the room Raven knelt before Naldo. "You can stay here where you'll be safe. I'm afraid your appearance right now would only frighten the villagers."

"Stay here. Tired. Not used to travel." Naldo stroked her cheek. "Sense peace inside."

"Yes." Even preparation for battle couldn't destroy her new strength.

"Beckett?"

She smiled. "I love him, Naldo."

He beamed at her. "Good."

"He asked me to marry him and I told him no." Raven stood up, catching a glimpse of Naldo's frown. "I didn't realize then how much I need him. He wanted me to give up space travel and I couldn't do it, but you know, Naldo, I don't think I'll ever enjoy space again if I don't have Beckett."

"So?"

"Once this fight is over . . . once we win . . . I'll accept his proposal." Just the thought of becoming Beckett's wife filled her with giddy excitement. "I belong with Beckett and he belongs on Alba."

"Give up stars?"

She hesitated. "Yes, if that's what it takes." She started for her room, unlacing her vest, then turned back. "Stay here on Alba, too, Naldo. You don't have to return to Erebus."

He closed his eyes, then nodded. "I stay. Too old. Telekinesis weak now."

A new fear gripped Raven. How long did Terellians live? How old was Naldo? "I'll be back after we win," she said quietly and entered her room.

No matter how many days he had left, at least he'd be here with someone who cared about him. The villagers would accept him . . . eventually.

Raven changed quickly and placed her laser into its holster. For a moment the weight about her hip felt strange. Raven grimaced. After today she'd probably never wear this outfit again.

She located Beckett by the village, overseeing the battle preparations. The other men surrounded him, sparring with partners or sharpening the edges of their swords. Once they spotted her they stopped and looked up expectantly.

At a nod from Beckett she held up her laser. "All the privateers will have weapons similar to this one. These are older weapons and fire laser pulses, which makes it easier for us. If you intercept the beam with the flat side of the blade, you can deflect it. If the beam hits you, it'll burn through your clothing, your skin and possibly your internal organs. It depends on how close you are. If you can't avoid a beam, try to take the hit on your shoulder or lower leg. That'll give you the best chance of survival."

The men muttered among themselves, their trepidation clearly visible. Raven drew in a deep breath and continued.

"They'll also have laser cannons. They're big weapons, longer and fatter than your arms. The beam from them is wider and much more powerful. It'll disintegrate you. If you see it coming at you, hit the ground. Don't duck behind a tree; it'll go right through that."

"We dinna have a prayer," one man shouted. Others added their own fearful exclamations.

"I think we do," Raven replied. "We'll practice with my laser. That will help you to prepare."

"Against sixty men?"

Raven paused and licked her dry lips. "I've traveled a lot through this universe. I've witnessed more battles than I care to remember. But nowhere have I seen the resilience, the courage and the skill that you have here. The privateers have weapons that can kill from afar. That's their advantage.

"But we have an advantage too," she continued. "You can move quickly, without a sound. You can attack with such stealth that they'll never see you coming. This isn't the type of fight where we stand in rows and wait for them to leave their ships. That would be suicide. We'll hide and pick them off. We'll show them that they've picked the wrong people to fight."

The men cheered and Beckett grinned at her. "We will defeat these pirates," he added. "They have become too dependent on their weapons. Once we rid them of these lasers they will fall." He lifted his sword. "We have our claymores. We have our Scot pride. They canna hope to defeat us."

More cheers arose as the villagers raised their blades to the sky. "Watch carefully as Raven and I demonstrate." Beckett motioned for her to fire her laser.

She aimed the beam beside him, but he shook his head. "Fire at me, Raven."

"No. What if you miss?"

"I willna." He gave her a wry smile. "I have some experience with this."

Though she couldn't remember seeing him fight lasers with his sword, she lifted her laser again and aimed for his shoulder. Her hand shook and she had to steady it with her other one. Though her mind screamed, she fired.

Beckett met it with his sword and deflected the beam into the sky. She fired. Again he rerouted it. "Do you see?" he asked his men. " 'Tis our speed that's needed here. Break into groups of three. I want one group at a time to practice with Raven. The rest of you scout out places for ambush. We canna let the pirates reach the castle."

The men formed trios and Raven steadied her breathing. This had to work. Without Alba . . . without Beckett, she had no future—whether Slade killed her or not.

Time passed too quickly for Beckett. Fortunately his men rallied, inspired by Raven's praise, and showed enthusiasm for the battle. As long as they believed in themselves, they had a chance.

He paused in digging a trench and watched Raven working with a small group. The sight of her skintight suit reminded him of their first meeting. He never would've guessed then that she would come to mean so much to him.

He loved her. Despite her negative response to his proposal, he didn't intend to give up. He'd hoped that her bonding with Kerr would convince her that children weren't as terrible as she feared. But even if he never had any more children, he'd still want Raven.

He glanced at the afternoon sky, knowing that soon invaders would descend from the stars. If not for Raven's help, his people wouldn't have a chance of defeating them. As it was, their chances were slim.

He'd been out there and had seen nothing to make him want to return. Why did Raven insist on going into space? Wasn't he enough to satisfy her?

With a sigh, Beckett returned to his ditch. It wasn't physical satisfaction she needed but freedom. A freedom that apparently only the heavens could provide.

What if he gave it to her?

If he had to let her visit the planets to keep her, could he do it? Space travel violated his ancestors' wishes. But they hadn't known Raven. Like the bird whose name she bore, she needed room to fly, to explore, or else he'd risk losing the spark that made her the woman he loved.

To have Raven for his wife he would give her that freedom. If she stayed, there would be changes. He knew that with an inevitability he could feel to the soles of his feet. Not immediately, but as with the waterseekers, she'd find a way to restore all of Alba's old equipment.

Beckett glanced up to meet her warm smile. It would be worth it.

A loud, low thunder reverberated through the sky. His heart skipped a beat. The pirates!

At his sharp command his men disappeared into their hiding places. Raven jumped his wide dirt wall and slid in beside him. He drank in her loveliness despite the ache in his chest. In a short time they could both be dead.

He cupped her head in his hand and seized her lips, tasting her mouth, determined to convince her of his love. She moaned, slipping her hands into his hair, her tongue stroking his. His body tightened.

The roar grew closer and they slowly drew apart, their breathing uneven. Raven's eyes shone as she stroked his face. "Beckett . . . be careful."

"Aye. Raven . . ." His voice broke. She couldn't be harmed. He wouldn't allow it.

She gave him a sad smile. Together, they turned to watch the privateers land on Alba.

Ships of all sizes, most of them larger than Raven's, plowed into the newly planted fields. Doors hissed open and men slowly emerged.

Beckett spotted their lasers at once. Every privateer held one ready as they formed a large group and approached the village. Scanning the surrounding trees, Beckett watched his men slide into action.

They moved silently from trees and rocks to follow the sides of ships and pick off those pirates lagging behind. One after another fell, their death screams silenced before they reached fruition. The privateers' numbers dwindled, but Beckett knew that soon—

"What's that?" A pirate spotted his men and the privateer group rounded on them, firing.

As villagers dove for cover, Beckett rose from the ditch and signaled his second group. Albans surrounded the invaders, removing several before they could react.

Fighting broke out in earnest. Beckett's pride swelled as he watched his men deflect laser beams with an almost casual ease. A cannon beam swung his way and Beckett threw himself down. A return beam zipped over his head and the cannon operator fell.

Jumping to his feet, Beckett acknowledged Raven's shot with a grim smile and attacked another opponent. As he predicted, removing the privateers' weapons rendered them defenseless. But getting close enough to knock away the guns—that was the problem.

To his dismay, Beckett noticed his men among the fallen. How many still lived? He couldn't pause to find out. Dodging and deflecting laser fire kept him too busy.

Searching for Raven, he found her on one knee beside the stone wall lining the slope to the castle, firing steadily at the advancing privateers. Beams blasted the rocks close to her, but she didn't flinch, her expression hard, her gaze cold.

A laser blast regained Beckett's attention. He ducked and rolled forward, managing to kick the weapon from the pirate's hand. With one fluid motion he plunged his sword into the invader. The man collapsed.

Once Beckett cleaned his blade he looked toward Raven. She was gone. A sudden rush of fear filled his blood as he scanned the area for her. There. Up the slope.

Raven ran toward the castle, apparently yelling, but

her words went unheard amid the noise of the battle. Glancing at the door, Beckett inhaled sharply.

Ciorstan!

What was she doing? Raven reached his daughter and seized her arm, dragging her inside the castle.

Beckett eased a sigh of relief. Now if only Raven would stay inside. Then he wouldn't have to worry about her.

With renewed vigor he approached another pirate. This one took longer to down, and as Beckett withdrew his sword, he examined the scorch mark skimming the top of his shoulder with disgust. He'd been too reckless. He wasn't about to die with the anticipation of Raven in his future.

He glanced again at the castle entrance and froze. Icy fingers drew circles around his throat and chest. He staggered forward two steps in disbelief.

Slade pulled open the castle door and disappeared inside. Raven must not have secured it.

Beckett started for the castle. Ciorstan, Raven . . . and Slade. Damnation.

A loud whooshing sound brought his head around and his eyes widened. Cannon fire filled his vision.

Chapter Twenty

Raven snared Ciorstan's upper arm and dragged her through the castle doorway. "What do you think you're doing?" She'd forgotten to breathe when she saw the girl on the slope. Spotting the sword in Ciorstan's hand, Raven figured out the answer even before the girl spoke.

"I wanted to help. I want to fight." She drew herself up straight, courageous despite her quivering lower lip. "I want to be like you, Raven."

"Oh, Ciorstan." Impulsively Raven hugged her. "I'm honored by that, but this is not who I am. I never want to fight and I've always done my best not to kill. It should always be the last thing, the only means of survival."

"But you have killed before?"

Faces flickered through Raven's mind—faces she'd never forget. "I can count how many men I've killed on one hand." She hesitated, remembering the carnage outside. "Until today."

"But I—"

"Ciorstan, if you went out there, we would lose this

fight. All our men would be too busy trying to take care of you, they wouldn't be able to give their full attention to what they're doing. I know you don't want that."

"Are we winning?"

"It's too early to tell." Raven turned Ciorstan to face the hallway. "Now get back to the great hall and stay there."

" 'Tis awful in there," Ciorstan said, but she started walking. "Everyone's crying or whining."

"Then maybe you should cheer them up."

Raven grinned at Ciorstan's exasperated expression. She couldn't blame the child for wanting to fight. At her age it looked glorious instead of the painful, dirty business it was.

She sighed. As much as she dreaded it, she needed to return to the battle. Her laser made a difference, but it hurt—terribly—to shoot at men she'd known half her life. Couldn't they see this was wrong?

Turning toward the door, she cast one last look at Ciorstan. Though she moved slowly, the girl was going. With a half smile Raven faced the entry and froze.

Slade stood just inside the door, his laser aimed at her, the Sword of MacLeod hanging in a scabbard at his waist. "So nice of you to meet me."

"Slade." His name escaped before Raven thought.

Though she spoke quietly, the sound traveled along the hallway and Ciorstan gasped. "Slade?"

He approached Raven, his evil gaze flickering behind her. "Ciorstan, come join us."

"No." Raven kept her body between Ciorstan and Slade. "Get out of here, Ciorstan. Now."

Slade pressed his gun against the base of her throat. "That will be enough out of you."

"Leave the child alone." Raven's heart hammered in her ears. "Take me instead."

"Oh, I intend to." His lips twisted in a sneer and he ran the nose of his weapon down Raven's chest, pausing to rub it over her breasts.

To Raven's surprise her hot anger faded—replaced by a coldness that invaded her veins and an unexpected calmness. "I know what you did to my mother," she said icily, meeting his dark gaze. "I know how you killed my parents and my brother."

Her revelation didn't faze him at all. He only grinned and reached up to cup her breast. "Now you know why I have to find out if you're as sweet as she was."

Raven trembled, glaring at him, rolling her hands into white-knuckled fists. She shifted her weight, waiting. . . .

"Let her go!" Ciorstan ran down the hallway, diverting Slade's attention, and Raven reacted, firing her knee into his groin.

He doubled over with a groan and Raven whirled around to seize Ciorstan's shoulder and pull her behind a wide table. She quickly flipped it on its side and pushed the girl down. "Stay there," she ordered, grabbing her laser.

Slade fired first and she ducked, cursing his quick recovery. Peeking over the top, she fired several shots, but Slade had taken refuge behind a heavy, thick chair.

They exchanged laser fire, neither achieving any success. Raven surveyed the large entry. She had to get closer . . . find an opening. "Stay put," she whispered to Ciorstan.

Using laser blasts as a shield, she vaulted from the table to the safety of a chair. "What do you want, Slade?" She couldn't believe he'd launch this attack just to find her.

"I want the secret of the sword. Give it to me and I'll leave."

"What secret?" Raven glanced at Ciorstan, who shrugged and shook her head.

"The secret to its magic. It doesn't work."

Raven laughed. "That's because it isn't magic. You fool. Why do you think we let you keep it?"

Slade bombarded Raven with a steady stream. The legs of the chair collapsed and she hurdled toward another. As Slade alternated his shots above and below her, Raven twisted, ducked and jumped. One pulse blast seared a streak across her back, and Raven cried out as she stumbled over her own feet, sprawling on the stone floor, her gun slipping from her hand.

She scrambled to her hands and knees in an attempt to retrieve it, but Slade placed his foot on her laser as he stood over her, anger flaring in his eyes. He held his gun to her head and motioned her up.

Swallowing the lump in her throat, Raven stood slowly. She stared at the laser, reviewing her options. It didn't take long. She'd fight Slade before she'd allow him to harm Ciorstan or herself . . . and she'd probably die. But maybe Ciorstan would get away.

Her muscles tensed, ready for action, as she watched Slade intently.

"This sword is magic," he snarled. "That little girl wouldn't have traveled across the universe to find it if it wasn't." He aimed the weapon at her forehead. "And I want its secret."

"You don't get it, do you?" Raven knew she was taking a chance, but anything she could do to keep him off balance could only help. "The sword's not magic. There's no such thing."

"You can't fool me. I know it's magic. I felt its power when I held it in my hand." The hand holding the laser wavered as he bent to touch the sword's hilt.

Raven bent her knees.

"Raven, catch!"

She turned at Ciorstan's voice to see the girl stand up behind the table and toss her a sword. As Raven snatched it from the air, Slade fired, his beam hitting Ciorstan's midsection, throwing her against the wall before she fell to the floor.

"Ciorstan!" Raven started for the girl, feeling as if she'd been hit, but Slade waved his laser in her face. Her cold calmness intensified as she lifted her head. "Now you're going to die, Slade."

She lashed out with the blade, slicing his shirt and nicking his skin, before he fired. She dropped and twisted, the beam flying over her shoulder. Regaining her posture, she tested the weight of the weapon, noticing it was lighter than the one she'd used before, but equally as deadly.

Slade shot and she met the beam with the blade. Though she'd worked with all the villagers on this procedure earlier, she hadn't done it herself. Was she quick enough?

She advanced on Slade, maneuvering with an agility she hadn't known she possessed, deflecting his shots. She had to get to Ciorstan. With a cry of rage, she whipped the sword over his hands and succeeded in throwing his laser across the room.

Stunned, he stared at her in surprise, then swiftly drew the Sword of MacLeod. The blade shone, its edge glistening with razorlike sharpness, and Raven caught her breath. Did she have a chance against this sword?

Slade gripped the ornate hilt and swung at her. She dodged the blow easily and parried his following thrusts. She quickly realized he had no skill with this weapon. Though she possessed only limited experience, it surpassed his.

Her callused palms absorbed the blows as her muscles responded to her actions. Despite Slade's superior weapon, Raven took the initiative, driving him back, recognizing the first flicker of fear in his gaze.

"You will die," he exclaimed. "This sword is magic."

"Only if you're a MacLeod," she responded. Though she'd wondered at the sword's powers, she hadn't seen a sign of anything other than a well-crafted blade. In Beckett's hand it would be lethal, but not in Slade's.

She met his blow and threw him backward. Holding her ground, she didn't flinch as he swung at her.

"Raven!"

Though she heard Beckett's strangled cry, she didn't pause in her forward thrust. Slade hesitated, and Raven slid her blade between his ribs.

He dropped to his knees, a startled look on his face. Raven ignored him. His death would follow soon. She ran across the floor toward the turned table.

"Beckett, it's Ciorstan."

"Ciorstan?" He joined her instantly and cried out in

pain at seeing the crumpled form of his daughter. Gathering her into his arms, he glanced at Raven. "Find Murray. He's the doctor. Last I saw, he was fighting by the waterseeker."

"Is she alive?" Raven blinked rapidly to keep back the threatening tears.

"Barely." Beckett's expression was grim. "I'll take her to her room. Hurry."

On her way to the door Raven paused. She'd need proof to convince the pirates of Slade's death. Since he'd killed Morgan, Slade had worn the older man's crest, a black engraved disc, around his neck. In one swift movement she seized the chain, then dashed down the slope, searching for the doctor.

Though many more had fallen, the fighting continued. Useless fighting. She leapt onto the rock wall.

"Slade is dead," she shouted. When no one responded she yelled again, louder.

Men turned to look at her—privateer and villager. "Slade is dead," she repeated. "Unless you have a very good reason for fighting these people I'd advise you to return to your ships and leave while you still can."

A visible shudder ran through the privateers. "Slade's dead?" one asked.

"Would you like to see his body?" she snapped. She lifted the disc so that it swung in the air. "I have Morgan's crest now." With it, she could claim leadership of the privateers if she desired. She didn't.

She threw the chain and disc at them. "You're free of Slade finally. Get out of here and choose your new leader."

They stared at her like lost sheep, then one man lowered his laser and started for his ship. As if in a daze, the others followed.

Recognizing victory, the villagers shouted with joy, raising their swords to the sky. Raven leapt from the wall and found Murray. "Come with me quickly," she said, grabbing his arm. "You're needed inside."

"I'm needed here," he replied, motioning with his arm to indicate the fallen villagers.

"It's Ciorstan."

He drew back and blinked. "Let's go."

Even as she followed him into the castle Raven's heart sank. None of this man's medical skills would save Ciorstan. She'd taken a direct hit.

Beckett waved Murray inside Ciorstan's room. He'd removed his daughter's dress, revealing the severe circular scorch mark on her stomach that gaped open to expose her insides.

Standing by the door, Raven inhaled sharply. With a wound like that, Ciorstan should already be dead. She watched with dread as Murray examined the girl.

Only one thing would save Ciorstan—a medtech unit. But Beckett despised that technology. It wasn't Alban in any way. He wouldn't allow it.

Raven swiped at her tears. Not even to save his own daughter? She bowed her head. He'd refused it to heal one of his people. No doubt he still believed in following their ancient ways.

As Murray shook his head, Raven's chest tightened. Beckett might be tied to his customs, but she wasn't. Even if he never spoke to her again, she couldn't let Ciorstan die.

Slipping from the room, she ran for the *TrackStar* as fast as her legs would carry her. She had to scrape dirt away to open the door, but once inside she located her portable medtech unit and cradled it to her chest.

Beckett would never forgive her for this betrayal. At least the waterseekers had been brought by his ancestors. This . . . this defied all his beliefs.

But she had to do it.

Tears streamed down her cheeks as she dashed back to the castle. She'd come to love Ciorstan as much as her father. She couldn't stand by and let the child die when she knew she could prevent it.

Visions of a future with Beckett died. He'd probably help her onto the merchant ship when it arrived after this. But at least Ciorstan would be alive . . . if Raven was in time.

She skidded to a halt just inside the doorway to Ciorstan's room. Beckett knelt beside his daughter's bed, holding her hand, his eyes glistening. Murray stood at the foot, his face grave.

Was she too late?

Unwilling to believe that, Raven felt Ciorstan's neck for a pulse. Though weak and uneven, it still beat. With a heavy sigh she bent her head.

" 'Tis only a matter of time," Beckett murmured, his words choked with tears.

"I know." Raven placed the medtech unit on the floor and activated it. As the box expanded to human size, Beckett jumped to his feet, his expression startled.

"Raven—"

Her hand shook as she drew her laser and pointed it toward him. "I won't let her die, Beckett. I don't care what your customs say."

Emotions played across his face—anger, hope, finally despair. "You've brought your healing box."

He approached and she fired over his shoulder. "Stay back. I don't want to hurt you."

His frustration showed. "Even your technology canna save her now."

"Would you not have me try?"

He hesitated, then dropped his gaze. "Nae."

Raven didn't look at him. The unit snapped into place and she hesitated before lifting Ciorstan and placing her in the box. Beckett could stop her while her arms were full, but he didn't.

He stood back, watching, his gaze unreadable as he rolled his hands into fists. He distrusted her technology, but obviously his desire for Ciorstan to live kept him back. Though Raven knew Beckett would hate her for interfering, at least he let her try.

Securing the lid, Raven started the healing program, her stomach churning until she saw the first yellow light. Diagnosis. The box revealed barely any life signs for Ciorstan but launched immediately into the healing process.

Red and white rays bathed Ciorstan's body, then circled over her wound.

"My God." Beckett stepped closer, watching the unit as if he wanted to look away but couldn't. His obvious unease and indecision matched her own.

The doctor, though awed, showed none of Beckett's distaste, only curiosity. "What is it?" he asked.

"It's the newest technology. We call it a medtech unit. It has the ability to heal most injuries."

"Can it save Ciorstan?"

"I don't know." Raven didn't dare glance at Beckett. "Perhaps. It is designed to repair laser wounds, but only if there's enough life left within the injured person."

"How does it work?" Murray extended his hand to touch the box, then paused.

"I couldn't tell you exactly, but somehow the healing process is accelerated. Broken bones can be whole in minutes. Wounds like Ciorstan's can be healed, the organs regenerated before they quit working."

"Fascinating."

Beckett still said nothing, only staring at the unit. Raven closed her eyes, dying a little inside. It was over—the future she might've had with Beckett, loving him, caring for Ciorstan and even Kerr.

Gone.

Her heart broke into a million pieces, the tiny shards invading every pore of her body. Now, when she'd finally found love and recognized its power, she'd thrown it away.

No, not thrown it away. She had no choice. The display showed the strengthening of Ciorstan's life signs. She couldn't regret this decision.

The red and white rays stopped as the display turned green. Suddenly nervous, Raven lifted the lid with shaky hands.

Ciorstan breathed. Raven could see her chest moving, but the girl still hadn't opened her eyes. A horrible thought pierced her mind: What if the unit didn't work the same on Albans?

No. Ciorstan was human. It was designed for humans. It had to work.

Raven brushed her fingers across Ciorstan's cheek.

"Ciorstan? Lass?" She used Beckett's endearment without thought.

Ciorstan's eyelashes fluttered. With painstaking slowness, she opened her eyes, then blinked. "Raven?" she whispered.

Raven smiled broadly and extended her hand. "Here, let me help you out."

As Ciorstan stood, she glanced down at her bare abdomen and touched her stomach carefully, a frown creasing her forehead. "He shot me," she exclaimed indignantly.

Nodding, Raven helped her step out of the box. "But you're fine now."

"You healed me?" She glanced at the medtech unit in awe.

"Yes."

"Ciorstan." Beckett barely whispered her name, his eyes damp. "Ciorstan."

She ran to him and he enveloped her in his arms, holding her as if he never meant to let her go.

Raven smiled until her gaze met Beckett's. "I'm sorry," she murmured. "I know how you feel about this, but I had to do it, Beckett." She turned away, unable to look at him any longer. It hurt too much. "Don't worry. The merchants should be here in a day or so and I'll leave then."

"Nae, you canna leave," Ciorstan protested, but Beckett said nothing.

"Will this box work on the wounded outside?" Murray asked.

"Yes."

"How do we carry it there?"

Raven reduced the unit to portable size again and lifted it.

"Murray . . ." Beckett's voice held a warning note, but Murray held up his hand.

" 'Tis my business to save lives, Beckett. If this thing can do it, then I'm all for it. Frankly, our ancestors had a good idea, but they've carried it too far. When I lose a patient due to a simple infection—something I know could've been cured easily in the past—then I wonder what we've really gained." He waved at Raven. "Come with me."

All the privateers had fled. While Murray tended to the less serious injuries, Raven used the unit to save those men on the brink of death.

When they finished she allowed herself some small satisfaction. Eight men now lived who might not have otherwise. How could Beckett see evil in that?

Despite the destruction, the women prepared for a celebration to be held in the castle, but Raven stayed outside, her pain too great to face Beckett again. With heavy steps, she retraced her path to her ship.

Now that she had to leave Alba, she didn't want to go. She never would've expected that when she first arrived.

Maybe she could return later—give Beckett time to forget this incident. Maybe then he'd be willing to forgive her. Hope flared, then died. What if she returned and he'd chosen another wife? Could she bear that?

No. She'd do better to go and never return.

Raven entered the *TrackStar* and slumped into her pilot's chair. Slade was dead, her past resolved, the universe waited to be explored, but none of it mattered. Without Beckett, adventure held no excitement, exploration no thrills.

A single tear slid down her cheek. "Fardpissle."

"Do you always swear at your computer?"

She whirled around to see Beckett standing in the doorway. "Mac's off-line right now," she replied automatically. She couldn't stop staring. Beckett wore an outfit she'd never seen before.

A dark jacket covered his usual white shirt and instead of pants, he was attired in a pleated skirt of his clan's distinctive plaid that hung to just above his knees. His boots had given way to heavy shoes and plain gray knitted stockings.

Raven had never seen a human male in a skirt before, but she couldn't say she didn't like it. The sight of his muscular legs only added to his masculinity. Her throat went dry.

"Wh . . . what is that?"

He paused and gestured at his skirt. " 'Tis celebration dress—my kilt. I confess I dinna wear it often, but tonight . . ." He grinned. ". . . tonight we have every reason to rejoice."

"Yes." Raven agreed, though the last thing she wanted to do was rejoice.

His eyes darkened. To Raven's surprise he fell to one knee and took her hand in his. "Raven, I ask again with all the love in my heart—will you marry me and be my wife?"

Raven couldn't help it. Her jaw dropped open. "I thought you'd never want to see me again."

He smiled. "Nae, 'tis my hope to see much more of you."

"But . . . but the medtech unit . . ."

Beckett sobered and stood up. "Using that machine went against everything I believed our ancestors wanted for us, but I understood why you did, Raven. 'Twas Ciorstan. I wanted her to live as much as you did. 'Twas hard to reconcile that with myself. Then I thought on what Murray said."

"Murray?" Raven tried to recall the doctor's words. She'd been too caught up in her grief to listen closely.

"When my ancestors decided to leave Earth 'twas the right and proper thing to do. We needed that chance to discover who we were and find our roots again." He paused.

"But . . . ?" Raven prompted, sensing his need to continue.

"But 'tis now two hundred years later. We have changed. The universe has changed. If such a machine can save people's lives, then 'tis foolish to find fault with it."

Raven gaped at him, unable to believe her ears. "Beckett . . ."

He took both her hands in his and gazed solemnly into her eyes. "Raven, I love you. Will you marry me?"

"I . . . yes." She had trouble speaking as joy dispelled her sorrow. "Yes, yes, yes." Flinging her arms around his neck, she met his lips in a fulfilling kiss.

When she could finally breathe again she smiled at him. "I love you, Beckett. I love you and Ciorstan and even Kerr."

" 'Twas all I could wish for." He kissed her again tenderly. "Come now; borrow one of Shauna's gowns and allow me to present you to the villagers as their future lady."

She snuggled close to his side as they crossed the fields, unable to believe the depth of her happiness. Glancing at the night sky dotted with a million points of light, she smiled sadly. That part of her life was gone now, but she couldn't complain.

"Will you miss traveling in space?" Beckett asked quietly.

"I've flown among the stars as long as I can remember. Staying on one planet will require some adjustment." She smiled and lifted her face to kiss him. "Just be patient with me."

"I canna take that away from you."

She gaped at him, stunned.

" 'Tis my hope that you'll be too happy here to want to go, but if you feel the need, then you have that freedom. I only ask to go with you."

"Go with me?" she echoed. This was too good to be true.

"I dinna think I can be without you for long." He grinned and pulled her close. His immediate arousal pressed against her loins and desire blossomed within her.

She molded her body along his hard length, her breasts swelling with longing. "Somehow, Beckett, with you as my husband I doubt I'll want to go far."

His kiss surpassed any thrill provided by the heavens.

Epilogue

"I'm back. Did you miss me?"

At Raven's words Beckett's heart leapt in his chest. He crossed the library in two large strides and gathered her in his arms. She melted against him and returned his kiss with enthusiasm.

His desire quickened and he nuzzled her neck, inhaling her unique scent. "I may have to rethink this space travel business," he murmured, knowing already how she'd respond to his teasing.

"This is the first time I've gone in the seven months I've been here, and then only for two days," she said indignantly.

"But 'twas two days too long."

She wrapped her arms around his neck and smiled. "You could've come with me."

" 'Nae. We had to finish the harvesting." He kissed her nose. "You could've waited."

"I couldn't sleep, I wanted dramberries so badly." She indicated a large package in the doorway. "I think I

307

have enough to last me through the rest of my pregnancy."

For a woman who had once said she never wanted children Raven glowed with contentment as she carried this one. In her tight jumpsuit Beckett could see the gentle rounding of her belly—their son or daughter. She'd been shocked to conceive almost immediately after her anti-pregnancy shot wore off, but she hadn't complained.

If anything, they'd been too busy. Their wedding ceremony had had to be squeezed in between the replanting of the fields and the rebuilding of the village.

But now he couldn't ask for more. He had a wife he adored, wonderful children, his village healthy and happy, and a large harvest, due mostly to the waterseekers and a slow but steady return to a normal rainy season. Darting a glance at the Sword of MacLeod mounted over the fireplace mantle, he wondered if it didn't actually have some magical powers.

"Da. Da. You're never going to believe this." Ciorstan ran into the room, her face alight with excitement. Kerr followed behind her, his steps still unsteady but determined. They paused, spotting Raven, and cried out together.

"Raven, you're home."

"Ma. Ma. Ma. Ma."

Raven hugged Ciorstan warmly, then bent to lift Kerr into her arms. He wrapped his arms around her neck and continued to jabber in a language only he could understand . . . and maybe Raven. She certainly acted as if she did.

Beckett grinned proudly. After they'd seen Kerr through teething, crawling and his first hesitant steps, he'd become as much their child as Ciorstan and the one growing in Raven's belly.

"What is it, Ciorstan?" he asked, breaking into the tirade of questions his daughter threw at Raven.

"Oh." She held up the faded yellow and red piece of silk they'd found with the Sword of MacLeod—the same one Beckett had used to bind Raven's wound.

"Kerr and I were playing with this and he found this button in a corner. It . . . well . . . listen."

She pushed on the odd-looking button fastened to a corner of the cloth and words emerged. Beckett glanced at Raven in surprise, but she didn't appear alarmed. More of her technology, no doubt. But what was it doing with the sword?

"My name is Devlin MacLeod. I'm one of the leaders in the Scottish relocation from Earth. While we all agree 'tis important to reestablish our heritage without the modern trappings that have controlled our lives in the past, I've wondered if we're doing the right thing.

"To that end, I wrote the riddle that led you to this planet, this cave and the Sword of MacLeod. I thought if life on our new planet, Alba, ever became such that someone was willing to leave it in search of this sword, then the time was right for a new era, for a joining of Alba with the universe."

Ciorstan beamed at Beckett and he smiled, a new peace filling him. He'd made the right decision after all.

"The sword isna magic," Devlin continued. *"However, this cloth is. 'Tis the MacLeod faery flag."*

The faery flag! Beckett had heard of it. Until his ancestors had left Scotland, it had resided in the Castle Dunvegan, but it had disappeared during the resettlement. Disappeared because it was used to wrap the Sword of MacLeod.

"As legend states, the flag has three magic properties. If raised in battle, it ensures a MacLeod victory; if spread over a MacLeod marriage bed, it guarantees a child; and if unfurled at Dunvegan, it charms the herring in the loch. After three uses the magic will be exhausted. 'Tis been twice invoked. Use it carefully."

"There is magic, Da," Ciorstan said, hopping from one foot to the other.

Beckett lifted the scrap of silk and looked at it dubiously. Magic? In this faded bit?

Raven shifted Kerr to one arm as she faced Beckett. "What do you plan to do with it?"

Hesitating, Beckett considered the flag's magical

properties. He'd already won all his battles and had a child conceived, and the loch, while restored to its former depth, didn't contain herring. "Let's put it somewhere safe. I dinna need its magic."

As Ciorstan groaned, he put one arm around her and his other around Raven. "With all of you I have everything a man could want."

Raven smiled softly, her joy reflected in her eyes. "That's because we have the magic of MacLeod, which is more powerful than any faery flag."

"The magic of MacLeod?" Ciorstan wrinkled her nose. "What's that?"

"Love."

Dear Reader,

I hope you enjoyed *Sword of MacLeod*. As someone who's loved science fiction and romance for most of my life, discovering futuristic romance was a special treat. Since I'd decided I wanted to be a writer at age twelve, I've created many stories set in the vast unknown of space, but always with a romance set in their heart. What could possibly be better than exploring strange new worlds and the love of a good man?

Sword of MacLeod first sparked to life in a writer's retreat located in the Colorado Rockies, where one assignment was to take the name Baku and use this person in a scene while listening to some unique African music. Everyone else saw a man dancing in the African jungle. Not me. I saw the bar from *Star Wars* filled with its wild assortment of aliens and Baku standing in the middle, looking for someone and ready for action.

From this scene Beckett MacLeod came to life. I quickly learned who he was looking for, why he needed the best tracker he could find, and the reason for his bewildered expression. I thoroughly enjoyed writing Beckett and Raven's tumultuous romance, and I hope you found that same pleasure in reading it.

My next futuristic will be available in 1997. *Somewhere, My Love* follows Tristan Galeron, a Scanner with telekinetic powers, as he seeks to bring peace in the war between his people and the Alliance of Planets. He kidnaps the Director-General's daughter in hope of persuading the Director-General to negotiate with them.

Unfortunately, he also ends up kidnapping Sha'Nara Calles, a member of the PSI Police, a division of the Alliance dedicated to tracking down and destroying the Scanners. Even worse, she's the daughter of the PSI Police Director.

Tristan knows he should kill Sha'Nara before she ruins everything, but how can he when she stirs his desire like no other woman? Please join Tristan and Sha'Nara to see if they can survive their inbred hatred of each other and bring peace to the Scanners.

311

Karen Fox

I love to hear from my readers. Please write to me at P.O. Box 4383, Biloxi, MS 39535-4383. If you wish a reply, a self-addressed, stamped envelope would be appreciated.

TIMESWEPT

Don't miss these passionate time-travel romances, in which modern-day heroines fulfill their hearts' desires with men from different eras.

Traveler by Elaine Fox. A late-night stroll through a Civil War battlefield park leads Shelby Manning to a most intriguing stranger. Bloody, confused, and dressed in Union blue, Carter Lindsey insists he has just come from the Battle of Fredericksburg—more than one hundred years in the past. Before she knows it, Shelby finds herself swept into a passion like none she's ever known and willing to defy time itself to keep Carter at her side.
_52074-5 $4.99 US/$6.99 CAN

Passion's Timeless Hour by Vivian Knight-Jenkins. Propelled by a freak accident from the killing fields of Vietnam to a Civil War battlefield, army nurse Rebecca Ann Warren discovers long-buried desires in the arms of Confederate leader Alexander Ransom. But when Alex begins to suspect she may be a Yankee spy, Rebecca must convince him of the impossible to prove her innocence...that she is from another time, another place.
_52079-6 $4.99 US/$6.99 CAN

KNIGHT OF A TRILLION STARS

DARA JOY

Fired from her job, exhausted from her miserable Boston commute, the last thing Deana Jones needs when she gets home is to find an alien in her living room. He says that his name is Lorgin and that she is part of his celestial destiny. Deana thinks his reasoning is ridiculous, but his touch is electric and his arms strong. And when she first feels the sizzling impact of his uncontrollable desire, Deana starts to wonder if maybe their passion isn't written in the stars.

_52038-9 $4.99 US/$5.99 CAN

Dorchester Publishing Co., Inc.
65 Commerce Road
Stamford, CT 06902

Please add $1.75 for shipping and handling for the first book and $.50 for each book thereafter. NY, NYC, PA and CT residents, please add appropriate sales tax. No cash, stamps, or C.O.D.s. All orders shipped within 6 weeks via postal service book rate. Canadian orders require $2.00 extra postage and must be paid in U.S. dollars through a U.S. banking facility.

Name _____
Address _____
City _____ State _____ Zip _____
I have enclosed $_____ in payment for the checked book(s).
Payment <u>must</u> accompany all orders. ☐ Please send a free catalog.

Futuristic Romance

Keeper of the Rings

NANCY CANE

"A passionate romantic adventure!"
—Phoebe Conn, Bestselling Author Of
—*Ring Of Fire*

He is shrouded in black when Leena first lays eyes on him—his face shaded like the night. With a commanding presence and an impressive temper, Taurin is the obvious choice to be Leena's protector on her quest for a stolen sacred artifact. Curious about his mysterious background, and increasingly tempted by his tantalizing touch, Leena can only pray that their dangerous journey will be a success. If not, explosive secrets will be revealed and a passion unleashed that will forever change their world.

__52077-X $5.50 US/$7.50 CAN

Futuristic Romance

Love in another time, another place.

On Wings of Love Saranne Dawson

"One of the brightest names in futuristic romance."
—Romantic Times

Jillian has the mind of a scientist, but the heart of a vulnerable woman. Wary of love, she had devoted herself to training the mysterious birds that serve her people as messengers. But her reunion with the one man she will ever desire opens her soul to a whole new field of hands-on research.

Dedicated to the ways of his ancient order, Connor is on the verge of receiving the brotherhood's highest honor: the gifts of magic and immortality. All will be lost, however, if he succumbs to his longing for Jillian. Torn by conflicting emotions, Connor has to choose between an eternity of unbounded power—and a single lifetime of endless passion.

_51953-4   **$4.99 US/$5.99 CAN**